I0685256

REALITY AND OTHER ILLUSIONS

A Spiritual Odyssey

JR Shepherd

Cover art and family tree: Luisa Galstyan

Illustrations: dreamstime.com

Certain passages are inspired by the wisdom and imagination of the ancients: Plotinus' *Enneads*, Ovid's *Metamorphoses*, Hesiod's *Theogony* and *Works and Days*, and Virgil's *Fourth Eclogue*, all of which are in the public domain.

ISBN: 978-1-7643650-1-7

Contents

CHAOS

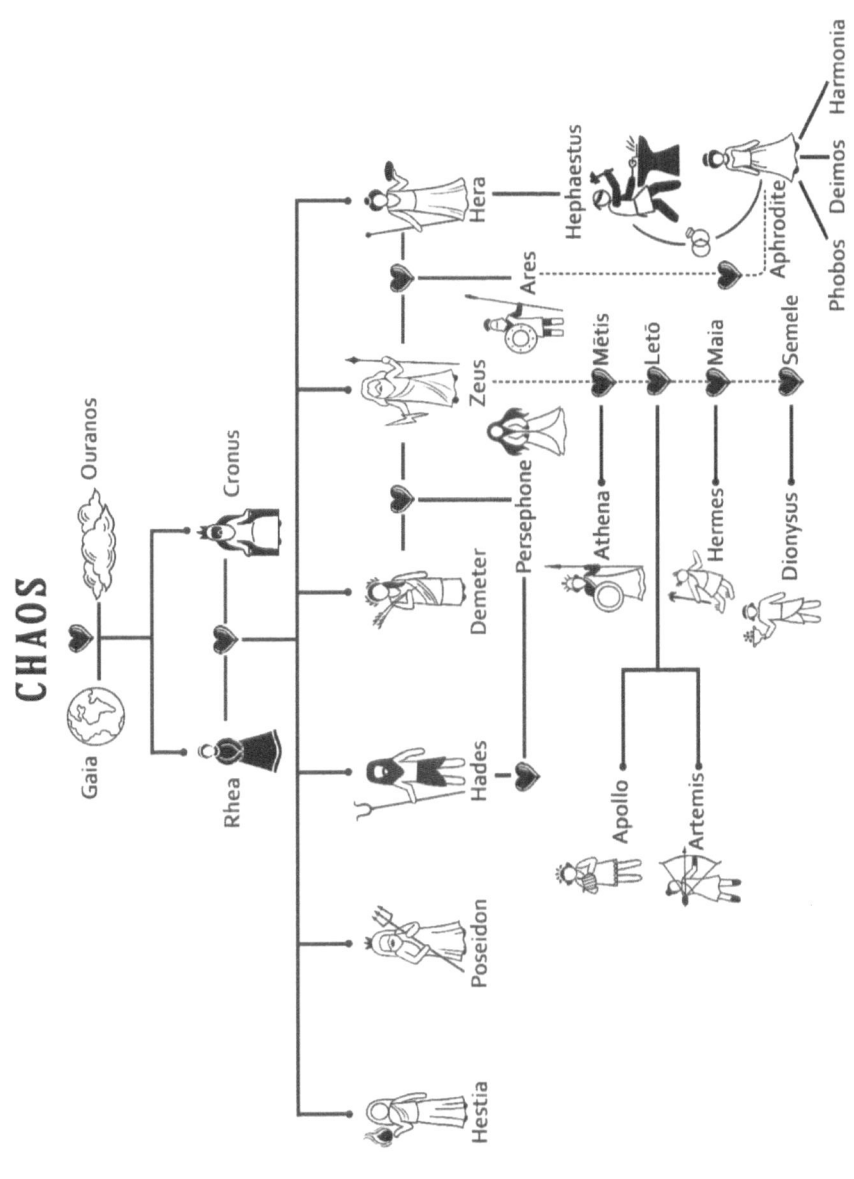

Prologue

From the Heliconian Muses, let us begin to sing, who hold the great and holy mount of Helicon, and dance on soft feet about the deep-blue spring and the altar of the almighty son of Cronus...

Over two millennia ago, and in a time yet to come, there lived a Greek poet by the name of Hesiod. Through divine insight, he perceived the human race as a vast family tree, its branches reaching high into the heavens. This he recorded in *Theogony*.

At that time, civilisation was young and the human mind inspired, expansive and poetic; more easily able to link Heaven and Earth. Thus, Hesiod could boldly state in *Works and Days* that 'gods and mortal men sprang from one source.'

In those far-off days, people recited stories in dactylic hexameter, a regular beat that lulled the mind and awakened the spirit. With the musical accompaniment of flute and lyre, portals opened, inviting the audience to soar beyond everyday mental processes into realms peopled by gods and goddesses.

The paradoxical nature of such stories appeals to the human psyche, as they speak to us of a deeper reality beyond the superficial constructs of our mind. Thus, parables, fairy tales and legends, recorded through the centuries, formed the template upon which history unfolded.

However, in recent times, the mystical approach gave way to the scientific, logical mind. People were encouraged to look elsewhere for answers and even ridiculed for daring to express their intrinsic nature, while deep within the shadows of denial, the narrative of the collective consciousness created a labyrinth of increasing complexity. Entranced by the comforting illusions, this twisted maze gradually imprisoned the human mind.

The time has come when we are beginning to see the self-imposed barriers that bind us to a world of endless problems and burdens. We long to discover a lost world of wonder and beauty within. The challenge looms before us, daunting and mocking, daring us to escape this web. Indeed, our very survival depends on it, as our shared sanity teeters on the edge of an all-consuming nightmare.

But we are jumping ahead, for every tale must have a beginning, and our story kicks off when our unfortunate friend finds herself in that very place where most stories end—the world beyond. In this realm, where death reflects the great unconscious, she sees her life through a dreamlike veil, making it difficult to distinguish between right and wrong, reality and illusion.

Shepherds of the wilderness, wretched things of shame, mere bellies. We know how to speak many false things as though they were true; But we know when, we will, to utter true things... Hesiod.

THE VEIL OF ILLUSIONS

1

The Guide

LIKE A PUFF OF wind, she flew from her now lifeless body that had been her home for the past thirty-nine years. In an instant, she hurtled through a tunnel, flying faster than the speed of light. The tunnel gave way to an ever-changing kaleidoscope of ethereal colours and patterns.

She floated gently. The experience felt strangely pleasant—as if rocked by a boat upon the waters.

I'm dreaming, she thought. *It must be time to collect my daughters from their sleepover.* She looked down at her hands... transparent, no longer flesh and blood. An arrow of fear sped through her.

What happened!

Instantly, a flotilla of swan-like beings surrounded her with soft wings, speaking to her in a language without words. "There is no place for fear in our realm. You're safe here."

Their voices sang a restful lullaby, and she gave herself up to the boundless comfort of their love.

After what seemed like an eternity, her eyes opened. Her ethereal body, light as gossamer, stood on black-and-white tiles. Potted palms lined the walls, and in front stood a blue doorway surrounded by tiles depicting mythical lions, tigers and goddesses.

An angelic being appeared before her, radiating an otherworldly glow. "Welcome home, Alison. I'm Angelo, your guide."

"My guide? Where am I?"

Angelo spread his arms. "You're in your foyer to the Afterlife, an extension of your worldly fantasy."

Fantasy was something Alison Maybridge had never thought about until now... life had seemed so real, so permanent.

She opened her mouth to speak, but words failed her. She blinked, and in an instant, a picture of an old-fashioned village square appeared on the wall. Alison recognised the image from the brochure she had picked up from the travel agent.

Her eyes widened. "Did I do that?"

Angelo smiled reassuringly. "This realm is nothing like the Earth plane, where sometimes you receive what you want and other times you get the opposite. Here, you create whatever you wish for."

The picture expanded into a lifelike hologram of stone buildings and trees surrounding a village square.

"Amazing," she whispered.

Angelo turned the handle and pushed open the blue door. An aroma of brewed coffee and the sound of children playing hopscotch on the cobblestones drifted from within. He held out his hand. "Come on. Let's explore your world of dreams."

Like movie stars on holiday, they strolled across the bustling piazza, Angelo in a white Armani suit and dark glasses, Alison wearing crisp white slacks and a floral top.

Beneath a spreading oak tree, schoolgirls in brightly patterned frocks chanted. "*When shall I marry? This year, next year, sometime, never.*"

They approached a stone well in the centre of the square. An ancient woman with wispy hair and a grey apron turned the handle until the bucket dangled over the well. Seeing Alison, she held out a penny. "Make a wish," she said, her pale eyes reflecting an otherworldly light.

"I wish to find happiness," said Alison as she tossed the penny into the well. It bounced against the stones before plopping into the water below.

The woman gave a toothless smile and offered Alison a glass of water. "Take my advice and drink from the waters of Lethe."

Alison turned to Angelo, her eyebrows raised. "Should I?"

His eyes met hers. "It's up to you. The Lethe is the river of forgetfulness. Drinking the water erases memories. It helps you move on... if you know what I mean?" He winked.

Alison reached for the glass. Holding it up, she watched the bubbles rise to the surface. "It looks like champagne," she said, bringing it slowly to her lips.

"No! Stop!" A shriek reverberated through the piazza.

Alison's arm jolted, and the glass slipped from her grasp, shattering on the cobblestones.

A woman limped towards her, waving her arms. "Sorry, I'm late. I'm Cora, your guide," she said breathlessly.

Alison stared wide-eyed at her purple dress and the untamed tendrils of hair poking out from beneath her hat. "But I already have a guide," she said, turning to Angelo.

Angelo gazed at her with doe-like eyes. "You have free will."

"What do you mean? What about my dream?" she asked.

He opened his mouth to speak. Cora interrupted. "He means you can drink from the Well of Forgetfulness and continue your dreamlike existence, or you can break free from the web of stories and remember who you really are."

Alison took a breath. Then, hearing the comforting hum of chatter and the clinking of glasses, she breathed out. The sun's rays filtered through the leaves, creating a dance of light and shadow on the cobblestones. "What should I do?"

"It's your choice," said Cora, her eyes flickering between Alison and Angelo.

Angelo's eyes overflowed with unspoken yearning. He reached out his hand.

Their fingers met, and Alison felt the tingle of his touch. She sighed, drifting into the orbit of his love. Part of her longed for him to stay, yet a deeper yearning erupted from within, bubbling up and threatening to engulf her.

The sound of chanting broke the stillness. "*What will my husband be? Tinker, tailor, soldier, sailor, rich-man, poor-man, beggar-man, thief.*"

An image of her daughters flashed through her mind, and with it came a crushing sense of loss. In an instant, the sights and sounds of the piazza appeared superficial and shallow, like a carefully constructed movie set. She turned to Angelo, but even he appeared two-dimensional, like the picture on the wall. She dropped his hand as if it were on fire. "I don't know why, but I can't do this." She lowered her eyes, her heart aching with regret.

Cora turned to Angelo, her eyes gleaming. "You heard her, Prince Charming. Goodbye."

His eyes widened, and he took a step back. "Farewell," he said. And with that, the dream faded.

Alison stared at the space where Angelo had stood. *What have I done?*

"Now, how about coffee?" said Cora.

Alison forced a smile. "That would be nice."

They crossed the piazza and stepped onto the footpath outside an outdoor café. A breeze ruffled the candy-striped awnings, and soft light filtered through the leaves, casting grey patterns on the tablecloths below.

They sat down.

Alison rested her head in her hands. The unending hum of voices buzzed like an army of cicadas.

Cora leant forward. "Great to see you again!"

Alison wondered where they had met before. She nodded. Her gaze shifted as she watched the people walking past.

"How was your transition?" asked Cora. Her tone seemed far too joyful for the occasion.

Alison clutched the serviette, attempting to maintain her composure, as she had long trained herself to do. "Everything happened so quickly. To be honest, I wasn't ready... not for death, or the Afterlife."

Cora tilted her head. "Very few are."

A vaporous mist swirled as the chanting increased in tempo. "*What will I be? Lady, baby, gypsy, queen.*"

Alison closed her eyes, hoping to banish the haunting images behind her eyelids. She longed to sip the champagne, to sink into oblivion. She opened her eyes. "Tell me, why did I have to leave... why?"

An elf in a green uniform approached, carrying a tray with mugs of coffee and plates piled high with hot buttered toast sprinkled with cinnamon and sugar. He smiled at Cora. "Anything else for the lady? A little pick-me-up, perhaps?"

"No, thank you, Avery," replied Cora.

Alison watched the elf as he walked away. "Who was that?"

Cora sipped her coffee. "Oh, Avery? He's a remnant of your long-forgotten world."

Alison took a deep breath.

"Now, getting back to why you had to leave. In short, there are no answers."

Alison's mouth slackened. She ran her hands through her ash-blonde hair. "And what does that mean? My life is over, and you tell me there are no answers?"

"Answers are an Earthly concept. In this realm, we see things differently—in time, you'll understand."

A slender man with a mop of red hair walked towards them, holding the hands of two dishevelled children. "Hi, Cora," he said as he passed. They sat at a nearby table.

Cora frowned. "Hey, Aidan, aren't they the twins from the explosion?"

He nodded. The children's eyes stared blankly, their faces distorted by fear and streaked with tears.

Cora pushed back her chair. "Excuse me, Alison. I'll be back soon." She hugged each child, and soon they were deep in conversation.

Alison took a bite. *Mm... cinnamon toast, my favourite.* She turned to watch the girls in their red and green patterned frocks. "*What shall I wear? Silk, satin, velvet, lace.*"

The girls disappeared, replaced by the faces of Alison's bright-eyed daughters. "Emma, Haley," she whispered. She reached out to touch them and the vision faded. Alison felt herself falling—down, down into a tunnel, spinning through time and space. Images from her childhood flickered like scenes from an old movie: her mother's homemade cakes, night-time stories, the schoolyard, playing hopscotch with her friends, her boyfriend, Bradley, their first kiss, the birth of her daughters, her hairdressing salon.

Life was good, wasn't it?

The newsreel continued: hide-and-seek in the backyard, her mother sobbing at night, her father yelling, her hiding place behind the water tank. She heard an ambulance siren, and her throat tightened. The air felt oppressively warm. The monotony of the endless chant drove a painful wedge through her mind. "*How shall I get it? Given, borrowed, bought, stolen.*"

Alison gasped. "Let me out of here!" she cried.

Faces turned toward her.

I must pull myself together, she thought. She took a deep breath and blinked away her tears.

Cora sat down. "Sorry about that. An explosion in the middle of a busy city. Aidan and I were there, lending our support, and just as I was about to leave, the two children accidentally slipped through their timeline and followed me into yours."

"What will become of them?"

"Once their little hearts are soothed, their relatives will take them home."

"Oh," said Alison. She watched the elf place bowls of chocolate chip and vanilla ice cream on the table. The children's eyes lit up with pleasure as they hungrily spooned the deliciousness into their mouths.

"How are you feeling?" Cora said warmly.

Alison slumped. "Terrible. I miss my girls. Can I go back?"

"Sure, anytime. Only they won't be able to see you. You're on the other side. That is the fantasy world—this is reality."

Fantasy? Alison recalled the events of the past few days... dropping the girls at school, vacuuming, washing the dishes, and then driving into town to her hairdressing salon. Her mind went blank. "How did I get here?"

"Don't you remember?" replied Cora.

Alison shook her head. "No, not really."

"Well, all I can say is, you're in an antechamber of your creation." Cora smiled. "Did you ever wish to be in a place like this?"

Alison gazed wistfully at the quaint buildings surrounding the piazza. "Oh, many times. It was my dream holiday. I even put aside money, but the more I tried to save, the more he spent..."

The chanting grew louder and more sinister. "*How shall I get to church? Coach, carriage, wheelbarrow, cart.*"

Her eyes clamped shut as her mind, distorted by confusion, spun out of control. A force gripped her throat. Seemingly out of nowhere, Stygian eyes glared, and a hot breath blew into her face. She forced a scream through clenched jaws. He slapped his hand over her mouth, and she descended into a vortex, spinning around and around.

She fell back against the chair, her arms hanging loosely at her side.

"Alison!" said Cora.

Alison trembled. "Huh, what?" She opened her eyes and stared vacantly as Cora's face fragmented into a kaleidoscope of shapes and colours.

"*Where shall I live? Big house, little house, pigsty, barn...*"

"I can't take this!" Alison cried, pushing out her chair. "Let me outta here!"

Cora reached over and held her arm. "Wait, stop. There's nothing to fear!"

Alison stared, wild-eyed. "No!" she cried, yanking herself free. She stumbled across the pavement and into the square, narrowly missing a man on a bicycle.

Cora stood helplessly on the footpath and watched her charge disappear.

Aidan caught her eye. "Free will?"

Cora nodded. "Something like that."

As if drawn like a magnet, Alison jogged along the road, faster and faster, until she broke into a sprint. Buildings flew by, and she had reached the edge of town before she knew it. She gripped a tree trunk to steady her thoughts—*what am I doing? Perhaps I should go back.*

The air shimmered like waves on the ocean as a sudden, sharp terror flooded her mind.

Her heart raced as she scanned the surroundings for an escape. Her eyes landed on a narrow lane that led into the countryside, and she took off like a hare across the vivid green hills under a pale aqua sky.

2

Snow White

ALISON RAN LIKE THE wind—free, no gravity, no tiredness, as if in a trance. The rhythm of her stride matched the beat of her heart.

The path took her high on a hilltop before taking her down, down into a tree-filled valley where the scent of lilies and maidenhair ferns filled the air and wild mushrooms dotted the forest floor.

A deer appeared on the path, its antlers like a regal headpiece. Alison hid behind a tree. *He looks just like the statue on my mantelshelf, the one Aunt Joyce gave me,* she thought.

His ears twitched, and he stepped lightly towards a pond. He looked around, put his head down and drank before bouncing off into the forest.

Curiosity drew Alison to the pond. Brushing aside the green ferns, she knelt at the water's edge, mesmerised by the light that danced across the surface. A trickle of water passed over mossy rocks before spilling into the water. Looking down, she watched the tiny fish dart in and out of their underwater palace.

"This place is so pretty," she said.

"Not as beautiful as you, my dear," said a voice.

Her eyes darted around.

"Down here!"

Alison took a breath and looked down at the water. The surface was as smooth as glass. She saw herself in the mirror, then ripples disturbed her reflection, and another face appeared.

"So lovely," sang the princess with the radiant eyes.

Alison gazed with longing at her silver earrings and fair hair.

"What is it you want?" asked the princess.

Alison's fingers touched the water, swirling around and around until they formed an eddy. "All I want is a handsome prince and a home, our castle. I want it so bad..." Her voice had a desperate edge to it.

"Look again. It's yours, all yours."

"Huh?" Alison looked down.

The water stilled, and a vision appeared on its mirror-like surface—a fairy tale bride in an off-the-shoulder gown sparkling with beadwork and lace. A tiara sat on her perfectly styled hair, and in her hands, she held a bouquet of pink and white flowers.

My dream wedding... Alison smiled.

The vision vanished in a whirl of ripples, and in its place stood an ancient hag, her eyelids hanging wearily over sunken eyes.

"It's a fantasy. Do you know the real you?" Her voice screeched like fingernails on a blackboard.

Alison shook her head.

"You're a failure," she hissed.

"No, no, I'm not!" cried Alison.

"Oh yes, you are—a useless piece of trash!" A hand shot forth, grabbing her arm in a vice-like grip.

Alison screamed as she hit the water, droplets flying, her arms churning like egg-beaters. "Let me go!" she cried.

"No escape—ever!" The voice cackled.

Down, down she went. Alison felt the weight of the water pressing around her, smothering her life force until she floated to the surface, limp and unmoving... then, like a helium balloon, she drifted upwards into the insipid blue sky.

She looked down at her hair fanned among the reeds. *Free at last... I don't need to think or feel anymore... I could drift like a cloud into nothingness.*

She heard the words, *'Then why are you still thinking?'*

A bolt of energy surged through her, and she plummeted. Alison threw back her head and gasped. She dragged herself out of the water, her clothes dripping and her hair matted with pond weed.

Sobbing, she stumbled into the woods and collapsed under a tree. Her anger and sorrow erupted in wild bursts as she beat the ground with her fists.

"Why? Why?!" she cried, her voice raw with anguish.

Finally, drained by the tornado, she drifted off to sleep.

The sunlight felt warm on her face. Alison awoke to the scent of lavender and the sound of singing.

She sat up... Her grandmother's favourite song.

Oh, Danny boy, the pipes, the pipes are calling.
From glen to glen, and down the mountainside.

The summer's gone, and all the roses falling.
It's you, it's you must go, and I must bide...
But come ye back when summers in the meadow,
Or when the valley's hushed and white with snow.
I'll be here in sunshine or in shadow.
Oh, Danny boy, oh Danny boy, I love you so...

Alison's eyes glistened with tears. *I love you too, Grandma.*

She watched a butterfly flutter in the breeze, following its path until it landed on a flower.

A cough sounded, and she looked up. On the bough sat an elf in a sky-blue suit.

He gazed at her through emerald eyes.

She blinked. *Not another one*, she thought. *This place is doing my head in!*

"Good morning, good evening and good day to you! It's all the same here." His voice had a lilt in it.

"Hello," she said as she straightened her top and pulled strands of pond weed from her hair.

His eyes sparkled. "Can I be of assistance?"

"Oh, thank you, but I'm fine," she said.

"Well, that's good. And where are you going?"

"I-I'm on my way home."

His forehead creased. "Which one? Home is a relative word in a multidimensional universe."

She stared at him. "My home on Earth, of course."

"Ah, of course. But why do you wish to return?"

So many questions... Alison sighed. "Well, for starters, my daughters need me."

"Oh!" The elf raised his eyebrows. "I see." He reached up and picked an apple and crunched it loudly. The juice trickled down his chin. "Is that why you ran away?"

Her eyes widened. "What? How did you know?"

"I have contacts." He smiled. "What were you running from?"

"Everything, but mostly this place." She shook her head. "It's so—bizarre."

"Ah, a common reaction. At least you're going somewhere; that's what I always say." The elf kicked the air with his boot. "Well, I'll be off if you don't need my help." He dropped the apple core and prepared to jump down from the branch.

"Wait! I'm sorry. What I'm trying to say is, I'm not ready for..." Her voice faltered.

"This level of transparency?" he said.

Alison sighed. "This place is like looking into a mirror."

"Surprising, isn't it?" he smiled.

She ran her fingers through her hair. "I don't want to be forced to look at myself."

"Relax! No one can force you to do anything. It's your story."

She shook her head. "It sure doesn't feel like it."

"That's because you're still in transit between worlds, so you're going to cling to what's familiar," said the elf. "In time, you'll come to see that life is as fragile as a butterfly in a field of flowers." He gazed at her. "You know, we too were forced to leave the Earthly plane."

"Oh, what happened?"

Resting against the tree trunk, he gazed into the distance. "Well, it's like this. We elves lived in harmony with humans for hundreds; nay, thousands of years."

"Thousands?" said Alison.

"It could have been longer or even shorter. Time means little to us." He sighed. "Life was good. The farmers followed the cycle of the seasons —planting, growing, harvesting, celebrating with a joke, a beer and a rollicking song. Humans left treats and gifts for us, and we played pranks on them so that their lives did not become too solemn. The cycle continued like a well-oiled clock until everything changed."

Alison's brow furrowed. "What do you mean?"

He frowned. "It all began when armies of workers laid railway tracks through our meadows and forests and, not long after, they dug for coal. The earth groaned as they pulled out the black lumps, and the sky filled with the smoke from their chimney stacks. As they dug up the land and blasted their way through the hills, we had no choice but to hide, only revealing ourselves to those living in harmony with nature; mainly the children. Then the war began, and the army used our homeland for target practice. That's when our story ended."

"How awful!" said Alison. "I remember Grandma telling me about the wee folk."

He tilted his cap. "I remember her well," he grinned. "She used to sing as she cooked, and afterwards, she left us gifts of biscuits and cakes on the windowsill."

"Gifts? Oh, that's because she left them there to cool..." She stopped and stared. "Hey, aren't you the elf from the café?"

"Common mistake. I'm Aldrin. That's my brother, Avery. We have to keep an eye on the newbies." He slid off the branch and landed softly on the ground. "We heard you're one of the special ones."

She felt a twinge. "I don't know about that. I'm just an ordinary mother, hairdresser and wife."

Aldrin looked up at her. "Ah, but those were the roles you played. Who are you, really?"

Her throat tightened. "Well, whoever I am, I feel like a failure."

"Oh, that's sad. We must find a way to cheer you up." The elf gazed at her with his emerald eyes. "I'm one of seven brothers, and we have a little cottage in the woods. We're looking for a housekeeper. Are you interested?"

Alison blinked. *How strange*, then a feeling of familiarity flickered. The more she thought about it, the more appealing the idea appeared—in fact, it seemed the perfect fit.

She nodded. "That would be nice."

His eyes lit up. "Oh, wonderful! Come on then," he said, setting off along the path.

As if in a dream, Alison followed.

They made their way deeper and deeper into the forest. Time seemed to slow. Trees loomed, their trunks and branches gnarled. Shadows flickered in her mind, and a feeling of foreboding came over her. She heard a voice. "Mirror, mirror on the wall, who is the fairest of them all?"

"Oh, no!" she cried, her heart pounding.

Aldrin turned. "Come on, we're nearly there."

Alison ran to catch up. Soon, they reached a cottage nestled in a clearing. A curl of smoke rose from the chimney. They arrived at the doorstep. Through the open door, Alison saw a fire crackling in the hearth and a wooden dining table set with placemats and cutlery for seven.

It looks so cosy, she thought.

"Come in," said Aldrin. "I'll warm the pottage. Avery will be home soon with cheese and freshly baked bread."

Alison was about to follow when a breeze blew her hair. She heard a voice.

"Oh, Alison!"

She turned and stared, wide-eyed.

On the path stood a goddess, her eyes as deep as midnight and her hair cascading over a rose-coloured gown. The goddess raised her eyebrows. "Do I detect a fairy-tale ending?"

Aldrin appeared in the doorway. Seeing the goddess, he bowed. "Greetings, Persephone."

"Greetings, Aldrin," said Persephone, then her eyes narrowed.

"Oh, I-I can explain," he stuttered.

Persephone smiled serenely.

"It was like this; I came across this lady in the forest. She looked lost and alone, so I invited her back to the cottage."

Persephone nodded. "And...?"

Alison piped up. "I just want to be happy."

"She just wants to be happy," echoed the elf.

Persephone gazed at Alison with a quizzical look. "Need I remind you how this story ends? Snow White eats a poisoned apple and falls into a deep sleep..."

Alison's heartbeat quickened as she recalled the eeriness of the twisted trees and the warning voice. She gasped. "Oh, I can't handle this!"

"Then leave!" said Persephone.

Alison blinked, trying to awaken from the dream. "It's not that easy."

Persephone's gaze met hers. "Try to remember who you are."

Alison faltered, fear rising like a tide within her. "I-I don't know," she said. The air stilled and, in an instant, the sights and sounds of the forest appeared flat, like an illustration in a book.

"Come on, Alison," said the goddess. "Trust yourself."

Alison drew in a shaky breath and recalled her daughters. A ripple of light spread from her heart; shadows cracked like glass. Slowly, the twisted forest began to straighten. *What am I doing?* She thought. *I can make my own choices...*

She turned to Aldrin. "I'm sorry, but who I am lies beyond this story."

His eyes glistened. "Are you sure?"

She nodded, still trembling, but steadier now. *I'm not Snow White...*

"See?" said Persephone. "You've begun to step out of the story. The rest will come in time." The goddess waved her hands, and with a burst of magic, the spell of Snow White shattered into a million pieces.

Alison threw back her head and breathed.

"Are you ready?" said the goddess.

Alison nodded, and they set off into the forest.

"Until we meet again!" Aldrin's voice echoed through the trees.

Alison frowned. "What did he mean?"

"No need to dwell on things you don't understand," said Persephone. "Now, it's time to discover the magic of who you are."

As they walked, Alison noticed her limp. "You remind me of someone," she said, frowning. "Aren't you Cora, my guide?"

"Yes, I am," said Persephone. She turned to Alison with a slight smile. "Arthritis, you know. It comes from years of living in the Underworld."

"But why?"

"I try not to overwhelm the newbies, at least not all at once, so I use my original name, the Kore."

"Oh, I see... I think," Alison's gaze lowered, "I'm sorry I ran away."

Persephone nodded. "Not unusual. I often find that humans are afraid of their own shadows."

Alison's eyes widened. "Really?"

They continued in silence, then Alison glanced over. "I must say, it's a beautiful gown."

"Oh, thank you," Persephone replied. "I wear it when visiting my father, Zeus. With his eyesight failing, he finds it difficult to distinguish the various goddesses unless they wear their traditional garb."

"Zeus?" Alison frowned. "I'm sorry, but I don't know much about ancient history. It was hard to concentrate. My high school history teacher was so cute."

Persephone smiled. "I too, was once at an age when my concentration lapsed and destiny took over."

Alison frowned. "Why? What happened?"

"I was gathering flowers with my friends in the fields when I spied a cluster of golden narcissus flowers," replied Persephone. "The moment I stooped; Hades arrived in his chariot and whisked me off to his home in the Underworld."

Alison frowned. "How dreadful. But what about your father?"

Persephone shrugged. "Zeus knew that my mother Demeter would not agree to the match, and so he and his brother Hades had arranged for my abduction."

"Abducted by your uncle! Whoa, that's creepy."

"Yes, but in those days, fathers decided who their daughters would marry, and they often chose uncles to keep their wealth in the family."

"How strange," said Alison. "But the story isn't real. It's just a myth, isn't it?"

"Are thoughts real?" asked Persephone.

Alison shook her head. "I don't know."

"Of course, you don't, which is why you can open your mind to my so-called myth, which is all about facing your shadow." Persephone's eyes bored into her. "While on your Earthly quest to find happiness, you ended up in the deep, dark depths. Is that right?"

The crunch of Alison's boots on the gravel magnified against the forest's stillness. She nodded slowly. "Well, yes."

"I too, felt desolate. I wanted to escape. That was until I discovered the secret of my happiness." She turned to Alison. "Speaking of which, Zeus offered to lend me his latest flying machine. Would you care to join me?"

"Oh," said Alison. "Is it a chariot with horses?"

Persephone shook her head. "Zeus has several horse-drawn chariots, but now the gods create flying machines using the latest technology. They still call them chariots, of course."

She smiled. "Oh, yes!"

"Very good." With a wave of her hand, Persephone changed into grey slacks and an ivory top, her hair tied behind. Then she slipped on a pair of designer sunglasses.

Alison stood transfixed.

"You'll get used to us after a while," she said as she pushed aside a waterfall of vines.

Alison gazed at the swan-like flying machine. "Wow, that's amazing!"

Persephone placed her hand on the bird's wing. "It sure is. Hop in, and we'll take it for a spin."

Alison clambered into the seat. She felt for the seat belt, but there was nothing...

Persephone slid into the seat next to her. The chariot gave a jolt as it lifted off the ground. A flock of red and green parrots flew, squawking, into the sky.

In an instant, they were hovering high above the trees. Then Persephone pressed a button, and the chariot shot forward, throwing Alison back against the seat.

She gasped.

Persephone grinned. "Let's live dangerously!"

3

The Wolf

ALISON GRIPPED THE SEAT, her hair swirling around her face as the chariot somersaulted through the air and swooped low over the hills.

Persephone smiled calmly. "Don't worry; there are no accidents in our realm."

Gradually, she relaxed her grip.

"Would you like to visit Zeus' domain?"

Alison's breath caught in her throat. "What, you mean, go home?"

Persephone nodded.

"Oh, yes," said Alison eagerly, thinking she could bail out as soon as they arrived.

Persephone touched the controls, and the craft blasted downwards, leaving a trail of silver vapour behind. They passed through a bank of clouds, and the continents came into view. They soared high above a maze of rivers and roads that looked like strands of spaghetti.

"Wonderful, isn't it?" said Persephone. "The emerald earth, the sky and the deep-blue ocean—the perfect theatre backdrop."

Alison frowned. It wasn't how she remembered it.

Flying over a patchwork of green and yellow reminded Alison of her honeymoon flight to the islands. She recalled the passion and the quarrels and winced.

The chariot swooped over the suburbs, so close they almost touched the red and grey roofs. Alison inhaled a mixture of sea breeze and car exhaust. "Home at last," she said, pointing to a two-storey house. "That's it. I promised to take my girls swimming and to their favourite café afterwards."

The craft slowed and then hovered.

Alison stared at the drawn curtains and the cars parked next to a taped-off area. "Hey, why are there police cars around my home?"

"There was a bereavement in the family," replied Persephone.

Alison's eyes widened. "Are my daughters okay?"

"Don't worry, I heard they're fine."

"Well, what about my salon?"

"Let's take a look," said Persephone. She touched the controls, and the chariot zoomed down the main street, weaving in and out of the traffic until it came to a row of shops. They hovered above the car park.

Alison pointed. "That's it. Style Leader Hair Design." She stared for a moment and frowned. "The blinds are closed; the place looks deserted. Where is my staff? Where is everyone?!"

"I guess they're coming to terms with your sudden departure."

Alison shook her head. "Oh, what?"

"How can I help you remember?" Persephone tapped her finger on her temple. "Ah, I've got it." She passed her hand over the controls, and the chariot sped towards the centre of town. Ahead stood a stone building that housed the local newsroom. The chariot hovered outside the first-floor window.

"Follow me," said Persephone, gliding out of the chariot and through the open window. "Over here," she said, positioning herself behind a journalist.

He shivered. Pushing back his chair, he walked to the window and pulled it shut.

Alison stared at the screen. "Another woman's life tragically lost. This week, yet another casualty of domestic violence, Alison Maybridge, a well-loved member of our community. Her husband, Bradley Maybridge, is under investigation."

Alison stepped backwards, eyes bulging. *No, not Bradley; he couldn't have.*

Then the realisation struck her like an oncoming bus. *It was late; he was drunk. We argued, and then he hit me.*

Her face paled, and she swayed.

Persephone moved fast, surrounding Alison in a force field. She quickly propelled them through the wall and into the chariot.

Alison curled up with her hands over her face. "No—stop!" she cried as she plummeted into a shadowy realm. Ghostly figures milled about like a murder of crows, mocking her with their whispers. *She deserved it... Her husband was a pushover... They're so naïve, humans.*

Alison squeezed her eyes. Her chest rose and fell as she struggled to make sense of the voices echoing in her head.

Persephone placed a comforting hand on her shoulder.

Alison opened her eyes and brushed the hair from her face. "I heard voices..." Her throat tightened. "They were mean."

"Don't worry; you're safe," said Persephone.

"But the headlines—I forgot it all."

Persephone's eyes softened. "Over time, you became used to shutting down your emotions, and so it was natural that you blocked the memory of your own death. Now, breathe and release. It takes courage to face your past, but you're not a victim anymore."

Tears ran down Alison's cheeks.

At last, she took a deep breath and wiped her eyes with the back of her hand. "I tried my best to be a good wife and mother, but nothing I did was right. He questioned me about my friends and how I spent my money. Oh, yes, he verbally abused me, but it wasn't until he started hitting me, I knew I had to leave."

"A common pattern," said Persephone.

"I told him it was over. I wanted to take the girls to a shelter, but what about my hairdressing business? It was all so complicated. I had nowhere to turn." She bit her lip. "Oh, Persephone, let's get out of here."

"A-okay." Persephone touched the controls. A zigzag of lightning flickered behind them as they ascended through the clouds.

Alison leaned back. "Oh," she groaned. "I feel like such a failure."

"That's just an old program playing in your head," said Persephone. "Do you recognise the spiral of negative thoughts that drag you down?"

"I never bothered about thoughts." Alison frowned. "But I see them now."

"You see them, but do you still believe them?"

"I don't know," replied Alison.

"Well, think about it," said Persephone. "Why should you listen to thoughts that highlight your flaws and prey on your insecurities? Yes, you suffered and made mistakes, and no, it wasn't fair or right, but give yourself a break. You can't change what happened, but you can choose how to perceive it. You can either remain a victim of circumstances or master the illusion."

Alison sighed. "I don't want to be a victim."

"Then know yourself as spirit, and spirit is powerful, beyond your wildest dreams."

The craft made a series of jolts as it sped through a dark cloud and out into the sunshine.

"The crossover between realms can be rough," said Persephone. "Look down there. We're passing over the Lake of the Hereafter."

Alison found the sight of colourful boats bobbing on the vast cerulean waters somehow soothing. As they flew on, she looked down at the olive-green valleys, clear blue rivers and open fields brimming with herds of wild deer and elephants. "It reminds me of a movie set," she said.

"That's right," said Persephone. "In the words of Shakespeare, all the world's a stage, and all the men and women merely players. They have their exits and their entrances."

Alison blinked. "I don't remember hearing that at school."

They passed over a range of tree-covered hills before descending into a valley below.

Alison's ears popped. "Where are we going?"

Persephone pointed to a rooftop. "Down there. There's someone I'd like you to meet."

The chariot touched down in a clearing near a fairy ring of thatched cottages. "Run along now. You don't want to keep your grandparents waiting."

"My grandparents?!" Alison beamed with delight. She pushed open the door and jumped down.

She gazed at the cottage surrounded by a garden full of colourful flowers. There was something strangely familiar about the scene. It reminded her of a picture book Grandma had read to her when she was a child.

Alison unlatched the wooden gate, and a shower of fairy dust blew up in her face. She brushed it aside. Remembering it was bad luck to step on the cracks, she skipped along the path. She stood on tiptoes to reach the metal knocker. It clanged.

"Come in," a voice growled.

Her eyes widened. Cautiously, she pushed open the door. Her footsteps echoed on the wooden floorboards. She walked along the musty hallway papered with faded yellow roses and opened the bedroom door. Beady eyes scrutinised her from beneath the bedcovers.

"My, what large ears you have, Grandma." Her words flowed, as though she was part of the story.

"All the better to hear you with," came a voice, low and menacing.

"Oh, and what bright eyes," she said.

The wolf smirked, revealing a row of long, white canines. "All the better to see you with, my dear."

"And Grandma, what big teeth..." Alison felt a stab of fear in the pit of her stomach. *Uh-oh, I remember how this story ends.* She spun around and ran down the hallway and out the front door.

Alison closed the garden gate and walked briskly down the path, not daring to look back. She heard a dog yap followed by a woman's voice. "Oh, Alison!"

She turned to see her grandparents at the gate, a black-and-white dog at their feet. "Grandma, Grandpa!" she ran back along the path.

Her grandmother wrapped her in a loving embrace. "Oh, Alison, how wonderful to see you again. Come in!"

How strange, thought Alison. The house looked fresh and bright. Gone were the faded wallpaper and the musty smell. Flowers on the coffee table filled the air with a sweet scent. She sat on the sofa. The little dog gazed up at her, tail wagging. "I remember this little fellow," she said.

"Jess has been with me forever," said her grandfather.

Hmm, this takes forever to a whole new level, she thought.

"How are you?" Her grandmother spoke in a lilting tone.

Alison sighed. "It's been a rollercoaster ride."

Her grandmother's eyes glistened. "Oh dear, your Earthly experience would test anyone's faith. Why don't you come into the kitchen while I make a pot of tea?"

She followed her grandmother into the kitchen, gazing at the lacy curtains and the old wooden table in front of the stove. A radio on the window ledge played an old tune. "What a cosy home you have."

"I'm glad you think so, dear," replied her grandmother. "It's been in the family for generations." She filled the kettle from the tap and placed it on the hot plate, then she sighed. "This place is pleasant enough, but we'd like a sea change."

Presently, the kettle squealed. Alison's grandmother poured the steaming water into the teapot. She turned to Alison; a thin line of worry creased her forehead. "Why did you run from the cottage? Did something scare you?"

"Would you believe I saw a wolf?" said Alison.

"Oh, my word, how annoying... he always appears at family gatherings. I wish he'd leave us alone," she muttered.

Alison blinked. "How strange. Can't you make him disappear?"

Her grandmother shook her head. "I enquired with the authorities, but they told me he is part of our family history, so unfortunately, he's here to stay."

Alison's eyes widened. "But why? Can you tell me more?"

"Well, dear, I was talking to your aunt..."

They heard a cough and turned. Her grandfather stood in the doorway. "What's keeping you, girls? Come on, I want to show you my powers of manifestation!"

"Coming," her grandmother said, picking up the tray.

Just as the conversation was getting interesting... she thought as she followed them to the dining room.

Her grandfather moved his hands back and forth across the table and muttered a few words. Instantly, platters of grapes, cheesecake, pavlova, cakes and delicate sandwiches appeared.

Alison's mouth dropped open. "Oh, Grandpa, you're a magician!"

He grinned. "Here, try some." He piled a plate with pavlova and handed it to her.

Alison spooned the gooey mess into her mouth. "Mm, delicious."

Her grandmother poured the tea. An earthy fragrance lingered in the air. "Do you have sugar?" She said, handing her a cup.

Alison nodded, stirring the tea with a spoon.

Her grandmother's face softened. "We were expecting you."

Alison looked up. "You were?"

"Yes. We were sorry to hear that your life ended; however, we had a feeling that something might bring you home earlier than planned."

Alison's eyes widened. "What, how did you know?"

"Just a little something I overheard while visiting the in-laws," her grandmother tilted her head.

"Really?" Alison whispered, wondering how they knew, after all, she had tried so hard to hide her marriage woes from the family.

Her grandmother dolloped cream onto a large scone. "No secrets here."

"It seems that way," Alison sighed wistfully. "All I wanted was a fairy-tale wedding, a comfortable home and two children. My wedding day was a washout, Bradley lost all our savings, and now this."

Her grandfather shook his head. "I'm sorry, Alison. I understand he was a gambler."

She sighed. "And an alcoholic, although he would never admit it."

"What he did was wrong, but he will face the consequences—we all do." Alison's grandfather gazed at her affectionately. "You did your best, and we're proud of you."

Alison's eyes glistened. "Thank you, Grandpa."

Her grandmother reached for a framed baby picture. "Haley and Emma. Aren't they beautiful?"

Alison gazed at the picture and smiled. "They're young misses now; teenagers." She sighed. "I hope to see them again."

"You will," her grandmother said. "I heard your father is looking after them."

Alison's eyes widened. "Oh, really?"

"Yes." Her grandmother nodded. "One thing's for certain; life on the other side can be a challenge."

Alison looked down at her empty plate. "I feel so helpless."

Her grandfather reached over and touched her hand. "Your Earthly life may have finished, Alison, dear, but your story isn't over yet."

She nodded slowly. "You're right. I have no choice but to move on."

"We can watch out for the girls if you like," said her grandmother. "I often check in on the family and give them advice." She smiled. "Mostly they ignore me."

"Remember the time you helped Jason turn the steering wheel?" said her grandfather.

Her grandmother nodded. "Just in time to miss an oncoming car."

"Wow, that's amazing," said Alison. "Thank you for offering, Grandma. That would be lovely."

At that moment, Jess jumped up and scampered to the door, yapping.

Persephone stood in the doorway. "Sorry to drag Alison away, but it's time we left."

They said their goodbyes, and her grandparents stood at the garden gate, waving white hankies.

The craft reached cruising altitude and then circled before soaring across the sky.

"How are your grandparents?" asked Persephone.

"They're great. Only my grandmother told me they would like to move house, but for some reason, they can't."

"Did she say why?"

"She wasn't sure. In any case, they seem happy enough."

"People are happy because they drink from the Well of Forgetfulness," said Persephone.

"Lucky for them." Alison sighed. "It would be so nice to forget the lies, insults and the late nights arguing..."

Persephone glanced over at Alison. "I advise you to keep your memories alive. Only by uncovering the secrets within do you encounter your light."

Alison frowned. "Speaking of secrets, I met a wolf in their house."

"Ah!" Persephone's eyes brightened. "The Wolf—a fascinating but not uncommon pattern."

Alison tilted her head. "What do you mean?"

"In times past, people didn't understand the critical voice inside their heads, and so they imagined their thoughts as monsters, wolves or negative spirits."

A quiet unease moved through Alison. She saw again the eyes watching her from beneath the covers. "So, the wolf is a family pattern?"

Persephone nodded. "When a woman devalues herself, she leaves herself open to abuse and, at the same time, passes the pattern onto her daughters. It works like a magic spell."

Alison frowned. "Sounds like a curse to me," she murmured. "How do we break the cycle?"

"With some difficulty," said Persephone. "It requires that you see it clearly, which means you must pass through the darkness of the story before you can transform it."

"I'd like to transform my story," Alison said quietly. "But I'm not ready... not yet, anyway."

Persephone nodded. "Which is why I suggest you keep your memories alive. Sometimes the pain of seeing the truth is necessary in order to break the spell."

A long silence followed. Alison felt the wolf's gaze, its eyes searching. She took a breath. "Speaking of magic, Grandpa manifested a beautiful afternoon tea."

Persephone raised her eyebrows. "Manifestation is also magic." She paused. "But even more, you can harness the power of your mind to see through the illusions."

Alison exhaled. "Easy for you to say; you're a goddess."

Persephone's eyes flashed. "You realise goddesses do not exist in isolation—we live within the consciousness of humanity."

"Really? They didn't teach us that at school."

"Reality was not a strong point in your school curriculum," said Persephone. "We can play catch-up. Shoot me a question, anything you like."

Alison rolled her eyes. "Um... well, if life is a theatre, where's the script?"

"Good question," said Persephone. "In ancient times, everything was new. Life was simple, and the blueprints of the script were unmistakable. However, as time passed, the human story expanded, and the original blueprint faded into mere myths and fairy tales."

"Oh," said Alison. "That reminds me, my daughters used to enjoy Sleeping Beauty."

"And just like Sleeping Beauty, your true self was asleep whilst you lived each day on autopilot," said Persephone.

Alison raised her eyebrows. "My true self, what do you mean? I made my own choices."

"It may have seemed that way, but think about it. Most people react to the life around them, mistaking their reactions for their true selves. They rarely question themselves, nor do they look within to examine what is happening. They make plans, and when things go wrong, they feel frustrated or depressed. Isn't that so?" She glanced over at Alison.

Alison faltered. Was that true of her? She wanted to deny it, but memories surfaced. She recalled the times she had acted out of fear or habit, without thinking why.

She took a deep breath. "I-I suppose so," she said, slowly. "But then, what was I doing all that time?"

"Sleepwalking, perhaps?" Persephone smiled.

Alison frowned. "So, you're saying none of it was real?"

"Real enough to learn from," Persephone said gently. "But not who you truly are."

They continued in silence. Alison looked up. "You know, to be honest, at times I felt different from the people around me but I just ignored my feelings and got on with it."

Persephone nodded. "Old souls often feel that way."

"You mean I lived before?"

"Yes," said Persephone. "Only you forgot."

A shiver ran down Alison's spine. She squeezed her eyes shut until the feeling passed, then she opened them again. "Where are we going?"

"The City of Dreams."

"Will I see my mother?"

"Most probably," said Persephone.

The chariot sped quietly through the sky, accompanied only by a group of multicoloured flying craft. On board, people chatted. One by one, the crafts joined in formation, swooping and soaring like flocks of birds. As they reached their destinations, the passengers bid farewell to each other with waves and smiles before their chariots peeled off from the group and went their separate ways.

"Who are they?" asked Alison.

"There are many sightseers in this world," replied Persephone.

The sun sank behind the hills. The sky turned russet, then darkened. From below, a cascade of lights illuminated a helipad on the ground.

The chariot landed.

"Well, this is it," said Persephone.

Alison gazed into the Twilight Zone. "You're leaving me *here*?"

Persephone nodded.

"But I thought you were my guide?"

"I'm only a thought away. Meanwhile, you need time and space to sort yourself out, and I need to get back to the Elysian Fields. But we'll catch up soon."

Alison frowned. "How do I get to the City of Dreams?"

"Don't worry, I arranged for a driver to collect you." Persephone reached into her pocket and pulled out a chain with a gold locket in the shape of a flower. "Wear this to remind you of your magic."

Alison clipped the chain around her neck and clambered down.

"The car will be here at any moment. I'll be off now. Ciao, bella." Persephone fluttered her fingers, and the chariot rose. "Remember, you are the driver of your story."

Alison watched until the light was just a speck in the sky. She rubbed her arms, chilly from the night air. Crickets hummed. Distant lights flickered, and church bells pealed their mournful tones.

Alison shivered. She had never felt so alone. As she walked towards the bus shelter, a high-pitched buzzing noise began, faint at first, and with each step it grew louder. Alison stopped and listened for a moment, then shook her head.

Must be traffic, she thought. She took another step, and a screech like feedback from a microphone blasted through her head.

She clamped her hands over her ears. "What the...!"

Alison walked faster, trying to escape the pain. Visions flashed across her mind's eye; snippets of memories, moments that seemed like a lifetime, The smell of Bradley's aftershave, the flowers he bought her after their arguments, his rasping voice, his apologetic attempts at compliments, his lips, his smile.

She recalled their honeymoon, the warm glow of exhilaration. The feeling she longed for—of being wanted and adored. The feeling of belonging that momentarily silenced the emptiness in her heart.

The buzzing continued. Memories rolled like a movie reel: quarrels over money, the yelling, the terror that ran through her veins as he walked through the front door. Suddenly, she froze. Trapped by fear, sparks began slowly behind the eyes, then a blinding flash. Her hands flew up to her head; the zigzag lines that come before a migraine.

'Mum has a headache,' she heard the girls whisper, knowing their mother would be out of reach for the next few hours.

Oncoming headlights dazzled her eyes, sending daggers into her head. Alison gasped.

A black Mercedes pulled up alongside her, and the window wound down. The driver leaned out. He wore a cap, and his smile was wide and toothless.

Her eyes sprang open, and she took a step back.

"Alison Maybridge?" he enquired.

She nodded.

The door swung open, and a driver in a suit and tie hopped out. His features, brown and knobbly, resembled a giant toad.

"At your service," he croaked.

4

The City of Dreams

THE CAR SPED ALONG the road, its headlights beaming snake-like in front. Alison stared at the driver's leathery skin and the warts on the back of his neck. "So, why am I being driven by a toad?" she wondered out loud.

The driver glanced in the rearview mirror. "Don't ask me, madam; it's your story."

Alison closed her eyes, trying to ease her throbbing head. Her mind swam with images of crocodile-infested waters. A toad with wide lips and bubble eyes loomed close. Her nostrils filled with a sour swamp odour as his lips puckered. "Kiss me," she heard him say. Suddenly, she clutched her stomach as a wave of nausea struck the back of her throat.

"Stop, I'm going to be sick!"

The car swerved onto the verge. Alison pushed open the door, stumbled a few paces and then lurched forward, expelling a mass of radioactive green worms. They squirmed and glistened in the dark. A sour taste filled her mouth. Alison leaned her hand against a tree and breathed deeply.

At least my headache is gone, she thought as she climbed back into the car.

The driver turned and handed her a drink. "Are you feeling better, ma'am?"

Seeing his brown eyes and trimmed beard, she blinked. "Yes, thanks." She sipped the iced tea. "I'm sorry. I don't know what came over me."

"It's okay, I've seen it all before," said the driver. "People feel freer once they purge their past."

He started the engine, and the car merged back onto the road.

Alison wound down the window, and a refreshing breeze tousled her hair.

"Excuse me."

"Yes?" said the driver.

"Why is the sun shining, and, uh... where's the toad?"

The driver glanced in the rearview mirror. "Newcomers often find the reflection of unconscious thoughts quite unnerving. I find a long drive always helps."

He swung onto a two-lane highway and merged with a cavalcade of fast-moving cars. "We're about to enter the City of Dreams. Who is your closest relative?"

"Oh!" said Alison. "My mother. She passed away quite recently."

The driver pressed a button on the console. "Number fifteen Buck Avenue." He exited the freeway and entered a suburban street. Passing a row of houses, he slowed down. Pulling over, he checked the flashing light on the console. "Look familiar?" he asked.

Alison stared at the white weatherboard cottage, the unkempt lawn and the ragged pink and blue hydrangeas in the front garden. "Y-Yes, that's it," she stammered.

The driver stepped out and opened her door. "Good luck, and may all your dreams come true."

"Thank you," she replied.

The car door closed with a thud, and he drove off.

Alison took a breath and started walking towards the front door.

A permed head popped over the wooden fence. "Hello, Alison dear."

"Oh!" said Alison, and then she remembered her neighbour. "Gladys, how lovely. I didn't expect to see you."

"Oh, well, here I am." Gladys grinned and held up the nozzle of the hose. "Watering, as usual. Arnold is inside watching the cricket. You won't find anyone at home. Your mother and aunt are at the mall chasing the weekly dream specials." She glanced at her watch. "They should be back soon."

"Gladdie...," a voice called from the window.

"I won't be long," she answered. "It's lunchtime, must go. Nice to see you again." Her face disappeared.

Alison wandered through the side gate and into the backyard. The metal swings, the vegetable garden overrun with weeds, the washing line and the old shed. It all looked so familiar. A tabby cat rubbed against her legs. Alison bent down to stroke her soft fur. "Oh, Tabitha, my dear."

She recalled the day her school friend's mother led her to the woodshed at the back of their house. They opened the door, and the kitten's eyes shone in the dim light. She had placed the tiny tabby carefully in her school bag and carried her home, where she had remained ever since.

Alison opened the back door, breathing in the familiar scent of laundry powder, toast and tea. Tabitha strolled along the hallway, her tail in the air. Alison followed. Cautiously, she opened her bedroom door and peered inside. The room was just as she remembered: the floral bedspread, piles of schoolbooks on the desk and her coat flung over the back of the chair.

The bed squeaked as she sat down. Alison opened the bedside drawer and pulled out her old diary, papered with hearts and roses. *I wonder,* she thought as she flicked to the last page and read. *'I went to the prom last night and danced with Bradley, my one and only.'* Her stomach churned. She quickly slid the diary into the drawer.

Gazing into the full-length mirror, she blinked. Looking back at her was a fresh-faced teenager wearing a red chiffon dress—the one she had worn to the school prom. Alison stood up. "I'm young again!" She switched on the radio. Her dress swirled as she danced around the room.

Baby, you don't know what it's like
...to love somebody... to love somebody
the way I love you...

A knock echoed in the hallway. Alison ran to the front door. A young man stood on the doorstep in faded blue jeans and a T-shirt. His nose was flecked with freckles and mousy hair flopped over one eye. Seeing her red dress, he smiled shyly, then pushed the hair from his eyes.

"Hey, Alison," he said.

"Ah...," Alison blinked. "I'm sorry, you are?"

"School, remember? Ian, Ian McKenzie."

School-day memories sped through her mind. Ian was a bookish boy who wore black-rimmed glasses and spent lunchtimes in the library. A smile spread across her face. "Oh, Ian. Yes, of course. You lived in the next suburb with your mum."

"Still do."

"I knew your mother had passed." She frowned. "I'm so sorry, I didn't realise you..."

"Hey, it's okay," he said. "I just wanted to say welcome. It's nice to see a familiar face."

"Thanks. It's kind of you to call." Alison stood for a moment, holding her breath, then exhaled. "Why don't you come in?"

"Sure," Ian said, stepping inside.

They sat in the living room staring at the old television set. "So, how did you know I was here?" she said, breaking the silence.

"Mum told me... it was bad luck."

Alison stared at the patterned rug. "You can say that again."

"She said you have two daughters."

Alison nodded. "I miss them so much. Emma is fifteen and Haley is two years younger." She swallowed, then she turned to him. "So, what about you? Do you still write poetry?"

Ian smiled. "You remembered…"

Alison nodded. "Of course. It was memorable."

"I still write, but it's mostly computer-related."

"Oh, I see. So, what did you do after you left school?"

"I had a scholarship to study computing and physics," said Ian. "After that, I did a master's degree in theoretical computing, and then I worked as a contractor for various computer companies."

Alison exhaled a sharp breath. "Wow, quite a career. Did you leave anyone behind?"

"No." A shadow passed over his eyes. "My girlfriend left me. She said, my work came before her."

"I'm sorry to hear that." Alison paused. There was something different about him, quieter, steadier. "So, how did you end up, you know… over here?"

"Last, I remember, my friend Joel and I were driving through a flooded river. He got out okay, but my door wouldn't open. In any case, I'm here, and he's there." He shrugged lightly. "It was fate, I suppose."

His calmness took her by surprise. "Do you want to return?"

"My mother is keen to get back to the Earth plane. She wants me to join her, but I'm not so sure."

"I'd like to get back," said Alison.

"You need to fill in forms, sign contracts and all that."

Her eyes widened. "I imagined it was just a matter of choosing your parents."

"I thought so too, but with so many trying to return, re-entry has become more complicated." Ian smiled. "You can't escape bureaucracy." He hesitated, then added. "Hey, I'm checking out the Re-entry Pavilion tomorrow. If you're interested, why don't you come along?"

"I'd like to, but are you sure?"

He nodded. "Of course. It would be nice to have some company."

"Thanks," she said, smiling.

"Great!" he said, standing. "I'll see you tomorrow."

Alison watched him leap sylphlike down the front steps. She smiled. *He hasn't changed;* she thought. For a moment, she lingered by the door, watching him disappear down the path.

Gladys' face appeared over the fence. "The shops are closing." She pointed the nozzle towards the mall. "Your mother will be home soon."

Alison waved. "Thanks, Gladys."

It wasn't long before the front door swung open, and her mother came inside carrying a large shopping bag. Alison's eyes widened. She looked so youthful in a green and white patterned dress.

"Alison dear, welcome home!" Beverly placed the bag on the table and embraced her daughter. "Lovely to see you again."

"It is," said Alison, beaming. "Oh, Mum, you look well. Last time I saw you..."

Beverly nodded. "I know—in the ward with an oxygen mask over my face. But that's all in the past." She looked over her shoulder. "Look who's here, Joyce!"

A mauve-haired woman with an armful of packages tottered through the door. "Well, I never! Let me put this loot down." She squeezed Alison tightly. "Lovely to see you! We were just saying how nice it will be when we're together again."

"And here we are," said Beverly, smiling. "Well, I don't know about you, but I'm exhausted. I'll just put a few things away, and then we'll have a cup of tea."

They went into the kitchen. Alison sat at the table as she had always done.

Joyce boiled the jug. Her eyes twinkled. "The proper stuff. None of those tea bags. Here," she said, handing Alison a plate. "Like a biscuit?"

Alison smiled. "Thanks, Aunt Joyce. Wow, it's been a long time since I had an Iced VoVo."

"The relatives were asking after you." Beverly's voice came from the depths of the fridge. She stood upright. "I told them you needed time alone."

"Thanks, Mum."

"And your room is just as you left it."

"Yes, I saw that." Alison gazed at the worn linoleum on the kitchen floor and the orange benchtops. In the background, the erratic hum of the old fridge. It was all so familiar, and yet she felt a tightness in her chest. She took a deep breath.

Beverly put her hand on Alison's shoulder. "Is everything okay?"

"Yes, I'm fine; it's just that I'm a bit confused."

Beverly nodded. "It takes time to adjust to the other side."

Joyce sipped her tea. "Things are not always as they seem."

"Tell me about it." Alison exhaled. "So, what do you do here?"

"Oh, anything and everything." Joyce winked. "This is easy street compared to the Earth plane. We have the best Euchre evenings, dances, not to mention dinner parties—so much fun. And the shops! We can't possibly wear the same outfit twice."

"Joyce won at bingo the other day," said Beverly. "But let me warn you, however much fun you have, nothing here is as real or satisfying as the earthly plane."

"Is that why souls want to go back?" she asked.

"Well, yes, dear. They want to experience their destiny."

"Was it my destiny to die, Mum?"

"Oh, my dear, who can say? It happened, and now you're back with us, and that's the main thing."

Alison sighed, "I miss the girls."

"I'm sure you do." Her mother smiled. "You'll be seeing them soon."

Alison's eyes widened. "What?"

"Your funeral..."

"Oh, of course," said Alison. "I completely forgot."

Joyce smiled. "Gladys told me that Ian dropped by."

Alison blinked. "News travels."

"That's right," said Beverly. "Ian's a good boy. He lives with his mum. Did you know she had multiple sclerosis?"

Alison shook her head.

"Towards the end, he did most of the shopping, cooking and cleaning."

"Oh!" said Alison. "I didn't realise."

"Are you going to meet up?" asked Joyce.

Alison nodded. "He invited me to the Re-entry Pavilion."

"Should be interesting," said Joyce. "I'm not going until I've seen old Stanley again."

"Speaking of Uncle Stanley, I saw him at the hospital recently. He didn't look well," said Alison.

Joyce's face beamed. "The old devil. He'll be home again soon, and we'll kick up our heels."

Beverly gazed at Alison and smiled. "You must be tired, dear. I'll run a warm bath. What would you like for dinner?"

"Something simple, Mum."

"What about baked beans on toast?"

"Sounds great."

Later, as Alison lay in the warm, lavender-scented bath, all her worries melted away. *If only life were so simple.* She sighed.

5

The Re-entry Pavilion

A SHINY BLUE CONVERTIBLE pulled up in the driveway. Alison appeared in the doorway in a yellow dress, her hair flowing.

"Nice car," she said, slipping into the passenger seat.

Ian adjusted his sunglasses. "I always wanted to drive one of these."

The engine hummed as the convertible sped along the highway.

"Where is the pavilion?" said Alison, holding back her hair.

"Over there." Ian pointed to a transparent multi-level structure bulging out of the mist. He swung into the car park and turned off the engine.

Alison stared at the lines of people moving about inside "Like ants in an ant farm."

Ian shook his head. "I don't know if I'm ready for this."

"You don't have to do anything if you don't want to," she said, taming her hair with her fingers and fixing it into a ponytail. "Hey, is that a carousel I hear?"

Drawn by old-time music, she swung her legs out of the car and wandered over, staring at the horses riding endlessly up and down and round and round.

Ian tapped her on the shoulder. "Thought you might like this." He held up a pink cocoon of fluff.

"Hey, fairy floss. Reminds me of my childhood."

They shared the sugary treat as they wandered through the trees, their leafy branches rustling in the breeze. Alison gazed at the ferns tucked away in mossy corners. "These gardens are so pretty."

Ian smiled. "Designed to calm frazzled nerves."

They passed by lifelike statues of scientists, artists, kings, queens and emperors. Alison gazed up at the statue of Leonardo da Vinci. "Imagine being able to travel through time and meet them."

Ian laughed. "In your dreams."

They entered the main doors. Alison wandered over to a large mural. She gazed at the intricate design.

"It's called the Flower of Life," said Ian. "A form of sacred geometry that contains all the patterns of creation."

"Beautiful," she said. "So, where to?"

"I'm interested in careers," he replied.

A line of green arrows on the floor led them to the lift. "Level one, Careers," said the robotic voice.

The door slid open, and they entered a vast gallery. Exhibitions dedicated to various occupations lined the walkways. They passed banners promoting the various professions: farming, medicine, nursing, law and teaching.

Ian wandered up to a banner with the figure of Venus reclining on a beach. "What are you here for?" he asked a young woman at the desk.

She gazed at him and smiled. "Why, the oldest profession, of course."

His eyes sprang open, and he stepped back.

Alison looked up from a fashion design brochure. "Did you find what you were looking for?"

Ian shook his head. "No, I'm looking for something, well... adventurous."

Alison pointed to the clowns in red and yellow costumes. "Well, if its adventure you want, perhaps you could join the circus."

Ian smiled. "That was my childhood dream, but these days I'm more interested in computer programming."

They wandered past the exhibitions. Ian spied a banner bearing the symbol of Ares, the god of war. "That's more like it."

Alison picked up the brochure. 'Fame and Fortune Computer Lifetimes. Do you want to be a member of the great brotherhood? Get a top-paying job with influence and power.' A stab of fear hit her stomach. "Let's keep moving."

Ian gazed at the symbol. "Not yet."

"Well, I'm going to look around," she said as she wandered over to another stall.

Ian walked up to the counter. A thickset man looked up. "What interests you, son?"

"I'm looking for a job that combines computing and adventure."

The man leaned over. "If it's adventure you want, we have a range of options, or we could design something special, a cyber-war expert, perhaps? There's money in it."

Ian's eyes glistened. "I often wonder what it would be like to be wealthy."

A man in a blue suit stepped out from behind the counter. "You've come to the right place. Wealth beyond your wildest dreams." He held out his hand. "Ian, isn't it?"

Ian shook his hand, then his eyes narrowed. "Do I know you?"

The man's mouth twisted into a smile. He handed Ian a gold business card. "Perhaps."

Ian slipped the card into his pocket.

Alison returned. "Are you ready?"

"Yes," said Ian briskly.

They came to a banner with the symbol of Hermes, the messenger god, and the slogan, 'Time flies when you have a broadband internet connection'.

Alison smiled. "This is more like it."

A man with a polished head sat behind the table. "Which of you is interested?"

"I am," said Ian.

He held out his hand. "Well, then, welcome to your new life. You're just the type we're looking for; dependable and working towards a pension plan."

Ian shook his hand. "Do I get to do anything exciting?"

"Of course. We can build in overseas conferences, or we can even arrange for you to be on reality TV."

"What's the downside?" asked Ian.

"Depends on your fate." He smiled. "Earthly life always brings surprises."

Ian frowned. "Not too many, I hope."

The man leaned closer. "I'll let you in on a secret. With a good attitude and a willingness to work, you can overcome anything." He smiled, "Here's my card. If you want to take up our offer, you'll need to undergo re-education."

"What's that?" asked Ian, slipping the card into his pocket.

"A mere formality," he said. "You can learn all about it at the Revolving Lifetimes Theatre."

Ian nodded. "Okay, thanks."

"Where to now?" asked Alison.

"I'd like to check out level two," he replied.

They returned to the lift, and Alison pressed the button. "Level two, Family Matters," said the computer voice. The door slid open, and they stepped into the foyer.

Ian looked around at the tangle of faces. "Where do we start?"

A poker-faced woman appeared with a name badge on her lapel. "Hello, I'm Hannah, your guide. Let me show you around."

They walked past families, catching snippets of conversation as they passed. A group of people stood around a boy. "No!" he yelled, stamping his foot. "I have too many friends. What I need is an enemy!" A man patted his friend on the back. "Finally, someone whose life will be more challenging than mine."

Hannah held up her hand, signalling for them to wait. She dashed up to a couple who were busily pushing and shoving each other. "This is not the place to sort out your domestic quarrels. The section that handles differences of opinion is down the corridor."

Hannah resumed her stride.

"What's the difference of opinion section?" asked Alison.

"Just one of our new initiatives to reduce the ever-increasing strain in relationships," Hannah replied.

She stopped in front of a row of supercomputers. "Here we are."

"They look like poker machines," said Ian.

Alison giggled. "Life is a gamble."

Hannah frowned. "This computer analyses your past life." She walked to the next. "And this is an imaging processor, designed to create holographic images of your new family. Here, you can make minor alterations."

"I was under the impression that it was just a matter of choosing your parents and hoping for the best," said Alison.

"Technology changed everything," said Hannah. "Just as they see the baby in utero, so you can now see your future family. It lessens the element of surprise."

Ian's eyebrows raised. "That's innovative. What happens next?"

"Once you approve your new family, you return to the front counter, where we record your agreement in your soul record. Then, you wait for the right conditions to come up. Of course, we can't advise on the waiting time, but it normally doesn't take long."

Ian stared. "Amazing."

"Any more questions?" she asked.

Ian shook his head.

A shriek echoed through the building, followed by a chorus of curses. A red light flashed.

"Sorry, emergency—must go." Hannah turned and strode away.

Alison stared at the bank of computers. "Are you going to give it a go?"

"I might as well," replied Ian. He stood in front of the machine, and a blue light scanned his forehead.

"Welcome." The voice sounded robotic. "Identity, past and future options—confirmed. Results complete." The machine spat a thin booklet into Ian's hands. He studied the cover. "It's the pre-birth plan from my last life."

"That sounds fascinating," said Alison. "How about we find somewhere to sit?"

"Sure," said Ian, reading the booklet as he followed. "Sorry," he said, bumping into a man.

Alison pointed to a sign that read Ye Olde Tea Shoppe. "Over here, Ian!" They found a table in the corner. Girls at a nearby table were debating loudly who was going to be born first.

Alison turned to them, a quizzical expression on her face.

"We're going to be twins in our next life," said one.

She nodded, "Oh, I see."

The waiter appeared. "Can I take your order?"

"Yes," said Alison. "A coffee for me, and do you have chocolate cake?"

"Oh yes, chocolate is popular here," the waiter replied. He turned to Ian, pen in hand.

Ian looked up, his eyes bright. "Yeah, I'll have the same."

The waiter left. Ian continued reading. Alison looked around.

A small group sat at a nearby table. A man turned to her. "Are you preparing to return?" he asked.

Alison shook her head. "Not yet. I'm still finding my feet. Are you going back?"

"Yes," he said, his eyes glowing. "We're among those preparing for the New Age. We're just deciding where to meet up again."

A woman piped up. "I say our mothers should enrol us in the same preschool."

Alison smiled. "Sounds like a plan."

The waiter returned with steaming coffee and chocolate cake.

They ate and drank in silence. "Are you okay?" asked Alison.

"Nothing is hidden here." Ian sighed. "The brochure says I made a pre-birth agreement with my mother. Apparently, I needed some lessons about caring for others. The twist to this story is that in a previous life, she was my child, and... I-I neglected her." He moved the crumbs around the plate with his fingers.

"Don't be hard on yourself, Ian. You did great. I mean, studying, looking after your sick Mum and pursuing your career? You should be proud of yourself."

"You may be right," he said. "According to this, I can look forward to an easier life."

"Wow, that sounds great. Do you want to see what the holographic imaging machine can show you?"

He nodded. "Okay. Why not?"

They finished their coffee and returned to the machines. Ian stood in front of the computer and, in an instant, a holographic image appeared on the screen; a father with slightly greying hair and a petite mother watching their three daughters playing on the floor. Their hands and eyes moved as though they were alive.

Ian exhaled. "Whoa, that's spooky."

"Don't be silly. It's a lovely family... hang on, which one are you?"

Ian moved closer and read the script. "Records show I've taken two male births in a row, so I'm due to take a female body in my next life." He pointed to the youngest daughter. "Lila."

A chubby two-year-old looked up and smiled.

"Oh, she's beautiful," said Alison.

Ian nodded. "Yeah, she's kinda cute."

"What do you want to do?" Alison asked.

Ian frowned. "I'll think about it."

"Okay, where to next?"

"I don't know," he replied.

"How about we check out the Revolving Lifetimes Theatre?" said Alison. "That might help you decide."

They returned to the lift. "Level three, Preparation for Re-entry." The door opened. Before them stretched a queue. An official in a red uniform stood at the door. He counted a group in, then held up his hand. "The theatre is full. Please wait for the next viewing."

Ian and Alison joined the line. In front, a group of girls chatted among themselves. Alison wondered where she had seen them before. She closed her eyes, then suddenly opened them again. *Of course, the piazza...*

A girl in a summery dress turned to her. "Hello," she said breathlessly. "I can't wait to be born. You'll never guess..."

Alison smiled. "Tell me."

Her eyes widened. "I signed up with Apollo. I'm to have a rich father and a super elegant mother. We're going to live in a gorgeous mansion in the country with lots of ponies. When I grow up, I'm going to marry a plastic surgeon. I'm planning my wedding already—a white gown with a bouquet of pink roses."

"Oh, what a beautiful dream. I hope it works out for you."

"Thanks," said the girl as the queue shifted forward.

"Until her surgeon husband runs off with his assistant," whispered Ian.

Alison gave a smile.

They reached the front of the queue. The official held up two pairs of glasses. "Do you want 3D or multidimensional?"

Ian pointed to the multidimensional. "I'll have those."

"Me too," said Alison.

"You can sit anywhere," said the official as he waved them through.

They found their seats, and the lights dimmed. The room began to move as the travelogue narrative began. "Come visit Earth, stay a while." The screen burst into life with a variety of scenes: cities, rural landscapes, river valleys, plains and mountains.

Ian slipped on his glasses. He nudged Alison. "Cool, eh?"

Alison put on her glasses. "Wow, yes." Iridescent colours that she had never seen before dazzled her eyes. Her imagination took her beyond the world to remote places where fairies, goblins and elves played.

The screen moved gradually over the continents. "Welcome to the re-entry session. The information provided here is to reassure you about the process of rebirth."

The images zeroed in on people of different races, genders and ages. "Many have questions about your physical form. However, regardless of your appearance, life is a wonderful adventure. For some, it will be a brief journey, and others will enjoy the fullness of life. You may even live to see your great-grandchildren. No matter how life unfolds, a warm welcome awaits you when you return."

Scenes of reunion followed, then the narrative continued. "Without one essential feature, people can accomplish little on Earth. Which of these is it—fire, food, or forgetting? You would be right to say all three. After all, fire is a gift of the gods, and food is a necessity. However, the most important element in the story is your ability to forget the past and fully immerse yourself in your present life experience."

The audience murmured.

"It is a condition of your re-entry passport that you drink from the Well of Forgetfulness. There is a fountain in the foyer. These sweet waters dissolve many of your memories and help you to re-enter the world with a clean slate."

Images of well-fed babies appeared on the screen. At the same time, Alison's glasses gave her a rare glimpse into the secrets of the soul. She watched as the spark of life entered its mother's womb, aware that their mortal lives were about to begin.

Then, images of schoolchildren flashed up on the screen. "Your new body carries its DNA inherited from your family along with the data you bring from past lives. These combine to form a new and exciting sense of identity with which you can create a life of your choosing. We hope for a safe landing and look forward to seeing you again in the future."

The theatre shuddered to a halt, and the lights came on. They made their way outside.

"You're quiet," said Alison as they walked across the car park.

Ian opened the car door. "I'm just taking it all in."

Alison slid into the passenger seat.

Ian turned to her. "This whole earthly trip doesn't hold the same fascination. I mean, they ask you to drink from the Well of Forgetfulness so you can wander around in what appears to be a hologram, mindlessly doing the same things over and over again. Most people don't know who they are or why they're there." He smiled. "If my mother heard me say that, she'd have a fit."

"I know what you mean," said Alison. Her eyes narrowed. "To be honest, after seeing this, I'm having second thoughts about returning."

"That's interesting," said Ian. "But what about those multidimensional glasses?"

"Oh, yes." Alison smiled. "They were magic. I saw all sorts of mythical creatures. I even had flashbacks to ancient times. We, I mean you and I were, well... together."

Ian's eyes widened. "Oh, really?"

She nodded. "Seems we've known each other in another lifetime."

He shook his head. "Hard to believe."

"How about you?"

"The glasses showed me a light beyond, so warm and loving. It felt like a beautiful homecoming." His eyes gazed into the distance. "I didn't want to return, but I heard a voice saying that I have a task to complete. Don't know what that was about," he said as he turned the key. The car hummed to life, and soon they were speeding along the highway.

"So, what are you going to do?" asked Alison.

"I need to think about it, but one thing's for sure—I don't want to forget. I want to remember everything. Isn't that the point of it all?"

"Oh, yes. That's what Persephone told me. She gave me strict instructions not to drink from the Well of Forgetfulness."

"What! You met the goddess Persephone?"

"Uh-huh."

He swung the steering wheel, veering the car off the highway onto the verge.

Alison grabbed his arm. "What are you doing?"

Ian turned off the engine. "What did she say, if you don't mind my asking?"

"Let me think." Alison paused for a moment. "Yes, she said we are actors in a cosmic play but we forgot the script. She also said we re-live family patterns. She told me other things, but I didn't think much about it. I guess I was preoccupied."

Ian nodded. "We all get wrapped up in our stories."

"It wasn't a story—it was my life!"

"I'm sorry, of course it was," said Ian.

Alison felt the locket around her neck. "She gave me this as a reminder to be the driver of my story."

Ian gazed at the golden petals. "Whoa, I can feel its power. You must feel different wearing it, I mean?"

She nodded. "Come to think of it, sometimes when I meet people, I can read them."

"What about me?"

She looked into his eyes. "I see someone who is seeking the truth."

"You may be right." Ian glanced in the rearview mirror. "Hey Alison, there's a car parked behind that bush. I think he's following us."

Alison turned her head. "Start driving and see what he does."

Ian turned the car out onto the highway. The car behind them hesitated for a moment before pulling out.

Ian frowned. "I'll have to shake him off." He slammed his foot on the accelerator and overtook the cars in front. "I know a side road, as long as he doesn't see me turn."

Alison clutched the locket, her heart pounding. "We need your protection, Persephone," she pleaded.

She felt an ethereal hand brush the top of her head. *'What troubles you?'*

Alison gasped. "We're in the car, and someone is following us."

Instantly, an invisible force field enveloped the car. Ian swerved around a corner and disappeared down the side road.

Alison turned around, her eyes wide. "He's gone," she said breathlessly.

"Thank the gods," muttered Ian as he sped down the road and into the sub-urbs. He pulled up outside Alison's house, switched off the engine and slumped forward, his forehead resting on the steering wheel. "I'm sorry," he murmured. "I don't blame you if you never want to see me again."

Alison shook her head. "Don't be silly. I enjoyed our little outing, and besides, you're one of the few people I can truly open up to."

He sat up. "Hey, that's good. I'm going to the theatre to watch the *News of the World*. Would you like to come?"

"I'd like to," Alison sighed. "But I have to attend my funeral..."

6

Hecate

BEVERLY STOOD IN THE doorway, dressed in a navy suit, hat and white gloves. "Alison, dear, are you ready?"

Alison waved her hand at the assortment of clothes strewn on her bed. "Oh, Mum, I can't decide. Perhaps I'll just wear jeans."

"You will not!" Her mother strode to the wardrobe and pulled out a gown. "This would be entirely appropriate. After all, your father paid a lot for it." She placed the white gown carefully on the bed.

Alison stood with her mouth open. "What's *that* doing in my wardrobe?"

"Items of significance tend to follow you around."

Joyce put her head through the bedroom door. "What's going on?"

"Mum says I should wear my wedding gown."

"Oh, and why not? You're our little angel," said Joyce.

"Come on, Joyce," said Beverly. She turned to Alison. "We'll be waiting in the front room."

Reluctantly, Alison pulled on the gown. She gazed at her angelic reflection in the mirror. *Perhaps it's symbolic,* she thought as she floated down the hallway. She found her mother and aunt standing in the living room.

Beverly took her hand. "We'd better fly quickly. I sense the thoughts of family and friends assembling in the chapel."

In a flash, a vortex pulled them into the earthly sphere. A gust of wind blew, and Alison found herself in the middle of a car park, her mother by her side. Around them, droplets of rain splattered on the road.

Joyce picked herself up off the gravel and straightened her black lace dress. "We seem to have missed our mark, ladies."

"Come on, let's get inside," said Beverly.

They flew into the chapel. Organ music played softly in the background while family, friends and colleagues milled about quietly.

The three of them hovered near the polished casket.

Joyce sneezed, and Beverly glared at her.

"It's the flowers," said Joyce.

Alison looked around at all the mourners. It suddenly struck her; *they're here for me.*

The music played softly, and everyone took their seats while ghostly apparitions, grandparents, great-grandparents, uncles, aunts, and distant cousins fluttered moth-like around the walls.

Her gaze turned to Emma and Haley, who sat quietly beside her father. Once a broad-shouldered man, Arthur now appeared somehow smaller. Tears glistened on her cheeks. "How sad," she said. "I can see the girls, but they can't see me."

Joyce handed her a tissue. "I brought a stack with me."

"Oh, good." Beverly took a tissue and dabbed her eyes.

Suddenly, an unearthly scream came from the rear of the chapel, followed by the sounds of a scuffle.

Alison's eyes widened.

Beverly glowered. "What's going on?"

Joyce fluttered away and then returned. "Bradley's ghostly relatives crashed the service, complaining about how he is now in custody. It's okay. Everything is under control."

Beverly pursed her lips. "Funerals bring out the worst in some."

The priest stood before the mourners, his words of comfort echoing as he spoke a sermon on a loving God who provides healing during times of loss.

Where was God when I needed Him? Alison wondered.

The sermon ended, and a school friend read the eulogy. Mourners blew their noses and dabbed their eyes. Then a cousin related their time growing up together, followed by a coworker who relayed, with humour, some hair mishaps, speaking touchingly of her caring attitude as an employer. Finally, her father shared how much he missed his daughter, complete with tears and stammering.

"How lovely of Arthur," said her mother.

How strange, thought Alison. *I feel they're talking about someone else, not me.* She twisted the tissue, turning it into a small ball in her hand.

The haunting notes of an organ filled the air as mourners, followed by the ghostly relatives, made their way to a nearby hall.

Flickering candles and floral arrangements graced the tables.

"What a pretty setting," said Beverly.

Alison sighed. "It feels so final."

Joyce smiled. "Cheer up, Alison. I love wakes. That's where you hear what they *really* think of you."

While the mourners sat around, nibbling on savouries and cakes, Beverly and Joyce fluttered about, catching up with ghostly relatives whom they only saw at weddings, christenings, and funerals.

Gradually, whispers gave way to talk, and the conversation buzzed. Everyone seemed to have something to say, yet they avoided discussing the manner of her death, as if it were part of a conspiracy of shame.

Alison gazed at her daughters. She remembered their once-smiling faces. Haley sat slumped on the seat, and Emma stared at the floor while a well-meaning aunt tempted them with pastries. She closed her eyes to escape the tangle of emotions that threatened to choke her.

Thoughts started spinning. *Why did this have to happen? I should have run, called the police or something, but I allowed it to come to this.*

Alison wrestled bitter memories, trying to change the past, but, frustratingly, the events remained the same. Her shoulders slumped. Through the teary window of her mind, a pathway opened, with steps leading down. Without thinking, she followed the shadowy figures who tempted her into a deep, dark cellar.

Suddenly, she heard a loud woof, and at once the shadows dissolved.

Alison's eyes sprang open. A dog stared up at her. Behind him stood a sorceress in a purple robe. Her heart raced. She looked frantically around the hall for her mother. She saw her talking to relatives on the far side. *I must be the only one who can see this apparition,* she thought.

"Calm down, you're safe," said the immortal. Her hood slipped back, revealing pale features and long, dark hair. "I am Hecate, the goddess that most humans choose not to see."

Alison wiped the tears from her eyes. "What are you doing here?"

"Rescuing you from your demons." Hecate's mouth hardened. "You should be more discerning about the thoughts you entertain."

Alison stared. "It's my funeral, and I can cry if I want to."

Hecate gave a crooked smile. "Mortals amaze me with their attachment to their stories. Why not be the phoenix who rises from the ashes?"

Alison shook her head. "But how?"

"You could start by not empowering every thought that comes into your mind. Look at me. What if I took what people said personally? Where would I be?" The goddess drew a pack of cards from her cloak and fanned them in her hands. "Take one."

Alison chose a card.

Hecate held up the picture of a building falling amidst fire and chaos. "The Tower card," she cackled. "It spells unforeseen change, crises and loss."

The hair lifted at the back of Alison's neck. Her eyes narrowed. "You remind me of a witch."

Hecate smiled. "Perhaps I am." Her smile faded. "Or perhaps I'm simply a reflection of the shadow that people refuse to acknowledge. Then, when everything collapses around them, they wonder why."

"How can you be so callous?"

"Call me what you will," said Hecate. "But I was the one who discovered Demeter alone at the crossroads. Demeter, the goddess of the harvest, mourning the abduction of her daughter, Persephone. I was so outraged by the injustice of it all that I devoted myself to helping her. Afterwards, I became a recluse, a guide and a goddess of the crossroads of life."

Hecate's eyes flashed. "I may not have won the hearts of human beings, but I know I have chosen well."

Alison exhaled. "Oh, I didn't realise."

Hecate sighed. "Demeter was broken-hearted. She'd lost all hope of ever seeing her daughter again, so much so that the harvests failed and the entire world suffered." She gazed into Alison's eyes. "Deep within the human psyche lies a stockpile of responses that surface each time your life takes a turn. At the moment, you are experiencing the despair of Demeter. Is that right?"

Alison's throat tightened. "What exactly do you mean?"

Hecate's eyes narrowed. "Separation from your daughters... alienation from yourself."

Tears welled in Alison's eyes.

"I often wonder how humans accumulate so much baggage in such a short time."

Alison expelled a quick breath. "Have you no heart?"

"Don't get me wrong," said Hecate, her tone softening. "I am not making light of your sorrow. I am simply encouraging you to see that you chose that ordeal to prove to yourself that you are powerful enough to plunge into the very depths of the human condition and survive."

Alison nodded slowly. "Oh... I never thought of it like that."

"Of course not, for that is the perception of a goddess." Hecate smiled. "So now you stand at the crossroads. Which path will you take?"

Alison shook her head. "I-I don't know."

Hecate's eyes flashed. "Well then, may I suggest you take the road less travelled—the one that leads to freedom from suffering? You are more than those old thoughts and memories. Nothing can hold you down. Whatever you aim for will come true. So, hold your head up, smile and tell yourself: *I love you*."

With that, Hecate vanished with her dog.

The words I love you lingered in Alison's mind. She whispered them softly, then louder; each repetition was a small act of defiance against the despair. Taking the reins of her thoughts, she guided them from the fierce waves of self-recrimination into the calmer waters of acceptance, and the heaviness in her heart lifted. With this, the room seemed to brighten, and Alison noticed the mourners. Drifting around the room, she blessed each one with the love in her heart. She lingered near her daughters, sending them her love and wishing them well.

Then she scanned the room for her mother and Aunt Joyce. Catching their attention, she said, "I think it's time we said our goodbyes."

7

The Siren

JUST AS THE TOWER card had predicted, Alison lay buried in a mess of bed-clothes. On the bedside table lay an empty box of cherry liqueurs, a cold cup of coffee and a half-eaten sandwich.

She had tossed and turned, recycling memories, trying to salvage the past. Each wakeful night had deepened the dark hollows around her eyes. A television in the corner blared. She flicked the remote and sighed. *Another renovation show...*

Tabitha lifted her head. Her ears flickered. She glanced at Alison, then yawned and went back to sleep.

After nineteen years of marriage, I never really knew him. "Why did it have to end that way?" She murmured.

"It always astonishes me when people think that life shouldn't be that way." A voice reverberated starkly.

Alison blinked, and her train of self-recriminating thoughts ground to a halt. She fumbled for the remote and turned off the television. "Who's there?" she said looking around anxiously.

A siren's face came into view; deathly pale, surrounded by an untamed mane of dark hair. Her blood-red lips moved.

Tabitha arched her back, leapt off the bed and scurried under the chair.

Alison gasped. "Tell me I'm dreaming."

The siren scowled. "I am no dream. I'm part of your story."

Alison shook her head. "No, you're not."

The siren moved closer. "Oh, yes, I am. I can fulfil your every desire," she grinned.

"Stop! Go away!" cried Alison, pulling the bedcovers around her neck.

The siren sneered, then, as a snake sheds its skin; her façade slipped, and in her place stood a goddess in a wine-coloured robe. Her lips wore a Mona Lisa smile.

Alison glared. "Why did you do that?"

Persephone beamed. "Fear is such an exhilarating feature of earthly life, don't you think?" She stared at the figure huddled among the bedcovers, a picture of misery and gloom. "It is not out of malice that I speak; however, what you judge as unfortunate is often advantageous from our point of view."

Alison's eyes widened. "What do you mean?"

"We immortals have our own way of interpreting life's little upsets," Persephone paused. "The simple fact is, unless the old self is sufficiently abandoned, humans do not awaken." She glided to the window and drew the curtains. A shaft of moonlight spread across the bed.

She stared out of the window. "Dark and light are equal and opposite. And just like the great immortals, you, too, were born to tolerate not only that which you desire but also that which is *not* to your liking."

Alison sat up and reached for a tissue. "I'm not in the mood," she said, blowing her nose.

Persephone spun around. "What was it you wanted?"

The question took Alison by surprise.

"Oh..." She faltered. "I-I just wanted a happy family life; marriage, family, all the normal things that seemed to be out of reach."

Persephone sat gracefully on the chair. "I can offer you normal, but is that what you *really* want?"

Tabitha peered out from underneath the chair, then scurried under the bed.

"So, how was your funeral?"

"Sad," said Alison.

"Naturally..."

"Hecate arrived with her tarot cards."

Persephone raised her eyebrows. "Dear Hecate, she tries to be helpful, though having an enchantress at one's funeral doesn't work for everyone."

"An enchantress?" Alison frowned. "I thought Hecate was a goddess."

"Hecate is a goddess; however, she came from an older lineage."

"Oh, really?" Alison nodded. "Well, in any case, she made me feel better. It's just that afterwards I faced a tidal wave of regret—all the stupid choices I'd made. If I had my way again, I would never have put up with all his lies and intimidation. How stupid of me to have pretended everything was fine. If I'd left him, my girls would still have their mother. I'm such a failure—blah, blah, blah. The thoughts continued, and I forgot everything that Hecate had said."

"Obviously," said Persephone, glancing at the clothes strewn on the floor.

"Sorry about the mess," said Alison.

Persephone shrugged. "I've seen worse. At the moment, you're travelling the rocky path of regret and blame, battling the frustration of not being able to change the past."

"When you put it like that," Alison smiled wistfully. "Hecate spoke about the road less travelled. I'm not sure what that means."

"Acceptance—the way of the goddess." Persephone gazed into her eyes. "Which path do you wish to take? Do you want to accept reality or to continue to resist what is?"

Alison shook her head. "I just want to be happy."

Persephone's eyes flashed. "Ask yourself, what is happiness? Is it a life where you are so dumbed down by lies that you forget who you are? If that's what it is—it's not working."

Alison gazed at Persephone. "I don't know what you mean."

"Of course you don't," said Persephone, returning her gaze. "You were programmed to think a certain way; a program so deeply embedded in your DNA that you don't even know it's a story. Look around and see how your family, friends and the wider community keep this narrative alive with promises of love, and, when you don't conform, they use guilt to shame you. Don't you see it?"

Alison stared at the blank television screen.

"Well?"

Alison turned to Persephone. "I'm trying."

"Well, try harder!"

Alison gazed at the faded curtains and worn furniture. She sighed. "I wanted love and respect, but deep down, I didn't believe I deserved it."

"Exactly," said Persephone. "Now embrace yourself unconditionally, for even in your darkest moments, you are an expression of the whole."

Alison felt herself floating and, for an instant, she felt blissfully connected and at peace with the world.

She took a deep breath and, as if a switch had flipped in her mind, she threw off the bedcovers and planted her feet on the floor.

"All I know is I can't carry on like this." She walked to the wardrobe and pulled on a dressing gown, tying the belt firmly around her waist. Then she went to the bedside table, opened the drawer and pulled out her old diary. "I know which path to take," she said, dropping it into the bin. "I want to be free."

Persephone's lips curved into a smile. "That's more like it," she said. Then the goddess vanished.

Alison scurried around, tidying the room, throwing the rubbish into the bin and straightening her bed. She stood in front of the mirror and brushed her hair, then stopped and stared.

"Where is it?" she said, her gaze darting around the room. Tabitha crawled out from under the bed as Alison bent down. Glinting in the dark lay the golden locket. Quickly, Alison clipped it around her neck and then stepped into her slippers. She turned to survey her room, and with a satisfied smile, she walked out.

Alison stood at the kitchen door. An old Beatles song played on the radio.

All you need is love...
La la la la Lah...

Joyce hummed as she washed the dishes.

"Hello Mum, Aunt Joyce."

Joyce spun around. "Oh, Alison!"

Beverly looked up from her magazine. "There you are. I was so worried. You haven't spoken more than a few words since the funeral, but I knew you'd get over it. Come and sit down."

"There's pizza in the oven if you'd like some," said Joyce.

Alison nodded. "Sounds good."

Afterwards, she listened to her mother and aunt talking about an upcoming sale. Her throat tightened. "Hey Mum, there's something I'd like to discuss."

Joyce frowned. "Does this include me?"

"Of course, it's a family matter," said Alison.

Beverly smiled. "What would you like to know, dear?"

"I'm concerned about Emma and Haley living with Dad."

"Arthur? But why?" asked Beverly, flicking imaginary crumbs from the table-cloth.

Joyce jumped up and switched on the kettle. "Anyone for tea?"

Beverly and Alison nodded. "Yes, please."

Joyce placed the cups in front of them and sat down.

"I'm referring to his alcohol intake," said Alison.

Joyce spluttered. She quickly dabbed the spray with her handkerchief.

Beverly put her cup down. "How can you speak like that about your father?"

Realising she was in too deep, Alison took a breath and ploughed on. "Let's be honest, Mum, family life was like a war zone. Arguing and yelling late into the night, and the next morning, it was as though nothing had happened."

Beverly's face flushed. "Well, Alison, I'm surprised you feel the need to bring this up. Your father had a lot of pressure at work, and I was busy too. Oh, I don't know." She shook her head.

"It's okay, Mum; I don't want to upset you. It's just that I'm worried about the girls."

"Of course, but there's no need to be concerned. Arthur was always kind to you. I would even say he spoiled you."

"He may have treated me well, but I saw how he treated you, and that pattern persisted. You see, I didn't even realise that my husband's behaviour was abusive, nor did I see the warning signs until it was too late."

Beverly scowled. "Are you blaming me for your marriage failure?"

Alison shook her head. "I'm not blaming you, Mum. Honestly, I'm only expressing my feelings. This veil of secrecy is not helpful. It keeps us playing the same old victim story." She stared at the patterns on the tablecloth, her heart racing. "Is there anything you can tell me about our family that explains why we continue in these abusive relationships?"

Her mother glared at her accusingly. "You do ask difficult questions, Alison. You must be over-tired." The chair scraped as she stood up. "I think I'll go to bed now. Goodnight."

Alison's shoulders slumped; she felt shamed, shut down. "Did I say something wrong?"

Joyce leaned over and squeezed her hand. "It's okay, Alison, you tried your best. Your mother is just not ready to face her past." She pushed out her chair, took the cups and rinsed them, then boiled the kettle again. "More tea?"

Alison nodded.

Joyce placed the cups on the table and sat down.

Alison sighed. "I hope she's okay."

"Don't worry. Beverly has a way of forgetting. Life will continue as usual." Joyce smiled. "Perhaps I can throw some light on the family. Stan and I argued all the time, and as you know, we later divorced. I blamed him, but at the same time, I sensed some strange friction within myself, and so when I arrived in the Afterlife, I came face to face with the wolf. It frightened me, and so I made inquiries to discover if by chance we were under a family curse."

"That's interesting. I saw the wolf when I visited Grandma," said Alison.

"Oh, so you saw him too? It seems that some of us see him while others don't. From what I know, that wolf has been haunting our family for generations."

"But why?" asked Alison.

"Well, I was able to locate family members who told me their stories. Your grandmother raised six children almost single-handedly. Her husband drank heavily, and after he died, she couldn't cope, and so she had to put some of the younger ones into care. Beverly and I were the eldest, and we went out to work. But this story was only the tip of the iceberg."

"Her mother, your great-grandmother, was in service until her employer seduced her. When she became pregnant, she lost her position. She later married a farmer who adopted her child as his own, but he never let her forget her shame. And before that, her mother had escaped a war-torn country with a child in her arms and one on the way. She travelled by boat to start a new life with her children." Joyce smiled sadly.

"So it goes, generation after generation. We inherit the grief of our ancestors without even realising it. But now that I know where my feelings of shame and guilt are coming from, I feel somehow lighter, freer. I'm even looking forward to seeing Stanley again."

Alison nodded. "Oh, Aunt Joyce, thank you for shining the light on our family skeletons. I want to let go of the past and create a new life for myself."

"That's a good idea," said Joyce. She gave a knowing look. "So, what about Ian?"

Alison hesitated. She gave a small smile. "I would never have considered Ian as my type, but I'm starting to see him in a whole new light."

Joyce chuckled. "Well, you never know how things work out." She tilted her head. "And how is his mother?"

"I'll find out tomorrow," Alison said. "We're going to watch the *News of the World*."

"Oh, the newsreel!" Joyce blinked. "Not very romantic, but it's a start."

Alison laughed, shaking her head. "It's not like that."

Joyce glanced at the door and lowered her voice. "Your mother didn't want to upset you, but I think it's time you knew. She made inquiries at the funeral, and her cousin told her about some parents who are planning to have another child. Beverly was waiting for the right opportunity to come along. She'll soon be gurgling in the cradle, as we say."

"Oh, really?" Alison sighed. "That's lovely for her, but it will be sad to say goodbye."

"And there's more," said Joyce. "I heard from an aunt that Stanley will be here soon. I can't wait to see him again." Her eyes sparkled. "I'll be staying with him and his family for a while until we sort out our plans. That means you'll have the house to yourself." Joyce winked.

Alison took a deep breath. "Oh, Aunty Joyce, I didn't see that coming."

She felt as if she were standing on the edge of a cliff, about to soar into the unknown.

8

Alfred Hangontight

ALISON AND IAN SETTLED into an old-fashioned booth. A waitress arrived with chocolate milkshakes and banana splits.

"Mmm, this is delicious," said Alison. "So, what's been happening?"

Ian took a bite and swallowed. "Well, my mother just left for Earth. She seemed happy enough. Her new mother is married to an air force pilot, and they already have a child. Apparently, she and her new mother were friends in a previous lifetime, so they share a bond."

"That's interesting," said Alison. "My mother is leaving too. She's in a flap, racing around and saying goodbye to everyone."

"Has she told you anything about her new life?"

"The only thing she said is that her parents are looking forward to their new baby. My mother believes that you shouldn't delve into your future. She prefers to let it all unfold." Alison smiled. "So, how are things with you?"

"I've been trying to find somewhere to live, somewhere I can think things through," said Ian. "I'd almost given up when I heard about a Taoist community on the foothills of the ranges outside the City of Dreams. Their lifestyle is in harmony with nature, and most importantly, they call for honesty rather than loyalty to any belief system."

"That sounds great," she said, taking another bite.

He sipped the milkshake and watched her for a moment. "You seem more at peace somehow."

"Maybe." She glanced at him, a soft smile in her eyes. "Attending your own funeral has a way of putting things in perspective."

"That's good to hear," he said.

She looked down at the banana split, tracing the edge of the glass with her spoon. "It wasn't easy, but I think I finally made peace with a few ghosts." She looked up and smiled.

"I know what you mean," he said. "I had a few of my own."

In the pause that followed, there was a lightness, a shared understanding, that they had both crossed something that had changed them in ways neither yet could name.

"So, what are your plans?" he asked gently.

"I'm not sure yet." Alison gazed out the window. "My aunt is leaving soon, so I'm thinking about renovating the old house, making it into something that reflects me."

"Hey, that sounds like an interesting project."

"Yes, it feels like a new beginning." Suddenly, she froze. "Hey, that man just took a photo of you."

Ian slurped the last of the milkshake and looked up. "Oh, yeah. Seems I'm under surveillance?"

She watched the man leave. "What? But why?"

He shook his head. "I'm not too sure." Ian glanced out the window, seeing the people walking towards the cinema. "Hey, it's time we caught the *News of the World*."

They made their way across the plaza and found their seats. Sinking into recliner chairs, Ian opened a packet of chips. The lights dimmed, and the flickering screen illuminated their faces.

The news began with a story about human cloning, with footage of scientists in white lab coats examining test tubes. Murmurs came from the audience. "What happened to nature?" yelled someone from the back.

The broadcast continued with the worldwide death count from earthquakes, floods and fires. Then came a segment on cyberattacks, with a story about hackers infiltrating foreign countries.

"Trouble ahead," said Ian, crunching.

"And now for the local news," announced the newsman. A mugshot appeared on the screen. Alison's eyes widened.

"A court sentenced Bradley Maybridge to a non-parole period of twenty-five years for the manslaughter of his wife, Alison. He pleaded not guilty. As he left the courtroom, a small crowd of onlookers heckled him. The increase in cases of domestic violence has fuelled a worldwide movement aimed at promoting family harmony."

The audience murmured.

Alison took a deep breath.

Ian leaned over. "Do you want to leave?" he whispered.

She shook her head. "I just need a moment." She closed her eyes. Memories surfaced, mingled with feelings of victimhood. *I can't let him get to me,* she thought. Her fingers clasped the locket as she reminded herself that these feelings were not hers alone, but echoes of stories carried through her ancestors. *I'm more than this story,* she affirmed. *I'm a survivor.* With this, her thoughts stilled.

The lights came on. They stumbled out of the theatre, blinking in the light.

"Would you like me to take you home?"

Alison took a breath. "No, I'll be fine."

Ian started the car and drove out onto the highway. The roof slid down.

She grabbed her hair and tied it back. "You know, Ian, I was shocked at first seeing Bradley; but then I realised something... He has no power over me." She held out her arms. "I'm free!"

Ian pressed his foot to the floor, and the blue convertible sped along the highway. "Where do you want to go?"

"I don't know," she replied.

Ian looked up at the chariots flying overhead. "Wanna take a flight?"

"Yes, why not?" she answered.

He turned down a side street and into a car park. The sign read, "Jimmies Joy Rides."

Alison swung her legs out of the car.

Ahead stood a red-faced man, his hands on his hips. Jimmy smiled. "Hi Ian, good to see you again. Who's the little lady?"

"Alison." Her tone was firm.

"Oh, pleased to meet you. Step this way. You're in luck; there's one glider left."

They clambered into a silvery machine with a red stripe down the side. An elf wearing a green pilot's uniform sat in the cockpit, pointy ears poking through holes in his cap. "Hello, I'm your pilot, Alfred Hangontight."

Alison's eyes widened. *What the...*

"Ready for take-off?"

"Yes!" said Ian.

Alfred worked a lever, and the craft rose vertically like a fast-moving lift. Soon, they were high above the City of Dreams. They swept across the cloudless sky, then he switched off the engine, and the ship went into gliding mode. Alison and Ian leaned back and closed their eyes as on and on they glided silently through space.

The sky glowed with the orange light of the setting sun when Alfred turned for home. The craft bounced lightly as it touched down.

"Thanks, Alfred," said Ian.

Alison's face glowed. "Yes, thanks for that."

"My pleasure. Come back soon." The elf jumped down from the craft and strolled away, humming to himself.

The moon shone brightly as they drove along.

"That was great," said Alison thoughtfully. "You know, the feeling of flying brought back a memory from my childhood, an out-of-body experience. I was playing in the backyard and suddenly I was looking down at myself."

"Funny, that happened to me as a child as well," said Ian. "I was at the circus with my mother when I felt myself floating as if I didn't have a care in the world."

"Perhaps it's our natural desire to return to the light," Alison said thoughtfully.

Ian turned the car onto her driveway. The headlights floodlit the peeling paint-work on the garage door. He switched off the lights, and they sat in the dark.

"I feel like I'm back at school," she said with a faint laugh.

Ian smiled. "Sometimes I think we re-live the same scenes over and over again."

She turned to him; her face was caught by the streetlight. "Some things I have to let go of."

"Talking of letting go, I was happy to live with Mum in our little world filled with trinkets, but now I'm ready to move on."

Alison frowned slightly. "Your future seems clear, but I'm not sure how I'll go about renovating this house."

Ian thought for a moment. "How about I contact my friend, Orion, from Wizard Home Styling Services? He plays a mean computer game."

She smiled. "Thanks. That would be great."

For a moment, neither of them moved, the air between them charged with the feeling that they must soon part.

Alison took a breath and pressed the door handle. "Will I see you before you leave?"

He nodded. "Of course."

She stepped out, and the cool night air brushed her cheeks as she watched the car reverse down the drive. The taillights glowed briefly, then vanished into the night. Alison stood a moment longer, her cheeks still flushed, before she turned and went inside.

Beverly looked up from her magazine. "Did you have a good time, dear?"

"Oh, yes. We went to the movies, and afterwards we went for a joyride."

"How lovely. Ian's a good lad. You could arrange to meet him on Earth. You'd have a great time together—a little place of your own and a kiddo or two."

Alison smiled faintly, sensing in her mother's words the echo of old dreams that no longer stirred the same longing. She shook her head. "Thanks, Mum, but right now, I have other things to think about."

"Oh?" Her mother sighed heavily. "But what could be more important than a husband and children, dear?"

Alison met her gaze with quiet calm. "I used to think that's what I wanted," she said. "Now... I'm not so sure anymore."

Her mother said nothing, only nodded faintly. The sound of the turning page filled the silence between them.

9

The Wizard

THE HOUSE WAS DEATHLY quiet without the chatter. The silence felt strangely unsettling. Alison gripped the handle of the vacuum cleaner and pushed it back and forth across the faded rug. She could still see her mother waving from the car. She recalled her saying, *'It's going to be so much fun this time around!'*

Meanwhile, news arrived of Uncle Stanley's passing. Joyce had beamed when she heard the news. *'Good luck!'* she had said, as she tottered through the doorway.

Alison gazed at the porcelain ducks lined up on the wall. She shook her head. *They'll have to go.* Then she looked over at the television set. *It must be at least fifty years old.* Surrounded by the past, her mind swirled. Suddenly, she recalled a dream she'd had the night before. Her husband, Bradley, lying in his coffin, eyes closed, peacefully decomposing.

"Oh," she sighed, as shadows of long-buried memories danced through her mind; love and loss, life and death; merging into an overwhelming sense of emptiness.

Alison dragged the vacuum cleaner along the hallway. She pushed it into the cupboard and shut the door. A familiar perfume drifted from her mother's bedroom. She stood for a moment, inhaling the fragrance.

I need coffee, she thought.

Her footsteps echoed in the hall. As she neared the kitchen, she heard the clatter of cutlery and froze.

"Who's there?" Her voice sounded shrill.

She took a deep breath and pushed the door. Shadowy creatures screeched and fluttered like frightened birds in a cage. Their flapping stopped, and they perched like vultures on the bench tops, staring down their beaks.

Alison gasped and stumbled backward. Heart racing, she spun around and bolted for the front door, but before she reached it, the door swung open with a creak. She pressed herself against the wall.

Tabitha sped through the open door and bounded up the nearest tree, her eyes staring from the refuge of the leaves.

Alison held her breath and dashed outside. She stood on the grass, eyes bright, like a creature caught in the glare of headlights.

Glady's face appeared over the fence. "Alison dear, how are you?"

Alison forced a weak smile. "Hello, Gladys. I'm good."

"Your mother left safely?"

"Yes, thanks."

"And I heard Stanley is back."

"Yes, Aunt Joyce went to meet him."

"Ah, life goes on..." Gladys' voice faded.

Alison exhaled. The grass felt cool under her feet. A gentle breeze ruffled the blue and pink hydrangeas, and birds flitted and chirped in the trees. She breathed in the scent of flowers and freshly cut grass. In the distance, she heard a dog yap and the sound of children playing on the swings.

What am I going to do? With trembling fingers, she felt for the locket around her neck. A voice whispered, *'Do not fear contradiction. Invite it in like a welcome guest.'* Alison exhaled. She slumped onto the front step. Tabitha jumped down from the tree. Bounding over, she sat and licked her paws.

A whoosh sounded, and Tabitha and Alison looked up.

A flying horse soared towards the house. With powerful strokes, he swooped into the front yard and landed on the grass. His wings folded at his side.

What the....! Alison sprang to her feet, while Tabitha scurried into the shelter of the hydrangeas.

A face leant out from behind the horse's mane. "Alison, isn't it?"

She nodded.

He slid down and strode towards her, a carpetbag in his hand. His frame was lean, his hair wild, his beard full. In his checked shirt and dungarees, he looked to Alison like a mountain man. As he drew closer, she sensed a mystical aura.

He held out his hand. "Orion from Wizard Transformation Services." He gestured. "And this is Pegasus."

"Oh!" she exclaimed as she shook his hand. "Ian's friend."

He nodded. "I came as soon as I could."

Eyes appeared over the fence.

"Thank you," she said. "I'd like to invite you inside, but the fact is..." Her voice dropped to a whisper. "Evil spirits have occupied the kitchen."

His eyebrows raised. "Ah... I see." He turned and waved his hand, and the horse vanished. "I can deal with that."

Alison blinked. "Where did he go?"

"He wanted to get back to his mares."

Alison led Orion into the lounge room. He set his carpetbag on the rug. "Now, what are your plans?"

"Well, this was my family home. My mother and aunt left recently, and I'd like to modernise the house, but I don't know where to start."

"That's interesting." Orion closed his eyes, focusing on the energies, and then he opened them again. "Your mother was a strong-minded woman."

"Yes, she was, but how do you know?"

"It's all in the energy," he said. "It takes a great deal of strength to suppress all the disowned parts of your family story." Orion gazed around the room. "So, you want to recreate this house?"

She nodded. "I'd like the place to reflect me."

"But do you know the real you?"

She raised her eyebrows.

"Okay," he said. "Let's start with your unwelcome guests."

They made their way to the kitchen. Alison stared at the door; her mouth dry.

Orion reached into his bag and took out a bundle of sage. He struck a match, and the smoke curled around his head. He murmured a protective blessing over Alison, then grasped the doorknob. "Follow me," he said, stepping inside. Tendrils of smoke drifted upwards, curling into the corners of the room. The shadowy creatures screeched and beat their wings.

"Now, repeat after me. You are free from the chains of this family story—make haste unto the light, where you will find peace."

Alison repeated the words, and their screeches turned to mournful wails. The creatures whizzed around the room like deflated balloons, becoming smaller until they disappeared.

"Amazing!" she said.

Orion smiled. "Now you can more easily discern the real you from your family story."

Alison felt lighter, as if a burden had lifted. She glanced at the pile of unwashed dishes. "Sorry about the mess."

Orion shook his head. "No problem, I thrive in disorder," he said, pulling out a chair.

Alison sat across the table. "I haven't come across a wizard before. What exactly do you do?"

"I transform living spaces," he replied.

She tilted her head. "So, what exactly can you do for this house?"

"I can't say until I find out where you're at." He closed his eyes and after a few moments, he opened them again. "Your dream showed that you're moving on."

Her eyes widened. "You saw my dream?"

"I see only what applies to my work. I understand you lost yourself in difficult circumstances, and now you're on a journey to find yourself again. Is that right?"

"Well, yes." She paused. "You certainly have a different approach. On Earth, it was only ever about renovating the house."

"In the Earthly realm, you refurbish the house and then you sit in your brand-new room and complain. In short, nothing changes."

"That's true," she said.

"A house is more than an outward appearance. It reflects the energetic frequency of the soul."

At that moment, Tabitha strolled into the kitchen, mewing loudly. Alison opened the fridge and took out the milk and poured some into a saucer.

Tabitha crouched down to lap.

"Your cat was more in tune with you than your parents." Orion removed a laptop from his carpetbag and typed in her name. "Now, let's dig deeper. Oh!" he said, his eyes wide. "A warning code came up. It states that a goddess is looking out for you. Is that right?"

Alison nodded. "Yes, Persephone."

"Well, now, that's interesting. According to the goddess, I can rebalance energies, but I am not to transform your living space. She insists you do it yourself."

"Oh!" Alison sighed, her shoulders slumped. "That'd be right."

"Are you happy to proceed?"

"I guess so."

"Good." Orion scrolled. "Let's begin. How did you feel on Earth? A little disempowered, isolated, needy... prepared to accept second best to get your needs met, perhaps?"

Her cheeks flushed pink. "Well... yes."

"I see you are making progress, but in order to unlock your full creative powers, you must rise above your story and realise your soul journey." Orion's beard quivered as his fingers flew across the keyboard. "Did you ever feel like a fish out of water, as if you didn't belong?"

Alison nodded. "I felt as if I belonged in another place and time."

He stared at the screen. "Hm, just as I thought. There was a time, long ago, when you possessed all your creative powers. You overflowed with happiness with the world and everyone in it. Do you remember?"

Alison shook her head. "Not really."

"Soul memory doesn't come easily to us humans. That's why I created a little computer program." Orion tapped the keyboard. "This allows you to see your soul journey." He spun the laptop around to face her. Splashed across the screen was a delicate leafy canopy and underneath a sea of flowers.

Instantly, Alison felt herself transported into the scene. She gazed at the deer nibbling on the grass. Then she saw a group of people in ornately decorated clothes step aboard their flying machines, and like birds they flew through the sky.

"Amazing," she said.

"The Dynasty of the Sun *was* amazing," said Orion. "Life was effortless. Souls were in tune with their life force. No emotional disturbances to block their energy."

He pressed a button, and they zoomed into a garden-like courtyard. "With the power of technology at their fingertips, their creativity was awe-inspiring." The screen took them through an arched entrance into an inner sanctum, moving through stately rooms with polished marble floors and walls inlaid with gold and covered in vibrant wall hangings.

A tingling feeling grew in Alison's chest. "How lovely. I want to go there now."

Orion shook his head. "There's no point in beautiful surroundings unless you are in harmony within; otherwise, you're simply not going to resonate," he said.

She sighed. "If only I could remember."

"Unlock your soul memory." Orion spun a vortex with his hands, and an image appeared on the kitchen wall. "This is an image of the Alpha point, the living Source. It is a powerful focus for those whose aim it is to awaken their original consciousness of purity, love and peace."

Alison gazed at the concentric circles and the golden lines radiating outwards.

"When you focus on a point of pure potentiality, you come into harmony with the universe," said Orion.

Alison focused her eyes. The concentric rays of light swirled as her consciousness expanded. She glimpsed past lives: a woman walking through a marketplace, a mighty king, an ancient healer whose knowledge of plant medicine brought relief to many. Faces of people of different ages in history appeared and faded.

Then, tears welled in her eyes as she saw herself in her most recent life; a victim of thoughts and imaginings.

"Long ago I was so happy, but in my last life I was so sad."

"Let it go," said Orion, taking a box of tissues from his bag.

Alison reached for the tissues as the tears rolled down her cheeks. In that moment of rawness, something shifted; the storm within her died, and a sense of peace filled her heart. It was then that she glimpsed a vision, a home set in spacious gardens. Alison quietly took in every detail, from the flowers lining the pathway to the stained-glass windows.

The hum of the old refrigerator broke the silence.

She opened her eyes. "I saw the home of my dreams."

Orion nodded. "Very good," he said. "Continue to focus on the light. Allow your consciousness to expand beyond the limitations of your story and emerge your original creative energies once more."

Alison smiled. "Thanks for everything." She gazed through the window at the horse grazing on the front lawn. "Pegasus is back."

"He always knows when it's time to leave." Orion picked up his bag, and they walked outside. "I look forward to your housewarming." The horse lowered his mighty head. Orion took hold of his mane and leapt onto his back. Pegasus spread his wings and flew into the sky.

Alison floated inside, as if in a dream. Standing in the kitchen, the atmosphere seemed so calm and clear.

Tabitha leapt onto the counter, picking her way delicately along the bench. She sat next to a pile of unwashed dishes and licked her paws.

Strange to think it's just me, myself and I. Alison quickly pushed the feeling of loneliness aside. Closing her eyes, she visualised a new kitchen with clean lines and large windows. She opened her eyes—nothing had changed. Remembering Orion's advice, she focused on the point of light. After a while, her mind calmed.

"I've got it!" she said. She opened the drawers and rummaged. "Ah, here they are." Alison grabbed a handful of garbage bags. "I'll start by cleaning out my bedroom."

10

Hestia

IT WAS LATER THAT evening. Tabitha curled up on the bed, her eyes open, quietly surveying the growing pile of garbage bags.

Alison finished packing up her old school clothes, records and books. She sat down, her thoughts drifting back to school days; the bustling lunchroom, standing in a line in front of the tuck shop window and brown paper bags. The whiff of sandwiches, ice cream and fruit mingled with the chatter. And yet, even among her classmates, she had somehow felt separate and alone.

Heaviness settled in her chest as she realised loneliness had always lurked like a thief in the shadows of her mind.

A voice echoed from the ether. *'Do not fear loneliness, for it is a portal through which you meet your higher self.'* A chime rang out, clear and pure, and within its crystal resonance, a goddess appeared. For a moment, time stood still.

Alison gazed at her flowing gown and the white lace veil draped over her hair.

"I am Hestia," said the goddess. Her gaze fell upon the garbage bags. "I sense you're grappling with creative inspiration?"

Alison's eyes widened. "Oh, sorry about the mess. I'm trying to transform my living space, but memories are holding me back."

"You made a start," said Hestia. "Now, I suggest you take these bags outside and meet me in the kitchen, for that is the heart of the home."

Hestia drifted down the hallway while Alison placed the bags near the back door. Entering the kitchen, she found Hestia peering into the cupboards.

The goddess shook her head. "Two cans of tomatoes and a packet of pasta. That's not much in the way of provisions."

Alison shrugged. "I haven't been shopping since my mother left."

"We can't have that." The goddess waved her hands, and in an instant, she stocked the shelves with bottles of milk, loaves of bread, slabs of butter, cheese, an earthenware jug full of yoghurt, and jars filled with plump figs and olives.

"Amazing, thank you!" Alison said, placing the perishables into the fridge.

Hestia turned to the dishes piled up in the sink. "Tut, tut," she said, waving her hands. As if by magic, the dishes washed, dried and stacked themselves on the shelves. Her magic continued, wiping the benches and cleaning the floor. A white tablecloth floated down and settled on the table, followed by a plate of sunshine-coloured cakes.

Alison's face flushed. The kitchen glowed with goodness. For a moment, she stood, breathing in the calmness and warmth. Her cluttered thoughts stilled. "Thank you," she said.

"It is my gift, for I am the goddess of the hearth and home." Hestia drew out a chair and sat down. "In ancient times, the fire burned at the centre of every home. Babies slept there, snug and warm, while people cooked, ate, and shared stories. All meals began and ended with a prayer to the goddess, and in return, I helped to make life easier."

Alison smiled wistfully; her love of family ignited. "How about I make some tea?"

"That would be lovely," Hestia said.

"Honey cakes; my favourite!" A voice chimed. A gust of energy sent a swirling mist into the kitchen.

Alison turned. In the doorway stood a statuesque goddess in a fitted gown—radiant, golden with eyes that held passion and laughter.

Hestia smiled. "I hope you don't mind, but I invited Aphrodite to tea."

"Of course not." Alison gazed wide-eyed at the goddess of love, radiant, unrestrained, everything she had forgotten to be. Then, seeing her bleached blonde hair, high cheekbones and rose-pink lips, she blinked.

"Yes, I know," said Aphrodite. "I may be a little older, but I'm still rocking it." She glided into the kitchen and gazed through her eyelashes. "Alison, I recall." Her eyebrows raised. "We have stories to share: the honeymoon on the islands—steamy. You two were soulmates until the tide of your destiny changed." She shrugged. "But that's life."

Alison inhaled sharply. "I'll just get another cup," she said, rummaging in the cupboard.

"These honey cakes look delicious, Hestia," said Aphrodite as she sat down.

"Why, thank you," said Hestia.

"But the real honey is between the sheets." Aphrodite turned to Alison. "Are you ready to find love again?"

Alison placed the tea-things on the table. "I'm not sure."

"Not sure?" Aphrodite tilted her head. "But love is all about completing your-self, finding your other half." She grinned. "I was married to Hephaestus, the blacksmith, but the love of my life was Ares." She gazed into the distance. "To the god of war, I bore seven children. But I also bore children to Poseidon, Hermes, Dionysus, Adonis and Anchises—and all behind my husband's back."

Alison poured the tea. Looking down, she saw she had overflowed the cup. "Oh dear," she said, carrying it to the sink.

"Your many offspring are famous," said Hestia.

Aphrodite tossed her hair. "Merely an expression of my unbounded passion." She took a bite, and a cascade of golden crumbs fell onto the plate.

Alison nibbled on honey cake. She wanted to interrupt, to ask Aphrodite how one learns to love again after the world has dimmed, but it was as though she didn't need to say anything. As they spoke, Alison found herself half listening, half remembering as their words flowed through her like music. Listening to their stories, something within her stirred.

Hestia smiled. "Speaking of which, what about the games you played with humans, starting with the little tryst you arranged between the prince of Troy, Paris, and Helen of Sparta?"

"Oh, that," said Aphrodite. "Athena, Hera and I competed for the title of the fairest goddess. Paris chose me, of course. And in return, I promised him Helen, the most beautiful woman in the world." She gave a mischievous smile. "Her husband, King Menelaus, was unhappy with this arrangement. It was most unsporting of him, and his jealousy led to the Trojan War. Naturally, I supported the Trojans. Ares had already promised Hera and Athena that he would be on the side of the Greeks. Then I convinced him to change sides." She chuckled. "We had so much fun!"

It's hard to believe the gods manipulate human feelings to play their little games, thought Alison, her gaze shifting back and forth between the goddesses.

"I'm surprised that the god of war and the goddess of love were compatible at all," said Hestia.

"Opposites attract. Ares embraced my passion, and I embraced his strength, and together we became a formidable team." Aphrodite brought the tea to her lips.

"Until Hephaestus caught you out."

She spluttered. "Ah, yes, a regretful incident..." Her eyes narrowed. "Hestia, truth or dare. Did you ever take a lover?"

Hestia shook her head. "I do not have your boundless passion for earthly affairs. I rejected the advances of both Poseidon and Apollo. Instead, I swore an oath before Zeus that I would remain a maiden all my days," she smiled. "But I'll let you in on a little secret."

"What's that?" Aphrodite leaned closer.

"As soon as Hermes detects the aroma of home-baked cakes, he's at my door. He'll devour whatever I put in front of him. In return, he tells me the latest news from Mount Olympus. That way, I stay in touch."

Aphrodite snorted. "And you believe everything that prankster tells you?"

"True, some of his stories are a little far-fetched; however, I don't mind. The comings and goings of the gods are an endless source of entertainment."

"Tell me truthfully, Hestia, what do you get out of life? Even to the gods, you remain an enigma. I mean, your existence as the goddess of hearth and home—so mundane."

"You may be right," said Hestia, putting down her cup. "In terms of worldly affairs, I achieved very little. But Zeus gave me the title of leader of the goddesses and blessed me with honour instead of marriage."

As they spoke, Alison felt their energy stirring inside her. Hestia's calm steadiness and Aphrodite's wild pulse were two aspects of life, like day and night, meeting at the horizon.

Hestia gazed into the distance. "I was the eldest child of Cronus and Rhea, the king and queen of the Titans. Cronus was fearful that his children would overthrow him and so after our birth, he swallowed us whole; first myself, then Demeter, Hades, Hera and Poseidon. Fearing for Zeus, her last-born child, Rhea replaced the baby with a stone wrapped in swaddling and sent her son to Mount Ida on the island of Crete to be raised by the nymphs. When Zeus reached adulthood, he slipped a secret potion into his father's drink. This caused him to bring up his children. I was the first to be swallowed and the last to emerge. Therefore, it is said that my part is at the beginning and the end."

Aphrodite laughed. "Zeus was only too happy to have his older sister out of the picture so that he could pursue his endless affairs."

"No doubt, Zeus was a schemer, but a charming one at that," said Hestia. "While my siblings became engrossed in worldly life, I maintained a constant connection with the light. My role was an enigma until now... for we are nearing the fullness of time."

"Well, my time is not over," said Aphrodite. "I'm having more fun than ever, which reminds me I have a rendezvous with Poseidon." She smiled. "It's been delightful to catch up with you, Hestia." The goddess of love turned to Alison and gave a playful wink. "I wish you well on your journey. Watch out for Eros' arrows." The air shimmered as she vanished into the haze.

Alison gazed at the chair where Aphrodite had sat. "She seems to know all about me."

Hestia nodded. "The goddess Aphrodite is the dream chaser." Her eyebrows raised. "No doubt, those who seek fulfilment in these earthly dreams are in for a rocky ride."

"I see." Alison gazed at the goddess. "At this time, I feel more drawn to being reflective."

"You are getting in touch with a long-forgotten part of yourself." Hestia smiled. "But do not discount Aphrodite; there is another side to her. Originally, she embodied the pure dimension of light and love, just like you."

"Really?" said Alison.

Hestia nodded. "The goddesses are within you, energies to be remembered." Then she faded into the ether.

Alison stood in the kitchen's quiet. The warmth of Hestia's gaze lingered, wrapping her in a gentle sense of belonging. Aphrodite's spark had stirred her imagination. Perhaps this was the renovation she had been waiting for—rekindling the fire of her spirit.

11

The Memorial Garden

THE GODDESSES STILL LINGERED in the air long after they had gone—Hestia's silent presence, inviting her to look within, and Aphrodite's unbounded warmth, encouraging her to express herself. But despite her efforts to open up to new possibilities, nothing seemed to change.

The following morning, sunlight streamed through the window. A hum filled the air as Alison pushed the vacuum cleaner over the faded rug. She flicked the switch, and the noise faded.

How long is this renovation going to take? She wondered. Flopping onto the couch, she wrapped herself in the soft folds of a blanket. *I visualise my dream house morning and night, but so far nothing has happened...*

Alison recalled Orion's words and focused her eyes on the point of light. Drifting inward, a realm of swirling patterns unfolded; chaotic yet strangely mesmerising. The ever-changing kaleidoscope drew her deeper. Fascinated, she watched the endless loop of patterns, falling apart, then returning to a peaceful symmetry, then falling out again. She was no longer a part of the patterns, but the observer of a narrative that reminded her of her duty to be a better person, and yet it was not interested in her truth or well-being. All it wanted was submission to its story.

Strange, she thought. *With every breath, I hear the familiar voice of an inner authority judging, shaming and reminding me of my failures.* She wondered, *is this me, or an identity whose very existence is based on conflict?*

She took a deep breath to steady herself as she realised this was not her conscience, but an oppressor, an inner voice that sabotaged her every move, and yet it was so much a part of her she hardly noticed.

Then, from beyond, came a thought; gentle, spacious and clear, *'You are not the inner battle of the ego, but the vast consciousness behind it; that of peace'*. A warmth spread through her, quiet and steady, like the glow of an unseen flame. She felt herself expand beyond her fears, beyond even her thoughts, into a stillness that felt familiar. For a few breaths, she simply rested there, suspended in peace. The swirling patterns dissolved into light, and the judging voice fell silent. What remained was the quiet hum of presence, nothing to prove, nothing to fix.

Gradually, the ordinary world returned. She breathed deeply. *I wonder if this is what Hestia meant when she talked about the eternal flame;* she thought.

She heard a car pull up outside. She looked up. Gazing through the window, she saw Ian's convertible. A knock soon sounded at the door.

"Come in," she called.

Ian strode into the living room. "Hi, Alison, how's the renovating going?"

She shook her head. "I'm not getting very far."

"Oh, why not?"

"Every time I try to renovate, memories surface."

"Tell me about it."

"You too?"

He nodded. "I call them shadow battles." His face brightened. "How was Orion?"

Alison smiled. "He was great. He cleansed the house of old energies and gave me lots of encouragement, but Persephone insisted I do everything myself. It's frustratingly slow. So, how are you?"

"I'm getting ready to leave for the Taoist community. Just wondered if you want to come for one last drive?"

Alison nodded eagerly. "Of course."

The convertible hugged the winding road as it ascended the mountain. Ian pulled up in a car park high above the City of Dreams. The wind carried a faint scent of pine trees and earth. They sat and watched the sunset, a glowing display of reds, oranges and purples. The sunlight faded, and their faces bathed in the moon's ethereal glow.

"Are you happy with your decision?" Alison said.

"Oh, yes," Ian nodded. "It's a fresh start, a chance to discover what I want out of life."

"That's good. I wish my future were as clear." A flash of doubt flickered across her face. "I planned everything so carefully, but it's just not happening."

Ian gazed at the twinkling lights of the City of Dreams. "Sometimes it's good to let it all go. Just step outside the box and see what happens. Which reminds me of a poem by *Lao Tse.*"

Just empty yourself of everything
Let the mind rest in peace.
The ten thousand things rise and fall
while the Self watches their return.
They grow and flourish and then return to the source.
Returning to the source is stillness
which is the way of nature.

Ian's voice was calming. Looking up, she saw the constellation Orion, its stars twinkling against the night sky. In the timelessness of that moment, she felt connected to something greater than herself.

Alison gave herself up to the ten thousand things running through her mind. She felt the stillness envelop her. After a while, she opened her eyes. She took a deep breath. "I know what to do," she said.

"What did you come up with?"

"Well," she said, her eyes gleaming. "You know my grandparents?"

He nodded. "I met them when I was searching for a community."

"They want to move house, and I think they might be interested in taking on a renovation."

"Hey, that's a great idea," said Ian. "Would you like me to contact them for you?"

"Yes, please." Alison sighed. "Oh, Ian. I'm going to miss you."

"I'll miss you, too." His voice carried a depth she hadn't heard before, and yet she sensed an undercurrent of unease.

"What's wrong?" She said, sensing the tension.

"Sorry," said Ian, his eyes focused on a distant star. "It's just that I get confused. The Re-entry Pavilion reminded me that life on Earth was a whirlwind of expectations. It left my head spinning. It made me realise what I don't know," he said, his voice tinged with frustration. "There's something missing in my understanding of the world. And my past; it feels like it's catching up with me." He shook his head. "It's hard to put into words."

"The Pavilion opened up questions for me, too. I feel that life is designed to distract us from something far greater than we can imagine." Alison nodded slowly. "Sometimes I wonder if we are really being told the truth about our earthly experience. Then again, I wonder if anyone really knows."

His eyes met hers, and for a moment the air between them shimmered with quiet understanding. "You have a way of getting to the heart of matters," he said. "It helps me remember who I am."

Alison smiled. "Maybe that's what we're here for—to remind each other."

A stillness settled. They didn't need to speak. Somehow, their thoughts seemed to merge.

"Whatever paths we take, we'll no doubt meet again," said Ian softly.

"I feel the same," she said.

A breeze rustled through the trees. Alison shivered.

"We should get back." Ian lowered the roof of the car, then they drove down the mountain in silence.

The convertible came to a stop in front of her house. "I guess it's goodbye for now," said Alison.

He reached over and took her hand. "This is only a pause in our journey."

Alison smiled warmly and squeezed his hand. "I hope so," she said.

Opening the car door, she stepped out onto the nature strip. Watching as the car disappeared down the road, she felt no emptiness, only the gentle touch of a deep and lasting connection.

The following day, Alison was in the kitchen when a knock sounded at the door. She glanced out the window and nearly dropped her cup. On the lawn sat a flying machine that looked like a huge purple grape. She went to answer the door.

"We received your message and came as quickly as we could," said her grand-mother.

"I'm so glad," said Alison as she stared at the grape. "What's that?"

"Oh, something I manifested," said her grandfather. "I was trying to imagine a bowl of grapes, and this flying grape appeared. It's handy for getting around."

Alison laughed. "Oh, Grandpa, you're so funny." She glanced over at the house next door. The curtains twitched as a face appeared in the window. "Let's go inside." She ushered them into the lounge room. "I called you here to see if you would be interested in taking on a renovation?"

Her grandfather smiled. "You mean move in here?"

Alison nodded.

Her grandmother glanced around the room. "Oh, yes. We could put in bigger windows so we can look out over the neighbours."

"Come on, dear, let's look around," said her grandfather. They wandered from room to room, chatting eagerly.

Alison caught up with them in the laundry, arguing about tiles.

"What do you think?" she asked.

"It has possibilities," replied her grandfather as they followed her to the kitchen.

Her grandmother ran her hand along the orange benchtop. "The room is a little dated, but the atmosphere is light."

Alison smiled. "Funny you should mention that. A wizard recently cleared the place of family secrets."

Her grandmother blinked. "Really?" She eyed the yellowing cabinets. "Look, we'll need new cupboards."

"Yes, my dear," her grandfather replied. "I'll have the place shipshape in no time."

Alison glanced from one to the other. "So, do you like it?"

"The house needs work, but the location is perfect." Her grandfather smiled. "I can see myself down at the tavern."

"Don't forget shopping and card evenings," said her grandmother. She turned to Alison. "But what are you going to do?"

"I'm not sure," she said, frowning. "But I'm working on it." Alison smiled. "How about a cuppa?"

"This is no time for tea." Her grandfather waved his hands. Immediately, a bottle of champagne appeared on the table.

They drank a toast to the house and everyone's future, then her grandfather stood up. "Well, Alison, dear, we're going to pack up our old place forthwith."

"And we look forward to hearing when we can move in," said her grandmother.

Alison showed them out, then waved as the purple grape ascended into the sky.

✳

Later, as Alison sat in the lounge room, a cheery voice sounded. "Yoo-hoo!"

Gladys stood on the doorstep in a green frock dotted with purple butterflies. "I've been thinking of you, all here on your lonesome. Would you like to come over for a cuppa?"

"That would be lovely," said Alison.

She followed her neighbour through her front garden; the beds filled with roses and snapdragons. Large pots overflowing with nasturtiums lined the path. They walked through an archway covered in vines and into the backyard. The contrast was astounding. Suddenly Alison found herself in the midst of a jungle of mottled light, palm fronds and rubbery green leaves. She breathed in the earthy fragrance. "This place is magical. I could get lost here."

"I often do," said Gladys as she climbed the stairs of the deck. She turned to Alison. "You go for a wander and enjoy the garden while I fix the tea."

A blue butterfly shimmered in the light, touching briefly upon a bush before drifting along the stone path. With a sense of wonder stirring in her heart, Alison followed.

A shimmering blue butterfly landed on a bush and then took off, fluttering above the stone path. Overcome with a childlike sense of wonder, Alison followed. She crossed a wooden bridge arching over a brook, where water trickled below and birds called softly above. The butterfly came to rest on a wheelbarrow brimming with feathery ferns, encircled by a carpet of blue flowers. Alison smiled, breathing in the stillness and the timeless beauty of nature.

It wasn't long before she heard a cheerful hum as Gladys set the table.

For a moment, Alison lingered before turning back toward the house. She climbed the stairs.

"Oh, there you are," said Gladys as she poured the tea. "What did you think of the garden?"

"It's magical," said Alison, sitting down. "What was your inspiration?"

"I created this as a memorial; to remind myself that no matter what life brings, everything is a gift." She shook her head. "Don't get me wrong, life was pleasant enough, but in the end, I couldn't remember a thing. I forgot my husband and my children. I forgot how to cook and clean. Everything I once took for granted disappeared."

"Oh, dear," said Alison. "How sad."

Gladys nodded. "After I passed, I remembered everything, and then I felt embarrassed. I saw myself as useless, a burden on my family and society. Then one day, while weeding the garden, a deep peace came over me. In the stillness, I heard God's voice: 'Do not listen to the trickster who judges you and your life. You are loved for who you are'."

"From that moment, I decided not to dwell on things I couldn't change, but to be grateful for life in all its myriad forms. That was when my creativity blossomed, and I created this sacred garden dedicated to the present moment."

Alison smiled. "How beautiful."

"I'm pleased you like it." Gladys offered her a sandwich, then she leaned closer. "I've been noticing a lot of comings and goings at your place."

Alison chewed and swallowed. "Oh, I forgot to mention, my grandparents are moving in."

Gladys' eyes widened. "Is that so? And where will you go?"

"I'm not sure yet."

Gladys smiled. "I'm certain it will all work out."

Alison returned home to find Tabitha asleep on her bed. She sat down and stroked her soft fur.

Gladys is right, she thought. *It's as though the trickster has something to say every moment of my life. A running commentary, whispering that I'm weak, useless, that I can never be enough.*

She sighed... *I want to express myself, but the inner judge paralyzes me before I even begin.*

Alison focused her thoughts on the point of light, and a feeling of peace came over her. She heard the voice of a higher self: *Don't be a victim. Turn the game around.*

Suddenly, she felt a surge of clarity, and the situation became clear. *Very well...* she thought.

If the trickster is trying to prevent me from creating, I'll do the opposite. I'll use my imagination and make something; anything—it doesn't have to be perfect, but it will be me, expressing myself; being free.

Alison looked beyond the faded curtains and the shag pile rug, seeing instead a large four-poster bed. Then, she imagined tapestries depicting scenes of mythical creatures on the walls.

With a fierce resolve, she jumped up. "A bedroom fit for a princess."

"Come on, Tabbie," she said, heading to the door.

Tabitha jumped down and followed her into the lounge room. "What do you think? How about an open-plan house with potted palms and enormous windows?"

Alison twirled gracefully, then stopped. "No! Let's splash out. How about a pink house with stained-glass windows and a magnificent dome on top? Oh, and I see it in a natural setting. No cars or motorbikes—a community of like-minded people."

Tabitha's almond eyes gazed at her. She mewed.

Alison laughed. "Oh, of course! Most importantly, the neighbours must have cats."

12

Temple to the goddess

ALISON HELD THE VISION of her dream house in her mind. Then one afternoon, as she pushed the vacuum cleaner across the faded rug, with each sweep, the colours appeared more vibrant. She paused, admiring the pattern, then startled as the ornamental ducks on the wall flapped their wings and flew away.

Alison's eyes widened as the rug quivered beneath her feet. She steadied herself as the rug swayed.

"I can do it, I know I can!" she cried as the rug rose. Higher and higher it floated until it popped through the ceiling until they hovered above the roofline.

Neighbours rushed out of their houses, pointing.

Suddenly, the rug took off. Alison gasped with delight as she flew like a bird above the towers and busy streets of the City of Dreams. Beyond the city limits, the landscape changed into rolling hills and green valleys, until at last, the rug descended into a tree-filled valley.

It landed gently, and Alison stepped onto the grass. A warm breeze blew through her hair. Before her stood a house with rose-coloured walls, stained-glass windows and a dome that gleamed like a jewel.

"Wow!" she breathed.

She heard a rush and looked up. Above her, a white horse circled, its wings silhouetted against the sky. He landed, tossing his head and folding his wings against his flanks. A pointed hat appeared from behind the horse's mane.

Alison smiled. "Orion! How did you know?"

"Pegasus has perfect timing," he said, sliding down.

She gazed at his red hat and blue cloak. "You look like a wizard."

He nodded. "I'm on my way to a Wizard Convention, and so I have to dress the part." He stood with his hands on his hips, gazing at the house. "Impressive style. Ancient feminine—a temple to the goddess, perhaps?"

Alison tilted her head. "Something like that."

"Have you seen inside?"

"No, I just arrived."

"Well then, lead the way," he said with a flourish.

They were almost at the door when the cat flap swung open. Tabitha's head appeared. Alison's eyes widened as Tabitha bounded along the pathway to greet them.

"Oh, Tabby, how did you get here?"

Tabitha's eyes met Alison's, then she blinked and sauntered away.

They reached the doorstep. Alison admired the crystal doorknob and wooden door inlaid with bronze. The door swung open at her touch, and a floral scent wafted from within. Stepping inside, her eyes widened. In the centre of the room lay a rug with overstuffed armchairs, warm and inviting. Green ferns spilled over pots. Wooden shelves held statues, and on the walls, artwork glittered with gold leaf. Off the main area, a gossamer fabric separated the living areas from the bedroom.

Orion stood beneath the clear, domed ceiling. He turned slowly in the spacious interior. "Mm... brilliant use of space and light."

The lithe statue of a dancing figure attracted Alison. She held it in her hands, and the vibrancy of the dance surged through her. She put the figure back on the shelf next to a statue of a goddess who appeared serene, compassionate, yet strong.

"Your inner goddess?" said Orion.

She smiled. "Perhaps." Her eyes fell on the beanbags. "Hey, this takes me back," Alison said, flopping onto a bag.

Orion smiled. "You are full of surprises." He sat in a beanbag and shifted his cloak around him. "After creating this, you still have doubts?"

Alison shook her head, but inwardly, a voice that resembled her mother's hijacked her thoughts. *'Don't you think of anyone but yourself?'* A current of dread passed through her. She reached for the locket around her neck and gasped. The chain was no longer there. Her head began to throb. She held her palm to her brow and closed her eyes.

"Sometimes I feel I don't deserve good things—you know what I mean?"

He reached out and brushed the top of her head.

The band of tension released, and she exhaled. "Oh, that's better." She gazed at him. "How did you do that?"

"I intercepted the energy pattern."

Her eyes widened. "Can I do that for myself?"

"Of course, just step into the experience. Do not fear it. Let it reveal its truth."

Alison closed her eyes and focused on her headache. Memories flooded her mind: the days when she couldn't work, her daughters, who knew when to leave her alone, and her husband, who blamed her for not being there for him. Endless visits to doctors, ever hopeful for that magical cure, and disappointment when nothing worked.

"Gather all of those memories into the present and hold them in the light of One," said Orion.

Her awareness lifted until she felt herself floating in the clear currents beyond the mind.

"Now," said Orion, his voice like a distant bell, "ask yourself, when did the pain originate?"

Alison was still for a moment, then a vision unfolded. She saw herself hiding behind the water tank, blaming herself for the conflict between her parents. After that, life continued as though nothing had happened, but from then on, she didn't feel safe. In the silence, the trickster crept in, whispering that it was her fault. No one had told her otherwise, and so its shame became her truth.

She opened her eyes. "I feel so helpless, so guilty. The same thoughts and feelings as when I had a migraine."

"Pain is a messenger. Now, bring it into the light and listen to your higher self," Orion said.

Alison focused on the light. For a while, she was silent. Then she spoke softly, "I am not responsible for others."

"What else?" he said.

"I am safe, I need nothing, I am enough."

"Good... and?"

Her voice dropped to a whisper. "My heart is pure."

She opened her eyes. "That's amazing!"

Orion nodded. "That's the power of divine light. It unmasks the illusion and restores what was yours all along. Soon you'll be ready to shine that light on other shadows in your past."

Alison frowned. "You mean my death?"

Orion's eyes softened as he nodded.

She felt a shiver down her spine. "Why? This is my sanctuary, my happy place!"

"Of course it is, but I also sense we each have a greater purpose, to heal ourselves and through that, to heal the world."

"What is healing?" she asked.

"Healing involves transforming your perception of the past. When your perception changes, you can make empowered choices in the present, which shapes your future."

"You make it sound effortless. Somehow, I can't imagine you having a tragic life, like mine."

Orion raised his eyebrows. "The road of trials is never easy. Each of us must face the obstacles necessary to awaken. For a perfectionist like myself, life and death can feel like such a messy business. But after reviewing a few lifetimes, I began to see the patterns—there was a hidden meaning in it all. And that is how I came to see life as entertaining; somewhat of a comic tragedy."

"How interesting. Could you tell me more?" asked Alison.

"I'd be happy to," he replied.

She smiled and shuffled the beanbag into a comfortable position.

"Let me see," said Orion, gazing into the distance. "I remember a lifetime where I thought I had mastered the game. In only a few short years, I learnt how to manipulate the world around me. Little did I know this type of magic came with its own set of shadows."

Orion's features faded, replaced by a pale man with angular features and hair parted down the middle.

"It was 1863 when Richard Galbraith had his first taste of the stock exchange. Instantly, he was hooked on the thrill of buying and selling shares. Richard was a partner at a law firm, and he provided well for his wife and three children. But Richard had aspirations to be a big man, so he left the firm and became a stockbroker, playing the market during the day and attending the club at night. He bought a large house and rode around town in a fine carriage. Then the market crashed, and he could no longer pay the bills. After his wife died in childbirth, Richard drowned his sorrows with alcohol and gambling. Eventually, he lost his fortune. One night, as he was strolling along a cliff face, he stumbled and fell, swallowed up by the waves below."

Alison shook her head. "Oh, dear."

"Oh, dear, indeed," said Orion. "And so, after reviewing Richard's lifetime, I decided it was time to unravel the tightly woven construct of my story."

Richard's face faded and, in its place, appeared a woman with auburn hair and round cheeks, partially hidden beneath a black lace fascinator.

"Charlotte Rose entered the world, red-faced and screaming. She grew up in a grey two-story house, where life remained regulated and predictable. Father read from the holy book every evening, and Mother, obedient and hard-working, rarely left the home except to do a weekly shop at the local market or visit her parents who lived across town.

"Little Charlotte quickly learned her place in a world that she despised: a world of housework and tapestries. She dreamt of running away and making a name for herself. The seed of this thought grew like a beanstalk until it became an obsession."

Alison's eyes widened.

"When Charlotte reached her twenties, her parents decided she should marry, so they found a suitable partner, a bookish pastor from the next county. Charlotte thought marriage was a waste of time, and the man they had chosen repulsed her. Preparations went ahead, and she cried herself to sleep at night. As the wedding day drew closer, her resolve grew. The day before the wedding, she packed a small bag and slipped out the back door. Heart beating, Charlotte walked quickly but resolutely away from a predictable life.

"She had just enough money to pay a coach driver to take her to a port city. There she worked her way up in the world, becoming the madam of a large and well-established bordello. Not only was she wealthy, but she had made a name for herself. When war broke out, Charlotte seized the opportunity to leave the country. She sewed her fortune into her petticoat, boarded a merchant vessel bound for an exotic land, and, while the guns roared, she spent her final years comfortably well-off in a guest house."

"Charlotte was quite a character," said Alison.

Orion nodded. "Charlotte's rejection of social graces helped awaken me from the dream, but I wasn't there yet. And so, with my next birth, I was ready to do something radical."

Alison watched as Charlotte's face re-formed into that of a boy with mousy brown hair.

"Ben was only fifteen when he died."

"Oh, so sad," said Alison.

"Ben grew up in a loving family with an older brother, Jamie. He never spoke a word, nor could he walk properly or play like other children. At four, his parents received a diagnosis of autism."

Alison nodded. As a hairdresser, she had heard such stories.

"Ben wasn't aware of life's difficulties. He was happy. He had everything he needed. In fact, he had no intention of dying young; however, things don't always go to plan."

"Ben's parents enjoyed camping holidays. His older brother, Jamie, often went along, although he preferred staying home and listening to music with his friends. On this day, his father stopped close to a river. Jamie had to look after his younger brother, but Ben gave him the slip. It wasn't Jamie's fault. Ben signalled he needed to go to the toilet behind a bush, and then he heard a gushing waterfall. Fascinated by the sound, he decided he would watch the water going over the falls."

"Higher and higher he climbed, over slippery stones, grabbing at the ferns to pull himself until finally, he achieved success, standing on an enormous boulder overlooking the marvellous sight, and the next moment, he was falling through space..."

Alison's eyes grew large.

"Ben felt light as a feather. Falling was fun until the rocks below loomed close. It was then that a flying horse whizzed past and scooped him onto its back. The horse flew down until Ben could see his family setting up camp. He saw his father ask Jamie where Ben was. Jamie shrugged. He saw his mother frantic with fear. Her voice echoed through the trees. Ben's father set off along the track, jogging breathlessly towards the waterfall. Somehow, he knew. The family searched everywhere, and when they couldn't find him, they dialled triple zero."

"Ben knew that number because he had called it before just to hear the voice. The police arrived with a tracker dog. Ben liked dogs. Late that night, he sniffed out his lifeless body. Ben was glad they had found his body. He wanted to hug the dog."

Alison shook her head as tears filled her eyes.

"Gratitude was a new sensation for Ben. It took him by surprise. As the ambulance drove away, he wondered why his family looked so sad. Suddenly he felt their pain, and with this, his heart exploded with love."

Ben vanished, and Orion's face re-formed, his eyes glowing. "I awoke from that dream, my awareness renewed. And here I am, the flying wizard..."

Alison smiled. "Wow, Orion. I would never have guessed that you went through so much."

"And there's more to come," he said. "I plan to be reborn."

"Oh, really?" said Alison.

He nodded. "I want to be there to help usher in a new consciousness."

Alison nodded. "I met others who are going to Earth with that aim."

"Oh, yes," said Orion. "The energy of change attracts many, but little do they know how difficult it is to awaken." He took a breath. "One needs the spirit of a wizard to see through the smokescreen of lies."

"What do you mean?" said Alison.

"As you know, the soul enters the world as a defenceless baby. Soon, expectations and social norms shape you into someone who fits a certain role. Then, as you grow older, desires emerge; thousands of years of conditioning." His voice lowered to a whisper. "The journey of awakening is a spiral that takes you to places you never imagined. You will remember who you are, and at other times you will forget and slip back into old ways."

Alison nodded. "I see, but how and why did we become trapped in the first place?"

"That secret lies beyond the web of thoughts and feelings that binds you to the story." Orion stood up and adjusted his cape. "Well, it's been a pleasure to see you again, but the convention is starting and I must away."

"Thank you for everything," said Alison as they walked outside.

"I wish you well," said Orion, his eyes aglow. He leapt onto the horse's back. Pegasus spread his wings and bounded into the air. Soon they were flying through the sky, his cloak flowing behind.

That evening, Alison heard a knock.

Her grandfather stood on the doorstep in a crisp sailor suit, and next to him stood her grandmother in a skirt and top and an enormous hat. Behind them, Alison glimpsed the purple grape bulging with possessions.

"How wonderful to see you!" she said.

"And you too," said her grandmother.

Her grandfather handed her a bunch of roses. "Congratulations on your new home."

"Oh, how lovely." Alison inhaled the perfume. "Come in."

"It was a little difficult to track you down," said her grandmother.

"I wanted a place away from the hustle and bustle," said Alison. She went to find a vase. Speaking from the kitchen, she asked. "Would you like a cuppa?"

"Oh, no, we can't stay long. It's getting dark, and we're moving in today," her grandfather replied.

Alison placed the flowers in a vase while her grandparents admired the play of red, yellow and green light streaming through the stained-glass windows.

"We must find some windows like this," said her grandmother. Her eyes sparkled, and she hugged Alison. "I hope you're happy here."

"Thank you, Grandma." A shadow passed over Alison's eyes. "I've been so preoccupied with the house, I neglected the girls."

"That's understandable." Her grandmother patted her hand. "But let me tell you, Emma and Haley are finding their way. Haley is getting good grades at school, and Emma has a boyfriend."

"How is my father coping?" she asked.

Her grandmother smiled. "Arthur is busier than he has been for a long time. The girls keep him active, and he spoils them rotten. And let me tell you a little secret." She leaned in. "I saw him empty his liquor onto the lawn. He's attending meetings and wants to be a role model for the girls."

Alison felt a wave of uncertainty. "I need to see them."

Her grandmother hesitated, then nodded. "If you wish, but be prepared, my dear. Those who are living, grieve in their own time." She smiled. "Let's take a look, shall we?"

The air shimmered, and Alison found herself gazing through a veil of light. There were her daughters—Emma at the kitchen table, staring blankly at a cup of untouched tea and Haley curled up on the sofa, her face hidden in her arms.

The room was heavy with silence. Alison reached towards them instinctively, but her hand passed through the veil. "Oh, my poor dears…" Her voice trembled. "I hope they are all right."

"They will be," said her grandmother softly. "But grief has its own time."

Then Alison's gaze shifted to her father. He was in the garden, a bottle in his hand. He stared at it for a long moment, then tipped it to his lips before placing it down with a curse.

Alison frowned. "I thought you said…"

"At least he's trying," said her grandmother.

The vision faded, leaving Alison in the afterglow of love and sorrow. She bowed her head. "They're still hurting… and I can't reach them."

Her grandmother shook her head. "You can, just not in the way you once did."

"Your grandmother is right," said her grandfather. "Keep moving ahead on your journey, and your strength will flow through to them."

Alison nodded. "You're right," she whispered. "I want to give them the strength that I couldn't give when I was alive."

Her grandmother smiled and nodded. "That's the way."

"Well, Alison, my dear, we must fly," said her grandfather.

They bustled through the front door, and Alison waved as the purple grape floated through the air.

That evening, as the sun went down, the lights in the house came on. Alison pushed aside the gossamer fabric and stepped into her bedroom. Before her stood the four-poster bed covered with a brocade quilt. Tabitha was curled up on the bed. The tapestries on the walls shone under the warm glow of the lights.

Alison slipped beneath the quilt. At last, she was in her own home.

An image of her mother appeared in her mind's eye, and with it came the realisation of her mother's pain and the unseen wounds that she carried from her own childhood. A quiet understanding blossomed of how over the generations, the harsh demands of survival had overridden the instinct to nurture.

It is hard; she thought as her eyes grew heavy, *but my purpose is clear—not to reject my family's story, but to heal it.*

13

Hades

ANAEMIC RAYS OF MORNING light filtered through the stained-glass windows, casting shadows on the bedroom walls.

As Alison awoke, thoughts swooped in like vultures.

You are nothing, a mere pea, insignificant. The force bore down, and a breath blew heavily on her neck. *No escape, there's no escape!*

She closed her eyes, trying to block the faceless shadows that darted menacingly close. "Get lost!" she cried. Clenching her fists, she sat up. An entity pushed her from behind, and another scratched her face. "Leave me alone!" she yelled, but the more she struggled, the more they pinched and pulled her hair.

What am I doing fighting these imaginary enemies? She threw her arms into the air. "Go to the light," she cried, as she threw off the bedclothes and struggled out of bed.

A gentle knock sounded. Alison pulled on a dressing gown and stumbled to the door. Tabitha scurried through her legs.

A young woman stood on the doorstep in a pair of jeans and a floaty top; her blonde hair in a ponytail. She held up a stick of herbs. "In need of some sage?" A thin curl of smoke drifted upward.

"Oh... yes," said Alison. She ran her fingers through her hair. "How did you know?"

"Occupational hazard of being human. I'm Flower, your neighbour. I live over there," she said, pointing to a hill.

"Hi, I'm Alison. Please come in."

Flower gazed around the room. "Wow, nice place you have here." The smoke drifted upwards. She muttered a verse while she waved the smoke around Alison's aura. Standing back, she nodded. "Feeling better?"

Alison looked down. Her pink dressing gown had morphed into a floaty dress, and her hair was brushed and styled. She smiled. "Oh... yes, that's lovely."

Flower glided through the house, waving the smoking herbs in the air. She returned. "That should help." She gazed at the statues and rows of books with golden spines on the shelf, then looked up at the dome. "Hey, this place is cosmic. Are you a goddess or something?"

"No," said Alison. "But I know one. Would you like a cup of tea?"

They sat in armchairs, bathed in filtered light, sipping lemongrass tea.

The cup clinked onto the saucer as Flower put it down. "So how did you die?"

Alison sat up. "That's a bit personal, isn't it?"

Flower shook her head. "Not at all. Here, it's a pleasantry; a greeting, as common as How are you?"

How strange, thought Alison.

Flower smiled. "The valley is a place of healing." She crossed her legs. "You're not quite ready to face your dark side, are you?"

The vision of her recent struggle flashed through Alison's mind. "I thought I'd left all that behind. What do you make of them, those malicious voices, I mean?"

Flower shrugged. "It's just the way things are, I guess." She paused. "Demons are elusive. Most people are not aware of them on Earth. Here they manifest, especially when you're feeling insecure. I have some of my own. Would you like to meet them?" She smiled, and her eyes turned blood red.

Alison blinked. "Later, perhaps. Could you tell me about the neighbours?"

"Of course. There's the old Professor who lives down the hill. He had a heart attack. He's a bit of a philosopher, always reciting poetry. Then there are the Biggley sisters. They take in cats and dogs and match them with humans in their next lives."

Alison smiled. "Tabitha will be happy."

"On top of the hill live the musicians, Peter and Paul. They host choir sessions at their observatory. Beautiful music—you like?"

"Oh, yes," she nodded.

"Then on the other side of the hill is Padma, the wise woman, who knows the past, present and future. She taught me how to sage a house. In one of her lifetimes, she died on her husband's funeral pyre."

Alison's eyes grew large. "How gruesome. So, how did you die?"

"I thought you'd never ask." Flower smiled, and her eyes flashed green and then blue. "I was only seventeen. We were at a music festival, my friends and I. They wanted me to try some pills, and so I did. Within hours, I was brain-dead. My parents had no choice but to turn off the life support. And there I was floating away, trying to make sense of it all."

Alison felt a rush of motherly concern. "Oh, my—so young. About the same age as my daughters."

"You had daughters?"

Alison nodded. "Emma and Haley. I barely recall their faces. Strange, isn't it?"

"The chain of love is never broken." Flower felt for a silver locket on a cord around her neck. She opened it. Inside was a tiny photo of two smiling faces. "Mum and Dad,"

"That's lovely," said Alison. Tears filled her eyes. "I just wish I hadn't been taken..."

"What?" Flower's mouth dropped open. "You mean...?"

Alison nodded.

Flower shook her head. "No wonder you were reluctant to talk. I'll call Padma; she'll know what to say." She closed her eyes for a moment, her lips moving. The air grew still. Then, a soft breeze stirred the air, and a matronly figure stepped forth, calm and radiant, draped in a sari of pale gold. Her steel-grey hair was braided, and her eyes, deep as though they could see through time itself. "Namaste, dear ones," she said.

Flower stood up, pressing her palms together. "Namaste Padma. This is Alison."

"Welcome to the Valley of Hope," she smiled. "How are you?"

Tears welled in Alison's eyes.

"I see," she murmured. "The school of life can be tough."

"I'll be off now," said Flower. "I'll see you later."

Alison waved. "Thanks for everything."

Padma leant forward. "Now, tell me your story from beginning to end."

Alison hesitated, then began. As she spoke, Padma sat motionless, listening as though she were watching the scenes unfold.

At last, Alison wiped her hand across her eyes. "...and that was that."

Padma's brow furrowed. "The events surrounding your ill-treatment and death were absolutely wrong."

Alison nodded, then she clasped her hands. "I know that, and yet sometimes I feel guilty."

Padma tilted her head. "But why?"

"I feel I failed myself... and my girls."

Padma reached out and rested her hand over Alison's. "Don't feel guilty. You didn't fail. You temporarily lost yourself, and now you are finding your way home. Tell me, what did you hope to achieve in that lifetime?"

"Oh... I don't know," said Alison. "I raised two children and ran a business."

Padma nodded slowly. "No doubt they were achievements. But tell me, beneath the doing, have you asked yourself what was the *real* purpose of your life?"

Alison shook her head. "I'm still trying to come to terms with everything."

Padma smiled. "Here in the Valley of Hope, we help souls resolve their past and make choices for their future."

"Then I am in the right place."

"Oh, yes," said Padma as she rose. "Come and meet our patron."

She led Alison to the far wall. They stood before a framed painting of a woman holding a jar. "This is Pandora, the patron of the Valley of Hope. According to myth, she opened the jar and released a multitude of ills into the world. When she realised what she had done, she quickly replaced the lid, and only Hope remained."

Alison noted a twinkle in Pandora's eyes. Suddenly, her lips moved. "Welcome, child," she said in a lilting tone. "Blessings be upon you. No matter your past struggles, here you can make a fresh start."

Alison stepped back, her eyes wide.

"It's okay," said Padma. "Pandora likes to welcome everyone personally."

Alison gazed up at the picture. "Oh... thank you."

Padma smiled. "I guess Flower told you about your neighbours?"

"Yes, she did."

"That's good. The Valley of Hope is a place of reflection and healing, a pause in your journey." Padma gazed around the room. "I sense you have an artistic flair?"

"I don't know," said Alison. "Apart from hairstyling, I focused on everyone else."

"Now is your chance to focus on yourself," said Padma as she walked towards the door. "I'll leave you to think about how you would like to express this phase of your healing."

Alison smiled as they said goodbye. For the first time, she felt that someone truly saw her.

She closed the door just as Tabitha burst through the cat flap.

"Oh, Tabby, you're back." Alison glided to the kitchen and poured milk into a bowl. Tabitha leapt onto the bench, her eyes large.

She mewed softly.

Alison listened. "You met the Biggley sisters... that's nice."

Tabitha blinked and mewed again.

"Oh, they have other cats. How many?"

Tabitha tilted her head to one side.

"Quite a few—I see," said Alison. She poured some milk into a bowl and placed it on the floor.

Tabitha jumped down and, with her engine purring, she went to find her milk.

Alison gazed out of the window. Multicoloured birds twittered and danced among the leaves. Across the way stood a pale cream cottage with a red roof. *Must be where the Biggley sisters live*, she thought.

An iridescent blue butterfly landed on the ledge outside. *How pretty* she thought.

Suddenly, she heard a voice. "Are you a butterfly dreaming you're a human, or a human dreaming you're a butterfly?"

Alison spun around. The room shimmered with a violet haze. A pair of eyes came into view, then a face appeared, followed by a goddess form.

Alison held her hand over her beating heart. "Oh, Persephone. What were you doing, sneaking up on me like that?"

"A little excitement never hurt anyone." Persephone laughed, and her diamante gown flickered. "How are you?"

"I'm okay." The words slipped from her mouth, a response from a lifetime on automatic. "No, I'm wonderful. I feel light and free." Alison twirled, and her dress floated around her.

"You should feel happy." Persephone's eyes scanned the room. "This house reflects your inner beauty."

"Thank you," Alison said, then her smile faltered. "But I lost the locket."

"You may have lost the locket, but you gained the magic within." Persephone gazed into her eyes. "Do you doubt your inner strength?"

Alison frowned. "If I'm so strong, why am I being attacked by demons?"

Persephone smiled. "Those are simply the shadows of your deepest fears."

Alison's eyes widened. "You mean I'm attacking myself?"

"That's it." Persephone met hers. "And what do humans fear most?"

From the corner of her eye, Alison saw the blue butterfly open its wings and fly away. "Death, I suppose…"

Persephone nodded. "Make peace, not only with your life but also with death, and the shadows will no longer haunt you."

"Really?" said Alison. "But how?"

"You've heard enough from me," said Persephone. "So, why don't we go straight to the horse's mouth?"

"What do you mean?"

"The Lord of the Underworld himself—Lord Hades."

Alison's eyes widened.

"Have no fear." Persephone smiled. "He won't bite you." She lifted her hands to the sky and spoke an invocation.

The shadows thickened, and the air grew heavy with unseen power. A god appeared—majestic, with dark hair and deep eyes. He wore a coal-dark cape draped over his shoulders.

"Persephone, my love, you called?" His voice resonated through the room.

"Yes, I did," she replied. She spoke to Hades in an ancient tongue—fluid and somewhat melodic.

Hades took a quick breath, and the atmosphere stilled. "There seems to be an epidemic of stupidity in the world." He inclined his head with graceful dignity. "Alison. It's a pleasure to meet you."

Alison smiled, lost in his fathomless gaze.

"Now then, how can I help?" he said.

"I know you're busy, my dear," said Persephone, "but Alison has some questions, and I feel she would benefit from hearing your side of the story."

"Of course." Hades removed his cape with a flourish and made himself comfortable in an armchair. "What would you like to know?"

Alison sat down. She tried not to stare at the god's wavy locks and shadowed chin. "I want to feel more comfortable with death," she whispered.

"My dear child, it is important at the outset that we get something straight—there is no such thing as death. The soul loses its physical body, but it remains a living entity."

Alison nodded. "Okay, but why did I have to leave?"

Hades drew a battered pipe from his cloak and packed it with tobacco. "The soul enters a body for an appointed span of time. The duration of each life is pre-set even before you leave for Earth. Once that time is over, the body returns to the Earth while the soul returns to its kind—among other souls." He placed the pipe between his teeth, struck a match, and inhaled until the tobacco glowed red-hot. "Tell me, Alison, do you remember arriving in the Afterlife?"

Alison shook her head. "Only vaguely."

"Ah, yes, understandable." A wisp of woody smoke drifted upwards. "Many rush through my realm." He gazed into the distance. "Not like old times. I took pleasure in renewing acquaintances with old friends. Over time, fewer and fewer came to dine at the palace."

Alison's eyes widened. "Oh, why was that?"

A cloud of smoke floated around his face. "People became absorbed in their own stories. But it was not always that way. Your ancestors accepted death as an inevitable conclusion. They saw their lives as part of a grand mythology. Thus, they honoured my sacred realm. However, as history progressed, many succumbed to the all-pervasive myth that they were sinners, and Hades became synonymous with hell."

Alison nodded. "I have to admit some fear. After all, we were never taught about the afterlife."

Hades' eyes flashed. He turned to Persephone. "You see how they avoid reality?"

"Yes, my dear," said Persephone.

Hades turned to Alison. "What else would you like to know?"

"I'd like to know what happens after we die."

"The transition to the afterlife is effortless, thanks largely to Persephone." He smiled. "The boatman ferries his immortal consignment across the river Styx. There, the newly arrived souls are met by guides and family members."

"I remember meeting my guide, Angelo, but then everything changed," said Alison.

Hades nodded. "Oh, yes. My wife has a habit of diverting souls from their well-worn paths. She wishes for everyone to return to the light." He turned to Persephone. "Isn't that so, my dear?"

Persephone sighed. "I do try, but not everyone appreciates my efforts. Most are happy to have a break and then continue with their same old stories."

"Persephone is right," said Hades. "Here in the Afterlife, souls are freed from the endless stories spun by the masters of illusion." His eyes flashed, and he gave a scathing snort. "Entertainment—I mean, what else do mortals do, except be diverted by the stories of the so-called gods? Just look at their endless love alliances, wars and pacts."

Alison sighed. "All I wanted was happiness."

"Of course, and, like most people, you sought one thing and found another." He sat back in the chair. "From the vantage point of my undying realm, the world of Zeus is nothing but dust."

Alison blinked.

"Yes, dear," said Persephone. "Now, tell Alison how you became the ruler of the Underworld."

"Oh, of course." Hades tapped his pipe over an ashtray. "After we Olympians overthrew the Titans, my brothers and I faced the question of how to divide the world. In the end, we tossed a coin." He smiled. "Zeus gained the sky, Poseidon the seas and I, the Underworld. Our sister Demeter became the guardian of the harvest, while Hera shared dominion with her husband Zeus, and Hestia chose the quiet hearth and home."

"It sounds like the gods gained control and the goddesses took supporting roles," said Alison.

"Hm... you are observant. But it is true. Zeus believed himself to be the omnipotent creator, but the fact was, he could only create through the feminine. Indeed, endless offspring sprang from the fruit of his loins."

Alison raised her eyebrows.

Persephone frowned. "I'm not sure Alison is interested in Zeus' dalliances—or yours for that matter."

"Of course, my dear." Hades turned to Alison. "We were young and full of the joys of life. But unlike my philandering brothers, I was faithful." His eyes glazed over. "The daughter of Demeter stole my heart, and so I tempted her with a cluster of golden flowers."

Persephone sighed.

"No doubt, it may have appeared somewhat dramatic with the golden chariot and black stallions. However, her attitude changed. Isn't that true, my love?"

Persephone smiled. "Once I recovered, I found the Underworld strangely compelling."

"Home to the riches of humanity's illustrious past." Hades cleared his throat. "Did you share your story of transformation from an innocent Kore to Queen of the Underworld?"

Persephone shook her head. "Not yet."

"Well, then you must, for it is a story worth telling." Hades stood up. "The problem is, humans cannot bear too much reality." Hades leaned over and kissed Persephone's hand. He stood up and threw his cape over his shoulders with a flourish.

Then his eyes met Alison's. "My dear child, it is good that you seek illumination, for the wisdom in this world has long vanished. Have courage and reclaim what is rightfully yours. And now I must make haste to attend a state funeral." The sombre notes of a Gregorian chant sounded as Hades dissolved into the ether.

Alison took a steady breath. "Hades is not as fearful as I imagined."

Persephone smiled softly. "Lord Hades may not be perfect, but his heart is in the right place." She rose from her chair. "I have duties to attend, but I will return." A violet mist surrounded her, and she vanished into the night.

Alison sat for a long moment, reviewing the events of the day. Life had certainly taken a turn, and now she was on a fresh path. She closed her eyes and recalled Padma's words, *'Now is your chance to focus on yourself.'*

I'd like to do something, but what? She wondered. She glanced over at the portrait of Pandora. Her eyes glimmered as though alive, urging her to undo the lock that held her heart captive—and fly free.

14

Persephone

BEAMS OF MORNING LIGHT shone through the stained-glass windows, bathing the bedroom in a rainbow glow. Alison tossed off the bedcovers, her resolve from the night before still firm in her mind. She dressed quickly, and as she passed the shelves, a title caught her eye, *Persephone's Story*. Settling into an armchair, she read.

The young maidens dressed in muslin gowns laughed and played together among the crocuses, irises, hyacinths and lilies. There were Styx, Urania and the lovely Galaxy, Athena, who rouses battles, and Artemis, who delights in the hunt. Among them was an unnamed kore, a slender maiden with long dark hair who knew nothing of the world outside, only her mother, the great goddess, Demeter, who blessed the fields with wheat, corn and barley.

Alison pictured the young maiden with a spray of white flowers in her hair, laughing and playing with her friends. The image lingered—sunlight, movement, the soft sound of laughter carried on the breeze. A knock at the door broke her reverie. She closed the book, resting her hand on the cover for a moment before rising to answer the door.

Padma entered with her warm presence. "I just dropped by to see how you are."

"Oh, thanks, Padma. I'm good." Alison smiled, then added, "In fact, I have an idea that I'd like to spend some time focusing on my inner self."

Padma nodded. "Very good."

"And... I want to express myself through art," Alison added, her eyes brightening.

Padma's face lit up. "Oh, even better! "I can arrange the art supplies and let others know you'll need some privacy."

"That would be wonderful," said Alison, a warm glow rising within.

In the days that followed, the beanbag became her refuge, a place to drift inward and untangle a lifetime of experiences. At times, her thoughts turned to her mother. *It was hard,* she thought, *very hard, not to have the comfort of motherly love.* Gradually, she saw she had chosen her mother, not for her nurturing or warmth, but because her brokenness was what she needed to inspire her own journey of awakening.

While part of her understood, part of her still whispered. *But why did it have to be this way? Why did I have to endure her silence, her rage, her distance?*

And from somewhere deep within came an answer. *It was not your role to receive love but to remember it...*

When the emotions grew too heavy to hold, Alison found release in the untamed corners of her garden, where she could breathe. One day, she brushed aside some branches and came upon a studio half hidden by the foliage, with a peaked roof and large windows. Dust motes danced in the sunlight as she opened the door. She immediately set to work, sweeping, airing and clearing.

It was late that afternoon when Flower dropped by.

"How lovely," she said, stepping inside the sunlit studio.

"I have to admit," said Alison, "I've never painted before. I don't know where to start."

"Maybe we could paint together," said Flower.

Alison smiled. "That would be great."

The next morning, boxes of paints and a pile of canvases arrived on Alison's doorstep. Later that day, Flower returned wearing a painter's shirt over her jeans.

The studio soon rang with laughter as they painted with wild abandon. "Just allow your imagination to run free," said Flower, splashing on bright colours and creating abstract shapes.

Alison felt something loosen inside her. She let go of her inhibitions and allowed the paint to flow. After that, she made daily trips to the studio. The canvases served as a safe place for her wild and unruly thoughts, her brushstrokes capturing her deepest longings and her fears.

Gradually, her painting became calmer. The bold splashes gave way to gentle tones. One morning she began a new canvas; a vision that had stirred in her dreams. With each brushstroke, her vision of the long-lost temple of the goddess emerged. Finally, Alison stood back and smiled. Her painting radiated the tranquillity of her inner peace.

✳

One morning, Tabitha joined her in the studio, curling up on a nearby chair, tail flicking lazily.

Alison reached for a fresh canvas. Standing back, she wondered what to paint. Standing back, she wondered what to paint. The story of the maiden, entranced by a cluster of flowers came to mind. Painting swiftly, she captured the innocence of the maiden at the moment when the earth split open and Hades, in his chariot, appeared. It was as though her hand moved with a force not entirely her own.

Once she finished, Alison stood back from the canvas.

A voice broke the silence. "I screamed. Hades slapped his hand over my mouth, and in an instant, he swept me into his chariot. The earth groaned behind us as we descended into the abyss."

Alison turned, dazzled by the shards of morning light. Through the glowing haze, a figure took form—radiant, her hair flowing over a white muslin gown. In her hand, she held a bunch of nodding daffodils.

"Humanity's fall from grace," she said, handing Alison the golden flowers.

"Oh, Persephone..." Alison smiled. "They remind me of spring days and bright sunshine."

Persephone smiled. "Clever, isn't it?" she said, "the way the bulbs hibernate over the frosty winter and burst into flower in spring. Their beauty is unsurpassed but at the same time fleeting, like trying to hold on to a mirage. I was naïve, so when I saw those blossoms, it was as if I were under a magical spell."

"So, you're saying we become attached to the physical world as if it's permanent and then we suffer?"

"Indeed," said Persephone. "Just like life's experience, the value of the flower lies not in its permanence, but in the beauty of its transience."

Alison sighed. "Strange, but I feel your story as if it were my own."

Persephone's eyes glowed. "What is life but a story that unfolds on many levels?" She glanced at Tabitha, who quickly jumped out of the chair. Persephone sat gracefully. "Are you ready to hear my story?"

"Of course," said Alison, sitting down.

"Then let us begin at the moment Hades bundled me into his chariot. I found myself in the dim light of the Underworld. Trees flashed by as the horses thundered across the plains. Then, abruptly, he pulled the horses up at the top of a hill. I caught my breath and looked around. In the distance stood a vast palace, set on a neatly manicured estate. Hades turned to me and smiled, saying, 'Welcome to my pleasure garden.'

"Feelings flowed through me like never before—a combination of excitement and dread. Then Hades took up the reins and bade the horses trot on. He was indeed the master of the illusion. We made our way up the palace stairs. Inside, life-size paintings of gods and goddesses lined the walls. Maids bowed low and addressed me as their queen, offering me a chalice filled with fragrant nectar.

"Hades smiled. 'We will meet this evening,' he said as the maids showed me to my room.

"After bathing, a lady-in-waiting stood by my bed holding a silken gown embroidered with tiny white roses. She slid it over my head. It fell in soft folds around my body. She dried and brushed out my hair, then pinned it in a style most becoming. A lacy train floated behind me as I walked through the door. Hades stood at the end of the corridor wearing a deep blue robe lined with a gold braid. His wavy hair tied back, with a few dark curls falling onto his forehead. My heart fluttered as Hades took my hand and brushed it with a gentle kiss."

Alison's cheeks turned pink. "Oh, how romantic?"

"The feeling was another first for me." Persephone smiled. "Together, we walked along the passageway. The double doors swung open, and the scent of wildflowers filled the air. We walked past urns filled with fragrant spring blossoms and guests dressed in their finest robes. The hum of conversation died down, and the guests smiled, bowed and whispered as we climbed the red-carpeted stairs and stood on the balcony.

"Hades turned to the crowd and addressed them, proclaiming, 'Tonight, and forevermore, we have the blessing of a goddess, daughter of Demeter and the great Zeus. I present to you my future wife, Persephone.' He kissed my cheek, and the hall filled with cheers. I smiled graciously, but I was furious inside—had I been asked?

"A young lad walked towards us dressed in rich brocade, bearing a velvet cushion on which sat a ring adorned with diamonds and sapphires. Hades took the ring and placed it on my finger. We were engaged. The crowd cheered, and the sounds of lute and drums echoed through the hall. We sat on velvet chairs while servants brought jugs of fruity ambrosia, which they poured into silver goblets. Music played, and the onlookers danced in merriment.

"Here I was, one moment a nameless kore, and the next I was Persephone, soon to be crowned queen of the Underworld with a powerful lord and palace at my fingertips. I felt a growing sense of isolation when Hades' interest in palace affairs waned. He often arrived home late; his face creased with concern. I questioned him, but he didn't want to worry me. Was I nothing but a trophy wife? I became anxious. Every noise made me jump. The maids whispered behind my back.

"One afternoon, as I strolled through the gardens, I glimpsed Charon, the ferryman. 'Do you mind if I join you?'

"'I am honoured,' he said, bowing.

"We strolled together along a tree-lined path, and I asked how things were. At first, Charon refused to talk, but I persisted until, finally, Charon held his hands over his face and let out a hoarse sob. 'Many are perishing in the world above. I ferry the boats back and forth, but they keep coming.' Charon looked up, his eyes filled with tears. 'I heard the story that Demeter refuses to bless the crops, and so famine has struck the land. The stench is terrible, as there is no one left to bury the dead.'

"'Demeter... my mother?'

"At the sound of her name, my sorrow increased, threatening to break open the dam of loneliness in my mind. She had not forgotten me. I hurried to my chamber, locked the door and threw myself onto the bed. Compelled by the pain of his story, I made a plan. That evening, I dressed for dinner and, afterwards, announced to Hades that I could no longer stand by and watch him leave for the river alone. I was going to be by his side and help him in whatever way I could. With shoulders slumped, he agreed. After all, what else could he do?

"The following day, I boarded Hades' chariot and together we flew to the fields of Asphodel. I stood on the bank, watching the boats full of shadowy figures arriving on our shores. Walking dead splashed through the water and struggled up the steep incline, despair in their eyes. I approached a woman, prematurely stooped. Beneath her dusty veil was a haggard face and dark holes where her eyes once shone.

"The thread-like line of her mouth moved. 'I am Callidora,' she said. Embarrassed, she pulled the veil across her face. 'I was once a strong woman with three healthy children and a husband who, with the good grace of the goddess, fed us with the bounty of the land. Each year, my husband ploughed the fields with the oxen, then he sowed the barley. But drought came, and hungry birds devoured the scattered seeds. White blossoms gusted from the trees, and vegetables wilted in the parched soil. We offered libations, but the goddess no longer heard our pleas.' A sob rose in her throat. 'After her daughter left, we heard Demeter had lost interest in maintaining the crops. They say she is punishing the gods.'

"'You deserve more than this,' I said, as I linked arms with Calliodora and assisted her to the shore where she could rest, then I busied myself meeting the shadowy, emaciated forms as they stepped out of the boats. It didn't take long to realise that there were too many for the current system to cope with.

"That evening, I proposed to Hades that we needed many more guides who could answer questions and assist newcomers in reconnecting with their relatives and friends. Hades murmured and nodded his head, and so I took his response to mean that he wouldn't stand in my way. And so, I organised teams of guides whose role it was to send the newcomers on their way with a lighter heart."

Alison's eyes glistened. "That's amazing."

"An unexpected twist to this was that it helped me. Gradually, the flicker of compassion fanned into a flame of love that spanned the universe. Hades and I grew closer as he recognised my flair for helping souls pass from one world to the next. Working together on the Elysian Fields, I discovered we had more in common than I had ever imagined."

"Ah... finally, you found love."

"Yes, but our little love story was soon to be tested. One afternoon, while on the banks of the River Styx, a horse galloped towards us. The messenger spoke breathlessly. 'My queen, the palace urgently needs you.'

"It wasn't long before I was striding up the palace stairs, two at a time. I stepped through the door. A mysterious guest was resting on a sofa in the parlour, his head bowed. He heard my footsteps and raised his head.

"I recognised the messenger god Hermes by his broad-brimmed hat.

"'Oh, my, d-d-dear Kore, it's been a long while, hasn't it?' The palace halls echoed with his mirth.

"Hades appeared in the doorway. Seeing Hermes, he held out his hand. 'Welcome to my realm, dear boy. How did you arrive?'

"'L-L-Lord Zeus lent me his finest horses and, of course, we know he can do anything he wants... well, within reason, and sometimes not within r-r-reason.' Hermes chuckled. 'He told me not to stay too long in the Underworld or I may not g-g-get out,' he said, his eyes flickering. 'And so, I'll come straight to the point. You see, Persephone's m-m-mother finally persuaded Zeus to bring her d-d-daughter home.'

"I trembled, remembering my mother, Demeter.

"Hades' cheeks reddened. 'Persephone is no longer a kore to be ordered around by her mother,' he said. 'She is queen of the Underworld.'

"Hermes raised his eyebrows. 'Well, I'm s-s-sorry, but apparently, they want her back,' he said. 'You must understand, Demeter is so enraged that she refuses to bless the crops.'

"I took Hades' hand in mine. 'We cannot deny the terrible effect of her wrath. I must see my mother again and put things right for all our sakes.'

"Hades remained quiet as he pondered the situation. Then he spoke. 'It pains me to say this, but we need to bring an end to this dreadful famine.' He paused again. 'Hermes, dear boy, please enjoy the hospitality of the palace. We'll meet you here when the full moon rises.'

"That evening, we sat together on the palace rooftop, watching the setting sun. The sweet call of a nightingale drifted through the air. A servant arrived with nectar squeezed from sweet pomegranates, and we toasted our kingdom and our lives. The fragrant liquid slipped down my throat, along with a few pomegranate seeds.

"Afterwards, we went to where Hermes stood in the chariot. He held out his hand, and I stepped aboard.

"Lord Hades looked up with tears in his eyes. 'Farewell, my love.'

"I felt torn. I wanted to stay in the Underworld with Hades, yet I yearned to be with my mother on Mount Olympus.

"Hermes took the reins, and the horses sprang to life, their wings reflecting the moonlight. Through the dark clouds, they soared as the chariot bumped from side to side until, eventually, they emerged into the clear light above. They landed gently in a field, and I breathed the sweet night air.

"'Here you are,' said Hermes.

"I looked around, recognising the grove of trees and the gleaming columns of the white marble sanctuary.

"Demeter is still sulking in Eleusis. I'll let her know you're back,' said Hermes. The chariot zoomed off with him singing at the top of his voice.

"A full moon hung overhead, and a cuckoo sounded a lonely call. I wandered the forlorn halls of my childhood, torn between the love of my mother and devotion to my husband until, exhausted, I lay down on a soft bed of reeds.

"The next morning, I rose early and splashed my face with spring water. Then, searching through the temple, I donned the simple white robes of my youth. Then, I sat on a rock and waited in the sunlight. A speck appeared in the sky. As the object drew closer, I saw it was Hermes, and next to him stood another. The horses landed, and my mother, in a hooded cloak, stepped down. Her hair fell in ragged locks around her face, and her cloak looked patched and worn. Her eyes lit up with joy as she held out her arms. We embraced together once more.

"'I -I-love happy endings,' said Hermes. 'But I must not linger any longer. I told Zeus I would return the horses before nightfall, and I have a few more, um, p-p-personal errands to run.'

"Arm in arm, we waved as the horses took wing, soaring high into the cloudless sky."

Persephone smiled. "And there I must leave the story, but it is not yet over..."

Tears welled in Alison's eyes as an ancient stirring rose within. "I don't know why I feel so moved," she whispered.

"That is the power of the story—an echo of your long-forgotten past." A swirling mist surrounded Persephone, and she vanished.

The studio glowed with the yellow light of the flowers. Alison turned to the canvases. *I know what I'll do,* she thought, *I'll paint a series; Persephone's descent into darkness and her awakening to the light.*

Images from Persephone's story, swirled in her mind. As she began to mix the colours, she wondered if she was a goddess dreaming, she was a human, or a human dreaming she was a goddess.

15

Hesiod

THE DAYS PASSED PLEASANTLY in the Valley of Hope. Alison met her neigh-bours; each committed to expressing higher versions of themselves. The commu-nity of the Valley of Hope embraced her in a spirit of friendship, and she began to unwind and enjoy herself.

It was mid-afternoon when she sat outdoors watching Tabitha chasing but-terflies across the lawn. Her thoughts turned to her latest canvas; the reunion of Persephone and her mother, Demeter. She thought about her own mother and sighed.

Alison looked up to see the Professor striding across the lawn in a grey suit, a long-stemmed bunch of flowers in his hand. They often took long walks together, the Professor discussing aspects of ancient history and philosophy. It wasn't only these discussions that intrigued her, but also the unexpected charm of his poetry and his polka-dot bow tie.

"From my garden." The Professor handed her the pink and white flowers. "Gladioli—the ancient Greeks referred to them as Xiphium. The name itself stemmed from the Greek word *xiphios*, which means sword of strength and faith."

"Thank you. They're beautiful," said Alison. She took the flowers inside and returned with a jug of lemonade and glasses. "What are you reading?"

The Professor looked up from his book. "Hesiod."

"Was he Greek?"

"Yes, a poet who lived around 700BC. Hesiod wrote two epic poems, which are still remembered today. These are *Theogony*, which is about the family tree of the gods, and *Works and Days*, which outlines how to live a good life and gives practical farming advice.

"Hesiod's own life story is fascinating. It began when he was quite young. Each morning, his mother, Pykimede, rose early and, with the help of servants, packed his midday meal of bread, olives and salted cheese. He placed the basket on a staff over his shoulder and took his father's sheep out to graze.

"While on the mountainside, he passed the time reciting poetry and epic verses, as was the practice of those times. Then, one day, his mind's eye suddenly opened and he found himself among the sacred Muses, who recited the history of the gods.

"Returning from their magnificent escapades, Hesiod recorded what he could, but words were inadequate. And there was information he dared not divulge, for fear that it would upset the hearts and minds of men whose opinions carried more weight than his own."

Alison nodded. "How fascinating."

He turned the page. "Here is a poem about Hesiod, written by Alcaeus of Messene, no less." The Professor took a deep breath.

When in the shady Locrian grove, Hesiod lay dead.
The nymphs washed his body with water from their springs
and heaped high his grave.
And thereon the goat-herds sprinkled offerings of milk
mingled with yellow-honey.
Such was the utterance of the nine Muses that he breathed forth
that old man who had tasted of their pure springs.

"Hesiod had a sad ending," said Alison as she poured the drinks.

"Indeed." A wistful smile played across his face. "His story holds a special place in my heart." The Professor took a sip of lemonade. "The concept of immortality consumed Hesiod. He wanted to be like the gods." He smiled. "In a way, Hesiod achieved immortality through his poems."

The Professor took a breath. "But getting back to the story. While in Delphi, Hesiod sought the advice of Pythia, the priestess of Apollo. She predicted he would meet his end in Nemea. And so, Hesiod, determined to prevent his fate, made his way south.

"Hesiod travelled with his friend Miletus, a servant, and his dog. Once they reached Locris, as was the tradition of Xenia, they sought the hospitality of a wealthy merchant. It was during their stay that Miletus became enamoured of their host's daughter. And being a loyal friend, Hesiod turned a blind eye to his indiscretions."

"Oh, that may not have been wise," said Alison.

"Indeed. Their host became enraged when he discovered the tryst. As generous as their host was, it was clear his daughter was not on the menu. After that, Miletus mysteriously disappeared, and their eyes turned to Hesiod. As a silent accomplice, he was considered as guilty by association. Henceforth, his host's sons carried out their father's punishment, taking Hesiod's life and that of his servant at the temple of Zeus in Nemea. Then they placed them on their boats and dropped them far out to sea."

Alison exhaled. "Oh, that is sad. And so, his life ended in Nemea after all?"

The Professor nodded thoughtfully. "No matter how carefully one plans for the future, one cannot avoid one's fate. However, his story didn't end there. It was afterwards that a strange event took place. A dolphin nudged the body towards the beach. Lying in the shallows, the waves gently rocked it back and forth."

Alison's eyes filled with tears. "How unfair."

"Alas, some may agree, while others may see it as a sacrifice to the god Poseidon. I take the latter view, for the former is a rejection of the intelligent universe in which we live." The Professor sighed. "And so, his story continued. As dawn graced the hills with its rosy light, a fisherman arrived on the beach. His eyes soon fell upon the gruesome sight. His cries rang out, and a horde of rowdy fishermen soon joined him. Amidst the chaos, his loyal dog bounded onto the beach. As soon as the dog caught sight of its owner, it barked frantically.

"The men followed the dog to the merchant's home and immediately stormed the house, confronting the merchant and his sons, who were trembling inside. After hearing their story and finding evidence of foul play, they wasted no time in banishing them to Poseidon's murky depths. Then the townsfolk loaded Hesiod's body onto the back of a mule and conveyed him to Oenone."

The Professor sighed. "One does not appreciate life until witnessing the preparations for one's funeral. His newfound friends poured a libation to the gods before burying the body. Not only did they grant the great bard a sacred burial, they also cared for his dog, and when he died, they buried him next to Hesiod."

Alison wiped a tear from her eye. "You bring the past to life as though it were only yesterday."

"And so will you, for it is our destiny to know your own magnificent story."

She turned to the Professor. "We learned the ancients were barbarians who struggled for survival."

"Oh, yes. One of many misconceptions." The Professor gazed at the clouds drifting across the sky. He turned to her. "When we turn to the past, we find philosophers whose vision shaped the very foundations of Western thought.

Consider the philosopher Plotinus, who painted a picture of a transcendent realm beyond the material, where God exists as the highest principle of reality. His vision encompassed goodness, virtue, happiness and beauty beyond human comprehension. Do you know what I mean?"

A gentle breeze blew through the garden. Alison closed her eyes, and in an instant, she felt herself transported to another time. She saw herself as a priestess draped in flowing robes, seeking communion with the divine. After a while, she opened her eyes. "I sense that life was deep and meaningful, even magical."

The Professor's eyes gleamed. "And it is this magic that we crave. For in devouring the earthly delights, humanity consumed the fragrant loaf that was ours to share, leaving mere crumbs on the breadboard of life. But all is not lost. According to Plotinus, through self-realisation, contemplation and purification, one can break free from the material world and ascend once more to a mystical state of unity and oneness with God."

Alison hesitated. "Do you really think that's possible?"

"I don't think. I know," said the Professor, his voice like rolling thunder. "As Hesiod said, we *descended from the mighty gods, and to the gods, we will return.*"

Alison's breath caught in her throat as her spirit soared. Was this the magic she longed for, and feared?

16

Demeter

THE DAY'S SHADOWS LENGTHENED. Alison returned to the studio, where the flickering glow of candles warmed the room. Tabitha lay curled up in a chair while Alison gazed at the blank canvas before her; an image danced in her mind, of the meeting between Demeter and Persephone. She dipped the brush into the paint and with each brush stroke she captured the tender reunion between mother and daughter.

"Diving into the Underworld I, see?" The candles flickered, and Persephone appeared in a traditional Greek gown. She gazed at the canvases propped up against the studio walls, studying each. "You capture the story, from the darkness of the Underworld to the bright light of reunion."

Alison smiled. "Thank you. I feel something is awakening within."

Persephone smiled. "It's a never-ending game of lost and found—waking up and then going to sleep again."

Alison tilted her head. "Is there really no end to this game?"

"Just as spring follows winter, so the end is also the beginning."

Alison frowned.

Persephone glanced at the chair and Tabitha jumped down and curled up on a cushion on the floor. "Take a seat, for my story is not yet over." She sat down, her eyes reflecting the light from the candles. "Now, where were we?"

"Your reunion with Demeter," prompted Alison.

Persephone nodded. "Oh, yes... my mother's hair was messy and her clothes were old. And yet her eyes glowed as radiant as ever.

"'My, how you've grown; you're no longer a child,' she said, releasing me from her embrace. We strolled arm in arm through the gateway and into the courtyard. There, we settled onto a stone bench and reminisced about old times, laughing and joking like old friends—and, suddenly, like the wind, her demeanour changed. 'Did you eat anything in that wretched place?'

"'Nothing, Mother... Only the pure nectar of the gods.'

"Demeter's eyes bored into mine. 'Are you sure?' I thought back to the last day when I swallowed a few pomegranate seeds.

My secret was out.

"Demeter was furious. 'I knew it! Hades is cunning, like his brother, Zeus! He forced you to return to the Underworld. How do you feel about that?'

"'If it is in my destiny,' I replied.

"Her eyes widened. "I find it hard to believe that you're willing to go back to that awful place."

"'Lord Hades is not so bad, Mother.'

"Demeter's cheeks grew red. 'You are no longer the dutiful Kore I once knew. What has my wicked brother done to you? Poor child, abducted and forced to work with the dead. Just wait till I see him again, I'll...'

"I held up my hand. 'Mother, please. If he'd asked for your permission, you'd have refused, and I'd have missed my calling as Queen of the Underworld.'

"Demeter rose to her full height. 'Well, if that's how you speak to your mother – and after all I did for you!' With that, she stormed into the temple, her hair and robes fluttering.

"I sat for a while, wondering what to do next, when a voice trilled in the morning air.

"'Anyone home?'

"A regal goddess appeared at the gateway; her auburn hair ornamented with jewels, and in her hand, she carried a large travelling bag.

"'Grandmother Rhea!' I jumped up and rushed into her warm embrace.

"'My dear child, look at you,' she said, smiling. 'You bear the name Persephone with honour.'

"'Thank you, Grandmother. How did you know I was here?'

"'Zeus informed me of your return.' She looked around. 'Where's my daughter, Demeter?'

"'Inside.' As I pointed to the temple, a plaintive wail sounded from within. 'I'm afraid we had a difference of opinion.'

"Rhea blinked. 'Oh dear, she was a highly strung child. I'll see if I can sort things out.' She hurried into the temple.

"Sometime later, Demeter and her mother returned. I noticed Demeter had styled her hair. She wore a new gown, the colour of young wheat. 'Isn't it lovely that we're all together again?' She smiled, but I detected an edge in her voice.

"Rhea reached into her bag and pulled out an earthen jug and three wine glasses. 'Mead,' she said, pouring the golden liquid into the glasses.

"We held our glasses high. 'May the goddess live forever in the hearts and souls of humanity,' toasted Rhea.

"The mead was robust, and gradually, my mother's mood improved. Seeing this, Rhea invited her to share her story, saying, 'A trouble shared is a trouble halved.'

"'Oh, Mother,' said Demeter. 'My anguish knows no bounds. I could not sleep nor eat while I searched the land and sea for my daughter. Amid my ordeal, the wicked god of the deep, Poseidon, pursued me. I avoided him by changing into a mare, but my disguise did not fool him. He changed himself into a stallion...'

"Rhea's eyes goggled. 'It was wicked of Poseidon... wicked.'

"Nine days and nights I walked. In the early hours of the morning on the tenth, I found myself at a crossroads. Exhausted, I fell under a tree. The baying of dogs awoke me, and Hecate, the goddess of the Moon, appeared, carrying a staff in one hand and a burning torch in the other. She helped me to my feet, and together we went to Lord Helios, the Sun god, who sees everything. I came straight to the point and asked Helios if he had seen my daughter. He told us he saw Lord Hades carry her into the Underworld. I was furious. I asked him why he had not informed the gods, and he replied it was the will of Zeus."

"Rhea nodded. 'Of course.'

"'Well, I would not stand for it. I was more determined than ever. Disguised as an old woman, I wandered the countryside until one day I reached Eleusis. A daughter of Celeus, the ruler of Eleusis, found me sitting by a well and took me to her home. Her mother, Metanira, suggested that I should be a nursemaid for their youngest, a son named Demophon. He was a lovely boy, and I fed him ambrosia, intending to make him into a god.

"All went well until his mother found me holding him over a fire to purify him. The silly woman screamed, and so I discarded my womanly disguise and appeared before her as a goddess. She screamed again, and the family came running. Seeing my true form, they fell at my feet, wanting to know how they could serve me. I requested a temple. After they built it, I sat alone in the temple, nursing my grief...

"'My poor daughter.' Rhea patted her hand.

"Demeter's eyes filled with tears. 'One by one, the gods arrived bearing gifts and imploring me to relent. Zeus even sent his messenger, Iris, to request that I take up my duties and bless the land with a bountiful harvest, but I refused to give in until Zeus agreed to release Persephone from the Underworld.'

"'Which he did.' Rhea smiled. 'And now your daughter has returned to you, all is well.'

"Demeter's eyes darkened. 'Not quite. That sly Hades fed her pomegranate seeds.'

"'Oh!' Rhea's eyes grew large. 'Then, there is only one thing to do – you must consult Zeus.'

"Demeter nodded. 'You're right, mother.'

"Rhea smiled. 'Of course.' Suddenly, she gasped. 'Oh, dear, I am becoming drifty. I forgot to pass on Zeus' message.'

"Demeter scowled. 'And what was that?'

"'He commands you to increase forthwith the fruit that gives men life.'

"'Oh, yes.' Demeter rose and glided into the temple. There she kindled the light at the altar of the great mother goddess and bestowed blessings on the elements. A rumble of thunder rattled in the distance.

"'Now the gods and mortals can look forward to better days,' said Rhea.

We stood and waved her goodbye.

"Early the next morning, Demeter and I set off to locate Zeus. We were halfway across the field when we heard a faint rumble that grew louder. Suddenly, the earth shook. My heart missed a beat as the ground opened up and Hades emerged in his chariot, drawn by two black steeds.

"Demeter threw up her hands in dismay.

'Hello my love and my dear mother-in-law.'

"Demeter scowled. 'Greetings, Hades.'

"'Where are you going?' he asked.

"'Thanks to you, we have a problem. We have to locate Zeus,' Demeter replied.

"'I heard he is in hiding. Let me take you there.' He reached out. I jumped aboard, and Demeter followed reluctantly.

"The horses flew swiftly over the forest and landed in a clearing. Before us stood a pink marble temple. As we climbed down, a willowy nymph emerged from within.

"Demeter craned her neck. 'Is Zeus about?'

"'I'll rouse him,' said the nymph as she disappeared into the temple.

"A voice bellowed from within. 'If it's my wife, tell her I'm not in!'

"'It's your sister!' yelled Demeter.

"A short time later, a bulky figure emerged, wearing a white robe casually tossed across one shoulder, his hair and beard in disarray. Zeus blinked in the sunshine.

"'Hades! Good to see you, dear brother,' he grinned. 'Greetings, esteemed sister Demeter, and your lovely daughter, Persephone.' He winked. 'To what do I owe the pleasure of your company?' Without waiting for an answer, Zeus gestured towards the temple. 'Don't stand on ceremony; you must come inside.'

"We followed him into the cool depths of the inner sanctum. There, we sat on marble benches covered with silk cushions as nymphs in diaphanous gowns arrived with crystal carafes of ambrosia. They filled our glasses and, as tradition has it, we toasted each of the gods and goddesses of Mount Olympus.

"Zeus beamed. 'I'm surprised you could find me. As you may be aware, I've had a little marital strife lately, so I'm flying under the radar.'

"Hades grinned. 'More offspring?'

"Zeus grimaced. 'Well, just a few. The mothers insist I am the father and, of course, Hera does not approve of these, err, rumours?' He cleared his throat. 'And how are you, Demeter?' Again, without waiting for a reply, he continued. 'I'm delighted you finally blessed the crops with abundance.'

"Seeing her scowling face, Zeus paused. 'Everything settled, then?'

"'My dear Zeus. While in the Underworld, and with your blessing, my daughter swallowed some pomegranate seeds, and therefore she is destined to return! Now I am in a quandary about what to do.'

"I thought I saw the hint of a smile, then Zeus nodded thoughtfully. He rubbed his beard, then his eyes met mine. 'What do you want, my child?'

"I sighed. At long last, someone was asking me. 'I am committed both to the glorious realm of Mother Nature and also to Hades' palace in the Underworld.'

"Zeus stroked his beard. 'An interesting dilemma. Perhaps you have a dual role to play, both as goddess of springtime and queen of the Underworld.'

"I nodded, 'Yes.'

"'Well then, dear child, why not spend half the year with Hades and the other half with Demeter?'

"Hades nodded. 'That sounds fair.'

"Demeter's eyes darkened. 'I do not approve!'

"Zeus's forehead creased. He tapped his fingers on the arm of the seat. 'Ah, well then, perhaps that should be one-third with Hades and two-thirds with Demeter.'

"Hades clenched his jaw.

"Demeter opened her mouth to speak, but Zeus held up his hand. My decision is final. Let us toast a goddess whose story will give hope to humans wherever they may be.'

"Our goblets clinked. The nectar rolled down our throats, then a clap of thunder sounded overhead, and the walls of the temple trembled.

"Hades leapt to his feet. 'We must make haste.'

"'We hurried outside just as a bolt of lightning lit the sky. Hades leapt onto the chariot and helped us aboard. We pulled our capes over our heads as the chariot flew uneasily across the stormy sky. The horses landed and shook the water from their flanks.'

"Demeter stepped down, then Hades drew me so close I could feel his heartbeat. 'I will wait for you, Persephone, my love.'

"I joined my mother, waving through my tears.

"'Hurry!' cried Demeter, and, arm in arm, we rushed into the shelter of the temple.

"After that, spring blossomed, and life soon settled into a gentle rhythm once again. Yet, remembering Zeus's words, Demeter and I devised a plan to offer hope to humanity in its darkest hours. And so were born the Eleusinian Mysteries. These sacred rites awaken humans to their inner journey from darkness into light.

"With her newfound enthusiasm, Demeter returned to her temple in the town of Eleusis, where she inspired a tradition. Each year, initiates went on a pilgrimage to Eleusis to celebrate the awakening of the spirit through a ceremony that wove life and death—the Underworld and the Heavens. This event became so popular among Greeks that it continued for thousands of years."

Persephone smiled. "Although the Eleusinian Mysteries ended, the memory of the story lived on."

Alison nodded. "It certainly is an epic story."

Persephone nodded. "In those far-off days, stories were heroic, for without such tales, humanity would have lost their way." She gazed at Alison, her eyes shining. "Just as I transformed from kore to queen of the Underworld, so too can you rise beyond the troubles of the world and walk through it with the grace and wisdom of a goddess." Then, with a glimmer of a smile, the goddess faded into the night.

Over the following weeks, Alison completed painting her series, including Persephone with her regal grandmother, Rhea, as well as emotionally charged scenes of Demeter during her awkward moments with Hades and Zeus.

One afternoon, as she put the finishing touches on a painting, Flower appeared.

Alison stepped back and viewed the canvas with its streams of initiates descending on Eleusis for the sacred ceremony. Their white robes shone, vibrant against the blue sky and green hills.

Flower gazed at the painting. "Wow, the colours are so bright. I feel like I'm there." She looked around at all the canvases. "Why don't you take them inside where you can see them?"

"Good idea," said Alison.

Together, they carried the canvases into the house and hung them on the back wall. Afterward, they sat and chatted as the daylight dimmed. The house lights came on, and the paintings glowed.

Flower and Alison strolled, pausing to study each canvas—from the descent into darkness, through the transformation into sovereignty and reunion with the goddess.

Flower smiled. "What an amazing story."

Alison's gaze lingered on the paintings. "Gods and mortals weave a never-ending tale."

17

Pandora

SPRING ARRIVED IN THE Valley of Hope, and with it came a burst of colourful flowers. Each morning, Alison awoke with a lightness in her heart, looking forward to the day ahead. Next door, the Biggley sisters bustled about, their lives a cheery jumble of cats and dogs.

It was sundown when Alison climbed the stairs to their veranda, with Tabitha following behind. Dot and Mavis sat in cane chairs, enjoying the last rays of gold descending behind the hills.

"Welcome," said Mavis as she opened the door for Tabitha, who dashed inside to play with her feline friends.

A Great Dane watched Alison closely, then gave a deep bark. Soon, the veranda filled with the wagging tails of dogs of various shapes and sizes.

Laughing, Alison settled into a chair and scooped a tiny dog into her lap. "They're all so happy." The terrier gazed up at her with adoring eyes.

Dot patted her knee, and a small dog jumped up and licked her face. "Unlike humans, they haven't lost their connection with their inner nature."

"What made you choose dogs and cats?" Alison asked.

Dot ran her hand over the dog's back. "Well, we sisters lived in separate towns and, strangely, we both developed incurable illnesses. Not long after I crossed over, Mavis followed. When we arrived in the Afterlife, our health was uppermost in our minds, and when we heard about the healing energies of the Valley of Hope, we applied to come here. They approved our admission, but only if we could bring in dogs and cats. I couldn't stand dog hair in the house, and Mavis was allergic to cats, but we agreed, didn't we, Mavis?"

Mavis nodded. "Changing long-held patterns was difficult at first. I sneezed and sneezed! However, eventually we came to see how out of touch we were. My sneezing stopped when I gave up judging every little thing and wanting everything to go my way."

"These fur babies worked their magic," said Dot, smiling. "Strange to think I used to be the mother from hell, obsessed with controlling everything and everyone around me."

"We learnt so much about giving rather than taking." Then Mavis eyed Alison. "Did you know Tabitha has been visiting us with a view to going back?"

"No!" Alison's eyes widened. "But why?"

"Probably because she didn't want to distress you," said Mavis. "Tabitha has accepted a life with a loving family, and she is preparing to leave."

Alison frowned. "But Tabitha is the only remaining remnant of my old life."

Dot gently touched her hand. "Our biggest challenge is to hold lightly to those we love and let go with grace and ease, for life flows like a river and nothing ever remains the same."

"Oh..." Alison sighed. "If it is her destiny, I must let go."

"We too are considering returning to the world of action," said Mavis.

"You're leaving?"

Mavis gazed at the tranquil surroundings. "Here, it's easy to be peaceful. It's only in the three-dimensional world that we really see how far we have come."

"That's right," said Dot. "The Valley of Hope is a place of healing. And now we want to spread our compassion into the world."

Alison nodded as she quietly wondered about her own future.

The sun descended behind the hills as Alison made her way home with Tabitha running ahead. The peaceful sound of a harp drifted through the air. She looked up at the observatory, the home of her neighbours, Peter and Paul. Peter had been a pianist, and Paul, a tenor. Their lives had ended tragically when their plane plunged into the sea. On arrival in the Afterlife, they were met with the most glorious sounds they had ever heard. Inspired by this, they came to the Valley of Hope to develop their musical skills.

She drifted through her garden and found Tabitha waiting at the door.

Later that evening, Alison heard a knock. She opened the door to find Flower clutching a large painting.

"I made this for you," Flower said, thrusting the canvas into Alison's hands.

"Wow, thank you," Alison replied, placing the canvas gently on a chair. She stepped back. The painting depicted a spirit emerging from the darkness and ascending a staircase that led to a vibrant new world.

"That's beautiful," Alison said, smiling.

"It's my farewell gift," said Flower. "I'm returning to the Earthly hologram."

Alison blinked. "You mean you're going back?"

Flower nodded. "I want to share my gifts with the world."

"I'm happy for you," said Alison, while deep inside, she felt a growing uncertainty. Her peaceful life seemed to be coming apart.

✳

The following morning, Alison awoke to find Tabitha gazing at her with her almond-shaped eyes. Tears welled in Alison's eyes, for she knew the time had come to say goodbye. Tabitha rubbed her face against Alison's cheek one last time and then jumped off the bed and darted from the room.

After Tabitha's departure, everything changed as, one by one, her neighbours departed.

The Professor was next. "Life is like a train," he said. "We are either stepping off or waiting on the platform to step aboard. And so, I prepare to board the train for another leg of my journey."

"What do you have in mind?" asked Alison.

"I'd like to continue my studies, but who knows what destiny has in store?" His eyes shone as he spoke. "And now, farewell, dwellers on Olympus, daughter of Zeus who holds the aegis—even those deathless ones who lay with mortal men and bore children like unto gods."

As she bid farewell, Alison had a strange feeling that their paths would cross again.

Not long after, Flower slipped away. Then Peter and Paul left, their faces radiant with celestial music. Finally, the Biggley sisters said farewell. Alison felt a bittersweet sense of loss.

That afternoon, she went for a walk. The once lively valley now seemed empty without her friends. She passed by beds of gladiolus standing straight and tall. *If only I had their strength and faith,* she thought as she walked towards the park.

Her feet made a hollow sound on the wooden bridge. She leaned on the railings and gazed at the stream below. She recalled Dot's words. *'Life flows like a river, and nothing ever remains the same.'*

If life is a river, where is it leading? She wondered.

Nowhere... came a bleak reply. *You're all alone, hopeless.*

Alison tensed as if standing on the edge of a precipice that spiralled downwards into despair. The hateful thoughts continued.

Jump—why don't you—jump!

She gripped the railing. *No... I can't let these dark thoughts get to me.*

Then, beneath the storm, a sound emerged. A gentle hum.

Aum...

She listened closely as the sound grew louder, permeating her being, dissolving the turmoil.

Aum...

The vibration filled her with a wave of comfort and belonging. Her consciousness expanded—that feeling of bliss she hoped would never end.

The thought crossed her mind that this could be God.

But I never believed... she thought.

And then, a voice replied within her: *Beliefs are a creation of the human mind. I deal only with reality.*

Her grip on the railing loosened, and she looked around. She wondered if she should speak and then thought, *Oh, why not.*

"Who are you?" she asked.

I am not of this world, yet I am as close to you as a friend.

Alison took a breath. "But how can that be?"

It is entirely possible when you realise that your mind is a powerful transmitter and receiver.

Alison blinked. "Really?"

Tune your thoughts to my frequency, and like a lotus flower, I will guide you from the murky waters of doubt into the radiance of your truth.

A wave of love spread through her. She heard the splash of a fish breaking the water and looked down. The surface settled, shining clear like a mirror. Her eyes shone with a brightness she had never seen before. *Is that really me?* She wondered.

You are a soul far greater than you can imagine, came the quiet reply. *Open your mind to unlimited possibilities.*

Alison closed her eyes and drifted into a hall of mirrors—images repeating through time and space: strange and beautiful symbols, monsters, dragons, humans and ancient gods and goddesses. She wondered what it was all about.

The voice replied: *This is the blueprint of a story that never ends. As enticing and wonderful as the story is, there comes a time when you say – enough is enough. The time is drawing near when you will come to know yourself, not as the body with all its needs and desires, nor the mind with all its razzmatazz, but as the gentle spirit, the conscious light within.*

The feeling of peace seemed to drift on forever...

Hearing footsteps on the bridge, Alison opened her eyes.

"Mind if I join you?"

"Oh, Padma, not at all." She exhaled. "I just had the strangest experience. I think God spoke to me. Am I mad?"

Padma smiled. "No, you're not mad. God speaks to us all the time, but do we listen?"

Alison exhaled. "Oh, that's a relief."

They walked over the bridge and into the park, where spring flowers bloomed and new leaves shone green on the trees. They sat on a bench in the shade of a tree.

Padma turned to her. "You've been in the valley for some time now. Are you ready to share what you learned about your past life?"

Alison nodded. "Yes, I've come to see how perfect the school of life really is," she said softly. "I discovered I gave away my power so I could understand my strength. Strange, isn't it?"

"It's not unusual," said Padma. "We choose experiences that rebalance our energies, like a seesaw. It's only through experiencing both the shadow and the light that we truly come to know who we really are. Speaking of which; your paintings of the journey from darkness to light were an inspiration to us all."

"Thank you for inspiring me to express myself," said Alison. "Painting helped me rise above my story and see it as a part of the whole."

Padma smiled. "This is the magic of healing. So, what would you like to do now?"

Alison sighed. "I'm not really sure. I'd like to remain here in the Afterlife, but I still want to help others."

Padma pondered for a moment. "Would you consider working with the goddess Persephone in the Underworld?"

A pang of self-doubt gripped Alison's stomach. "What? Work with the goddess? But I'm just a mortal!" Instantly, her energy streamed into the atmosphere, twisting and warping the very fabric of existence. In an instant, the once glorious trees and flowers appeared two-dimensional, like a page from a book.

Alison gasped. "Oh, did I do that?" She held her hand over her mouth.

"You did!" answered a voice.

They turned to see a woman standing on the bridge; her silvery hair adorned with jewels, and her gown fastened at the shoulder with a diamond brooch.

Padma stood up. "Pandora! How lovely to see you!"

Pandora smiled. "And you too, my dear, Padma." She looked around at the two-dimensional scene, the abstract trees and the flowers. Then she turned to Alison. "Making some modifications to the blueprint, I, see?"

Alison stared wide-eyed, unsure of what to say.

Pandora doubled over with mirth. Wiping the tears of laughter from her eyes, she stood upright. With a straight face, she looked Alison in the eye. "What thoughts led to this?"

Alison's face crumpled. "... I'm just a mortal."

"My dear child, you must realise the creative power of your mind. The idea of just a woman, man or child arises from the pithos of limiting beliefs and therefore is not in line with the way things are."

Alison frowned. "Pithos?" she said.

"It's a Greek word for jar," whispered Padma. "Symbolic of the human mind."

Pandora descended from the bridge and sat down. "What is it you desire?" she asked.

"I used to think it was happiness," Alison replied softly. "But now my deepest longing is to know myself and why I'm here."

"Very good." Pandora nodded. "To know yourself means to hear your story that echoes from the very beginning of time." She gazed at Alison. "It began long ago, when Zeus ordered the god Hephaestus to create a maiden out of clay. And so, he shaped every curve and feature with his hands. Once he finished, the gods endowed her with their special gifts. Aphrodite gave her beauty and charm. Athena granted her wisdom and courage and dressed her in a beautiful gown adorned with sparkling jewels. They named her Pandora, the first woman."

Alison's eyes narrowed. *Sounds like a fairy tale,* she thought.

Pandora took a breath and continued. "I was but a fresh-faced beauty with golden hair and rosy lips, and yet they married me off to that tedious old Epimetheus, the dreamer who regretted the passing of the Golden Age. He delighted in telling tales of how human beings once lived like gods, free from sorrow, toil and grief. But I had no interest in the past. Life was an open book. I had my future ahead of me." She sighed. "After our marriage, he ignored me. Imagine that? The most beautiful creature in the world."

Alison shook her head. "But why?"

"Why indeed? Perhaps I did not live up to his dream. He said I was but a replica, an imitation of the goddess. What do you think, Padma?"

Padma shook her head. "I think it was most unfair."

Pandora frowned. "Do you know, Zeus had asked Hermes to give me a shameless mind and deceitful nature? Legend has it I became a manipulative, complaining shrew. But that's not all. Zeus gave me a wedding gift of a pithos. He told me not to open it."

Alison's eyes widened. "And you did...?"

Pandora chuckled. "Oh, yes. I opened the lid to spite him. To my surprise, a swarm of spirits flew out, swirling like flies—envy, remorse, desire, ignorance and fickleness. There was never a dull moment after that."

Alison couldn't hold back anymore. "It sounds like a fairy tale to me!"

Pandora raised her eyebrows. "And your life wasn't?"

Alison's smile faltered.

"One spirit stayed behind in the jar. She was Elpis, the spirit of hope."

"Oh, yes." Alison nodded. "I was ever hopeful."

"Of course you were. But is hope enough?" Pandora's eyes flickered. The afternoon light surrounded her face in a golden haze.

"Now, free yourself from the limitations of this story and know yourself as you truly are. You are bold, fierce and brave, and you are also silent, sweet and loving. You are human, but you are also divine—both a lion and a deer." Pandora smiled, her eyes shining. And with that, she glided across the bridge and disappeared into the pantheon of stories.

For a long moment, Alison stood in silence. She looked at the park, flat and unreal, like a page from a book; a stage set built from her own belief that she was *just a mortal*.

From deep within she heard the quiet voice, *you are a soul, far greater than you can imagine.*

An intuitive knowing arose; a feeling of lightness.

She heard the voice again, *open your mind to unlimited possibilities.*

Something gave way inside her. An old image of herself; small and two dimensional. A warmth spread through her chest. She no longer felt like a character inside a story, but a storyteller awakening from a dream.

She opened her eyes.

The air shimmered. The park had come alive, pulsing with depth and light. All around, the trees and flowers had expanded into their three-dimensional forms.

"Wow," she whispered. "Did I do that?"

"You did," said Padma, gazing at the park with wonder. "Now tell me, what of your future; would you work with the goddess?"

Alison smiled, her voice steady. "When do I start?"

THE ROAD OF
TRIALS

18

The Tribunal

It felt like only yesterday that Alison had arrived in the realm where the boundary between life and death blurred. Months had passed, and she had found a quiet contentment, working as a guide on the banks of the river Styx.

As Alison stood waiting for the ferry, her thoughts turned to the Valley of Hope. She recalled how Persephone had arrived in a fawn-coloured travelling tunic and sandals. Alison had bid farewell to Padma. She boarded the chariot and, through a vale of tears; she watched as the dome of her house grew smaller until it disappeared from view.

Persephone had flown to a cave, a secret portal, high into the mountains. Hearing jangling in the shadows, Alison's heart had skipped a beat. As her eyes adjusted to the cavern's greenish glow, she saw a chariot with horses champing at their bits.

They climbed aboard, and the horses sprang. She remembered clinging to the rails as the chariot plunged downwards. That was just the beginning of her adventure. Her eyes widened upon seeing the grandeur of the Palace of Hades. It took a while for her to become familiar with its imposing pillars and massive stairs.

Persephone had introduced her to Aidan, her supervisor. His frizzy mop of hair looked familiar. She recognised him as the guide who had helped the children when she had first arrived in the Afterlife.

There was more that she had to become accustomed to. Hearing the howls of Cerberus, she had trembled. Aidan had reassured her that the three-headed dog was only there to prevent the dead from leaving. Then seeing the souls for the first time, disembarking from the boat, her heart had felt heavy. Aidan had reminded her that death was just a myth invented to scare young children.

He explained that those who tried to hide their guilt would face their inner demons in Tartarus. At the same time, those who led an ordinary life with few achievements had to look forward to an uneventful time in the Meadows of

Asphodel, and those who tried to achieve greatness would find refreshment in the Elysian Fields.

In time she came to see, just as Hades had said, that the passage from life to death was an effortless transition.

Through the mist, the ferry came into view. Alison gazed at the familiar sight of Charon, the ferryman, standing at the helm. But today was different as high above, a royal flag fluttered from the mast. The ferry was secured and a twenty-one-gun salute sounded as the boat rocked gently against the dock. The woody scent of incense hung in the air and a distance, the melodic voices of a choir. The walkway went down, and the queen glided ashore in a coronation dress, complete with a glittering crown. Kings and queens from times gone by, wearing their regal regalia, stepped forward to pay their respects. It looked like something out of a fairy tale.

The ceremonials ended, and the queen stepped aboard a royal chariot drawn by winged horses. Everyone departed, and all was quiet.

Not long after, another ferry arrived.

Alison joined the guides waiting at the dock. Amidst a flurry of activity, the ghostly passengers made their way down the walkway.

Aidan called on Alison to help him check for stragglers. Once aboard, they saw a body lying lifeless on the deck.

"Could you see to him while I look inside?" said Aidan.

"Sure," Alison nodded. She drew closer.

He stirred and looked up, his face pallid and his eyes icy blue. Alison stepped back, almost falling over a rope, then she hurried towards the cabin.

Aidan emerged. "All clear inside. How's the invalid?"

She swallowed. "He needs help."

Aidan hurried over and knelt beside the man. "So, what brings you here? Murder, robbery, ex-girlfriend?" His tone was jovial.

The man cleared his throat. His lips moved, and a chill like ink on blotting paper crept along Alison's arms.

"Please hear me out," he said, as though he carried a burden.

Aidan nodded. "Go ahead."

"I spent the morning at the casino until I ran out of money, so I got some from my wife. That night I arrived home, and it was then that a power came over me. It was stronger than an impulse." He flinched. "It was like a black cloud—a demon of rage. It was not of my doing. Afterwards, the demons abandoned me to my fate."

"We'll look after you," said Aidan as he lifted the ghostly form. He carried him down the gangplank and placed him gently on the riverbank. He turned to Alison. "Could you keep an eye on him for a moment? I have to attend to someone else."

Her eyes widened. "But..."

"I'll only be a minute."

Alison sighed. "Oh, okay."

The stranger propped himself up on one elbow. He winced, then looked at her through half-closed eyes. "Happy to see me?" he rasped.

Alison's heart thudded. "Is that you, Bradley?"

He nodded weakly. "Yeah, it's me." A faint smile crossed his face. "Hey, you look like an angel."

She felt her throat tighten. "That's because I am."

"What?" Bradley's head swivelled. "Where the hell am I?"

"You're in the Afterlife."

He sank back with a sigh. "Oh, that'd be right. A wasted life..." He lay still for a moment, then his eyes opened. "The guys back at the prison said they'd take care of me. I didn't think it would be so soon. All over a stupid pack of cigarettes." He let out a bitter laugh. "The officers didn't give a damn. One less inmate to deal with."

Alison exhaled. "I don't know what to say."

He looked up with pleading eyes. "Please forgive me, Alison... I was a victim, too," he whispered.

Aidan approached. "Hi, I'm back. How is–?" He stared at her ashen face. "Hey, what's up?"

"He's all yours." She turned to Bradley and glared. "May God forgive you," she said as she walked away.

It was later that evening when Alison heard a knock. "It's me. Aidan."

She opened the door.

"Are you coming to dinner?"

Alison shook her head. "I'm not hungry."

"I'm sorry; I didn't realise."

"It's okay," she said.

"Do you want to talk about it?"

She nodded. "Come in." She sighed. "Oh, Aidan. I thought I was above all these feelings..."

Aidan smiled. "Don't be too hard on yourself. We all have our baggage."

She sighed. "I know, but some are worse than others."

"To be honest, Alison. I was in a bad way when I arrived."

"What?" Alison frowned. "But you're so kind."

Aidan shook his head. "Only after I broke my ties with the forces that controlled me."

"What do you mean?" Alison asked.

He tapped his fingers on the arm of the chair. "Do you really want to know?"

"Please," she nodded. "It would help."

"Well, it was like this," Aidan took a breath. "In my last life, I was CEO of a giant communications organisation and I disregarded the needs and feelings of those under me."

"Really?" said Alison.

Aidan nodded. "I was obsessed with power, and so I created a ruthless plan to downsize while continuing to haul in an exorbitant profit. Machines replaced many of the staff. It meant nothing to me that after years of faithful service, many were unemployed and some even ended up living on the street. I was on a roll, growing wealthy on the backs of others. Then one day I suffered a massive heart attack."

She shook her head.

"I was stunned," said Aidan. "I didn't build death into my five-year plan. In the afterlife, I came face-to-face with the Tribunal. The lords Rhadamanthus, Minos and Aeacus read my record and, without even blinking, declared that I was without a conscience. Then they banished me to Tartarus."

She gasped, "Oh, no."

"Oh, yes. Hearing their verdict, I ran as fast as I could back to the boat that had carried me here. I was a few steps from the gangplank when Cerberus stepped into my path, drooling, his heads growling and baring their teeth. Scared out of my wits, I fainted.

"I awoke alone in a cave, cold and hungry. After what felt like an eternity, a radiant image appeared. He was not an angel, but a being unknown to me. I inhaled the aroma of coffee and toast. My mouth moistened. I longed for what I could no longer enjoy. The beast's lips curled back in a grin.

"He said he was the Prince of Darkness and that he could give me more money, power, and pleasure than I could ever have imagined. I asked him what other options there were, and he replied. 'Well, either you serve me or starve to death.' He smiled a false smile of the devil, then he left me to think about it.

"I felt sorry for myself. I had led a full life, always busy, but now I was alone and starving. But I had time to reflect—all the time in the world. And so, I began working backwards. In the agonising weeks that followed, I relived every scene of my life, from CEO down to small-time solicitor. All that effort to achieve greatness—for what?

"Time passed, and gradually the shadow of self-interest lifted from my mind. I concluded that being without a conscience had aided my passage to the top. And then the awful realisation dawned on me—I knew this beast, not as some mythical prince, but as the person I had become!

"It was an ugly discovery. For the first time, I felt ashamed. Complaints from those I had wronged bombarded my newly awakened conscience. My mind raced. I wanted to die, but I was already dead."

"I remember yelling, 'Please, God, help me. I'll do anything. Just get me out of here!'

"It was then that a goddess appeared. Her fingernails were painted black, as were her lips. Even so, I sensed her fairness. She introduced herself as Styx, the goddess of Justice. I immediately informed her I had been falsely accused.

"Her eyes shone like torches. 'You're lying, and obviously in the right place.'

"As she turned to go, I felt a wave of remorse and struggled to my feet. 'Stop! It wasn't me who said that. Please! Please help me.'

"'What are you prepared to give up?' she asked.

"'I'll give up my selfish desires, just get me out of here,' I replied.

"'Well, it may be a bit of a comedown, but my husband, Pallas, needs a farmhand. We keep a herd of cows at our palace at the mouth of the River Styx.'

"Cows...? I was far from enthusiastic, but it was a way out, and so I agreed. Each morning, I rose before dawn to listen to the goddess Styx as she recited the stories of Justice. She told me her story, how whenever someone accused the gods of lying, Zeus would send Iris, the messenger goddess, to the river to collect a cup of water. The gods then summoned the goddess Styx, the oath maker, to be present while the god drank the water. If they were lying, they collapsed, and when they awoke, they found themselves temporarily banished from Olympus.

"During the day, I worked for Pallas, shovelling manure. While I worked, I had time to contemplate my crappy past. Pallas inspired me to make amends. After that, I worked even harder, so much so that one day, the goddess Styx announced

I was now free. She asked me what I wanted to do, and I replied I wanted to serve humanity, so she introduced me to Persephone... and here I am."

"Oh, Aidan!" Alison sighed. "You've given me a lot to think about."

That night, Alison went for a walk in the garden. A full moon hung low. She followed the misty pathways flanked by daylilies and hedges trimmed in the shapes of peacocks and elephants and sat beside a fountain. A silvery cat appeared, gazing at her with almond-shaped eyes.

"Can I help?" he asked.

"I don't know," she replied

"What don't you know?" asked the cat.

"What should I do?"

"It depends, really."

"On what?" she said.

"On whether you choose to please yourself or others. Cats don't have that problem." He ambled off into the mist, tail in the air.

Alison closed her eyes, her mind in a whirl.

She heard footsteps approaching and looked up.

"Here you are," said Persephone breathlessly. "Aiden told me about your unfortunate incident. Meeting the old troops is never easy." Her gaze softened. "Are you okay?"

Tears welled in Alison's eyes, and she shook her head.

"Come on, let's walk."

They started along the path; the gravel crunching beneath their feet.

"To be honest," said Alison, "I was frightened even though I knew Bradley couldn't hurt me. And then came the anger." She sighed. "I'm disappointed in myself for not being able to forgive him and move on, but I just can't do it."

Persephone placed her hand on Alison's shoulder. "You invested everything in that dream. He was your knight in shining armour; your reason for living. What he did was the ultimate betrayal. But are you going to let that define you?"

Alison shook her head. "I don't want to, but somehow, I feel trapped."

"You do not have to be trapped unless you choose it."

"What do you mean?"

Persephone stood quietly, then she spoke. "You see, individuals decide on pre-arranged contracts, and that sets them on a path. But these contracts do not bind you. When the learning is complete, then the contract dissolves."

Alison gazed at the goddess. In that moment, she sensed how her thoughts and feelings continued to bind her to the past. She took a deep breath. "I must end this contract once and for all—but how?"

"Perhaps you could be present at the Tribunal?" Persephone offered.

A knot of fear tugged at Alison's heart. "It's one thing to face Bradley, but the judges may question me as well."

Persephone's eyes narrowed. "Just like the great immortals, you, too, were born to endure that which you desire but also that which is not to your liking."

"Oh, so you mean own my story?"

Persephone nodded. "Exactly."

It was midnight, and the Underworld was shrouded in darkness. Alison stood alone in the shadows, her heart racing. High above, on a rocky ledge, a pale light illuminated the three kings, Minos, Aeacus and Rhadamanthus, their cloaks stirring in an unseen breeze.

Bradley stood in a shaft of moonlight below, surrounded by a cluster of ghostly apparitions.

The kings opened the tribunal with a hymn to Styx, and then the questioning began.

Bradley spoke at length, recounting his worldly achievements from the day he was born until the day he died. His story included a flawless tale of himself as a father and husband.

Alison shook her head. *He's delusional.*

Without warning, a beam of light shone directly on her face. *Oh no,* she gasped. Bradley swung around, his eyes wide.

"Alison Maybridge," said King Minos. "What is your version of the story?"

Her voice caught, then suddenly she blurted. "Bradley is lying." The words came haltingly at first, then spilled out in a torrent of anguish. "Our marriage was a sham," she cried. "He destroyed me! Not just physically but emotionally, too!"

"And what do you say to that, Bradley?" asked the king.

Bradley waved his hands in the air. "No, no, she's got it wrong!" He argued his case.

Alison had heard it all before; his selfishness, his faulty reasoning. An old ache flared, and her throat tightened as she recalled the memory of those helpless years.

Her shoulders slumped as tears rolled down her cheeks. Overwhelmed by the memories, she fought the urge to run, to escape the pain, but the kings' gaze held her; not in judgment, but as witnesses to her truth.

Bradley faltered. For a moment he seemed to feel her pain. His legs weakened, and he bowed his head. "Forgive me," he whispered.

Alison's eyes widened. "Forgive you?" she said hoarsely. "How could anyone forgive you after what you did? What about your daughters? Did you ever think of anyone but yourself?"

Bradley looked up, his eyes pleading. "I never meant..."

"You didn't even try," she interrupted.

"I tried... truly I did." He bowed his head. "But I had no control."

A hush descended, each lost in their own thoughts.

When Alison finally spoke again, her tone was quieter. "I can't change you, Bradley. I can't change the past either."

The kings exchanged solemn glances.

"Bradley Maybridge," said Minos. "You tore apart the family unit. What is your plea—guilty or not guilty?"

Bradley hesitated. Ghostly figures fluttered closer. He listened to their murmuring and then he looked up. "Not guilty," he said. "Please... have mercy!"

"Mercy must be earned," said King Aeacus.

Bradley shook his head. "I will change, I promise."

King Aeacus conferred with the others, then he turned back to Bradley. "It is time to bring this session to a close. You must decide where you will go. Are you ready to reflect on your actions?"

A ghostly figure whispered in his ear. Bradley shook his head. "No, I'm moving on."

"What?" Alison gasped in disbelief, and the familiar feeling of futility returned like a headache from the past. She recalled the words of Orion. *'Gather all of those memories into the present and hold them in the light of One.'* Her awareness lifted until she felt herself floating in the clear currents beyond the mind. The feelings were there, but they no longer owned her.

Her energy had shifted. She began to think; to breathe again. *I may not be able to change the past, the betrayal and lies, but I can change my attitude; after all, I did the best with what I had at the time.*

Then, something within her softened—an understanding that ran deeper than forgiveness. She saw her daughters, their young faces luminous with resilience.

She thought of her parents, of the generations bound in silence and survival. This was the knowing that carried her forward in her journey towards peace.

She looked up. "I have more to say."

All eyes turned to her.

"Go ahead," said Aeacus.

Alison's heart pounded, but her voice remained steady. "For years I tried to please everyone, smoothing over conflicts and shrinking myself. But today is different. Today, I choose self-respect. I will no longer carry this burden." She turned to Bradley. "You are no longer part of my story, and so I set you free."

The strength of her words dissolved the invisible cords that had bound her to the story.

Alison felt a weight lift off her shoulders. She felt lighter, not because the pain had vanished, but because it no longer defined her. And in that moment, she realised she no longer needed anything from Bradley—he was free to face his demons on his own.

19

Athena

Word of the Tribunal spread swiftly through the realm. The guides gathered around Alison, offering their love and support. Slowly the echoes of that lifetime faded; transformed into something she could hold without fear.

Buoyed by their presence, she regained her composure and returned to her role as a guide; quieter now, but somehow feeling more whole.

Time flowed like the River Styx, drawing Alison deeper into the mystery of the Underworld. Then, one day, everything changed. Was it fate? To Alison, it felt like the universe had shifted—as if the stars themselves had conspired against her.

It all began in the faded light of the early morning. A ferry pulled in and a group of souls disembarked, wide-eyed with questions. Relief washed over them as, one by one, the guides listened to their concerns, offered reassurance and helped them on their way.

"It's so busy here," remarked one lady, "and you've been so helpful. Do you ever tire?"

Alison smiled. "Helping souls cross over is a labour of love."

Out of the corner of her eye, she saw Aidan waving. She excused herself and hurried over.

"Urgent message," he said, handing her a scroll.

"What?" she said, breaking the seal. She unrolled the parchment and frowned. "Oh, it's from the monks. Ian is missing!" She took a breath. "They fear he was abducted."

Aidan frowned. "You must find him before it's too late!"

Alison's eyes widened. "Who, me?"

"Of course," he said, waving to the driver.

Before she knew it, Alison was back in her room. She quickly changed into her civvies.

Persephone met her on the palace steps in her pink dressing gown and slippers. She clicked her tongue. "Be careful; there are evil forces out there."

Alison's face paled.

A chariot arrived bearing the emblem of the Underworld. The driver reached out and helped her aboard. He gave a signal and, with wings outstretched, the horses bounded.

"Find Ian and bring him here!" Persephone called in a shrill voice.

The chariot sped through the air, and the horses disappeared into the clouds. "Hold tight, we're about to hit turbulence," said the driver.

Alison's breath came in sharp gasps as she clung to the side of the chariot. "What on earth am I doing?" she muttered as the chariot rocked and rolled.

"Nearly there!" he shouted, the roar of the wind almost drowning out his voice.

They burst into the bright light of the realm above, and it wasn't long before they circled high above the City of Dreams.

"Where to?" asked the driver.

"I don't really know," replied Alison.

"Is there someone who might have tried to influence him?"

It was then that Alison recalled the computer stall and the banner of Ares. "Well, there was the Re-entry Pavilion..."

"That place is full of charlatans," said the driver, as he turned the horses.

They landed in the car park, and Alison stepped out.

The driver tipped his cap. "Call me when you find him," he said, and then he flicked the reins.

"Call you?" Alison watched the chariot rise. "Oh, why is this happening to me?" she muttered as she made her way into the pavilion.

Alison entered the lift and made a beeline to the computer stand that read, 'Time flies when you have a broadband internet connection'. She approached the man behind the counter. "I'm looking for Ian. Do you remember him?"

"Oh, yes. I never forget a face," the man replied. "But he hasn't been back."

Alison pushed her way through the crowd, searching for the Ares banner, but the stand was nowhere to be seen. A woman at a nearby stall told her they were using underhanded methods to recruit, and so they were asked to leave.

Alison sighed. "What am I going to do?"

"You can try the administration section," offered the woman.

Alison hurried down the corridor. An official in a green uniform listened while she explained how the agent on the Fame and Fortune stall was interested in Ian and that now, he's missing.

The officer nodded. "We know the crowd. Recruiters who work for Ares, the god of war."

"Can you find him?"

The officer's brow furrowed. "According to our rules, we can't interfere in the fate of human beings."

Alison's eyes narrowed as a supernatural power came over her. "What! Ian is in danger, and you're worried about rules?" Suddenly she seemed taller and stronger, like an immortal.

The officer's eyes widened.

Bystanders murmured, shaking their heads disapprovingly. One man leaned on the counter. He narrowed his eyes. "You'd better help the lady," he said.

The officer gulped and then quickly typed his password into the computer. "I need his full name, birthdate and city of birth."

Alison blinked in astonishment. She gave him the details, and he pressed the button.

"Hmm, just as I thought. The movement of the planets indicates power struggles, strong desires and potentially destructive behaviour."

"Do you think they may have kidnapped Ian?"

"I don't know. All I can say is, it's potentially dangerous for his soul."

"We need to find him," she said.

The officer's brow furrowed. "According to our rules..."

Alison glared at the officer, her expression firm. "I'm not leaving until you do something."

The murmurs of bystanders grew. "You heard her. Do something," said the man behind her.

The officer's face twitched. He hesitated for a moment before picking up the phone. "I-I'll call head office," he said, punching in the numbers. "We have a situation here that requires immediate attention. Ah, yes, realm sixty-six." He looked up. "They're sending a car."

Alison exhaled.

The officer reached for his hat. "We must move fast."

They hurried down the corridor to the lift. 'Going down,' said the voice.

They rushed through the front door, where a car was waiting. Alison slid into the back seat, and the officer sat in the front, next to the man in blue. The vehicle took off along the Highway of Dreams, siren blaring.

The officer glanced in the rearview mirror. "I must warn you, if he's already programmed, get the hell out of there because you'll be next."

Alison felt a surge of fear. "How do I know if he's programmed?"

"Easy. Look into his eyes. They'll be vacant."

The car veered off the highway. "We're entering realm sixty-six," said the officer as the car glided down a road lined with dilapidated buildings.

The car pulled up opposite an alleyway. Reaching into the console, the officer in blue took out two bars of chocolate and handed one to the officer in green.

"Mm, rum and raisin, my favourite," he said. He turned to Alison, his mouth full. "Over there—red door, number twenty-six, four loud knocks. Err... call us if you need help."

Alison's eyes widened. "What! You're not coming?"

The officer in blue shook his head. "There's nothing we can do. It's classified as a domestic."

I don't believe this; she thought as she opened the car door. She hurried down the alleyway. Faces stared through curtained windows as she passed. Her legs felt weak as she stood in front of the red door. She knocked four times.

A man appeared. "Hello ma'am, what can I do for you?"

She took a deep breath. "I'm looking for my friend, Ian."

He stared at her in disbelief, then turned to someone behind him. "It's a chick."

"What does she want?" A flabby man with jowls and hooded eyes came to the door. He looked her up and down, his eyes glimmering. His voice deepened. "Come on in."

Alison shuddered. "Oh no, I-I can't stay. I just want to know if my friend Ian is here."

"Who?"

"Ian. I was told he's here."

The man scratched his head. "Who told you that? Hey, boys, listen to this." A pair of thugs burst through the door and into the alleyway. The man with the hooded eyes stood behind them.

Alison flattened herself against the alley wall. "Help, officer!" she called.

"Help, officer, help!" repeated one of the men.

"They won't help you," said another. He drew a knife from his pocket. Hooded eyes glared at her, and she felt his hot breath on her face.

Alison screamed, and a man slapped his hand over her mouth.

"Ha!" He laughed. "Another recruit," he said, dragging her into the house.

"Lock her in the front room," barked the man who gave the orders. He shoved her into a room and shut the door with a thud.

Her heart beat frantically as she looked around at the bare walls and shabby curtains. A painting of Ares hung on the wall. His gaze seemed to follow her every move.

"Persephone, please free me!"

'You're already free,' answered the goddess.

"Oh, Persephone, please help me, or they'll brainwash me and turn me into one of their slaves."

'Do you want that?'

"No!"

'Well then, why don't you tell them?'

Her shoulders slumped. "Oh, what's the point?" Her heart pounded as she scanned the room for a way to escape. "Persephone!" she begged.

'Don't be such a drama queen. Be still and focus on the energies within. What does this show you about yourself?'

Alison took a deep breath and closed her eyes. "I see a fortress surrounded by an enormous field. Oh, there are armies and warriors—it's an ancient battlefield."

'Okay, now, look closely. What else do you see?'

"I see gods and goddesses hovering above the armies." She blinked. "What does it mean?"

'You're witnessing the conflict of the inner story. Now, rise beyond the inner battle and invoke the warrior within.' Persephone's voice faded.

"Come back, Persephone. Don't leave me!" The sound of her pleading bounced off the walls. She closed her eyes. "I just hope I can find Ian."

"Hope is not a strategy," replied a voice.

Alison's eyes sprang open. She saw a glimmer of bright eyes, then a goddess appeared with a helmet, shield and spear. "Athena at your service. How can I help?"

Alison's eyes widened. "Oh, Athena. Thank goodness. I need help to rescue Ian."

"You can trust me on that." The goddess gripped her spear. "This is spiritual warfare. The force of illusion is powerful. They will try to deceive you into believing who you are not." Her voice sounded clear like a bell. "Do not allow doubt to cloud your mind. Know your enemy and act accordingly."

A wave of courage filled Alison's heart. "Thank you," she said, then her eyes narrowed. "It was you, wasn't it? You gave me the strength to stand my ground."

Athena smiled. "Just as I encouraged the heroes of old, so I stand with you now. Call on me whenever you need wisdom, courage or a strategic mind."

Alison exhaled. "I certainly need courage. I don't know if I can do this," she said, her voice trembling.

"Have no fear. You were born to rise above it all. Now, go forth and be victorious." And with that, the goddess disappeared.

Alison took a deep breath, trusting herself and drawing upon the depths of her being.

Soon, the door unbolted, and a man with scruffy blond hair stood in the doorway. "You're in luck. Class is about to begin." He hustled Alison along the corridor and into the classroom. Faces turned as they entered.

"Here is your seat," he said.

Alison pulled out the chair and sat down. Seeing Ian on the other side of the room, she smiled and fluttered her fingers. His eyes sprang open in surprise.

A patriotic song blasted through the speakers, and a military man entered the door. He stood in front of the portrait of Ares and saluted.

On the front desk sat a globe and a black flag with a gold border. "Welcome to the Universal Fame and Fortune Lifetime Program," he said. "I am your instructor." He flicked the globe, and it spun. "We will recite our allegiance to the code."

People are bad for the planet.
Fewer people, better planet.

The students repeated the creed.

"You know what this means, right?"

They nodded dutifully, and the introductory session began.

"Psst, Ian, what are you doing here?" whispered Alison during the morning break.

"Impressive, isn't it?" he said, biting into a cinnamon scroll.

She shook her head. "I wouldn't call it that."

"I wouldn't either, but I had no choice."

Alison exhaled. "Thank goodness you're okay. So, how did you end up here?"

He glanced left and right and then leaned closer. "I was with the monks in the mountains. While I was there, I continued working on my computer project. It was going well until I thought about making a name for myself. It was only a fleeting thought, but recruiting agents were on the lookout, ready to grab hold of anyone with a desire for infamy—and well, it seems my thoughts gave me away and here I am."

Alison gasped. "Do you realise that they're planning a worldwide takeover and there may be no one around to honour your so-called achievements?"

Ian swallowed. "I hadn't thought of that."

Alison rolled her eyes.

"Anyway, it's a bit late now," he said, reaching for a chocolate slice. "So, what are you doing here anyway? I thought you weren't interested in computers." He took a bite. "Hey, this chocolate thing is good. You wanna try some?"

Alison wondered if it was too late to help him. "I'm not hungry. I'm here because I received a message that you were missing, possibly abducted." She looked at him with pleading eyes. "Come away, Ian, please."

A woman approached. "I'll have to separate you." She took Alison's arm and marched her back to her desk. "Now, sit there and stop disturbing the others."

The students returned to their seats, and the instructor took his place in front of the whiteboard. "Attention, everyone, turn to page eight. This is a practical session about the latest malware designed to hack into the weapons division of the armed forces. It's a simulation, of course, but the experience will be useful. Next week, we'll host representatives from various nations who will watch your progress through a two-way mirror. If successful, you'll have a chance to achieve fame and fortune in the country of your choosing."

The students clapped.

"Thank you, team. Now, get to work," said the instructor.

Hurriedly, they typed the codes into their computers. Alison stared at the book in front of her. The title read, 'Malware for Dummies'. *How did they know?* She wondered. The first few lines of text were harmless enough, but as she continued to read, the letters seemed to twist and blur together. Her eyes grew heavy, and a pleasant sensation came over her. *This isn't so bad after all...* she thought, sinking into a hypnotic state.

A sudden gust of wind rushed through the open window. Alison looked up and her heart skipped a beat as she glimpsed Athena's glowing form.

With a glint in her eye, the goddess soared across the room, her hair trailing like a comet's tail.

"Now!" said the goddess as she whizzed past.

Alison blinked, and suddenly her thoughts flowed strongly. *I mustn't forget who I am and why I'm here.* She slammed the book shut. "None of this makes any sense!"

Heads turned towards her, glazed eyes blinking in astonishment.

Scraping her chair, Alison rose to her feet, legs shaking but determined. "I don't know about all of you, but this is ridiculous! We need to help the world, not hinder it!" Her voice grew steadier. "Yes, stare all you like. I don't care what anyone thinks!"

She strode across the room, grabbed Ian's hand and pulled him to his feet. "Come on, we're outta here." He grabbed his bag and stumbled after her. She pushed him through the door and turned to face the class. "And if you have any sense, you'll get out of here, too."

The instructor stood speechless. This had never happened to him before. He was about to give chase when someone tackled him and he fell to the floor.

Alison slammed the door behind her. "Come on, Ian. There's a car waiting."

Ian's eyes flickered. "Oh, okay."

She grabbed his hand and started towards the front door, and he stumbled after her.

A pair of burly henchmen blocked the door.

"Hey, where are you going?" said one. He lunged towards Ian, twisting his arm, while the other grabbed Alison.

"Yikes, that hurts," cried Ian.

"The boss won't be pleased."

"Yeah, he'll make sure you end up on the trafficker's list."

Ian's eyes glared. "Trafficker's list?" His mind suddenly clicked into gear. "What the hell are you talking about?" With one deft movement, he freed himself and aimed a powerful kick first at one and then the other.

Alison jumped back, heart racing, as the men doubled over with pain.

"Come on," said Ian, grabbing her hand. They sprinted through the door, the alleyway rushing past in a blur, and scrambled into the back seat of the car.

Alison's face flushed with exhilaration. Breathing hard, she had never felt so alive.

The officer in green swivelled his head. "Seems you didn't need us after all."

Ian grinned, still catching his breath. "Those karate lessons came in handy," he said, as the car sped along the road leading out of realm sixty-six.

Alison gazed at the city lights as they flashed by. *Now I know the courage of Athena,* she mused.

20

Thrace

THE PALACE HOSTED A welcome-home party for Alison and Ian, and everyone was invited. The only one missing was Hades himself, but his absence did not dampen their enthusiasm. Music filled the hall as they sang and danced into the night.

As the party came to a close, Ian stepped onto the stage. "Thanks, from the bottom of my heart to everyone who helped with my rescue, and especially to Alison. At least here in Hades, I'm protected from my own ruinous desires." He pulled a funny face. Alison smiled, and the residents of the Palace of Hades cheered.

Persephone stepped forward and pinned a badge on his lapel. "In honour of your escape and as a reminder not to do it again."

To the delight of all, Ian was accepted as a guide. His enthusiasm was infectious. He had a way of bringing everyone together in a spirit of friendship and good humour. In the evenings after dinner, Ian shut himself in his room.

"A project," he said.

Occasionally, he emerged with a request for a rare gem or metallic rock, supplies of which were plentiful in the Underworld.

Meanwhile, the river Styx was a hive of activity with an ever-growing influx of souls. Despite the workload, Alison had never felt happier—until one day, when everything changed.

The morning began with an ominous silence. Suddenly, the sky that was serene only moments before burst into flames of reds, oranges and blues, followed by the mournful howls of Cerberus.

"Awesome," said Ian.

Alison's eyes widened. "I wonder what this means."

That evening, the atmosphere around the dinner table was heavy with dread. Ian held down a swede with his fork. As he cut into it, his knife slipped out of his hand and fell noisily to the floor.

Alison jumped, and everyone stared. "Talk about cutting the air with a knife," she whispered.

A red-faced elf appeared at the door. "Come quickly. Hades has called an urgent meeting."

Hurriedly, they pushed their chairs from the table and jostled to get through the door. Outside, the inhabitants of the palace spilled out of every doorway. Alison and Ian squeezed through the throng. Hades and Persephone stood on the balcony, with palace officials strategically standing behind.

Hades' voice was solemn. "I returned from Mount Olympus, where I met with Zeus and Poseidon. The situation is dire. The future of the human race and of the gods is in jeopardy."

Murmurs arose from the crowd.

Hades stood quietly, and the noise settled. "It appears that Ares, the god of war, has launched an unprovoked attack on the world through his human agents. Not only are the rights of people threatened, but so too are those of the gods. His aim is to become ruler of the three realms."

The crowd gasped.

Hades continued. "The world is now divided. Zeus, who heads the Allied powers, has tried his best to maintain communication with the Axis powers. Throughout the whole affair and despite discouragement, he struggled hard to prevent a breakdown of discussions. He has repeatedly made it clear that he doesn't want war, and he has said that if war came to the world, it would be of Ares' making.

"I ask you, the residents of the Underworld, to stand firm and united in this time of trial. The task will be difficult. There will be dark days ahead. As you know, war is no longer confined to the battlefield. But we can only do what is right and reverently commit our cause to Zeus."

The onlookers shook their heads in disbelief.

"In the coming days, my time will be spent in the war room with the Grand Council. Meanwhile, Queen Persephone will manage the day-to-day running of our realm.

At the mention of her name, a cheer went up.

Persephone stepped forward. "Dear ones, please be assured that we will convey all that we know. Stay calm, stay safe and keep the wheels of Hades turning."

The residents disbanded and returned to their various stations.

"That explains the increasing influx of souls," said Alison as they returned to their rooms.

Ian nodded. "Sadly, it looks like we'll see more."

The following morning, the ferry arrived as usual, its wooden hull creaking. The passengers stepped onto the dock; a look of bewilderment and anguish etched on their faces. They spoke of mysterious diseases, endless suffering, unspeakable atrocities, sudden deaths and more. Teams of guides worked all morning, consoling and sending them on their way.

By mid-afternoon, Alison flagged. "Sorry, Aidan, it's not like me to complain, but the atmosphere is so heavy. I just need some time out."

He nodded. "I know what you mean. I'm feeling it too."

Alison returned to her room. As she sank into her armchair and closed her eyes, a familiar sound rose within her, softly at first, then spreading like ripples through her being.

Aum...

Enveloped in the peaceful vibration, her thoughts stilled.

From within the silence, words emerged: *'The threads of the story of good and evil are unravelling. Life has lost all meaning. Souls feel scared and confused. Do not be afraid. Reveal the light and let them know who they really are.'*

The message lingered, glowing faintly in her mind. Feeling reassured, Alison drifted into sleep.

✳

It was late afternoon when she awoke. She found Ian in his room, leaning over his computer, his fingers tense on the keyboard.

"Hi," she said, sitting down. "What are you doing?"

He looked up. "Working on a program to break through the barriers that separate the realms."

"Oh, what for?" asked Alison.

"I want to talk with souls anywhere."

"You mean someone on Earth?"

He nodded, his jaw tight. "The problem is, I can't quite make the connection." He hit a key harder than necessary. "It's infuriating."

"Don't be upset, Ian; it's only a computer."

He turned to her, his eyes burning with frustration. "It's more than that, Alison. It's everything I worked for; the culmination of all my research into electromagnetic signals, resonance fields, the possibility of transmission—it's my life's work."

"Your earthly job, you mean?"

He nodded slowly. "I never told you, but I was a defence consultant; classified electronic communications."

Alison's eyes widened. "Wow, is that why Ares kidnapped you?"

Ian's shoulders slumped. "Partly, yes."

"What do you mean, partly?"

He looked down. "I wasn't kidnapped. I agreed to go."

Her breath caught. "You *what*?"

He met her stare for a moment, then looked away. "The lifestyle was good, the meditation, the quiet mountains, but old desires surfaced, and that's when Ares' agents intercepted my thoughts. They said I could complete my research, change the nature of consciousness itself."

"And you believed them?"

He shrugged. "I found their proposal interesting," he said quietly. "They appealed to the part of me that wanted to be successful, important."

Alison shook her head. "I risked everything to save you!"

"I know, and I'm grateful. Truly I am." His voice cracked. "Honestly, Alison, I went into it blind, not realising the level of mind control. I just wanted to finish my project." He picked up the booklet. "As I was leaving, I grabbed this. But there isn't enough information."

Alison shook her head. "If I'd known, I would have left you there."

Ian winced. "I'm sorry." He gazed at her with pleading eyes. "Don't be too hard on me. I admit my mistake. Being in this realm has forced me to reflect on my past, and now I'm coming clean." He took a breath. "They promised me all the riches and pleasures my heart desired. I fell for the illusion, trapped like a fly in a web. It's only now that I see the cost of chasing after empty promises and material gain."

For a moment, silence filled the room.

Finally, Alison exhaled. "At least you see it now. But you'll have to rebuild the trust you've broken."

"I know," he murmured. "I'm thinking of returning to the Taoist community and spending some time in reflection, to find myself."

"Honestly, I think you need some advice," said Alison. "Why not speak to Persephone?"

He nodded. "That's a good idea, but she can be rather... unpredictable."

Alison smiled. "I'll go with you if you like."

He managed a faint smile. "Thanks. I don't deserve your kindness, Alison, but I'll try to earn it."

It was late that evening when Ian and Alison ascended the palace steps. An elf directed them into the library. They sat on a chaise lounge and waited. It wasn't long before Persephone glided into the room, wearing a long black gown and elbow-length gloves.

She greeted them with a solemn expression. "How are you holding up in these difficult times?"

"It hasn't been easy," said Alison.

"No, it hasn't." She turned to Ian. "And how are you?"

Ian drew a slow breath. "I'm thinking of returning to the Taoist community."

"Oh!" Persephone's brows lifted. "Do you think that would be wise?"

"I'm not too worried. I've learnt my lesson. The main thing is not to attract the dark forces with my ruinous desires."

"Desires?" Persephone's eyes narrowed. "What exactly do you mean?"

"I was trying to build a communication system to break through the veil between realms."

"He wants to talk to people on Earth," Alison added.

Persephone's eyes widened; a flicker of intrigue flashed across her face. "Now that *is* interesting."

Ian hesitated. "The problem was, I was using it to achieve wealth and prestige."

"Of course, it is human nature," Persephone said dismissively. She leaned forward. "Are you sure that giving up is the right decision? It sounds to me that such a device may benefit humanity and even the gods themselves."

Ian nodded. "I'd like to think so, but Ares holds the information I need to finish my project."

"Dear me, how inconvenient," said Persephone. She paused, eyes glinting. Suddenly, her eyes sprang open. "Then why not go directly to Ares' palace in Thrace?"

Ian stared at her. "You can't be serious. That's walking into a hornet's nest?"

Persephone smiled. "They're always in need of human servants, so you'd blend in perfectly."

"It sounds dangerous to me," said Alison, her voice tight.

The goddess grinned. "What is life without a little danger?"

Ian shifted nervously. "Uh, how do I get to Thrace?"

"By cloud dragon, of course. They're quite reliable."

Ian exhaled. "My knowledge of ancient history is sketchy. Apart from computer games, I know very little about this guy, Ares."

Alison gave him a quick jab. "He's not a guy, Ian."

Persephone's eyes widened. "Indeed, he is not. Ares is a god, born from the union of Hera and Zeus."

Alison frowned. "Wait, so Zeus is your father, too?"

"Indeed," Persephone sighed, then a faint smile crossed her face. "I remember young Ares. He was, what can I say... a little perverse. I recall him shooting wayfarers with deadly arrows and ruthlessly hacking his way through childhood with hooked spears. The scent of blood and acts of evil brought the child great pleasure."

Ian grimaced. "How awful."

Persephone nodded. "Ares had no respect for others, which is why he was unpopular among the gods, except for Aphrodite, who found his charms irresistible. He fathered the twins, Deimos, the god of fear and Phobos, the god of terror; along with Harmonia, named in honour of the short-lived harmony between wars. Ares also fathered demigods to mortal women, but his offspring often inherited their father's violent temper."

"What dreadful sons," said Alison.

Persephone shrugged. "What more can I say except that they take after their father? The three of them take great pleasure in creating chaos. They love the din and roar of battle, the slaughter of men, and the destruction of towns and cities. They aren't fussy about winning or losing. Sometimes they assist one side and sometimes the other. But it's not only war that inspires them; they also revel in plagues and epidemics."

Ian's brow furrowed. "But that's pointless. Why create so much pain, death and misery?"

Persephone's eyes narrowed. "It may seem meaningless to you who are fed by the fruits of the Earth, but everyone, including the gods, needs an energy source. Ares provokes conflict, not for the sake of battle as much as the tumult, confusion, and horror it creates. And that's because the gods of war feed on the fear and terror of their victims."

"Oh my," Alison gasped.

"But it still doesn't make sense," said Ian. "How does he convince people to kill each other?"

Persephone nodded slowly. "You must realise, war is a lucrative business. Ares entices others to do his bidding with promises of wealth, power and prestige. As a result, he has a bevy of allies in the top echelons. Their quest is to create a new world order."

"I've played enough computer games to know what that means," said Ian.

"Oh yes, world domination is an age-old obsession. It is the pinnacle of power and glory. The ancient Greeks called it kleos, but in Ares' case, glory comes at a tremendous cost to humanity." Persephone gazed into Ian's eyes. "Now, are you willing to go?"

Ian exhaled. "I can see what's at stake for humanity, but what if I'm caught?"

"I hear the castle is a busy place. They're always having meetings and conferences. If you go together, you could blend in without raising suspicion, and you may even gain the information you need."

Ian nodded. "That's true."

Alison frowned. "You can't be serious. After all you've been through, do you really want to take that risk?"

He turned to her, his eyes pleading. "But, Alison, it may be the only chance we have."

Alison felt a chill run down her spine. Her mouth went dry. She could feel the web tightening around them. "All right," she murmured. "I'll go."

"Splendid!" said Persephone. "I'll meet you in the garden tomorrow morning at cockcrow. Don't be late."

Alison shook her head in disbelief. This was not what she expected, nor wanted, but there was no turning back. Somehow, she knew they had just agreed to something far larger than either of them understood—something that would forever alter their fate.

21

Egor

THE MORNING MIST HUNG gloomily as they made their way through the trees.

"What was that?" Alison squealed. "I felt something breathing down my neck."

Ian chuckled softly. "Looks like you made a friend."

Alison peered into the mist. She could just make out the form of a dragon with wings.

"Giorgio won't hurt you," said Persephone as she emerged from the shadows. "Here," she said, slipping a necklace over Alison's head. "Within the pendant is a mini camera, invented by the gods."

"Thanks," said Alison.

"I forgot to tell you," Persephone spoke softly. "We meet on Mount Othrys in a few weeks to celebrate the Eleusinian Mysteries."

"I know that mountain," said Ian. "It's near the City of Dreams."

"Good, I'll see you there."

Alison's eyes widened. "But..."

"Now, all aboard. You must leave before the sun comes up." Persephone helped them onto the dragon's back. "May the blessings of the gods be with you."

Giorgio stretched his wings and took flight. The wind whipped their faces as the dragon soared higher through the clouds. Soon they were flying over mountains and valleys.

As dawn cast its rosy fingers over the land, Giorgio spiralled downwards into a dense forest. He landed on a well-worn track.

They slid down and Alison gazed up at his enormous head. "Thank you, Giorgio."

The dragon let out a low snort before flying away. He circled briefly, then he disappeared into a cloud.

"There's no going back now," said Ian.

A distant, rhythmic thud echoed through the forest.

"Hey, listen, what's that sound?" said Alison.

"Hoofbeats—they're approaching fast." Ian grabbed her hand and pulled her behind a tree as soldiers in chain mail galloped past. In the distance, trumpets sounded. "Come on, we must be close," he said, setting off along the track.

They rounded a bend, and the forest gave way to an open field. Ahead stood an imposing castle with a drawbridge. Armoured sentries wearing helmets paced back and forth on the turrets above.

Ian stopped. "That must be Ares' palace."

"More like a fortress," said Alison.

The two stood in silence, staring at the castle walls.

Alison's gaze shifted nervously. "How are we going to get in?"

A tall, lean man walked along the track with a basket over his arm.

Ian gazed at his beret and a white apron. "Ah, excuse me," he said.

"Hello, can I help?" said the man.

Ian smiled. "Ah... y-you see," he faltered before speaking clearly. "We're visitors. We've heard about the wild majesty of this realm and the noble traditions of this castle. Can you tell us anything about the place?"

"Well then, welcome," said the man. "There certainly is a lot of history here. People say the stones they used to build the castle fell from the planet Mars."

"Really? That's interesting," said Ian. "Do you work at the castle?"

"Between lifetimes." He held out his hand. "I'm Donald, head chef."

Ian shook his hand. "Pleased to meet you. I'm Ian."

"And I'm Alison," she said, shaking his hand. Her gaze went to the basket. "What are you gathering?"

"I like to wander the forest during my break time. I found these mushrooms for tonight's meal," Donald said, removing the cloth from the basket.

"Wow, nice," said Ian, looking at the brown caps. "You must have a large kitchen."

"Oh, yes," Donald replied.

Ian smiled. "To be honest, we're fascinated with old castles and would love to work in one."

"We're always looking for more staff," said Donald. "Can you wait tables and clean dishes?"

"Sure, I was a cleaner, and Alison."

"Oh...," she said, "I worked at a pizza bar."

Donald's eyes lit up. "That sounds perfect. At the moment, we're preparing for a conference. Guests will be coming from all over." He paused. "Are you ready to start right now?"

"Yes, chef," Ian smiled.

"Excellent, then follow me."

They made their way to the drawbridge. On either side stood sentries guarding the massive gates. An officer on horseback rode by, hooves clattering. They walked through the towering archway and into the central courtyard.

Alison gazed at the statues of cavalry horses and war elephants, complete with howdahs on their backs.

Ian looked up at a towering statue of a god holding a spear in one hand and a shield in the other. He read the words, 'Ares, the supreme god of war.'

Donald turned to him. "Impressive, isn't it?"

"It certainly is," said Ian.

Donald pointed. "The kitchen is this way."

Their footsteps echoed on the stone steps. A housemaid greeted them with a blank expression on her face. She led them through a maze of winding corridors, stopping outside a small cell. "This is your room," she said to Ian as she unlocked the door.

The housemaid turned to Alison. "Follow me." She walked along the corridor and unlocked another door. "This is yours. Come up to the kitchen when you're ready."

Alison stared at the stone walls, the narrow, lumpy bed and the oil lamp on the sideboard.

Ian appeared in the doorway.

"So much for the rustic castle experience," she said, smiling.

"Well, at least we're in," said Ian. "Let's go upstairs."

The kitchen buzzed with activity. The sounds of sizzling pans and clanging pots mingled with the scents of herbs and spices. Counters gleamed, and appliances appeared sleek and modern.

"That's a relief," said Alison. "I had visions of cooking over hot coals."

Donald greeted them and showed them around. In the days that followed, they became accustomed to stacking the dishwasher and mopping the floor while keeping out of the way of the temperamental cooks and their equally moody assistants. The staff appreciated Alison's pleasant nature and efficiency. Meanwhile, Ian attempted to maintain a low profile, taking on jobs that kept him out of the spotlight.

In the evenings, they met in Ian's room, where the glow of an oil lamp cast shadows on the walls. "There's not much we can see, working in the kitchen," he said.

Alison nodded. "Don't worry. Guests are arriving, so an opportunity may come up."

The following morning, Donald approached, his face flushed from the warmth of the stove. "The conference starts tomorrow, and Ares is hosting a sit-down luncheon. Alison, I'd like you to wait on tables, and Ian, you can continue cleaning."

They nodded in unison. "Yes, chef."

The following day, Alison donned a waiter's uniform and joined the line of servers pushing the trolleys through an underground tunnel that connected the kitchen to the servery.

Alison wheeled her trolley into the grand hall. Reptilian faces leered as she approached the table. She tried not to stare at the scaly creatures with humanlike bodies. Suppressing the urge to gag, she placed an entrée of slimy boiled snails drizzled with a thick, dark blood sauce and a plate of fried cockroaches in front of them. Alison shuddered as their claws reached greedily.

With a practised smile, she collected the empty plates and served the main course: succulent roasted rodents atop a bed of fried crickets and wild fungi. Back in the servery, she discreetly opened the door to allow the sound to drift into the room.

"Ladies, gentlemen and guests, on behalf of the Olympian god Ares and his sons Deimos and Phobos, I welcome you. We are here to host the fifty-sixth meeting of the Order of Iniquity, which sees us steadily moving ahead in our mutually beneficial plan. This year, we aptly named our conference, 'Three Realms, One Regime.' Please let us know if you have any special requirements. We hope you enjoy your stay here."

That night, Alison and Ian met in his room. "Did you get a good look at them?" he asked.

"I sure did," she said, nodding her head. "Looks like there are different groups. Some appear human, while others are more like reptiles. Someone told me it's because of their nature. Apparently, they adopt normal bodies on Earth." She smiled. "It's surreal, but fascinating. I want to gain access to their meetings so I can learn more."

"That would be helpful, but how?"

"I'll think of something," she replied.

The next morning, Alison approached Donald in the kitchen. "I noticed that many of the guests have peculiar dietary needs, and they are always hungry. What do you think about providing an around-the-clock snack service?"

"Mm... good idea," said Donald. "What do you suggest?"

"May I suggest potato chips, battered mice and crispy earthworms washed down with a cold beer?" said Alison.

Donald nodded. "Sounds great. Would you be prepared to dedicate the next few days to making sure the service runs smoothly?"

"Sure," she said.

"Well then, I'll arrange the catering."

Alison passed Ian on the stairs. "I'm in charge of the snack service, so I can access their meetings," she whispered.

"Well done, but just be careful."

She nodded. "Don't worry, I will."

That afternoon, Alison pushed a trolley filled with snacks and drinks through the tunnel. Her footsteps echoed on the stone floor. Passing through the servery, she made her way into the grand hall. She stood the trolley inside the door. As she was early, she looked around.

A raised stage stood at the front of the hall, over which hung a gold shield engraved with an image of Ares. Along the walls hung portraits of legendary conquerors. She wandered around the room, studying the portraits of the rulers who had sought earthly power through conquest: Alexander the Great, Alaric the Visigoth, Attila the Hun, King Cyrus, Hannibal, Julius Caesar, Scipio, and Sun Tzu.

Alison returned to the snack trolley. She had just finished setting up when the guests arrived. It had been a while since the banquet, and some were peckish. Guests took packets of tasty morsels and drinks, and soon the sounds of muttering, crunching and slurping filled the room.

"The worms were most enjoyable. May I have another?" said a guest.

"Certainly," said Alison, handing him a packet.

"I'll have one, too," said a woman in a grey suit.

Alison smiled. *They are not at all concerned about my being here*, she thought.

The lights dimmed, and an anthem belted through the speakers in military style. The guests rose as imposing figures in battle dress of the gods entered the hall. Following was an entourage of suited men in dark glasses. The leaders made their way to the stage, and the guests sat down.

The chairperson stood up. "Honourable gods, Ares, Phobos and Deimos, men and women from all corners of the globe, welcome to the 'Three Realms, One Regime' conference. You will find in front of you a folder containing an outline of the plenary sessions. In your free time, we invite you to partake of the delights of Ares' palace. Included in your welcome package is a map of the castle, highlighting the many game rooms. Now, without further ado, we will begin with a few words from our esteemed leader."

Ares loomed over the audience, eyes blazing and hair cascading around his chiselled face.

Alison's legs trembled.

His voice boomed through the speakers. "Welcome, future world leaders. For a thousand years, we have been preparing for this moment: orchestrating wars, toppling civilisations, erasing history and replacing it with our own." His sons came up behind him and positioned themselves on either side of Ares. He placed his hands on their shoulders. "All this time, the twins, Phobos and Deimos, supported my goal to spread chaos and terror throughout the world."

Deimos and Phobos grinned.

Ares continued. "I am pleased to announce we have infiltrated every high-level organisation in Zeus' earthly realm. Only last week, we took the City of Dreams. Our next conquest will be the Underworld!" His eyes gleamed. "We are on the brink of achieving our goal of world domination!"

Alison gasped as the hall erupted into cheers.

With a raised hand, the god silenced the room. "Zeus is growing weak. His grasp on Earth is slipping. It is time for me to rise and claim my rightful place as ruler. We will wage war, and no one will stop us. We will emerge victorious!"

Deimos took the microphone. "All honour to Ares!"

Everyone stood, and the room resounded with the sound of, 'Ares, Ares!' Their voices echoed like a battle cry.

Ares smiled proudly as he took his seat.

The meeting continued in a lively fashion, with representatives from various nations recounting tales of recent wars and terrorist attacks, advancements in military domination, along with the staggering numbers of dead and displaced humans. Excitement filled the air as each speaker expressed their support for Ares' cause. The meeting finally drew to a close, and Ares and his sons strode from the hall, followed by the guests.

Alison glanced around the empty hall. A conference program lay on the table. She fumbled for her camera and pressed the button.

That night, she met Ian in his room.

He held the pendant up to the light. "Hmm... I wonder how this works." He connected the camera to the computer, and the image appeared on the screen. "I see it now. 'Three Realms, One Regime. The psychology of fear, control and authority. Three days of iniquity, followed by blood sports under the lights.' Wow, that's quite a program."

"You won't believe this, but Ares has control of Zeus' realm," Alison blurted. "Last week he took over the City of Dreams, and now he plans to conquer Hades' as well. His goal is to control the three realms. From what I've seen, Ares has been working on this plan since the beginning of time. He's like a puppeteer, manipulating the story to his own ends."

Ian shook his head. "I never would have imagined. And to think I fell into his hands."

Over the following days, Alison snapped photographs and gathered snippets of information, which she filed in her mind for later. In the evenings, she met with Ian to discuss her findings.

On the last day of the conference, Alison guided the trolley towards the recreation room. Inside, unearthly creatures stared at computer screens. A toad snatched a packet of dried tadpoles from the trolley and turned back to the screen. He bounced on the chair and clapped his hands, then he broke open the bag and munched.

He looked around. "Man, these are good. Any more?"

"Sure." Alison handed him another packet. "What are you watching?"

His eyes glowed with a strange luminescence. "The world news. It's brilliant," he said.

"Why, what happened?" asked Alison.

"Terrorist plot—it's all part of the plan." He smirked. "The more we strike fear into those helpless humans, the more compliance we have. It won't be long before we can do anything we like." He snorted with laughter and turned back to the screen.

Alison quickly snapped a photo. *I had better not look too interested*; she thought. She moved the trolley around, handing snacks to the guests, then glided through the automatic doors that led to a lavish smoking room furnished with glass coffee tables and velvet lounge chairs. On the wall hung portraits of Deimos and Phobos. Tall men in princely attire sat in a row in front of silvery computers. Others played pool at a large table. They waved her over, took some packets and drinks, then returned to their game.

Alison was about to leave when Phobos appeared at the door. She quickly hid behind the trolley.

The guests stood as Phobos entered the room, followed by men in dark glasses. "Greetings, Princes of Darkness," he said. "I am here to offer a preliminary trial of my latest computer game." His lips curled into a cruel smile.

Alison quickly felt for the pendant around her neck and pressed the button.

Phobos handed his assistant a microchip. The assistant slid it into the computer and punched in some commands. "Game launcher installed," he said.

"In this game," said Phobos. "Not only do we implant thoughts into the minds of human beings in real-time, but they also obey our script. Watch this." He moved the mouse over the image of a man driving a truck and manipulated his mind so that he fell asleep at the wheel. In an instant, his truck ploughed into the back of another car. Soon, there was an enormous pileup, and ambulances and police arrived on the scene.

The onlookers clapped and cheered.

Phobos smiled. "Instant horror—who are we?"

"Rulers of the globe!" they answered back.

"I'll leave an operational booklet of the game for anyone interested. Please enjoy." Phobos strode jubilantly from the room.

Alison leaned on the trolley to steady herself. *Oh, my... It's like Ian's communication software. Only evil.*

"Over here, love." A man with lush lips and a gold earring beckoned. Reaching for a packet of fried crickets and a bottle of beer, she took them over to the man.

He looked her up and down and licked his lips. She backed away. Alison placed a row of snacks and drinks on the shelf next to the guests. She was about to leave when a holler sounded.

"Bloody hell, I caught a fish!"

The Princes of Darkness rushed over. "Hey, guys, this new game is wild. Look, humans playing with drugs, knives and guns and stuff." He wheezed with excitement; perspiration dripped from his forehead as his breathing increased. He moved the mouse. "Got him! Oh, yes, kill!" he yelled at the top of his voice.

His colleagues elbowed each other to get to the screen. Their obscenities reached a crescendo. They yelled and punched each other, egging the fighters on.

Hyenas at the kill, thought Alison. Her heart raced as they huddled over the computer. She seized the chance to flick through the booklet, snapping photos of each page. I must get this back to Ian, she thought, as the trolley wheels sped silently along the corridor.

A side door opened, and a man stepped into the corridor with his hands on his hips. Alison turned to run. He reached out and grabbed her wrist and pulled her into the room, shutting the door behind them. She gasped as he threw her onto a chair.

"And so... we meet again." His lips tightened. "You're a spy, aren't you?"

Alison stared, wild-eyed. His florid cheeks and receding hairline looked familiar.

Where was it? She closed her eyes, remembering Ian's rescue. Suddenly, her eyes snapped open. *Oh yes, the City of Dreams.*

"Thanks to you, we lost a member of our team, a valuable resource," he snarled. "I should turn you over to Ares to be shut away in the dungeons of hell for eternity, but..." He smiled. "I find you fascinating. Your eyes, your hair; you exude an air of mystery. You're my kind of woman."

A surge of fear shot through her like a lightning bolt, but her eyes remained fixed. "You're keeping me from my duties, Mr..."

"My name is Egor." His jowls wobbled like jelly. "This time, there's no escape." He grabbed her wrists, dragging her to her feet.

Alison looked him directly in the eye. "No, you don't." She flew at him with all her strength, head-butting his bloated stomach.

"Oomph." Egor fell like a tree trunk and lay motionless on the floor.

She stood for a moment, stunned by what she had done, then turned and ran towards the door. Her heart pounded as she fled down the stairs, but just as she reached the bottom step, someone grabbed her arm with a vice-like grip. Alison tried to scream, but a hand covered her mouth.

"Come with me." He spoke in a deep monotone.

Alison looked up at the massive soldier and, without hesitation, kicked him firmly in the shin.

"I feel no pain," he said as he dragged her through a doorway and down a dark flight of stairs. Alison struggled and fought, but he swung her onto his shoulder and carried her through the maze of underground corridors.

Later, amidst the bustle of the kitchen, Donald approached Ian. "I'm sorry to tell you, they found Alison's snack trolley in the corridor."

Ian's brow furrowed. "But where's Alison?"

Donald shook his head. "We don't know," he said. "From time to time, workers go missing... It's best not to ask questions." He turned and walked away.

Ian grabbed the broom and began sweeping furiously.

22

Aphrodite

THE METAL DOOR SLAMMED shut. Alison heard the key turn in the lock and the echo of boots on the flagstones. She held her stomach, feeling bruised from being carried on the shoulders of the brute.

She looked up at the remnants of fading light that filtered through a high window. "That's done it," she muttered. She remembered Donald telling them that the stones came from the planet Mars. Up close, they appeared menacingly thick and impenetrable.

Something stirred above her. They looked like bats.

"Persephone!" Her words echoed in the empty cell.

As night fell, the bats stirred. Suddenly, like angry bees, they swooped, wings beating, screeching and squealing; their claws tearing at her. Frantically, she covered her face with her hands, but it was useless. They were everywhere.

"Oh, Persephone, please help me!" she cried frantically.

'Where are you?' replied the goddess.

"In a prison cell. I'm being attacked by bats!"

Suddenly the air shimmered, and a force field surrounded her. The bats retreated to the ceiling. There they hung upside down, their beady eyes following her every move.

"Oh, thank you," breathed Alison.

'Trapped again?' Persephone's voice rang out.

Alison sighed, preparing herself for what was coming next.

'You seem to make a habit of this,' said the goddess. *'Have you ever stopped to wonder why you find yourself in these situations?'*

"I ask myself the same question," whispered Alison.

Persephone pressed on. *'Is it because you can't control your thoughts, or is it something deeper?'*

Alison sighed. "I don't know. Bad things just keep happening to me."

'*Of course you know,*' said the goddess. '*You're simply not ready to face it. Perhaps a little solitude will help you self-reflect.*'

Tears filled Alison's eyes. "Oh, what's the point?" Her heart pounded as she scanned the cell for signs of escape. "Persephone, please!" she begged.

'*Don't be such a drama queen,*' Persephone's voice faded.

"Come back, Persephone. I need you!" The sound of Alison's pleading bounced off the walls and faded into the silence. She took a deep breath and steadied her thoughts. *At least the bats have gone.*

The door grill squeaked, and a guard pushed a lump of bread and a bowl of water through the opening. The grill closed, and footsteps echoed down the hallway.

Hunger drove her to finish the dry, hard loaf, then she lay back on the wooden bench. *Persephone is right; I need to figure out why I'm here.* Alison closed her eyes, and an image emerged in her mind—a wounded self, huddled in the shadows, a fragile identity created in her younger years, a victim of circumstances, defenceless against the unknown.

It was then that she heard Persephone's voice. '*Look in the mirror. Are you that false self behind a locked door, or are you the one who is holding the key?*'

Alison stared into the mirror of her mind. There she saw it; the subtle, silent program controlled by a tyrant, urging her to yield, to shrink her true self in order to please everyone around her.

Persephone continued. '*Can you see the survival mechanisms you adopted; how you learned to become smaller, quieter, and more submissive? This state of inner exile may have helped you as a child, but as an adult, it became a prison. Now, break free from your own self-imposed walls.*'

Alison's vision blossomed into a kaleidoscope of colours that exploded behind her eyelids; reds and oranges, greens and blues. Colours swirling together, both exciting and terrifying at the same time. The patterns drew her deeper into herself until she confronted an immense wall built out of the ancient stones from Mars.

She heard a voice commanding her not to go any further, lest she should perish. Hearing the screams of warriors and the roar of Ares' battle cry beyond the wall, her breath quickened. Gathering herself, she climbed to the top. From there she saw a battlefield with shouting, weapons clashing and the sound of Ares' cry. And there, alongside Ares, she saw Aphrodite, the goddess of love. Tenderness and violence intertwined—the paradox of love and war.

Alison heard a key turn in the lock, and her eyes sprang open. The door creaked, and a flickering light illuminated the stone walls.

Egor entered, carrying a lantern. He stood for a moment, metallic green eyes shining and wispy hair floating above his flaccid face.

Alison's stomach churned.

"So, my little firecracker, I finally caught up with you." He looked around the cell. "Not the most pleasant surroundings, but under the circumstances, it's the best place for an impetuous girl like yourself." His gaze lingered, hard and calculating, then it softened. "I can make things easier for you, of course."

Alison stared. "What? You want me to sell my soul for total control?"

Egor's mouth twitched. "Don't get me wrong. That's not what I meant at all." He leaned closer. "I have a confession." His eyes gleamed. "You are looking at a man in love. Your shining eyes, your vision... Come with me. You and I together... our future is bright. I've seen what lies beyond the chaos, and you, of all souls, were meant to stand beside me."

"Are you out of your mind?" she muttered.

Egor smiled. "After they clean up the plutonium and replant the forests, there will be a silence, a purity. Vast lands untouched, and waiting for us to claim as our own. Together we'll lift the world from its ashes. We could build a sanctuary—a new Eden." His eyes gleamed.

"Why me?" she groaned.

"Why not?" he smiled. "I fell in love with you the minute I saw you. Together, we will rule the world, or at least our little corner." He gazed at her with pleading eyes. "Don't you see? The goddess within you has already chosen me."

Alison stared in disbelief. "My answer is no! I'd rather stay here than go with you."

"What!" Egor looked visibly shaken. He had offered her the world, and he didn't expect to be refused. He smiled, undeterred. "Well then, my little flower, I'll leave you to think about it. Perhaps a few days in solitary will help to change your mind." Egor knocked twice, and the guard opened the door. He turned. "If you continue to resist, we may have to arrange a little encounter with one of our lions. Goodbye, my dear. I'm sure you'll make the right decision."

The door slammed, and the key turned in the lock.

A shiver ran down her spine. *Let me out of here!*

Alison lay on the bench and closed her eyes, drifting into a dreamworld. No longer in a cell, but on a sunny beach. The sand felt pleasantly warm beneath her toes, and the light sparkled on the water. A pod of dolphins dove playfully through the waves. They swam closer. "What is it you want?" they said.

She gazed across the vast ocean and the endless sky. "Freedom," she replied.

"Then come with us."

"With you? But I'll drown..."

"Don't worry, we'll take care of you. Come join us." They said as they surfed the waves.

"Why not?" Alison said, entering the water, walking deeper until her head submerged under a wave. She emerged on the other side, gasping for breath. A dolphin swept underneath her, lifting her onto its back. She gripped the fin, and the dolphin skimmed through the water as they headed out to sea.

The water ahead began to bubble and churn. The dolphin slowed as a goddess emerged from the depths, draped in an emerald gown. Light surrounded her, and her hair shone like spun gold.

At once, Alison felt herself enveloped in a love as boundless as the ocean.

The goddess introduced herself as Aphrodite. Hovering above the waves, she asked, "What brings you here?"

"I wish to be free," replied Alison.

Aphrodite gazed into her eyes. "You will never be free as long as you hold discord in your heart instead of love."

Alison blinked. *Is this the Aphrodite I met at morning tea?*

As if hearing her thoughts, the goddess responded. "I am the goddess of love; elevated and pure." She smiled. "You will know me when you transcend the inner struggle and embrace the paradox of your inner goddess, the one who rides the tiger."

"Oh!" exclaimed Alison.

"Is there anything else?" asked the goddess.

"Yes," replied Alison. "A practical question. How do I get out of this place?"

"You know their little game, play it..." Aphrodite winked, then disappeared beneath the churning waves.

With a jolt, Alison sat upright. The dream had seemed so real.

She heard boots on the flagstones, then the key turned in the lock. The door opened. "Morning, miss." A guard entered with a tray on which sat a bowl of steaming porridge, a mug of hot chocolate and a tiny vial of blue liquid. "Aphrodite requested this for you," he said, placing the tray on the bench.

Alison stared at the tray for a moment, then she slid the vial into her pocket.

The day passed quietly. As it drew to a close, Alison heard muffled voices outside her cell. The guard pushed open the door. "You have a visitor."

Egor stepped inside. "I hope I'm welcome."

Alison forced a smile. "Oh, Egor, it's nice to see you."

He raised an eyebrow. "You've changed your tune. You obviously had time to think."

Her expression turned solemn as she nodded. "Yes, I have. And I've made my decision. I accept your offer."

"Oh, how delightful." Egor grinned like a schoolboy with a bag of lollies. "Well then, let's go." He offered her his hand. She felt the webbing between his fingers and shuddered. "Come, I prepared a cosy repast in my den." He rapped on the door. The guard opened it, and they strolled out, hand in hand.

They made their way through the corridors, Egor chatting all the way. As Alison entered his room, she saw a table adorned with an array of delicacies: soft cheeses, crusty bread and plump olives.

Alison's stomach rumbled. She pulled up a seat. "This food looks delicious," she said, reaching for a piece of cheese and bread.

Egor's grin widened. "Try the wine. It's from my Château." He poured two glasses. After handing a glass to Alison, he guzzled.

Alison sipped. The wine was rich and full-bodied, with hints of oak and berries. "This is superb," she said, reaching for the bottle. "Have some more," she said, refilling his glass.

"Thanks, but I must, eh..." He stumbled to the bathroom.

Alison took out the vial and quickly poured the liquid into his glass. Then, seeing his guitar, she picked it up. She had never played before, but suddenly she felt the urge. Inspired by the goddess Aphrodite, her hands moved over the strings as if she had played all her life.

Egor stood in the doorway. "You play like an angel." He sat on the couch and took a gulp of wine. "I feel rather thirsty," he said, gulping another. Lulled by the music, he lay back and gazed at her sleepily. "Time for bed." His eyes closed, and soon he was snoring.

Alison tiptoed towards the door.

His eyes flickered. "Where are you... going?" he mumbled.

"Don't worry, I'll be back soon, my love." Alison opened the door and slipped out.

She hurried along the corridor, then raced down the stairs, her hands brushing the damp walls. She dashed through the tunnel and emerged into the bustling kitchen. All eyes turned towards her. She gave a reassuring smile, and they resumed their work.

Seeing her, Ian's eyes glowed. He smiled and quietly pointed towards the door. They took the stairs two at a time, hearts hammering. At the top was a door. With a sharp tug, he wrenched it open. They ran along the passageway. Shadows leapt along the walls as their footsteps echoed.

"This place is massive," she said, catching her breath.

A shout rang out behind them. Ian grabbed her hand. "Come on, we're almost there."

She stumbled after him as the light from the door grew brighter. They burst out onto the battlements, and Ian quickly reached for a rusty chain. "Giorgio!" he shouted as he yanked it and a clanging bell echoed through the fortress.

A rumble of wings responded to the sound. Hot air whipped past the battlements as the dragon circled above them. But the soldiers had also spotted him, drawing bows and shouting warnings.

Ian grabbed Alison's hand, pulling her toward the edge of the battlements. "We have to jump together!"

Alison hesitated, eyes wide.

"Trust me," he said.

They leapt just as arrows whizzed past, thudding into the walls around them. Giorgio angled down, wings spread, and they landed with a thud on his back. Alison clutched the fur, heart racing.

Down below, soldiers fired. An arrow bounced off Giorgio's thick hide.

"Hold on!" yelled Ian.

Alison braced herself, feeling the wind rush past her. Below, the castle receded into a blur. Giorgio soared over forests and hills until finally he descended onto a rocky ledge, high on a mountainside.

The air was fresh, and the wind gusted. Around them, fairies perched on branches, singing in high-pitched tones. They slid off the dragon's back.

Alison threw her arms around Giorgio's neck. "We did it!" The dragon puffed his warm breath into her face, then he spread his wings and flew.

A low rumble rolled across the heavens, followed by a giant clap of thunder. The mountain trembled, and the fairies squealed and chattered as the wind blew steadily through the trees.

Alison looked around. "Where are we?"

"Mount Othrys," said Ian. "Now, to find shelter." Pushing his way through the undergrowth, suddenly, he froze. He stared at the bushes ahead. "I saw something moving."

A black-caped figure brushed the branches aside, her face partially hidden by her hood. "You're here at last," she said.

"Persephone!" cried Alison, and the fairies shrieked with delight.

23

The Priestess

A BLAST OF WIND threatened to blow them off the mountain. Alison grabbed a branch and held on tight. Persephone pulled her cloak around her. "Zeus is displaying his wrath. Let's get inside."

Alison and Ian struggled against the oncoming gusts while the fairies flew into the cave's refuge, making themselves at home in the nooks and crannies within the walls.

Once inside, their eyes adjusted to the warm glow of flickering lamps.

Alison sighed with relief. "Whew, we made it."

Persephone tossed back her hood and shook her hair. "It was either that or end up in the lion's den."

Alison scowled. "You omitted that detail."

"There had to be some surprises." Persephone grinned. "So, how did you go? Get the information you needed?"

Alison clasped the locket around her neck. "I hope so."

"Very good. Well then, make yourselves comfortable. The Eleusinian ceremony begins tomorrow, and I have much to attend to." She pointed to a corner of the cave. "Over there, you will find hammocks. The fairies will take care of your immediate needs." And with that, the goddess disappeared.

Alison undid the locket from around her neck and handed it to Ian. "I took some photos in the games room. I think you'll find them interesting."

He plugged the camera into his computer, and soon an image of Phobos flickered on the screen. "Mm, so that's the god of fear and panic," said Ian. "What are they doing here?" he said, gazing at the picture of the games room.

"They're using a game to project evil thoughts into people's minds," said Alison. "I also managed to get the manual."

"Very good," said Ian, carefully reading each page. After a while, he sat back. "It appears the demons have a direct line to the collective consciousness."

"What does that mean?" asked Alison.

"Well, imagine that we all exist as characters in a play, and our every thought and emotion connects us to the main script."

Alison nodded.

"The gods access this connective energy while feeding thoughts that divide us from each other and our Source. Weakening our collective link allows them to fill our minds with their thoughts and desires."

"Whoa, really?"

"The gods think they run the show, but that's part of the illusion. In reality, it is humans who truly hold the power." Ian flicked back and forth in the game's manual, carefully reading the instructions. "Okay," he said, as his fingers moved rapidly across the keyboard, "I think this should work now."

The communication light blinked, casting a faint crimson glow over the cave. Ian's eyes widened. "Hey, someone is coming through."

"Alison, where are you?" The voice sounded shrill. "It's me, Alison, dear."

"It's Grandma. I can hear her, but I can't see her."

"I need to work on the video settings, but at least you can hear her voice," said Ian.

The crackle of the transmission filled the cave. "I don't have much time. Just want to say goodbye. I love you and hope to see you again one day."

"What do you mean, Gran? Where are you?" said Alison.

"Oh, my dear..." her voice softened. "Everything has changed in the City of Dreams. We're not allowed to make our own choices since Ares seized control. They even reconstructed the Re-entry Pavilion. It's now just a gigantic processing plant."

Alison gasped. "Oh, Grandma, it can't be true."

"Last week, the army came knocking on our door, forcing us to return to Earth. They took your grandfather. He had no say in the matter. Oh, Alison, I'm scared. They assigned me to a distant country plagued by famine. I will be born as the youngest of eight." She stifled a sob. "But, my dear, I don't want to burden you. I simply wanted to tell you how much I love you."

Alison choked up. "I love you, too, Grandma." They heard a faint goodbye, and the crackle of the transmission faded.

Alison's eyes filled with tears. "Oh, Ian, we can't stand by and let this happen," she cried.

"There's not much we can do unless I can communicate with the Earth plane." His eyes flashed as his fingers flew across the keyboard. The screen glowed with lines of code as he located the keys to unlock the secrets of other realms.

Outside, the sky darkened. Waves of thunder rolled across the heavens, and the mountain trembled. The sky opened and rain fell. Rivulets of water ran down the slopes. They swelled and joined, forming larger streams until a huge current flowed like a waterfall over the opening of the cave.

The fairies fluttered like tiny birds and settled on a large rock. Alison heard the faint sound of an accordion and a fiddle. Soon, they started dancing.

Ian looked up from his computer. He tapped his foot to the music. "Hey, I've been meaning to ask you about the Eleusinian mysteries. What's it all about?"

"It's the celebration of Persephone's ascent from the Underworld, her return to her mother, Demeter. Apparently, the ceremony itself is a release of the mortal fear of death and an experience of the sacred vibration that carries the essence of immortality."

Ian nodded. "Sounds cool."

Alison gazed into the distance. "Wouldn't it be wonderful to travel back in time to ancient Greece and take part in the ancient ceremonies?"

Ian raised his eyebrows. "Time travel, anyone?"

A clap of thunder reverberated through the cave, and Alison jumped. "Oh, that sounded close."

The music ended, and the fairies prepared a spicy dish of rice and vegetables in an earthenware tagine. They spooned the meal into bowls, which they offered to Alison and Ian. The fairies ate their fill, after which they curled up in hiding holes in the walls and were soon gently snoring.

"How's it going?" asked Alison later that evening.

Ian looked up and smiled. "I did it. I broke through the veil. Not long now, and I'll be talking to people on Earth."

She smiled. "You're amazing!"

He shook his head. "I couldn't have done it without you."

"What do you mean? I didn't do anything," she protested.

Ian's smile faded. "Alison, you risked life and limb to get this. You were locked in a cell, alone. You're becoming unshakable, like a goddess."

"I don't know about that," said Alison. She looked down, feeling both self-conscious and thankful.

"No, I mean it," Ian said softly. "You take yourself for granted. Few would have the courage to do what you did. I didn't always deserve your trust before, and yet you were there, anyway."

Alison's eyes softened, and she smiled.

He closed his laptop. "I'll continue in the morning." Stretching his arms above his head, he looked across to the hammocks longingly. "I bags this one," he said as he climbed into a hammock strung between two boulders. Within moments, he was asleep.

Alison watched him settle, the quiet rhythm of his breathing. She gave a contented sigh. They had been through fear, frustration and even betrayal, but now somehow the threads of trust were weaving stronger than before.

✳

Alison climbed into her hammock. She closed her eyes and listened to the sound of rain flowing down the mountainside. *Hmm... time travel*, she thought as she drifted off to sleep. She felt herself spinning through space, then everything went quiet as she drifted into a tranquil stream running between the epochs. Alison felt a jolt and opened her eyes. She stood on a stony beach, gazing at an old-fashioned cargo boat as it sailed away across the sea.

Where am I?

She ran her hands over her gown, tied at the waist with a fine cord. The sea breeze tousled her hair.

Two young women dressed in flowing robes ran across the beach towards her.

"Euthalia, you're back." They hugged her warmly.

"Iona, Tamara, how good it is to see you." The moment she spoke, the memory of Alison faded. She was now Euthalia, a woman in ancient Greece.

They struggled up the rocky shore, stepping onto a path that led up the hill towards the temple. Sunlight warmed the wooded hills, and birds sang in the trees. There was a festive atmosphere on the temple grounds. A flute played in the background as they shared the sun-ripened fruit, cheese, olives and bread. It was early summer, and the air was hot and still.

Euthalia walked towards the shade of the spreading tree. There sat the High Priestess, who enjoyed hearing about her visions and dreams. "Welcome back, Euthalia. Do you have anything to share?" "Last night I had a vivid dream," said Euthalia. "The goddess Artemis told me I would travel by boat, but I only just arrived. What does that mean?"

The High Priestess frowned. "Perhaps it's the fact that I will soon choose the initiates to be sent for training at the temple at Ephesus on the coast of Iona."

Euthalia gazed at the lines of ants that scurried along the ground. "I had another dream, but I have no wish to upset the gods."

"Your heart is pure. What could you say to upset the gods?"

"I saw a vision of the future; a world where there is no goddess."

The High Priestess took a breath. "That is a warning. I cannot tell you the meaning, but I know prophecies are the sign of a true oracle."

Euthalia exhaled. "Then I am relieved of this burden?"

"Speak no more of this," said the High Priestess. "No matter what happens, you must trust your nous—your inner knowing, for that is your link to divinity. Now enjoy the festivities."

As she walked towards the temple, she felt lightheaded, and then she fell. Lying on the ground, Euthalia heard a voice. *Alison…* the name drew her into a vortex that sped her through the barriers of time. Suddenly, she found herself in a dimly lit cave gazing at a woman in a hammock.

Thunder rolled like a freight train across the heavens. Alison felt a jolt, and her eyes sprang open. The light flickered on the walls. She felt a presence and looked around. A figure stood silhouetted against the lamplight.

Oh, my goodness… Alison stared, spellbound. "I awoke from a dream and here you are."

The light illuminated Euthalia's face, and the words flowed softly from her lips.

"Tell me, how long has it been?" said the priestess.

Alison frowned. "Around two thousand years, give or take."

"So long…" She gazed into the shadows. "You're in a cave. Who are you hiding from?"

"The forces of darkness," Alison replied.

"And where is the goddess?"

"What?"

"The goddess, the warrior, the protector?"

"Of course, we know about the goddess," said Alison. "But it's the gods of war who rule this world."

A flicker of sadness passed over Euthalia's face.

"So, my vision was true; the goddess vanished."

Alison nodded. "You were right."

She ran her fingers through her hair.

Strange, thought Alison. *She even has the same mannerisms as me.*

"I come as a messenger." She smiled. "I can tell you from as early as I can re-member, I lived between two worlds—immortal and mortal. At times, immersed in a divine consciousness, and at other times, plagued by the petty demands of the gods."

Euthalia sighed. "I went to the temples, where seekers gathered from Egypt, India and Persia and Greece. They all agreed on one thing: we stood on the edge of change. More and more, hearts were being led by power, desire and fear. The inner peace that once guided humanity was slipping away."

Alison's eyes widened.

"It was at the Eleusinian Mysteries that I received the gift of divination. I could see into the future, a world that was a mere shadow of its former glory. I saw visions of conflict and the fall of great kingdoms; some crumbling in the desert heat, while others submerged under rising waters or buried under lava flows." She smiled sadly.

"But I was not content with visions; I wanted to see for myself. And now I have fulfilled my wish. Now I know we are children of the Ocean. You belong to the rising tide, whereas I belong to its flow."

She gazed at Alison as if looking into a mirror. "I leave you with a message: trust your intuition, sweep your house clean of fear and reclaim your power. A time will come when you will once more walk the sparkling shores of the ancient world..." Then Euthalia faded into the morning light.

Ian jogged past. "Hi, you're up early. At least the rain has stopped. Time for my Tai chi. Going to join me?" He burst out of the cave entrance and into the morning sunshine.

Alison made a cup of mint tea and followed. The mountainside sparkled after the rain. She sat on a rock while Ian completed his morning ritual. Around her, birds twittered and fairies fluttered in the morning light.

Ian brought his hands into a prayer position. "Well, that's me done. I'm going inside to work on the computer program."

Alison gazed at the mountains shimmering in the distance. Strains of flutes and temples swirled like veils in her mind, then suddenly, out of nowhere, came a deafening roar as a V-formation of war chariots zoomed overhead. The fairies scattered under bushes, their wings quivering.

The chariots turned and soared low over the mountain. Alison grabbed her cup and ran into the cave.

Ian looked up from his computer. "What was that?"

"Warplanes," she said, breathlessly.

He frowned. "Ares must know we're here." He looked up, and his face broke into a triumphant grin. "I did it!"

Alison's eyes widened. "What, really?"

Ian nodded. "I've been talking to an old friend, Joel. He's a computer programmer."

"I bet he was surprised?"

"He was. Would you like to meet him?"

"Of course!"

Ian pressed a button, and a face appeared. "Hi, Joel, this is Alison."

Alison peered at the screen. From his broad shoulders and long hair pulled back into a ponytail, she saw Joel was a sturdy man. But despite his strength, there was a haunted look in his eyes.

She waved. "Hi, Joel. Nice to meet you."

"Hi Alison. It sure is."

"It's been a while since I've been on Earth. How are things?" she said.

Joel shook his head. "I doubt you'd recognise it. We're no longer individuals. Artificial intelligence tells us what to eat, where to go, and what medications to take. Money is just numbers on a screen. Everything is expensive. I'm working long hours just to survive."

"I'm sorry to hear that."

"And that's just the beginning," said Joel. "Right now, there are food shortages and people are looting. There's danger everywhere. Humanity is a thing of the past. No justice, no God, no human rights—all run by a pantomime of clowns. Last week, my friends had had enough. They took their backpacks and headed for the hills. I thought about joining them, but it's not worth a few days of freedom. When the food runs out, what do you eat, each other?"

Joel exhaled. "I was on the balcony of this seven-storey unit when Ian's message came through on my phone." His voice broke... "Ian saved my life."

Alison exhaled. "Oh, thank goodness."

Ian leant over. "Hey, Joel, I'm with you, man."

"You are fortunate, Joel," said Alison. "Many think death is the easy way out. Though you may be free from your physical body, you will not escape the turmoil in your mind." Joel nodded. "So, Ian told me. But meanwhile, how to survive this dystopia?"

"Remember when we played computer games?" said Ian.

"Sure."

"Well, now the game is no longer on the computer. It's happening in real life. In other words, view it as if you are an onlooker," said Ian. Then he paused.

"Speaking of computers, why don't we join forces and collaborate? There's a lot we can do if we work together."

"I'm in, buddy. Thanks for giving me hope," said Joel.

They said goodbye, and Ian closed the computer.

Alison smiled. "You are clever, being able to talk to Joel like that."

"Thanks," he said, his eyes gleaming. "I couldn't have done it without you."

24

The Eleusinian Mysteries

It wasn't long before the sounds of drums and panpipes drifted through the cave. Drawn by the music, Alison and Ian hurried outside. A flock of chariots hovered overhead.

As each craft landed, Alison felt the excitement rising. Princes and princesses in regal attire, and priestesses in ceremonial robes, descended from their chariots. The air echoed with their banter as they made their way through the cave.

Ian and Alison followed. The sand felt soft beneath their feet as they made their way through the dimly lit passages that led to a cavern in the heart of the mountain. They stopped at the earthenware jars where others were sipping the nectar of the gods. After taking a drink of the sweet nectar, they made their way inside. In the centre of the cavern, a sacred fire burned brightly, the flames reflecting on the crystal walls.

"How magnificent," said Alison, gazing up at the cathedral-like ceiling.

Ian nodded. "It sure is."

They heard the steady beat of drums. Alison joined the throng that moved slowly and rhythmically around the fire. The drumbeat guided their movements, building in intensity, faster and faster, until they moved in unison. Their spirits soared as the primal beat carried them into an otherworldly realm, each becoming part of something greater. As the music faded, they closed their eyes, basking in the silence that enveloped them, no longer feeling separate but united as one.

"Welcome to the Eleusinian Mysteries." Persephone's voice resounded through the cavern.

Alison opened her eyes.

In her hand, Persephone held a cluster of white narcissus flowers. "I hold a symbol of an illusory desire to possess the beauty, abundance and joy that the material world provides, a time when humanity made a universal decision to forgo the spirit and enter a physical realm. And in this foreign land, the spirit became a distant memory."

Persephone threw the flowers into the fire, and they hissed and melted. "Gradually, humanity lost their way in the maze of doctrines, boundaries and regulations, forgetting their origins as beings of light." Her eyes shone. "It is time to embrace the mystery of renewal!"

The light dimmed, and the sweet notes of the flute floated through the air. The ethereal goddess Hestia stepped forth, her hair flowing over her gossamer gown. In her hand, she held an unlit torch.

So pure and clear was the goddess that tears glistened in Alison's eyes.

Finally, the goddess Demeter emerged in a rippling golden gown. In her hands, she carried a sheaf of ripened wheat. Her jewel-like voice echoed through the cavern.

I sing of the sacred spirit,
the descent into darkness,
the plea for release
and the ascent into the light.
I sing of the reunion of the holy goddess
and her child Persephone,
whom Hades seized under the eye of Zeus,
the one who sees far and wide.

Demeter threw the sheaf of wheat into the flame. "As this wheat burns, so do your illusions." Her eyes glowed in the firelight. "We welcome you, one and all, to this sacred space, safe from the forces of darkness that hover like vultures outside our door. I call upon Persephone to lead us in a ritual journey from darkness into the light."

Persephone stepped forward. "In your desire for that elusive narcissus flower, you succumbed to the voices of those who promised you riches and power, only to be left with a hollow ache for what you left behind. The soul became a prisoner of the mind, and as a result, both life and death became a struggle. But now it is time to shatter the illusions and break free." She paused for a moment. "Breathe deeply and release the stories of your past."

The drums began a rhythmic beat. Alison breathed deeply and with each exhale, she released all her heaviness, her doubts and misgivings. Her thoughts and feelings mingled with those of others, drifting upwards until they formed a black, oily cloud over their heads. She looked up and trembled as monstrous faces stared back at her.

"Prepare yourselves for the ritual of purification," said Persephone.

Hestia held her torch in the flames, and with fierce resolve, she stepped into the gathering.

Alison quickly moved aside.

Holding the flaming torch high, Hestia declared, "Stand firm and have no fear of what is coming." Then she thrust the burning torch into the oily haze. The cloud burst into flame, and smoke billowed, thick and dark.

Alison gasped and fell to her knees, joining the others who were already on the ground, gasping for air. The cavern glowed brightly as the flames grew higher. Explosions sounded above them, along with the shrieks of dying demons.

Gradually, the clouds dispersed. The crowd rose to their feet, coughing and spluttering.

Hestia placed her torch in a holder on the wall and with a sweep of her hands, a cool, clear light washed over the gathering.

Her voice floated through the cavern. "Behold the mystery, how you emerge from the dark night of winter into the light of spring."

The musicians took their positions. The melodic notes of the flute and the soft beat of the drums floated through the air as faces reflected the radiance of the goddess.

A warm feeling of belonging washed over Alison. With eyes half-closed, each breath filled her with an intoxicating sense of peace. Time slipped away, stretching into what felt like an eternity... She heard the crowd murmur and she opened her eyes.

A god stood before them, his face ruddy, with sunburnt lips, dressed in cargo pants, a red sweatshirt and hiking boots with an orange beanie. "Greetings," he said, nodding to Persephone. "P-Please forgive my appearance. I was hiking the Himalayas when the boss, er... Zeus, commanded me to deliver this message."

Persephone smiled. "Dear Hermes, what message do you bring?"

Fumbling in his bag, Hermes pulled out a rolled parchment. It fell to the ground along with a protein bar. "S-Sorry about that—frostbite." He smiled. "Could you please?"

Persephone scooped the parchment from the floor, then reached for the protein bar.

"Thank you," said Hermes, stuffing the bar into his pocket.

"No time to linger—my hiking companions are waiting. I w-wish you well," he said, waving gaily as he vanished through the crystal ceiling.

Persephone smiled as she broke the royal seal. "It's from Aunt Hera." Reading ahead, her smile faltered. "This is not good news," she said in a low voice.

Demeter sighed. "Not another infidelity. Read on."

Persephone took a breath, and a hush came over the crowd. 'My dear sisters, Demeter and Hestia, my niece Persephone and heroic humans, please accept Zeus' and my blessings for the Eleusinian Mysteries. I write to you with pressing news. Over recent centuries, Zeus' eyesight and hearing have deteriorated. And now, without his confidante, the goddess Metis, who gifted him with divine wisdom, his story is wavering. Lord Zeus wants me to share the unfortunate news that Ares, his son and rival, may take his throne. Affectionately yours, Hera.'

Whispers circulated among the throng. The mighty Zeus, king of the gods, losing his kingdom? It seemed impossible.

Persephone rolled the parchment. Her gaze turned to Demeter as she posed the question that burned in everyone's mind. "What does it mean?"

Demeter nodded slowly. "The truth can no longer remain hidden. All along, the great god Zeus secretly relied on the wisdom and power of the goddess!"

Silence came over the cavern. The only sound was the crackle of the fire.

All eyes turned to Demeter, and then a priestess spoke up. "An unknown goddess has emerged, and we know little about her."

"Metis was originally a Titan," said Demeter. "I met her long ago. The goddess of wisdom helped us in the war against our father, Cronus. After our victory, she and Zeus were married. Everything was fine until Metis received a prophecy in a dream, that she would give birth to a child who would be mightier than his father. Fearing this, Zeus promptly swallowed her."

"Such is life. We must keep calm and carry on." Demeter smiled. "I will forthwith convey our best wishes to Zeus and Hera." She turned to Hestia. "I call upon Hestia to offer our blessing to Metis, the goddess of wisdom, wherever she may be."

Hestia's eyes reflected the light of the flames. She held out her hands as though spreading her invocation through the universe.

I call upon the Titan, Metis,
daughter of Oceanus and Tethys' gentle streams.
First mother of counsel,
shaper of thought,

Mother of grey-eyed Athena.
You are the hidden wisdom
the deep-flowing stream.
Metis, freed from the bonds of Zeus.
Come now, all-wise one
receive our blessings,
and shine wherever you dwell.

A temple bell sounded, and a wave of joy spread through the gathering.

Demeter stepped forth. "Beloved ones, the hour is upon us. Our task is great. We must rouse all who dwell on the Earthly plane and guide them once more to their immortal roots. And now I call upon Persephone to offer her final blessings."

Persephone stepped up with a pomegranate in her hand. She split the pomegranate with a stone, crimson seeds scattering like drops of blood on the ground.

"These seeds symbolise the paradox of life and death, bondage and freedom, mortality and immortality. Hold the image in your hearts as a reminder to remain awake within the dream and walk through it in freedom, power and love."

Demeter smiled. "Farewell, dear ones, and may the goddess be with you."

The musicians struck up a lively tune as the crowd dispersed.

Ian tapped Alison on the shoulder. "That was cool."

Alison turned to him in a dreamy haze. "Sure was."

"Where are we going?" he said.

She shook her head. "Hade's castle?"

"I don't think it's wise to return to Hades amidst a takeover by Ares," he said. "What about the City of Dreams?"

Alison shook her head. "I'd rather go somewhere safer."

Ian shrugged. "Okay, how about we just follow the others?"

The crowd made its way through the cave. Ian picked up his bag. Outside, the sky was ablaze with sunset hues of pink and orange. The air buzzed with excitement as, one by one, the chariots ascended into the sky.

A goddess appeared before them, tall and regal. "May I be of assistance?" She said, drawing them in with her alluring eyes.

"I don't think we've met," said Alison.

"Ah, forgive me. I'm Eris, daughter of Zeus and Hera." She gestured towards a gleaming chariot. "My carriage is at your disposal. Where may I take you?"

"We haven't decided," said Ian.

"Well, in that case, I know a place where you'd be most comfortable."

Alison shook her head. "No, it's okay."

"Even when it's everything you ever wanted?"

"Like what?" asked Ian.

Eris's lips curved into a smile. "A paradise," she purred. "A mansion on a secluded island, with beaches, palms and tropical fruit falling from the trees."

"Hmm, sounds interesting," said Ian. He turned to Alison. "We need a holiday. What about it?"

"Oh, Ian, is that really what you want?" Alison locked her arm in his and guided him away. "I think I should head back to the Underworld to help Persephone," she whispered.

Eris stepped in front of them. "The Underworld is a dreary place." She turned her gaze towards Alison and beamed an image of tropical palms and beaches into her mind. Speaking in a hypnotic tone, she said, "Trust me, you'll love it."

Alison sighed. "Well, maybe you're right. A break would do us good, but afterwards, we must get back."

"Excellent!" Eris smiled. "It's settled then." She led them down a path towards a sleek black chariot.

Alison's eyes widened. "It looks like a stretch limo without a roof."

Eris chuckled. "Even better." She guided them into the back seat. "Make yourselves comfortable," she purred, offering them wine, chocolates and a selection of videos. As they settled in, she slipped into the driver's seat and pressed a button that locked the doors with a soft click.

Alison gazed at the black upholstery with the gold trim. "Hang on, this looks more like something Ares would dream up."

"You're right." Ian's eyes darted around frantically, his heart pounding. He pushed against the door. "Damn—we're trapped."

Suddenly, the chariot lifted off. They looked over the edge, but all they saw was the mountain shrinking below them.

Alison felt her spirits drop. *Duped*, she thought.

The goddess turned to them, with eyes shining like onyx. "You will love it, I promise." Her lips rolled back into a wide grin, revealing wolf-like teeth, long and sharp.

25

Artemis

THE CHARIOT SOARED LOW over a sandy beach, and the salt wind whipped their hair.

What a letdown, thought Alison. Her eyes watered, partly from the wind, but mostly from her own folly.

The chariot travelled farther out to sea.

"Looks like an island," Ian said brightly. "At least she was right about that."

Alison clenched her jaw and stared straight ahead.

They landed on a cliff, high above the crashing waves. Ahead stood a stone fortress, its perimeter lined with barbed wire. Grim-faced jailers strode towards them, keys jangling on their hips.

"The prisoners are here, safe and sound," declared Eris. She turned to Ian and Alison, her lips twisting into a smile. "Out!" she snarled.

The door clicked open, and they scrambled down.

"Enjoy your holiday, earthlings," she sneered. The chariot blasted upwards and swept across the sky.

Alison frowned in dismay as she looked around at the windswept saltbush and the tussocks that stopped abruptly at a cliff face. "We finally made it to the gates of hell," she whispered.

Ian took a step, and a guard grabbed his arm. "This way, buddy."

The guards marched them up the stairs and along a stone passageway amid a cacophony of groans, rattles and clangs. A heavy wooden door stood open. The guard pushed Alison inside. "There you go, my lovely. And you too, pretty boy." He shoved Ian through the door and slammed it shut. The clump of boots grew softer as a deathly quiet closed in.

Alison sank onto a stone bench, covering her face with her hands.

A sliver of sunlight fell on a pail of water. Ian filled a mug and drank, then he filled the mug again and placed it on the bench next to Alison. "Are you angry with me?"

She reached for the mug. "What do you think? You want all the good things, and all the time you play into the hands of those demons!" Her voice cracked with frustration and fear.

Ian sat on the bench opposite, shoulders slumped. "I'm sorry," he said, then his eyes brightened. "At least the guards didn't search us." He patted his jacket.

She sighed. "I had a bad feeling about Eris. When am I going to learn to trust my intuition?"

"Don't blame yourself," said Ian, smiling. "As a software engineer, I would say you may have a virus in your program."

"What?" She glared at him. "Speak for yourself. Your track record is legendary."

"Let's not fight," he said. "We're in this together."

Alison stared, her anger giving way to relief. "You're right," she admitted.

They sat in silence for a moment, feeling the comfort of each other's presence. She smiled. "At least I'm not alone."

Time passed, and the last rays of sunlight faded into darkness. Pale moonlight seeped through the window.

Alison's gaze lingered on Ian, slumbering peacefully on the bench. She looked around at the stone walls. *Here I am, trapped again. No point in asking for help. Persephone would only say, 'You're the architect of your own fate'.*

She focused on the light of One. Soon, the tranquil hum of *Aum* floated through the air. A feeling of peace washed over her, loosening the threads of tension. Her thoughts slowed.

From the stillness came the words: *Face the shadow of your own making and, as you do so, your worldview, once upside down, will turn the right way up again.*

Her shoulders relaxed, and she let go and surrendered to the silent embrace of sleep.

The first rays of morning light cast a faint glow over the cell. The sound of boots echoed down the hallway. A plate containing lumps of dry bread and cheese shot through a slot in the door.

Ian took a bite of the bread. "Tastes like sawdust."

As midday approached, the door swung open. "Time to go," barked a guard. They led Ian and Alison along a corridor and up a flight of stairs. At the top loomed a door marked Senior Officer Hazard.

The guards ushered them inside. Behind the desk sat a man dressed in full military attire. He peered at them over his glasses. "Enjoying our little island retreat, are we?"

Ian smiled. "It's lovely."

The officer slammed his fist on the desk. "I will not tolerate insolence here." He glared. "I know everything about you." He glanced at his notes, and his eyes narrowed. "You were spies in Ares' castle. Is that true?"

Ian shook his head, and Alison stared at the wooden floor.

Hazard raised his voice. "I'll ask again, were you spying? Tell me the truth, or I'll extract it from you."

A flame ignited in Alison's heart. She glared at the officer. "What if we were?"

Hazard stared helplessly, his mind spinning like a wheel. "You treasonous vixen! I'd have you shot at dawn if I could." His shoulders slumped as if he had just lost a high-stakes game of cribbage. The Afterlife was not an easy place to work without the fear of death.

He leaned forward and studied the inmates. "Well, since you're here, perhaps you could make yourselves useful. We have openings for cleaners, servers and kitchen assistants. Are you interested?"

Ian frowned. "You're asking us?"

"Of course." His voice boomed. "You have a choice—either hard labour or languishing in a cell."

Ian swallowed. "Where's the work?"

"A resort on the other side of the island."

Ian glanced at Alison.

"Take it," she whispered.

"Okay," replied Ian.

Officer Hazard fumbled in the drawer and took out a cigar. He lit it slowly while glaring at them. "The oceans are full of sharks, so don't even think about escaping," he said. A puff of smoke rose in front of his face. He reflected for a moment, then sighed and waved his hand. "Okay, take them away."

The waiting Jeep roared to life and raced up a hill. As if by magic, they descended into a forest, fresh with the scent of green foliage. Beyond, lay palm trees and sparkling white sand.

"Nice, eh?" said Ian.

Alison nodded. "Looks like you'll get your island holiday after all."

They passed a sign that read, Celestial Resort. The Jeep rumbled down the tree-lined driveway towards a white Venetian-style mansion. They pulled up near the side door and stepped out. The guard knocked.

The housekeeper answered, her face stern. "Who do we have here?"

"New workers, compliments of Officer Hazard," said the guard.

"Oh, is that so?" she said. "Come in and mind your feet."

She led them down a flight of stairs to their rooms. The servants' quarters were simple. Just a bed, a chair and a dressing table.

"I'll fetch your uniforms," said the housekeeper, before disappearing down another hallway. A short time later, she returned. "Put these on and report to the kitchen."

Alison quickly changed and caught up with Ian. "Did you notice the officer didn't even call us by name?"

Ian nodded. "To them, we're disposable worker bees."

"Slaves, more like it," said Alison.

They made their way to the kitchen. A thickset woman with a ruddy face stood at the stove, vigorously stirring a pot. "You can call me Cook," she said, holding up a spoon. "Kayla, will you show these two around the resort?"

"Sure," said Kayla, grateful to be released from washing-up duties.

They walked the pathways, while Kayla pointed out the guest quarters, gym and various buildings, purpose-built for leisure and comfort. They learnt the island was one of the major destinations for the rich and famous and that the calendar overflowed with meetings, parties and conferences.

The tour ended, and they returned to the kitchen, where Kayla made them a cup of tea.

The Cook threw off her apron and pulled up a chair. "Oh, it's good to sit down. Do you have any questions?"

Alison tilted her head. "Can you give us any advice?"

Cook slurped her tea. "My advice? Lights out early; you'll need your beauty sleep."

Alison nodded. "What time do we get up?"

"Five sharp, and you work until you finish, even if it's late."

Ian grimaced. "Do we get a day off?"

"I haven't had a day off in eighteen years."

Alison shook her head. "How do you stand it?"

Cook yawned. "Only two years to go."

Alison's eyebrows raised. "Gosh, that's a life sentence!"

"I knew that when I came here."

"You chose this place?" asked Alison.

Cook nodded. "There's plenty of gossip floating around, so you might as well hear my story," she said, sipping her tea. "In a previous life, I was the son of a king. I had everything and everyone at my fingertips, but I still had a burning desire for more. So, I surrounded myself with advisers who were as grasping as myself. My father, the king, died under mysterious circumstances. Some people claim it was poison. Regardless, I inherited the throne. While the peasants toiled in the fields, I spent their taxes fighting wars in foreign lands and building pleasure palaces.

"My obsession with power was boundless, and my temper legendary. Those who served me were in constant fear, trying to keep up with my outrageous demands. Then one day during a siege, one of my officers stabbed me in the back. My last thought was, 'How unfair.'"

Alison took a breath.

"When I arrived in the afterlife, they threw me into solitary confinement. It didn't take long for me to realise that through my grasping for wealth and power, I had gained nothing at all."

A wistful smile played on her lips. "Now remember, early to bed. Oh, and another thing: if you want to stay safe, keep your mouth shut." She pushed the kitchen door and hobbled out.

"Whew, what a story, but at least she chose to be here." Alison pursed her lips. "Makes me wonder why we're here."

Ian shook his head. "I need to think this through. How about we meet in the courtyard tomorrow night?"

Alison nodded. "Okay, I'll see you then."

The following day flew by in an endless round of washing-up, cleaning and sweeping. It was late when Alison sneaked out of the kitchen door and scurried across the lawn. A night owl called, and shadows moved in the walled garden.

Ian turned to her; his face bathed in moonlight. "Hi, how was your day?"

Alison sat on the wooden bench beside him. "Busy, how was yours?"

He yawned. "I never want to see another bathroom. I cleaned at least twenty today."

They sat quietly, listening to the gentle swish of the waves.

Alison sighed. "Pity the beach is off limits." She turned to Ian. "So, how's Joel? He's not thinking of joining us on the other side?"

"No, he's going to ride it out." Ian turned on his laptop. "Hey, he's coming through." The laptop light blinked, and Joel appeared.

Alison leant over and waved.

"Hey buddy, how are things?" asked Ian.

"Hi, guys. It's getting tricky. The police shot at me over the weekend. See…" Joel lifted his T-shirt and revealed a series of purple and red weals on his back. "Rubber bullets."

"Jeez, how savage," said Ian.

Alison frowned. "Anything serious?"

"Not really, but the whole thing shook me up. Spent the night in a cell. The police released me with a warning. Three convictions and I earn a free trip to a re-education camp, do not pass go, do not collect two hundred dollars." Joel gave a small smile. "But then, a strange thing happened. I was on a train, and a guy sat next to me and started talking about meditation. He seemed genuine, so I attended a class later. I discovered we are souls, not just our bodies. I'm going back tomorrow for another lesson."

"That sounds great," said Ian. "Let us know how it goes."

"Will do—see you later," said Joel.

Ian turned off the laptop. He shook his head. "You never know what's coming next."

"All I know is we're trapped." Alison took a deep breath.

"Let's clear our minds of any thoughts or expectations about who we are and why we're here," said Ian.

They sat in silence, tuning in to the gentle swish of the waves.

"I remember the words of Lao Tse," said Ian quietly.

The ten thousand beings rise and flourish
while the Sage watches their return.
Though all beings exist in profusion,
They all end up returning to their Source.

A bird fluttered in the branches overhead.

Alison's eyes widened. "I hear someone coming."

A wolfhound bounded into the courtyard, closely followed by a goddess with loosely tied hair and eyes that shone a greyish green. A tunic hugged her muscular frame, and she carried a massive bow. On her back, she carried a quiver with an arsenal of arrows. Another wolfhound trailed behind, growls rumbling from his chest.

"Greetings, Earthlings! I heard there are wild boars on the island, so I thought I'd come prepared."

"What?" said Ian.

Alison stared wide-eyed.

"Elek, Theron, down," she commanded. "I am Artemis of the hunt." The goddess placed her bow and arrows on a bench. "A little birdie told me you were here."

"Oh." Alison's eyes grew large. "Was it Persephone?"

Artemis smiled. "Yes, she said to congratulate Ian on his powers of discernment."

Ian grimaced. "I seem to make the same mistakes."

"Good or bad, right or wrong, without the divine wisdom of the Great Mother, human beings are totally senseless." Artemis sat on the seat opposite. "So here you are, enjoying a working holiday."

Alison shook her head. "We're slaves."

"We're hoping someone would spirit us away. You know, get us out of here," murmured Ian.

The goddess raised her eyebrows. "So, you desire freedom from pain and suffering? Do you wish to avoid facing uncomfortable energies that may lead to personal growth, to confront your inner demons or heal your ancestral karma? What about your chance to serve humanity and make a positive impact on the world?"

Ian swallowed.

Alison felt a tightness in her chest. "I'm confused. You're saying we shouldn't have made that choice, and yet you say it's not bad after all."

"It's destiny that brings you to a place of maximum discomfort." Artemis turned to Alison, her eyes glowing. "Most humans are lovers of pleasure. They want to be free of effort and responsibility. They interpret painful experiences as negative, but pain is not necessarily bad when it is an opportunity to learn. After all, you cannot escape that which is fated."

"Is it my fate to be cleaning bathrooms?" muttered Ian under his breath.

The wolfhound growled.

Alison nudged him. "Be careful!" she whispered.

"In the past, we punished men who disrespected the goddess. Isn't that right, Theron?" She leaned over and patted the dog's head. His tail thumped. "These days we are more lenient."

"Whew, that's a relief," said Ian. "I simply want to help the world."

"I understand. Even Zeus acknowledged my free-spirited nature and my willingness to help the vulnerable," said Artemis.

Alison's eyes widened. "So, Zeus was also your father?"

"Of course," replied Artemis. "My mother was Leto, a nature goddess. It was a marriage of heaven and earth. Only Zeus was already married. Hera, his wife, became furious and forced Leto to take refuge on an island, where she gave birth to twins. I entered the world quickly, but my brother, Apollo, was slow to be born, and so I acted as a midwife."

"Wow, so young and yet so strong," said Alison.

Artemis smiled. "I was blessed with vigour."

"Did you meet Zeus?" Alison asked.

"Oh yes. I was three years old when my mother presented me at the court of Olympus. I remember it well." She smiled. "It was a festive occasion, and all the gods and goddesses were present. They made a fuss of my long blonde curls and had me laughing, but then, when I saw my father's bearded face, I burst into tears. Zeus smiled and told me funny stories until I laughed again. Then he declared that because I was fearless, I could have anything I desired."

Alison's eyes widened. "Really?"

Artemis nodded. "Hera jumped up, her eyes wide with indignation, but Zeus held up his hand. 'Hera, my dear, this child is so charming that even you cannot stand in the way of my decision.'"

"What did you ask for?"

"I declared myself a nature spirit, born under the feminine sign of the moon, and so I asked for the freedom to roam the world and help those in need."

"Zeus replied, 'Then a hunter and not the hunted you shall be.' He ordered the finest bow and arrows and invited me to choose the best hounds in his stables and the liveliest nymphs to accompany me. I was so pleased. Seeing the delight in my eyes, my mother beamed with pride."

"So, you never married or had children?" said Alison.

"Oh, no. My essence is freedom," replied the goddess.

Alison sighed. "I was never free on the earthly plane, and even now, I feel trapped," she said, her voice tinged with frustration.

"Your time will come, for your spirit shines bright," said Artemis. "Just re-member, it takes two to tango." She paused; her eyes shifted. "I hear a wild boar." Artemis reached for her bow and quiver of arrows. "Elek, Theron, let us go!" And with that, they soared into the night sky.

Ian blinked. "These goddesses are quite extraordinary. So, getting back to our situation, what are your thoughts?"

Alison shook her head. "All I know is we're here to stay."

26

The Oneiroi

THE RESORT CATERED TO all culinary tastes, and the kitchen was constantly in high demand. It had been a long day. It was late by the time Alison retired to her room.

She heard a knock.

A woman in a hotel uniform stood at the door. She smiled. "Hi, I'm Grace. I saw you in reception the other day and just wanted to say hello."

"Yes. I picked up a delivery there," said Alison. "Come in."

Grace sat down. "You're new here?"

Alison nodded. "Have you been here long?"

Grace sighed. "Too long."

"It is quite a resort," said Alison.

"Yes," said Grace. "It's currently being expanded. They're bringing in more workers."

"Where do they come from?"

"Oh, here and there. Many are on their way to Earth, and the resort is just one of the many perks they receive on the way. Strange, aren't they?"

"They sure are," said Alison. "Whenever I try to strike up a conversation, they stare at me, like I'm speaking another language."

Grace chuckled. "They act like automatons, but from the light in your eyes, I see you're normal."

"I don't know about normal." Alison shook her head. "I get depressed at times."

"At least you have feelings, unlike those zombies."

"Zombies?" said Alison. "What are they?"

"Non-thinking humans, shut down by fear and numbed by the twisted ideas implanted in their minds." Grace shook her head. "Sad, really, seeing them go through the motions of life without really living. But this is what the leaders want, a population of compliant slaves."

"What do you think of them, the Princes of Darkness?"

"I see them as shapeshifters and masters of illusion," said Grace. "I'm wary of their charms. They could fool anyone."

"They can't fool me," said Alison. "So, how did you end up here, on this island?"

Grace took a breath. "I was still on Earth when the values I took for granted unravelled before my eyes. Everywhere, from schools to hospitals, collapsed like a pack of cards."

"Wow, that must have been a shock."

"It was." Grace nodded. "Those who protested were silenced. Strange, but most people failed to recognise the perpetrators, much like when one marriage partner bullies the other into submission, but the victim remains loyal."

"I understand," said Alison. "Tell me, how did you survive?"

Grace took a deep breath. "I was part of a group. We met in secret to support each other and raise our awareness. The sense of belonging helped us remain steady whenever a wave of atrocities struck." A shadow passed over her eyes. "I was working in childcare when, one day, a group of soldiers burst in and began assaulting us with their rifles. They ripped the screaming children from our arms..." Her voice broke.

Alison's mouth dropped open.

"The incident didn't even make the news. The authorities were in denial, and the distraught parents couldn't get answers."

"That's shocking," Alison whispered, her thoughts turning to her daughters.

"It wasn't long after that God spirited me away."

"You ascended?"

Grace nodded. "I like to think so. There was an illness going around, and my body wasn't strong enough to fight it. In a way, I was relieved to be out of there, but when I arrived in the City of Dreams and heard they were demanding everyone be reborn, I fled to the mountains. Eventually, they caught up with me, and because I refused to return to Earth, they sent me here." She sighed. "So, how did you arrive?"

"I came here with Ian."

"Ian?" Grace paused. "I don't think I've seen him lately."

Alison shook her head. "I haven't either. I think he's on another part of the island. Anyway, we were duped. We accepted an offer from the goddess Eris, who promised us a holiday." She exhaled.

"Eris, you mean Ares' sister and comrade?"

Alison nodded slowly. "Yes, I know it wasn't a smart move."

"Don't be too hard on yourself," said Grace. "It doesn't matter where you go these days; there's no escaping their web of maliciousness."

Alison smiled. "You seem so calm and level-headed."

"I try to stay positive, but it's a constant struggle. I think of it as a battle of good and evil, and I can tell you now, I don't always win." Grace stood up. "I should get back to my post now. It was nice talking to you."

"And you," said Alison. As Grace walked through the door, she felt comforted knowing that she had an ally in this strange and hostile place.

That night, as Alison lay on her bed, memories flooded her mind. She longed to see her daughters; to tell them she loved them one last time.

The dream spirits, the *Oneiroi*, intercepted her thoughts, taking her deeper and deeper into the world of dreams until she no longer existed as a human, but as a tiny bird trapped in a cage. Her wings beat frantically against the bars as she tried to escape.

Phobeter, the phantom of nightmares, opened the cage door. "Fly free," he said. She clung to her perch, trembling. Suddenly, he grabbed the cage and tipped it upside down. Frozen with terror, she spiralled downwards through time and space, landing on a grassy verge. People hurried past her on the footpath; their eyes fixed on the glowing screens. Headlights dazzled and sirens wailed.

Terrified, the tiny bird fluttered into the air. Higher and higher she flew until she came to rest on the railing of an apartment balcony. Behind the glass door, a woman and a man sat in front of a flickering screen. Gazing through the glass, she realised. *That's Emma, my daughter!*

No sooner had she recognised her daughter than the bird that had carried her awareness vanished and her ethereal form emerged. She floated into the room, her presence unseen.

A knock sounded at the door, and another woman entered.

"Hi, sis," said Emma, smiling as she held up a packet of nuts. "Want some?"

"Thanks, I'm famished." Haley took a handful and settled onto the lounge. "What are you watching?"

"Nothing much, just the news." Emma reached for the remote and switched it off.

Alison smiled. *My girls... how they've grown up.* Through the veil, she felt their energies—Haley's quiet strength, Emma's gentleness. Emma's hand drifted to her belly. Alison sensed the new life within.

"How have you been?" Emma asked.

"I'm okay," Haley sighed. "Work's exhausting. We're short staffed again, turning patients away." A faint smile crossed her face. "But at least I'm helping where I can. And you?"

Emma hesitated. "I'm doing all right; it's just that I'm nervous—what will happen when the time comes."

"I'll be there for you," said Haley. "Don't worry. You'll be fine. You've always been strong."

Emma exhaled. "Thanks, sis."

Alison wanted to whisper that she was proud, but then Emma's husband appeared. He set some drinks on the coffee table. "Did you hear about the neighbours? They sent them to a re-education camp. Apparently, it was to correct their thinking."

Haley's brow furrowed. "Oh, no. What's going to happen next?"

"Who knows?" he said, nodding grimly, and went back to the kitchen.

The sisters sat in uneasy silence. The world outside seemed fragile, trembling on the edge of change.

Alison drew closer. A longing grew within her. *They need hope;* she thought. *Not comfort but truth.*

Emma was the first to sense her mother's presence. She froze. "Did you feel that...?" she whispered.

Haley followed her gaze. Seeing a shimmer in the air, her breath caught. "Oh, my Lord... It's Mum, isn't it?" she murmured.

Alison hesitated; afraid her presence might scare them. Then, seeing their tear-filled eyes, she conveyed a message from her heart to theirs.

Do not fear the collapsing world, she whispered across the veil. *The world you know is changing. Look within, remember who you are... beings of light.*

Silence hung in the air.

Alison wasn't sure if they'd caught her meaning.

Emma's eyes grew wide. She pressed her hands to her heart. "I always knew she would be back." Her lips trembled. "It's a message. I can feel it. She's telling us to stay centred, to remember who we are. To hold our light, even when everything changes."

Haley nodded. "I need to learn how to meditate."

"It's something I've been wanting to try as well," said Emma.

Alison smiled. Her daughters had sensed her heartfelt message. Warmth filled the room as her form faded and she became a bird once more. She fluttered through the open window.

Her daughters followed. From the balcony, they watched the little bird fly away.

On and on she flew, her heart bursting with joy. Flying felt so natural, so exhilarating.

Her reverie ended, and Alison opened her eyes.

Oh... what a beautiful feeling, she thought as she longed for a few more moments of blissful freedom.

❋

The following morning, Alison, Winnie and Kayla sat at the kitchen table, enjoying a batch of freshly baked scones.

Suddenly, the door burst open, and the housekeeper rushed in, waving a piece of paper. "Attention, everyone. Fifty guests are arriving for a special three-day event." She handed the memo to the Cook and left the room.

The cook glanced at the piece of paper. "Hosted by Phobos. Must be important."

At the mention of his name, Alison felt the dread creep up her spine.

Winnie looked up from her magazine. "I hope it's not like the last time—three days of existential chaos."

Kayla nodded. "Yeah, like a jumping castle full of two-year-olds."

Alison's eyebrows raised.

The Cook glared. "There's no need for that."

Winnie flipped the magazine page. "There he is, the man of my dreams."

Kayla leant over. "Domitius, the Roman gladiator."

"He's so handsome," sighed Winnie.

"Now, ladies, time to get back to work," said the Cook, abruptly.

That evening, in her room, Alison heard a rap at her door.

The housekeeper handed her a bundle. "You'll be required to wait on guests tomorrow," she said.

"Can't I stay in the kitchen?" asked Alison.

The housekeeper shook her head. "Sorry, we're short-staffed."

Alison undid the bundle, and a frilly apron unfolded in her hands. "Oh, dear," she said as she placed it on the dresser. She undid her ponytail and ran a brush through her hair.

The door opened behind her. She spun around.

"Ian!"

He closed the door quietly behind him. "Sorry, I can't stay long. I just wanted to drop by to see how you are."

Seeing his eyes ringed with shadows, she reached out to take his hand. "Are you okay?"

"I'm fine," he said, wrapping his arms around her in a warm embrace.

"Where have you been? They're not trying to brainwash you, are they?"

"No." His hands rested lightly on her shoulders. "I can't say any more."

Alison sighed. "Have you spoken to Joel?"

Ian nodded. "Yes, he's doing a lot better now that he's meditating."

She smiled. "Give him my love."

"I will," said Ian. "Sorry, but I have to go."

"When will I see you again?" Alison blurted.

"Soon, hopefully."

With a heavy heart, Alison said goodbye.

What's the secrecy? she wondered as she drifted off to sleep.

27

The Magician

ALISON AWOKE TO PEALS of laughter and the sound of footsteps running up the stairs. She hurried along the corridor, catching up with pyjama-clad girls who jostled for a position in front of the window. She strained her neck. Outside in the early morning light, a fleet of black limousines crawled towards the motel. One by one, the car doors opened as otherworldly beings spilled out in their glittering finery, traipsing towards the front entrance.

"I hope they keep their hands to themselves this time," said one girl.

Behind them, the housekeeper clapped her hands. "OK, show's over. Time to get ready for work."

The morning went quickly, and later Alison returned to her room. She pulled on the frilly uniform, applied some lipstick and tied her hair in a bun. She gazed at her reflection in the mirror and smiled. This is all just a performance, she mused.

The ballroom glittered with white tablecloths and vases filled with roses. The dance floor, polished to perfection, caught the light of the chandeliers. On stage, the musicians tuned their instruments. Soon they struck up a gentle melody.

Alison and Winnie set each place with silverware, glasses and napkins.

"Hey, Winnie, who are the guests?" asked Alison.

"I call them humanoids," Winnie smiled. "They try to pass as human, but they're shadowy and fickle. They can transform from pleasant to fiendish in a second."

Alison shook her head. "How strange."

"You'll see."

The guests swept inside in their elaborate gowns and sparkling jewels. Seated at the tables, the scene resembled a royal banquet. They engaged in genial conversation while servers glided around with trays of steaming soup and bread rolls. The appetisers ended, and the main course appeared.

Alison carried a large plate and a spoon. "May I offer you some carrots, peas and potatoes?"

"What, no blood?" remarked an excitable woman in a crimson gown.

"Sorry, ma'am," said Alison.

A bearded man fingered his dinner knife. "Do you have anything sharper?"

Before Alison could answer, the man next to him drew a large knife from his pocket. "Perhaps this will suffice."

Alison quickly stepped aside.

The meal ended peacefully, and a Magician stepped onto the stage. The guests sat back in anticipation as he drew an endless array of scarves and flowers from a hat. They smiled and applauded, caught up in the magic of it all.

Winnie leant over. "Be careful of Shay," she whispered.

"Why?" said Alison.

"She once worked for a cartel smuggling drugs and weapons. Her weapon of choice is dual daggers. Whatever you do, don't mention her ears."

Alison gulped. "Thanks for the warning."

The Magician ended with a flaming display of sword swallowing. As he breathed out, flames escaped, setting the stage alight. Thinking it was part of the show, the guests whistled and cheered.

Alison's eyes widened. "What's going on?" she whispered.

Winnie shook her head. "I don't know."

A trombone player quickly grabbed a fire extinguisher and put out the fire just before it reached the curtains. The Magician fled the charred stage, and the orchestra struck up a tune.

Laughter and chatter echoed as groups drifted out onto the lawn. Inside, they cleared the hall, ready for the ball.

A waltz began as the orchestra played, and the dance floor soon filled with women in glittering evening gowns gracefully twirling and spinning in the arms of their tuxedo-clad partners.

Alison and Winnie returned their trolleys to the kitchen. The housekeeper did a quick headcount. She frowned. "We're down one. Where's Kayla?"

"Last time I saw her, she was collecting plates," said Alison.

"Come with me," she said as she stormed from the room.

Alison followed her into the night. A full moon cast shadows on the lawn. They made their way to the guest quarters. Suddenly, they heard a scream. Alison looked up to see Kayla waving from a balcony. A figure grabbed her from behind and dragged her inside.

The housekeeper pursed her lips and strode through the front door. The lift flew up to the third floor and shuddered to a halt. They hurried down the corridor and halted outside room thirty-four.

The housekeeper knocked firmly, then waited. She jangled the keys. "Percival, open the door, or I'll use the master."

Alison heard the sound of footsteps, and the door swung open. A man appeared. He leaned on his walking stick. "Hello, Marion, my dear. What can I do for you?"

"You know what I want, Percival. Give her back."

His face fell. "You know I wouldn't do her any harm. I just wanted someone to talk to."

"Of course," said the housekeeper. "Now, where is she?"

"But I haven't finished with her yet." His eyes glinted, and his teeth grew until they protruded from his drooling mouth.

Alison's eyes widened, and she took a step back.

"No need to impress me with your werewolf impersonation," said the housekeeper. "We're about to serve dessert, and Kayla is on duty."

"Dessert... oh!" he said brightly.

"All your favourites—pavlova, tiramisu and cupcakes."

"Cupcakes?" Percival's fangs receded, and the old man took his walking stick and shuffled towards the bathroom. "Kayla, there's someone here for you."

The housekeeper pushed open the door.

Kayla sat dejectedly on the rim of the bathtub.

"About time," she said.

Alison and Kayla followed the housekeeper down the corridor.

"Has this happened before?" whispered Alison.

Kayla nodded. "Oh yes, it's all part of the game. Speaking of games, as we were coming up, I saw Ian going into room thirty-eight."

"Ian?" Alison's mouth dropped open. "What's he doing here?"

"We'll soon find out," said the housekeeper as she swung around and marched back along the corridor. She thumped on the door with her palm. An elfin creature with pointed ears answered. "Oh, it's you, Albit," she said. "I'm looking for Ian. Have you seen him?"

The elf stared at her blankly. "Umm... maybe?"

Ian's head appeared around the door. "Here I am."

The housekeeper's cheeks flushed a deep shade of crimson. "Ian, you know very well that the guest rooms are off-limits." Her eyes darted nervously along the corridor.

Albit held up his hand. "It's okay. He has permission from Phobos."

The housekeeper's eyebrows shot up in surprise. "Oh, you're working for him?"

Albit nodded. "We sure are."

"Well, in that case, I'll arrange for food to be sent over. What would you like?"

"Some snacks would be great," said Ian.

"Much appreciated." Albit closed the door.

They hurried back to the kitchen. The housekeeper filled a basket with cakes, fruit and biscuits. She waved to Alison. "Here, take this over to Albit and be smart about it."

Alison carried the basket to room thirty-eight and knocked on the door.

Ian opened it. "Hey Alison, come in." He closed the door behind her.

She placed the basket on the coffee table and looked over at Albit, who sat in front of a bank of buzzing computers. Her eyebrows raised. "Oh, computer games—lucky for some."

Ian smiled as he walked her to the door.

"So, who is he?" she whispered.

"Albit?" said Ian. "He's Avery's cousin."

Alison nodded. "Oh, of course."

"I'll tell you more later," whispered Ian as he opened the door.

The full moon cast ghostly shadows on the lawn. A wave of uneasiness coursed through Alison as she walked along the path. She stepped into the kitchen and looked around. The Cook appeared red-faced and flustered.

Winnie sat at the table, her arms folded. "I'm not going back," she said.

"Hey, Kayla," whispered Alison. "What's going on?"

"It's Domitius, the Adonis. He took offence when the knight Glynn cut in on Antonia, the princess with the poofy dress. A fight began on the dance floor. When Shay brought out her daggers and started egging them on, we had to get out of there quick."

"Perhaps it's the full moon," said Alison.

"Humph!" Winnie exhaled. "Seems it's always a full moon with this lot."

The housekeeper hurried breathlessly through the kitchen door. "All is clear. The guests are outside. Don't worry, they'll soon burn themselves out."

"Okay, girls," said the Cook. "You heard the housekeeper. It's safe for you to take the sweets to the servery."

Grudgingly, Winnie stood up and together they pushed the trolleys to the ballroom. The sounds of yelling and cheering drifted through the open window. After filling the servery, they hurried over to look outside. Moonlight illuminated the white sand. The guests had separated into opposing camps. Some were brandishing knives and swords. Others hid behind large shields. Suddenly, they launched a full-on attack, charging at one another.

Alison gasped, and Kayla giggled.

"Back here, girls," called the housekeeper.

After a while, the sounds of battle cries and clashing steel faded. The guests wandered in, dishevelled and pumped with energy.

Percival hobbled up to the dessert bar. His eyes twinkled mischievously. "Marvellous how the sea air gives one an appetite. I'll have a slice of everything."

A bearded man approached, sporting a fresh wound above his eye. "Invigorating, absolutely invigorating," he said. "Love this place, but you need to sharpen those knives."

"I always bring my own," said Shay as she straightened her ballgown. "Damn these gowns; they always get in the way."

A broad-shouldered gladiator strode in, a victorious grin on his face. His ripped shirt revealed his muscular chest. He whispered to one of the serving girls, who blushed and lowered her eyes.

Antonia followed demurely, the hem of her poofy dress wet.

Glynn, the knight, limped up to the dessert bar. He pointed. "What's that concoction?"

"Pavlova, sir. It's very nice," said Winnie.

"Oh, good. Be a dear and bring me a double portion." He limped away.

The guests ate peacefully while the band serenaded with a medley of songs from the First World War. Their music faded, and the stage curtain slowly opened to the thunderous beat of drums.

A mist swirled, and a figure in a top hat and cape stepped out. The Magician was back!

A hush fell over the room as all eyes turned to the stage.

With a flourish, he tossed back his cape. "And now, for my last act of the evening, I present to you a special guest." He reached into his top hat and pulled out a furry creature with enormous eyes. The creature whirred, and its fur changed from pink to green. "I give to you the Little Ones!" he declared.

The guests gasped with delight.

The Magician looked out into the crowd. "Can I have a volunteer from the audience?"

Antonia thrust her hand into the air.

The Magician pointed. "Princess Antonia, come on up."

Antonia hurried up the stairs, stumbling in her high heels. She took the tiny creature and held it to her chest. "How adorable," she said as it purred with delight. "Can I show him around?"

"Why, of course," said the Magician. "There's more where that came from."

The creature made contented noises as the guests stroked its silky fur. The ladies giggled when it changed colour from green to blue and then pink again.

"The Little Ones make ideal pets," he announced.

Shay raised her hand. "Can I have one?"

Others waved their hands. "I want one, too," they cried.

"Only if you promise to feed and care for them," said the Magician.

"Oh yes," they nodded eagerly.

"Well, then, come on up." The Magician drew Little Ones, one after another, out of the hat.

Cradling the creatures, the guests wandered outside. "I think I'll call him Domitius," crooned Antonia as she walked by.

Alison turned to the housekeeper. "Can we have one as a mascot?"

The housekeeper looked at her aghast. "Not on your life. Now get to it and collect the cutlery and bowls."

It was later that evening. Alison and Winnie were washing up in the kitchen when they heard a knock at the door. Antonia stood there looking bewildered, her hands lacerated and bloody. "Have you seen the Magician?" she asked.

"No, why?" replied the housekeeper.

"He didn't tell us the little devils grow spikes, and not only that, they have an enormous appetite and gobble everything in sight. They're taking over the guest quarters and giving us hell!"

"Sorry, dear, I hear he checked out after the show." The housekeeper closed the door, wiping a tear of laughter from her eyes. "Dear me," she said. "It happens every time."

"Without fail!" said the Cook, laughing and slapping her thigh. "Now, where did I put the Pied Piper's number?"

28

Bogaris

THE KITCHEN WAS A constant hive of activity: cooking, serving and washing up. Weighed down by the tedium of it all, Alison trudged through the day. She yearned for something more, something beyond the daily routine, a spark of excitement, a glimmer of adventure, anything to break the monotony of the routine.

The following morning, she scanned the roster, and there it was: 'Cleaning Duties' next to her and Winnie's names.

The air was sweet with the scent of flowers as they stepped outside. Alison took a deep breath. "It's good to get out of the kitchen."

"Sure is!" said Winnie.

They strolled along the footpath, past couples sitting on benches, while others strolled beneath leafy trees.

"Strange how enemies can become friends in this place," said Winnie.

"Maybe those pesky little creatures were a blessing in disguise," said Alison. "They seemed to bring everyone together. Did you hear, they had to hire a Pied Piper to get rid of them?"

Winnie smiled longingly. "Yes, I saw him. He was so handsome, I wouldn't mind following him myself."

Alison's pace slowed. "Strange, but I dreamt last night of a Romeo who swept me off my feet."

"Wow, lucky you," replied Winnie. "Perhaps the goddess Aphrodite paid you a visit."

The lobby door slid open. They passed by the fernery with a waterfall trickling over rocks.

Winnie emerged from the storeroom, pushing a trolley with cleaning supplies. The lift took them up. The doors slid open with a soft hiss. They made their way along the hallway, stopping to clean each room. Finally, they reached a door with a plaque that read Royal Suite.

"I heard Ares stays here," said Winnie.

Alison's eyes widened. "Let's look inside." She pushed the door and gazed at the plush rugs and mirrors adorning the walls. The beds with their white embroidered quilts looked like clouds.

Winnie sighed. "I'd give anything to live like this."

"But at what cost?" asked Alison.

"Who cares?" said Winnie.

Alison fought the urge to shake her, tell her to wake up, but in her heart, she realised everyone chooses their own path. She closed the door and pushed the trolley to the lift and then out into the lobby. A flurry of activity signalled a fleet of limousines.

"Let's stay awhile," Winnie whispered.

Alison nodded. "Okay. We need some light relief."

Alison pushed the trolley into the storeroom. "Come in," she said. "We can watch from here."

A flock of elegant men and women swept into the lobby. Their stylish clothes and jewellery sparkled under the lights. A woman in a glittering gown planted a kiss on a man's cheek. "Hello, darling," she cooed. "This is such fun, isn't it?"

"Oh, yes," he replied, his voice oozing with charm. "Each time I see you, you look younger."

"My dear, you flatter me." Her laughter echoed as she sauntered towards the lift.

A group of designer humans entered the lobby like living dolls with their perfectly composed façades.

"Wow, they're gorgeous," Winnie whispered. "They must be the new breed of trans-humans. We'll soon be obsolete."

Alison smiled. "You'll never be obsolete, Winnie. Have you seen enough?"

Winnie nodded, and they slipped out of the storeroom and walked towards the door, just as a group of men in black suits and sunglasses strode inside. Alison recognised them from Ares' castle. One of them locked eyes with her. Her heart rate quickened. Thinking quickly, she grabbed Winnie's hand. "Come on. Let's go." She hurried to the door.

Seeing their uniforms, the man turned away.

Alison hurried down the stairs, almost colliding with a man in a tailored suit. "Sorry," she said. For a moment, his gaze met hers. She looked away quickly, trying to hide her blush.

They returned to the kitchen to find everyone bustling about in a flurry of activity.

The housekeeper approached Alison. "Phobos is arriving tonight. He and his secretary will have their meals in the penthouse suite. Can I leave you in charge?"

Alison's face paled. "Okay," she ventured.

That evening, Alison made her way to the West Wing with a gleaming trolley filled with hors d'œuvres, main course and sweets. Grace waved to her as she entered the lobby. "Pop in when you're finished."

"Sure," said Alison as she pushed the trolley into the lift. She pressed a button, then waited.

"Penthouse," said the voice.

Alison knocked. The door opened, and the scent of cologne and freshly cut flowers wafted towards her. She recognised the suave gentleman she had almost collided with on the stairs. His presence made her heart flutter.

"I have a meal order for Phobos," she said.

He smiled. "I'll make sure he gets it."

She placed the containers on the side table and turned to leave.

He reached into the inner pocket of his coat and pulled out a gold-rimmed card. "Here," he said, handing it to her.

She glanced at the card. It read, 'Mr Bogaris Themis, Private Secretary'.

"And you are...?"

"Alison," she replied, tucking the card into her pocket. With hurried steps, she pushed the trolley out of the room. Once on the ground floor, she left the trolley in a corner and made her way to the reception desk.

Grace smiled. "Hi, Alison. How are you?"

Alison leaned on the desk. "Confused."

"Oh, what's up?"

"I find it strange that we should run around like old-fashioned servants. After all, these gods have the power to have anything they want?"

"It's confusing all right, but the fact remains: the gods revel in tradition. They enjoy the attention that humans give them. Our servitude is a token, a reminder of who's in charge—who is serving whom."

"I guess you're right," said Alison. They chatted for a while and then Alison returned to the kitchen.

That night, she fell into bed, her mind in a whirl.

If only I could talk to Ian, she thought as she drifted off to sleep. It wasn't long before the ruggedly handsome Bogaris entered the fabric of her dreams, like a knight in shining armour, releasing her from the drudgery of everyday life.

She awoke to see a glimmer as a small creature disappeared through the wall. *Hmm, the Oneiroi,* she thought.

Alison met the housekeeper in the kitchen. "Only two for breakfast this morning. One on the first floor and another in the penthouse suite. Phobos is hosting breakfast on board their super-sized yacht," she said.

Alison and Winnie placed the meals in heated trolleys and pushed them towards the guest quarters. Winnie took the meal to the first floor, and Alison continued to the penthouse.

She knocked on the door, her heart racing.

Bogaris answered the door dressed in casual jeans and a blue shirt. "Come in," he said.

She placed the containers on the sideboard and turned to leave.

Bogaris moved towards the door.

"Do you have a few moments to spare? I was wondering if you'd like to take a stroll along the beach tomorrow evening."

Alison's heart leapt at the thought of the waves and warm sand between her toes. She replied hesitantly, "It's off limits for us."

"Listen, if anyone says anything, I'll take full responsibility," Bogaris smiled. "I'll meet you near the dunes after work."

After a moment's hesitation, Alison nodded. "Okay, but I won't be able to stay long."

Alison pushed the trolley along the path, giddy with excitement. *The handsome prince and the maiden at the palace gates.*

Winnie's voice disturbed her fantasy. "Only two more days," said Winnie. "After the ball, I'm leaving."

"Oh?" Alison's brow furrowed. "Where will you go?"

"I'm going to parents who will love me."

A pang of longing filled Alison's chest. "Oh, Winnie, I'll miss you, but you're right; you don't deserve this servitude. You deserve a loving family."

Love... her thoughts returned to her own fantasy as she wondered, *who is this mysterious prince who sweeps me off my feet?*

✳

The following day flew by. Buoyed by the promise of a clandestine adventure, Alison packed the last of the crockery onto the shelves, then she opened the kitchen door and crept into the night air.

There he was, standing in the moonlight, looking more handsome than ever.

Bogaris' eyes glistened. "Alison, how lovely to see you."

"Hello," she said shyly.

They made their way across the lawn and were soon out of sight of the kitchen. Once on the sand, Alison kicked off her shoes and sank her toes into the warm sand. "How wonderful!" she cried, racing down the dunes, the breeze blowing through her hair. Splashing through the shallows, she flashed a playful smile.

Afterward, they strolled along the beach. She turned to Bogaris. "Why are you interested in an ordinary mortal like me?"

"You're hardly ordinary," he replied.

"Oh, really?"

"Tomorrow is my last day here, but I want to stay on. I'd like to get to know you better."

Alison shook her head. "Sorry, but I'm working."

"I can get you time off. I have connections in high places," he smiled. "I'm Prince Bogaris, named after the majestic snow leopard. And in the future, I'll rule the world, or at least part of it."

Alison's eyebrows arched. His words sounded strangely familiar.

She felt the water lapping around her ankles. *Oh, what the heck,* she thought, *why not enjoy the moment?*

They reached the headland, and Bogaris sprang onto a boulder. He held out his hand and pulled her onto the weather-worn outcrop. Alison wandered across the rocks, stopping to gaze into the moonlit pools, marvelling at the tiny sea creatures.

Bogaris fought the urge to run his fingers through her hair. "Do you believe in love?" he whispered.

"Of course," she answered. "Isn't it everyone's dream to have someone special?"

"I like that about you, the way we share the same dream of love divine." A soft smile spread across his face. "Love isn't just between two people. It's the current that binds the cosmos. You and I, we've touched that love before."

The dream of love divine... the words echoed in her mind. She saw herself as a fresh-faced teenager in the red chiffon dress, her hair falling stylishly over her shoulders. Alison opened her eyes and twirled, her dress swirling.

"You look stunning." His voice was low. "Do you ever long for your very own Prince Charming?"

"Oh, yes," she sighed. Overcome with euphoria, the jagged rock beneath her feet vanished, and in its place, a polished wooden floor. Waltz music filled the air, enveloping her in a long-forgotten grandeur.

With a flourish, Bogaris held out his hand. "Let us dance, now and forever, across the lifetimes?"

She laughed. "You make it sound eternal."

"We are eternal, you and I. Don't you feel it?" He drew her close, and together they spun across the dance floor, their bodies moving to the rhythm of the music. The stars above shimmered, and for a moment, everything else slipped away.

The music faded, but the feeling of warmth remained. He leaned in, his voice tender. "Alison, my dear," he whispered, dropping to one knee. "Marry me. Unite both heart and mind. Together we will create a paradise in this broken world."

Alison stepped back. "Oh! I'm flattered, I really am, but we only just met. I can't make such a commitment at this stage."

"Why not?" Bogaris gazed up at her, his eyes bright with ardour. "I fell in love with you the moment I saw you. You are the light in my life, my other half." He extended his hand, and the webbing between his fingers glistened in the moonlight. "We're soul mates, remember? Together, we will rule the world, or at least our little corner of it."

His hands—his words? Alison froze as if trapped in a dream. She blinked, trying to awaken. In his eyes, she glimpsed a frozen wasteland; the domain of the snow leopard. A chill ran down her spine. Beneath her feet, the dance floor disappeared, leaving her standing on solid rock once more.

She took a deep breath. "It's late," she said, trying to hide her unease. "I really should head back."

"Nonsense," he replied. "The night is young. Let us walk and continue to get to know each other."

Fast-moving clouds veiled the moon, and the salt wind gusted. A stabbing pain of fear gripped her belly. "They'll send a search party."

He sensed the urgency in her voice. "Don't worry, my dear. I arranged it all with Phobos. We can stay out as long as we like."

The waves crashed against the rocks, sending spray high into the air. Alison shivered.

Persephone, please help me! She pleaded.

A voice replied. *'Sorry, I don't do beach scenes.'*

Alison blinked. *What?*

'Try Athena instead.'

Alison looked up at the night sky and sent her plea into the silent space.

Goddess Athena,
warrior of the night
I could really use your help right now
Help me see what's real.
And what's just in my head.

A streak of light flared across the heavens. The shooting star drifted downwards, its radiance expanding. The goddess appeared, bathed in light.

'How can I help?' Athena conveyed her words silently through her mind.

I feel like I'm trapped in a dream, Alison answered.

'A dream? Athena's gaze shifted to Bogaris. *But he looks real enough to me.'*

Athena's light flared, and all at once, the goddess of war became visible to his eyes.

Bogaris glared. "Who is this who dares challenge the great Snow Leopard?"

The goddess held her sword high. "Athena, the goddess of war!"

He sneered. "Goddesses are nothing but mere legend—fantasy."

Athena's eyes narrowed. "Of course, how remiss of me. I must have missed the part when you tried to erase our story—because we're still here!"

His eyes widened. "Are you questioning history?"

"History was no more than advancing your own agenda, and to what end?" Her eyes flashed. "What exactly is your goal?"

Bogaris' chest swelled. "To create Utopia on Earth."

"And for whom?"

The veins in his temples bulged. Bogaris raised his voice. "For us, of course—the Princes of Darkness. We are the conquerors of this world, now and forevermore!"

Athena's eyes narrowed. "And what of humanity, when they rise against you, as they have done many times before?"

"Foolish humans." Bogaris' smile widened into a sinister grin. "We will crush the spirit of anyone who stands in our way."

Athena raised her sword. "There is more to power than physical might." With a cry, she brought her sword down, sending Bogaris crashing to the ground. "Know this—the goddess will always be victorious!"

Bogaris lay on the rocks, his chest heaving. Then, with a roar, he leapt to his feet. "You cannot destroy me."

Athena's grip tightened. "Maybe not, but I can reveal your true nature," she said in a low voice. She swung the sword, unleashing a powerful flame that ripped through Bogaris' façade. With a bloodcurdling scream, his handsome face melted like glass, revealing a twisted and repulsive creature.

Alison gasped. Before her stood Egor, the shape-shifting egomaniac with bad breath and a dangerous temper.

Egor's eyes alighted on her, and his grin widened. "Humans need us—they like us." He walked towards her, arms outstretched.

She quickly pushed him away.

Athena raised her sword high, her eyes blazing. "This war will not be fought on a battlefield, but within the hearts and minds of those you oppress in pursuit of your delusional dreams." Without hesitation, she threw the glowing sword toward Alison. "Cut away the old narrative that keeps you trapped in this web of delusions and remember who you are."

"But—" Alison froze, eyes wide. "I thought you'd save me!"

A wave of despair crashed over her as Athena's form faded into the night.

Alison looked down at the sword pulsing in her hand. For a moment, she didn't know what to do. Then warmth flooded her arm, spreading through her chest. She heard a whisper. *'Nothing can separate you from your innate power.'* Her fingers gripped the hilt. "All right," she murmured. "Let's see what we can do." The sword glowed like a living flame in her hands. Alison lifted it instinctively, feeling the weight and balance as though she'd wielded it before.

Egor's face blurred, his features melting and reforming until Bogaris stood in his place. He smiled. "Now, where were we before we were so rudely interrupted? Ah, of course," he said, as if remembering his lines. His gaze softened. "You carry a flame I have sought across lifetimes. I see you, I understand you, my dear," he said, leaning closer.

His words struck a chord. "You do?"

"To resist is to deny yourself... to deny the universe." Bogaris crooned, leaning closer.

But as he drew nearer, the smell of decay filled her nostrils. Revulsion surged through her. The illusion shattered. In that instant, Alison saw the inner pattern of seeking validation and acceptance from others. She shook her head. Gripping the sword, she affirmed her strength. "What do you want from me?!" she cried.

A sly grin formed on his lips. "I only want the love we shared. We go back a long way, remember?"

Alison's mind stilled. It was then that the veil fell, and she saw through the far-off mists of time to a mountain, wild and remote, where people danced a frenzied invocation to the gods.

She took a deep breath. "We go back a long way, but the party is over," she declared. "I never want to see you again."

"*Never* is a long time. Come with me. I'll give you everything you wanted." Bogaris held out his hand.

"I've heard that line before, and it's a lie." Alison raised the sword and brought it down on his hand.

Bogaris let out a bloodcurdling cry as his body contorted and twisted, transforming into the demon Egor. She felt a searing pain shoot through her cheek as his hand struck her. The sword slipped from her fingers, clattering against the rocks.

Egor's eyes blazed. "Do not defy me," he growled.

Alison reached for the sword, and Egor's foot came down heavily on the blade. Instantly, the sword ignited, and he cried out in agony. He staggered backwards from the scorching flames.

Alison grabbed the hilt and glared at the demon. "I order you to leave—now!"

Egor advanced, his mouth twisted into a snarl. "I give the orders here."

A gust of wind blew through her hair. "No, you don't." She swung the blade, and with a shriek, Egor collapsed, shadows coiling around him.

Alison stood, hands on her hips. "I'm no longer a pawn in your twisted game."

As she spoke, the shadows shifted. When they cleared, it was not Egor who stood in front of her, but Bogaris. "You don't seem yourself, my dear. Are you in your right mind?" Concern lined his forehead, and his voice was soft and measured.

Alison frowned. "Of course, I am." She drew a deep breath, steadying herself, but his carefully chosen words had unlocked a tremor of self-doubt.

His eyes softened. "Then why do you question my motive when all I did was care for you?"

Her voice faltered. "You... did?"

"Of course," Bogaris said with a smile. "Without me, you would never have made it in this harsh and unforgiving world."

Suddenly, the sword pulsed in her hand, its light erasing the haze that clouded her mind. The hypnotic dream faded. She glared at him. "You cared for no one but yourself!"

Bogaris' face flickered, then dissolved and Egor reappeared, his eyes burning with fury, his breath in harsh gasps. "How dare you insult me when I gave you everything your heart desired?" His words echoed into the darkness. "You need me. I'm your inspiration, your judgement, your *everything*! Without me, you'll perish alone... in the void!"

Alison's grip tightened on the sword. Her eyes narrowed. "I do not fear the void half as much as I fear your version of reality. It was grand, but in the end, it was only an illusion."

Egor's face twisted with hatred. "Then you leave me no choice," he said and unleashed a tidal wave of self-recrimination that crashed against her mind.

Alison's throat tightened as his thoughts, sharp as arrows, pierced her consciousness, each one dredging up a past mistake, a doubt, a poor decision.

The weight of hopelessness pressed in, but she stood firm. Her fingers tightened on the sword. She felt the power surging through her, lifting her awareness above the battlefield until she stood in a place of stillness, a place of oneness within.

Aum...

The sound filled her being, steady, luminous, eternal. Peace washed through her, and with it, her perception shifted. Looking down, she saw herself, not as a vulnerable woman fighting for her life, but as a spirit, timeless and unbroken. "At times I may have been sleepwalking," she said. "But I did my best with what I knew. Ultimately, it was my choice to experience life and learn from it."

As she spoke, the urge to fight faded. Looking down, she saw that the sword in her hand had become a single red rose. Peace filled her heart knowing that everything would be set right again. In that moment she realised it was not herself, but Egor, who was fighting for his life.

With the rose in her hand, Alison welcomed his curses, allowing them to wash away every trace of self-doubt and judgement until only pure consciousness radiated from within. Her heart filled with love, and the realisation struck her: *I am not the ego self, this mind-made monster, but a soul, loved for who I am.*

As the light in her eyes grew stronger, Egor's hope diminished. He slumped heavily onto a rock.

Alison looked at him calmly. "Do you have anything else to say?"

His eyes flickered. "Not really," he said as he dragged himself to his feet. He took one last glance at Alison, then jumped down from the rocks and trudged across the sand.

The clouds drifted, and the moon cast a silvery glow across the sea. She spread her arms. And like a phoenix rising from the ashes, she felt weightless and free. It was as if at any moment she could fly away. Then the memory of Ian tugged at her heart and the thought of their unfinished business.

Clutching the rose in her hand like a warrior of peace, Alison retraced her footsteps along the shoreline.

A gust of wind whipped her from behind as Athena zoomed by, her hair like a fiery comet's tail.

Alison's brow furrowed. *I wonder why the goddess is in such a hurry?*

29

The Deception Breaker

ALISON RAN UP THE dunes. She found her shoes and strolled across the lawn. As she neared the courtyard, she heard a sound.

"Psst..."

She stopped. Cautiously, she peered into the leafy arbour. "Ian!"

"Hey, Alison," Ian said hoarsely. "I've been looking everywhere for you."

She stepped inside, her hair tousled and sand still clinging to her feet.

"Thank goodness you're safe." He reached up and took her hand. "Where have you been?"

"At the beach."

His eyes widened. "What? Don't you know how dangerous that is?"

She handed him the rose. "I do now."

The perfume wafted into his nostrils, and the tension in his shoulders relaxed. "Oh, Alison, I'm sorry I neglected you, but work—you know."

"It's okay." Seeing the rings around his eyes, she frowned. "You look tired. What's going on?"

He leaned against the wall, his eyes half closed. "I've been putting in long hours to program a video game. It's Phobos' latest project. It's his pièce de résistance; version five of *Shadow Dreams*. He's going to launch it tomorrow after the ball."

"Not another game," she said.

Ian frowned. "This one's different. Through this, the demon's plan to tighten their net over the entire world."

"Oh, Ian." Alison exhaled. "How did you get roped into this?"

"Sorry, my fault," said Albit.

Alison turned.

The elf wandered in and sat down. "Phobos employed me to iron out the glitches."

"They trusted you?"

"They're under the impression that elves share their disdain for humans." Albit winked. "I did my best to fix the errors in the game, but we needed a human programmer, so that's where Ian came in."

"I had to sign a non-disclosure agreement," said Ian.

"So that accounts for the secrecy."

Ian nodded. "Yes, but I can't keep quiet any longer. This is not a game; it's cyberwar, and they have the upper hand." He sighed. "I helped create a monster, and now I don't know what to do."

"Why don't you alter the outcome of their game?" suggested Alison.

Albit nodded. "Yeah, that's what I've been telling him all along."

Ian shook his head. "Sure, guys, but what if I'm caught?"

Alison frowned. "You're concerned about yourself. What about humanity?"

He shook his head. "I-I just don't know."

Alison pondered for a moment. "Why not seek the advice of Athena?"

Albit raised his eyebrows. "The goddess of war?"

"That's right," said Alison. "Did you know Athena was born from Zeus' head?"

"Oh!" said Albit. "The goddesses are a mystery to me."

"How can Athena help?" said Ian.

"Why don't you ask?" came a voice from beyond. The courtyard filled with a soft haze, and Athena descended, her grey eyes glowing, shield and spear in hand.

"I took a tour of the island. Nice, isn't it?"

"Except for the guests," murmured Alison.

"I gather they can be troublesome at times." Athena smiled, then she turned to Ian. "Now, what's the problem?"

Ian took a deep breath and exhaled. "Phobos is about to launch a video game designed to infiltrate the minds of humans. If they release it, it's game over."

"Phobos, eh? And what is your role in this?" asked Athena.

Albit and I are programmers.

"Oh, I see." Athena frowned. "So, you're in a spot of bother."

Ian nodded. "You could say that."

Athena gazed into the distance. "Ares and I go back a long way, to the time of the Trojan War."

"So, you're familiar with their tactics?" said Ian.

"Absolutely. He and his sons, Phobos and Deimos, have been changing the face of war. For centuries, I struggled to prevent the expansion of the House of Ares. However, with every conflict, they only become stronger. Now, it seems we can no longer stop the escalation of their plans."

Ian frowned. "If the gods can't stop them, what hope have we?"

"Hope is not a strategy," said Athena. "What you need is a war cabinet." She laid down her weapons and sat on a nearby bench. "As you see, it is out of our hands, for the gods can no longer control them, but fear not, dear ones, humans possess great power, more than you realise. With your strength and cunning, you can easily outmanoeuvre the House of Ares and defeat their twisted plans."

"Do you really think so?" said Ian.

"Of course. This one-way game created by Phobos lacks the element of choice. In other words, it presumes that humans will follow their directions. You could add a little something to make it a two-way game."

"What do you mean?"

"I mean, given that you have free will, you can either choose to follow the directions of the demons or reject their age-old story and tap into the highest power and wisdom of the universe."

Ian's eyes widened. "So, you're saying we should corrupt their game?"

"Why not? After all, the demons are trying to corrupt you." Athena's lips curved into a smile. "Expose their plan, turn the game to your favour, and you can shift the tide."

Albit shot Ian a smug glance. "That's what I've been saying all along."

"Albit is right." Athena locked eyes with Ian. "Use your intellect and see the situation clearly. The theatre of war has changed. The battle for supremacy is no longer out there in the world anymore—it's in here." She tapped her temple. "In the mind."

Ian frowned. "What do you mean?"

"It's a subtle war," she said. "The weapons are your emotions—they use words to create fear, labels to create division and beliefs to undermine your very power. In this way, they turn people against each other, weakening their will."

He nodded slowly. "So, it's about control."

"Exactly." Athena's eyes flared. "Smoke and mirrors. Keep humans confused, and they stay compliant."

"How do we fight back?"

"Discernment," said Athena, "adds an element of transparency so people see through it all. Once they do, they will remember who they are—peaceful, compassionate and powerful. Difficult to scare or manipulate."

She reached over and fastened a small badge onto Ian's collar. "The owl stands for discernment. It's never deceived. It sees its prey, even in the dark. Do you understand?"

Ian nodded. "What you're saying is, humans are more powerful than the gods."

Athena smiled. "The secret is, human beings have autonomy and free will. These are your greatest weapons. While they may upset your plans, restrict you or change your surroundings, they need permission to manipulate your mind." Athena stood up and reached for her weapons. "No matter what happens, do not comply with fear. Guard your thoughts, for they are your own." She smiled, and with a rush of air, she vanished.

Ian stretched his arms. "Whew, that was some war cabinet." He turned to Albit. "What do you think?"

Albit smiled. "It should be easy enough to make it into a two-way game."

"What can we call it?" asked Ian.

They sat silently for a moment, then Alison spoke up. "It appears the demons are masters of deception. So how about *Deception Breaker*?"

"I like it," said Albit.

Ian smiled. "They'll be fuming when they discover what we've done." He turned to Alison. "That reminds me, I have to attend the launch, but afterwards, we need to get out, and quick."

"Okay," said Alison. "But what about Albit?"

The elf's eyes sparkled in the moonlight. "We come and go as we please. Put your trust in divine magic; that's what I always say." He rose from the bench. "Goodnight, my friends," he said, and sauntered away.

"We had better go too," said Alison.

Together, they walked along the path. Ian stopped at the kitchen door. "See you tomorrow," he whispered.

Alison nodded. "Good luck," she whispered back. She slipped inside and crept down the stairs. She opened her bedroom door and froze. In the dim light, she saw a shadow sitting in her chair. "Who's there?"

"It's just me," said Grace.

Alison flicked on the light switch. "Oh... Grace, are you okay?"

Grace shook her head; her eyes filled with tears. She sniffed. "I feel awful. My mind is spinning—I can't think straight anymore."

"Sounds like you're feeling the vibe," said Alison.

Grace blinked. "Why, what's happening?"

"Phobos is planning something big. It's a video game designed to enslave the minds of every human on the planet."

"Oh!" Grace gasped. "How dreadful. I don't feel safe here."

Alison nodded. "The general mood is deteriorating. I'm finding it harder to separate illusion from reality." She took a breath. "We're not waiting around. Once the video game launch is over, Ian and I are leaving."

Grace wiped her eyes with the back of her hand. "Can I come with you—please?"

Alison frowned. "It'll be dangerous, and we really don't have a plan..."

Grace's eyes widened. "I can wing it!"

"Of course," said Alison. "Why not?"

Grace jumped up and hugged her. "Oh, thank you!" she said, her voice trembling with relief.

As Alison watched Grace fade into the shadows of the hallway, she suddenly felt a pang of unease in her chest.

30

Phobos

ALISON WOKE EARLY AND made her way to the kitchen, where preparations were underway for breakfast.

"Last day," said Winnie.

Kayla sighed. "What a relief."

"Stop gossiping, girls, and give me a hand with these croissants," barked the Cook.

They had almost finished when the housekeeper's face appeared at the door. "What's happening down here? The guests are calling for breakfast. Fill the trolleys and take them up immediately."

The dining room was abuzz with activity. Alison and Winnie replenished the servery, and soon guests carried plates piled high with hash browns, baked beans and toast back to their tables. Kayla filled the croissant tray and placed bowls of fresh fruit on the table.

Alison checked the tea and coffee supplies. Then she saw him—Bogaris. He poured himself a coffee and walked away, not a flicker of recognition in his eyes. Only then did Alison realise she'd been holding her breath.

Breakfast ended, and Kayla, Winnie, and Alison returned the trolleys. Nearing the kitchen, they heard clanging and yelling.

"What's going on?" said Alison.

Kayla smiled. "I heard it's a team of artistically brilliant chefs. Here to create the ultimate fine-dining experience."

Winnie chuckled. "They're temperamental. We've seen it all before."

"Don't just stand there gawking, get busy," said the Cook.

With the washing up finished, they returned to their rooms for a break. Walking down the stairs, Kayla remarked. "There's a fancy-dress theme for tonight's ball—Olympian gods and goddesses."

"That should be interesting," said Alison.

Winnie turned to her friends with a glimmer of sadness in her eyes. "I'll be leaving tonight. Just in case things get hectic, I'll say goodbye now."

Alison and Kayla threw their arms around her. "Oh, Win, we'll miss you," they cried.

"I'll miss you too," said Winnie. She smiled sadly before going into her room.

Alison closed the door behind her and drew a sharp breath. All at once, reality struck—Phobos, the launch and their planned escape, not to mention Grace! Her stomach tightened. She gripped the back of the chair, her mind spinning.

Then, centering herself, she focused on the One.

A soft hum rose within her—

Aum...

The sound flowed through her, steady and luminous, and with it came the words: *Remember who you are. You are not the victim of your fearful thoughts, but an ever-powerful soul.*

Alison sat in the stillness until she had regained her composure. When her breath settled, she tied the apron around her waist, did her hair and returned quietly to the kitchen.

It wasn't long before Alison, Kayla, and Winnie were trundling gourmet food to the grand hall.

The guests swept in; the women in flamboyant robes and golden feathers and the men in colourful tunics and togas. As they took their seats at the grand table, they looked to Alison like a pantheon of gods and goddesses.

The guests eagerly devoured all the haute cuisine dishes put before them. The courses kept flowing until finally they came to an array of crispy and velvety sweets accompanied by chocolate and vanilla bean ice cream and fresh berries.

Just as the guests scraped their bowls clean, Alison heard a commotion in the hallway. The door swung open, and the housekeeper entered, a smile on her face. "Ladies and gentlemen," she announced. "May I present your chefs for the evening?"

The chefs, wearing aprons and tall white hats, entered to the sound of applause.

The banquet was a resounding success, but the night was not yet done. They threw open the ballroom doors, and the gentle sounds of waltz music drifted across the lawns. Outside, guests stood around, play-fighting with swords.

"They just can't help themselves," Winnie remarked as she stacked the trolley.

Alison felt a tap on her shoulder and turned around. "Oh, Ian." She turned to Winnie and Kayla. "I won't be long. I just need to step out for a few minutes."

"Sure," they said.

Alison and Ian made their way to the lift.

"How was the banquet?" Ian asked.

"It went smoothly. At least it was better than the night before." Alison smiled. "It must have been the fine dining experience."

'Lower ground,' said the lift. Ian pushed open the conference room door.

"Wow," said Alison, gazing at the theatre that sloped to a stage, each chair with its personal computer. She followed Ian down the stairs and pulled up a seat at the console.

Ian entered his login. The screen flickered briefly, then a message flashed: 'Warning! Strong language and toxic violence.' Then the display burst into glorious colour with a map of the world.

"Now to contact Joel." Ian moved the mouse, honing in on the longitude and latitude.

"Wow, this is great," said Alison, staring at the screen. "Is that his apartment."

"That's it," said Ian as he tapped Enter. "No one in the lounge room. I'll try the kitchen." He moved the mouse. "There he is." Joel appeared on the screen in shorts and a singlet, standing in front of an open fridge.

Ian pressed the speaker key. "Hi, Joel."

Joel spun around. "Oh, it's you, Ian." The screen zoomed in on Joel's hand as he reached for a block of cheese. "I just got some supplies—I'm starving."

He cut a wedge of cheese and wolfed it down. "I haven't heard from you in a while. How's it going?"

"Sorry, I've been busy programming this computer game," said Ian. "I have some vital information, but we haven't much time."

"Okay." Joel grabbed a packet of biscuits and hurried to the dining room. "Let's go," he said, sitting in front of his computer. He tore open the packet. "Where are you?" he said, munching.

"I'm at the launch of a war game called *Shadow Dreams*. It's designed to infiltrate human consciousness and enslave everyone on the planet."

"Whoa!" said Joel, his eyes wide. "Who's behind this?"

"If I told you, you wouldn't believe me."

"Try me," said Joel, reaching for another biscuit.

"Okay," said Ian. "It's Phobos from the House of Ares."

"What, a god?" said Joel, spraying crumbs onto the keyboard. "I don't believe you!"

Ian glanced at Alison, who smiled uncertainly. He turned to the screen. "Let me explain. The world is made up of layers upon layers of interconnected energy.

Some take physical forms like humans, and others exist in more subtle realms, like the gods. But what all living beings have in common is the need for an energy source—like biscuits."

Joel nodded. "Okay, I get that. But what do the gods eat?"

"Devotion sustains most gods; however, the gods of war need more than that. They feed on the energies of fear, terror, and dread."

There was silence at the other end.

"Are you there?" said Ian.

"Uh huh...," said Joel. "Just processing. Go on."

"This game is a means through which they implant divisive, conflict-ridden thoughts into human minds. Their goal is to infiltrate the collective consciousness by flooding it with fear and terror so they can seize control of the world," said Ian. "However, the good news is we installed a *Deception Breaker* into the game, based on the human qualities of free will and the power of discernment. So now humans have a fighting chance."

"So, do I have this right? This war game is being played out in human minds, and we need to defend ourselves."

"Exactly," Ian replied. "Through the lens of *Deception Breaker*, you actively fend off the divisive thoughts of fear and instead connect to the consciousness of peace. And it doesn't end there. Fearful situations become opportunities to overcome your fear-based programming."

Joel's eyes widened. "So, you're saying we become like superheroes?"

Ian smiled. "Kind of, but instead of physical capes and masks, you wear the cloak of spiritual power and the mask of discrimination."

"Excellent," said Joel. "Can anyone use it?"

"Yes, anyone," Ian nodded. "No matter who, we are all souls, children of the One. When you are no longer battling with deception, you can more easily empower yourself by connecting with the Source and remembering your original state of peace and love."

"That's what we need right now," said Joel. "So, I guess their greatest fear is that we withdraw our energies from their little games."

"You got it," said Ian. "Once you focus on your higher good, their entire system crumbles."

"Okay. I'll spread the word online." Joel's fingers flew across the keyboard. "Let the games begin!"

"Hey, you!" roared a voice behind them.

Ian whipped around, his hand hovering over the escape key. "Sorry, Joel, gotta go. I'll catch you later." With a keystroke, he ended the transmission.

Alison and Ian stood up.

Phobos and his guards stood in front of the doorway. The god looked as impressive as a Greek statue.

"Who are you?"

"I'm Ian. Err... just doing a last-minute check, sir."

Phobos scowled. "So, you're the programmer?"

Ian nodded. "Yes, sir."

Phobos' eyes flashed. "You'll be here tonight?"

"Yes, sir. I'll make sure everything runs smoothly."

"Good." Phobos' gaze swept the room before settling back on Ian. "Looks like everything is in order. We'll get down to business as soon as the ball is over. I want this to be a success."

"Yes, sir. It will," said Ian, nodding.

Then Phobos stared at Alison. "And who is this?"

"I'm Alison, Mr Phobos!" she squeaked.

Phobos stared for a moment. "Pretty little thing," he muttered, then he strode off.

"Whew, that was close," said Ian.

Alison took a deep breath. "I'll head back."

Ian nodded. "Okay. I'll see you here after the ball."

Alison slipped quietly into the ballroom. Waltz music filled the air, and colourful gowns swayed like wildflowers in the breeze.

"Sorry, I'm late," said Alison.

"You haven't missed a thing," said Winnie, polishing a wine glass.

Kayla smiled. "She means, they haven't got going yet."

The waltz ended, and a couple dressed as Zeus and Hera sat at a nearby table. They began arguing loudly. The woman turned towards the bar and raised her hand.

Alison approached. "Can I get you something?"

"I'll have a martini," said the woman.

"And a beer for me," said the man.

Alison carried their drinks on a tray, and the woman promptly tossed the martini into his face. Alison stepped back in surprise. "Would you like another?" she asked.

"You're a rude girl," said the woman. "I have a mind to report you."

"What for?" asked Alison.

"Don't you dare answer me back! Come on, my love, we're leaving." He grabbed his beer and followed obediently.

Alison shook her head. "How strange."

Winnie tried to keep a straight face.

Kayla smiled knowingly. "I told you." She whispered.

A man in white appeared in the doorway. He beckoned to Winnie. She dropped the tea towel. "Looks like I'm off! Bye, Alison, bye, Kayla."

"Goodbye and good luck," they said.

Winnie walked over to meet him. She turned and gave a smile before disappearing into her new life.

Alison picked up the tea towel and started polishing the glasses.

A couple wearing Roman robes sat down. "He'll have a gin and a wine for me," said the woman. She lit a cigarette in a long holder. Kayla took them their drinks.

"Just delete him," the man said, waving his hand dismissively.

The woman took a drag. "I'll arrange for a hitman tomorrow," she said, blowing out the smoke.

Alison felt a wave of frustration. "Why can't you all get along?" she blurted.

Kayla's eyes widened, and she ducked behind the bar.

"What?" the man exclaimed, his face turning pink and then a deep red. "How dare a serving wench speak of our affairs?"

"Now, calm down, Helios," the woman said soothingly. "I'll just add her to our revenge list."

The guests turned to watch, with a look of sheer glee on their faces.

"Wow, you sure stirred them up," whispered Kayla.

"I-I couldn't help it," Alison stammered.

"This place is getting to me, too." Kayla grabbed the handle of a trolley. "I'll just take this back to the kitchen."

The musicians struck up a quickstep, and guests pulled their partners onto the dance floor. The night was young, and the guests danced it away with a foxtrot, tango and lastly their favourite waltz.

Instantly the music ended, they flocked to the bar.

Alison glanced at the door. *Kayla should be back by now.*

"Hurry up, I'm dying of thirst," yelled a purple-faced man dressed as Apollo.

Alison hurriedly handed him a vodka and then began pulling beers one after the other until her arm ached.

A white-bearded creature jumped onto the counter like a mountain goat. "Where's my gin and tonic?"

Alison poured him a drink and handed it to him. He bleated happily.

Then a tall man dressed as Dionysus pushed his way to the bar.

"I was in front!" wailed a blonde-haired Aphrodite.

Ignoring Aphrodite's wails, Dionysus roared. "Enough of the alcohol. I want plasma."

Others took up the cry. "Plasma, plasma, plasma."

I can't take this. Alison slammed her hands on the counter.

"Enough! Either you line up sensibly, or I'll close the bar."

They stopped for a moment, stunned by her audacity, and then the chanting started again.

Alison closed her eyes. *Please—somebody, help!*

A woman in a sparkly red gown and high heels strode up to the bar, positioning herself between Alison and the irate guests. She held up her hand.

"Now, one at a time!" she said with a note of authority.

They worked steadily to serve the remaining guests.

The lights dimmed. As the orchestra struck up a slow waltz, the guests drifted onto to the dance floor.

"Thank you, I'm so grateful..." Alison stopped and stared. "Is that you, Persephone?"

The goddess chuckled. "What fun! I always harboured a wish to attend one of these balls, and tonight, with the dress code, I blend right in."

Alison stared in astonishment as Persephone poured herself a martini. She held up the glass. "Cheers, bella," she said before breezing into the crowd.

Alison shook her head. *This just tops it off.*

She threw down the tea towel and slipped out of the hall, hurrying along the corridor and down the stairs. Once in her room, she changed, brushed her hair and she closed the door behind her.

The lift doors slid open on the lower ground floor. Grim-looking officials stood on either side of the conference room door. Their eyes turned towards her, and her heart missed a beat.

Suddenly, Ian stepped out, striding through the door. "Here's your name tag," he said, leading her inside. "Sit near the stairs," he said, pointing to a chair at the back of the theatre. "I'll be down there by the stage."

"Good luck," she whispered, with a faint smile.

Alison sat down. She took a deep breath and watched the drama unfold. Some of the more intoxicated guests were in a fighting mood. One pushed a guest out of his way. "How dare you!" he said.

An official hurried down the stairs. "Now, sirs, please. There are seats for everyone." The guest released his hold and followed the official quietly.

A large man pushed past Alison. He squeezed into the chair next to her. Breaking open a bag of chips, he began crunching loudly.

Finally, the lights dimmed, and all eyes turned to the big screen on the stage.

The voice of Phobos echoed through the speakers. "Esteemed gods, goddesses, and honoured guests, welcome to the launch of my latest video game. Before we begin, I would like to extend an apology on behalf of Deimos. He wanted to attend the launch tonight but couldn't because of a prior engagement at a conference on divisive narratives. And now, we will take a moment to honour our glorious leader, Ares."

Rousing music played as the screen burst into life with a montage of scenery from the four corners of the world. The image faded, then cheers arose as Ares, in his golden chariot, galloped across the screen. Scenes of war followed from antiquity up to the modern day.

The lights came on, and Phobos stepped out. The guests showed their appreciation, stamping their feet and clapping.

Phobos held up his hands. "And now, the moment we've all been waiting for, the crème de la crème of computer games. I present to you, the one and only, *Shadow Dreams!* This game uses the latest technology to manipulate the fabric of consciousness, inducing humans to the depths of fear and terror, thereby leading to our ultimate conquest of the world!"

The man next to Alison inhaled suddenly, promptly choking on his chips. Alison thumped him on the back, and he breathed again.

"Thanks," he said, gasping.

She smiled and nodded.

Phobos leaned into the microphone. It squealed suddenly, and he stepped back. "Ah, the joys of modern technology," he said, frowning. "Now, I'd like to introduce Ian, our consultant programmer. He handles the fine-tuning. Ian is here to answer questions."

Ian stood up.

"It's a dirty, stinking human!" exclaimed the man next to her. He turned to Alison. "I can smell him from here."

"Is that so?" said Alison, taking a calming breath.

"And now for the rules of the game," said Phobos. "We have assigned each computer to a target group. This will appear on your screen. The more you influence your humans to act out of vengeance, the higher you will score. Grading will be based on evil thoughts, words and actions, with acts of violence receiving the highest. You will find the scores from the different regions displayed on the screen." Phobos grinned. "Which region will come out on top?"

Guests waved their hands. "Ours!" they yelled.

Phobos smiled, his eyes gleaming. "Then, let the competition begin!"

Like children in a candy store, the guests quickly became engrossed in the game. They tapped eagerly at their keyboards as they watched the drama unfold.

Ian walked up and down the aisles, answering questions and pointing out the program's features.

Alison turned to the man next to her. "I don't know a lot about computers. Can I watch your screen?"

"Of course," he said, leaning back. "The target is my local neighbourhood. This is my old nightclub. See that man heading to the bar? He has a revenge issue." Using his mouse, he zeroed in on the man. Then, choosing thoughts from the drop-down suggestion box, he implanted evil thoughts in his mind. Suddenly, the man grabbed someone and started shoving him.

"Oh, sweet maliciousness," the gamer remarked, smacking his lips.

A woman in front of Alison threw up her hands. "This is excellent! It's only been a few minutes, and already I'm planting jealous thoughts in this woman's mind. She fell for it, and now she's screaming at her husband. I'll put a watch on this conflict in case it escalates."

Alison felt her stomach churn. *These malevolent beings are stalking people and hacking their thoughts. I can't take much more.* Her eyes scanned the room for Ian.

Suddenly, with a shriek, a guest stood up. "I caught a fish. He's a biggie! He's threatening to unleash the army on his people!"

Phobos pointed. "Over there, Ian. You can really create havoc now!"

"Thanks, Phobos, but I think everything works well," said Ian. "It's about time I left."

Alison's eyes widened as she held her breath.

Phobos turned to Ian with a wry smile on his face. "That's not possible," he replied in a low voice.

"Why not?"

"We can't let you go now, you and that delightful piece up the back." Phobos glanced up at Alison.

"What are you talking about?" Ian stood firm as he stared evil in the eye.

Some guests looked up.

Phobos waved and smiled. "Don't make a scene. We'll discuss the details of your payment later."

Ian stood firm. "We're not discussing payment—we're not discussing anything. I'm leaving, and that's that."

A bodyguard stepped up. "What do you want me to do, boss?"

"I'll interrogate him first," said Phobos.

The bodyguard lunged.

Ian jumped back, then he looked up at Phobos. "You are nothing but *stardust!*"

Phobos' jaw dropped in astonishment. No one dared speak to the son of Ares like that. "What did you say?"

"*Stardust!*" repeated Ian.

This is looking grim, Alison thought. She pressed her palms together and silently invoked Athena.

Instantly, she heard a whoosh as the goddess flew towards the stage. Lights flickered, and a breeze scattered papers across the floor.

Phobos frowned. "Not more technical failures."

Then the room went quiet, as though time stood still.

Seeing this, Ian seized the moment. He spun around and ran up the stairs two at a time. Taking Alison's hand, he walked calmly through the door. It was as though an invisible force field surrounded them. The officials let them pass, unaware that they were now fugitives.

Alison headed for the lift, and Ian pulled her away. "We'd better avoid the main entrance," he said as they hurried down the hall.

A man in a grey suit stepped out. "This way," he said coolly.

Alison froze momentarily, then she felt the clarity of Athena urging her to stay calm. In that moment, she saw in his eyes the gentle strength of the snow leopard. His grace and independence, a sacred guardian of the mountains.

"Come on, Ian," she said.

He grabbed her arm. "No, Alison, don't."

"It's okay. I know him," she said.

He led them down a corridor, then he took out a set of keys and unlocked a door. "This leads to an underground tunnel that will take you directly to the beach."

"Thank you, Bogaris," said Alison.

"No trouble," he said. "It's the least I can do."

She glanced at the snow leopard for the last time and then turned. Entering the dimly lit tunnel, they ran as fast as they could.

"I hope this is not a trap," said Ian.

"Not far to go. I see moonlight up ahead," said Alison.

They burst out of the tunnel somewhere between the sand dunes and the sea.

"Whew," said Ian. "Let's make a run for it."

Suddenly, they heard a shout. Grace burst through the front door, closely followed by a band of soldiers.

"Get out of my way!" she cried, pushing a soldier out of the way. "Alison, wait!" she yelled as she ran across the lawn.

Ian rolled his eyes.

Alison held her breath. "Oh, be careful!"

The soldiers took aim, firing rounds of bullets until Grace fell. "You go on ahead," she cried as they dragged her away.

The soldiers marched steadily closer, rifles pointed. Ian and Alison inched backwards towards the sea.

A cold sweat trickled down Ian's forehead. "It's just a story, isn't it?"

Alison stared wide-eyed. "Of course," she said. "Remember the *Deception Breaker* and tune your frequency to the light of One."

Instantly, Ian's fear evaporated.

Together they stood silently, encircled in divine light.

"Not the light!" the soldiers shrieked. They began moving like marionettes, their bullets whizzing overhead.

"That slowed them," said Alison. "Now, let's go."

"Where to?" said Ian.

Alison pointed to the headland. They sprinted along the beach and climbed onto the rocky outcrop.

"What next?" he said breathlessly.

"Albit said to rely on magic, so here goes." Alison turned her face to the sky:

Queen Persephone,
boundless goddess.
Blessed by gods and humans.
You who embody life and death,
may you reveal your divine form.

The response came immediately. "Hang on, I'll be there in a tick."

"What?" said Ian.

After a long minute, Persephone stepped out of the ether, her red gown crumpled and high heels scuffed, her hair cascading in unruly curls. "I trust the matter is pressing enough to interrupt a thrilling game of whist?" Her voice betrayed the effect of one too many gin and tonics.

Alison's eyes widened. "We need your help, Persephone. Please! Soldiers are after us, and we have to get out of here fast!"

Persephone sniffed. "I had the perfect hand, too."

Alison sighed. "So, you had a good time?"

Persephone tossed her hair. "Oh, it was wonderful. First the ball, then a soiree with old friends and some enemies." Her eyes glistened as she crooned. *"Should auld acquaintance be forgot..."*

The goddess sighed wistfully and then turned to Ian. "Looks like your brush with the demons is ending. Are you sad?"

Ian stared at the troops, who had regrouped and were steadily making their way towards them. "Not at all," he said, shuffling his feet.

She smiled. "Well, as long as you don't have any regrets."

He shook his head. "None whatsoever."

"Please hurry," urged Alison, her heart pounding.

"Nothing worse than regrets... they weigh you down, you know," said the goddess.

Alison glanced at Ian, her eyes wide. He nodded, and together they focused their thoughts on the One. Instantly, their fear vanished, and a beautiful peace washed over them.

Persephone smiled. "Okay," she said. "Hang on to your hats."

Alison and Ian ascended like rockets, landing in a cloud-like realm.

Gazing through the mist were large, sapphire eyes.

THE SACRED MOUNTAIN

31

The Realm of Possibilities

THE MIST THINNED, REVEALING giant birdlike creatures that resembled white feather dusters.

"They're cute," Alison said with a smile.

Ian reached out with his hand. "I wonder if they're friendly?"

The birds hopped back, then inched forward again, their sapphire eyes blinking. Suddenly, in unison, the birds advanced, surrounding them in a feathery circle while humming a soothing tune. Their serenade finished, and the birds drifted away.

Alison exhaled. "I feel so peaceful..."

Ian smiled. "Not a care in the world."

Alison looked around at the moonscape. "Where are we?"

"I have no idea," said Ian. "This place looks strangely empty."

From the mist, a figure emerged, clad in a brown robe and flowing cloak. "You mistake emptiness for the void, and yet it is a reservoir of infinite possibilities."

He leaned on his staff, his voice like rolling thunder: *"Unwearying flows the sweet sound from their lips, and the house of their father. Zeus the loud-thunderer, is glad at the lily-like voice of the goddesses as it spreads abroad, and the peaks of snowy Olympus resound."*

Alison's jaw dropped. "Is that you, Professor?"

"Hello, Alison," he beamed.

"It's wonderful to see you again." Then her head tilted. "But I thought you had returned to Earth?"

"Oh, yes," he nodded. "That was my plan, but upon witnessing the deplorable state of affairs, I felt my calling lay in the higher realms."

Alison smiled. "Professor, meet Ian."

Ian nodded. "Honoured to meet you."

"I, too, am deeply honoured," said the Professor. "And delighted that you made it here safely."

"It wasn't easy," Alison replied.

"The spiritual path may not be easy, but it is the only path that leads somewhere real."

"Where exactly are we?" asked Ian.

The Professor gestured broadly with his hands. "You're in the Realm of Possibilities, where multiple timelines co-exist."

"What do you mean?" asked Ian.

"I refer to one's perception," replied the Professor. "In the world of *Chronos*, we have a single timeline from birth to death. Here, in the Realm of Possibilities, we draw upon the power of *Kairos* to perceive multiple dimensions, beyond time and space."

"Sounds fascinating," said Ian. "But who is *Kairos*?"

The Professor's eyes glimmered. "*Kairos* is an ancient god of the opportune moment. He represents the space where possibility occurs, the fleeting instant that, if missed, is gone forever. If you know what I mean?"

Ian nodded. "Yes, I've had a few of those, but I still don't understand the difference between *Chronos* and *Kairos*?"

"Let me explain," said the Professor. "Think of *Chronos* as the clock on the wall. It tells you when the sun rises and sets, when to work and when to rest. But *Kairos* is not measured by clocks—rather, it is felt by the soul. It is the pause between thoughts, the moment of reflection, the silence before a word is spoken. To enter *Kairos* is to step beyond the narrow construct of the mind into the limitless possibilities of the soul."

"Oh, I see." Ian looked around. "And the birds?"

"Ah, the Observers, the silent keepers of introspection; those who practice the art of self-reflection."

The birds ruffled their feathers and chirruped. Their curiosity satisfied, they wandered away.

Alison frowned. "I'm a little confused. I thought *Chronos* was the father of Zeus."

"You refer to Cronus, the king of the Titans and father of Zeus, who attempted to hold back time by devouring his own children," said the Professor.

"Oh yes, I remember now." Alison frowned. "I have to admit, this place is a little confusing."

The Professor's eyes shone. "It will take a while to settle in; after all, it's quite a leap from *Chronos,* where achievement comes through *doing.* Here it is through *being* that one awakens the magic within."

Alison took a breath. Was this the magic she had longed for and feared?"

His gaze softened, as if he had heard her unspoken thoughts. "The magic within you is not to be feared, for it is your own essence—your original self, waiting to be remembered." He smiled. "Now, let me show you around."

The Professor gestured with a sweep of his arm, then paused, his hand in the air. "Actually, there is not much to see in this realm, as it mostly takes place in here." He tapped his forehead.

"What do you mean?" asked Ian.

"Well, here in the Realm of Possibilities, you do not merely react to your surroundings. Instead, you create the scene through your thoughts. In other words, you are not merely a traveller through time and space, but you become the master of your own reality." He smiled. "Rather like a computer game."

Ian smiled. "That's unreal. How does it work?"

"Let me demonstrate," said the Professor, waving his hand. "Behold Sunset Point." As if on cue, a hot-air balloon appeared, yellow against the pale blue sky. The balloon landed, and the trio climbed into the basket. They floated silently upwards until they were suspended in space. The balloon drifted on the breeze, then, suddenly, the Professor pulled a lever and they descended with a bump. He opened the latch on the door and they stepped onto a giant rock.

He waved his staff. "Here you are—the perfect view."

Alison gazed at the distant mountains painted in sunset hues of pink and gold. "It is beautiful."

Ian walked to the edge of the cliff and spread his arms. "I can fly!"

Alison gasped. "Come away, you haven't got your wings yet!"

Ian returned, grinning.

"Oh!" Alison exhaled. "I've had enough excitement for one day."

"The roller coaster of excitement is the drug that the ego craves," said the Professor. "It brings no lasting fulfilment. It is only by living in accordance with one's higher purpose that one achieves a state of total fulfilment. The ancients knew this as the bliss of *eudaimonia.*"

Alison's brow creased. "But that would take a lifetime to achieve."

"Not necessarily," said the Professor. "Through the portal of *Kairos,* one is able to reach the state with ease." He looked around. "Now for practicalities. This is your base camp, the place where you go forth on your inner journey."

Alison stared at the flat rock. "You mean here?"

"Don't be fooled by appearances. The wonder of creation lies within."

"Amazing," said Alison. "So, where do we begin?"

"Start by asking questions. The answers will come, even if they aren't what you expect or want to hear. But that's what makes it even more interesting."

"Where is your base?" Ian asked.

The Professor's eyes gleamed. "Among the ancient scrolls in the Library of Alexandria. There, I explore the profound truths that were once thought to be lost to time." He blinked. "Which reminds me, I have a lecture to attend." And with that, he flung his cloak around his shoulders. "The Observers will take care of your immediate needs."

The Professor stepped into the basket, and with a whoosh, the balloon lifted off the ground.

"Whew...," said Ian. "What have we got ourselves into?"

Alison smiled. "At least it's a step up from our so-called island holiday."

"No doubt about that," he said.

Alison and Ian stood gazing at the setting sun. Suddenly, there came a buzzing noise, like an enormous swarm of bees. They turned to see a flock of Observers flying towards them. On one bird sat a woman, her arms flailing.

"It's Gracie!" cried Alison.

The Observers flapped awkwardly as they landed.

Grace ran towards them. "At last, I caught up with you," she said breathlessly. They hugged warmly.

"I'm sorry we had to leave without you," said Alison. "How did you get away?"

Grace took a deep breath. "Well, Persephone arrived just as the soldiers were dragging me away. She could have rescued me then and there, but I had an inner struggle. You should have seen it—on one side was the goddess, and on the other, the demons. I was so frightened I couldn't think straight. I yelled and struggled, but they refused to let me go. Then, I remembered to channel the light. Oh, you should have heard the screeching of those wretched demons. They threatened me with all sorts of terrible consequences, but I remained unmoved. It was then that Persephone whisked me away."

A smile spread across Alison's face. "I'm so relieved. You know Ian, of course?"

"Hi," said Grace. "I saw you in the lobby with that little elf."

Ian smiled. "Yes, Albit."

Grace gazed at the rock and frowned. "This place looks deserted. Where are we?"

"The Realm of Possibilities," replied Alison.

"Really?" Grace sighed. "Well, I don't know about you, but I'm exhausted."

The Observers gathered in a feathery circle, squawking among themselves. Suddenly, they stepped aside, revealing a giant red sofa with brightly coloured cushions and woollen throws. They hummed in unison as if satisfied with their efforts, then they waddled to the cliff face. Spreading their wings, they flew away.

"Oh, look at that. Just what I needed!" Grace collapsed onto the sofa and closed her eyes.

Ian turned to Alison. "So, this is how it works."

"Yeah," she replied, nodding slowly.

They sat on the sofa.

Leaning back against the cushions, Alison let her gaze drift. The soft light shimmered around her. She frowned, half amused, half bewildered at the strangeness of the realm. *What is this place?* She wondered.

Then, like a familiar current, she felt the peace of *Aum*. And with it came a quiet understanding. A whisper arose within her mind: '*Not so strange when you remember that everything you see is energy... even you.*'

She smiled faintly.

After a while, she heard Ian stir.

"Hi Joel," he said.

"Hi, Ian. Greetings from the great misconception."

Alison leaned over and waved.

"What's the latest?" asked Ian.

"Where do I begin?" replied Joel. "Corruption and coercion are widespread. We are being enslaved by technology, the health care is destroying our health, and the education system is stifling our ability to think logically."

"Wow, sounds like you're in a void," said Ian.

Joel sighed. "It feels like time is spinning backwards. There's little common sense left in the world. But news of the *Deception Breaker* is spreading. People are weary of the constant conflict in their minds."

"That's wonderful," said Ian.

Alison gazed at the screen. "Life certainly sounds tough down there."

Joel nodded. "I used to miss the carefree days of summer and the laughter of friends. But those days are gone. My mission now is to be true to myself even in the middle of chaos."

Suddenly, gunshots sounded while an order to take cover barked over a loud-speaker: "Everyone inside, get inside!"

Joel glanced at the window. "Speaking of chaos, I'd better go."

"Bye, Joel," said Alison.

"Take care," said Ian, as the screen went blank.

The air felt warm, like a summer afternoon. Ian closed his eyes. His thoughts faded as he drew deeper into inner tranquillity.

Alison gazed at the mountains, reflecting on her journey. She recalled her meeting with Persephone and how the goddess warned her not to drink from the Well of Forgetfulness, but to face her memories, no matter how painful. With each encounter, Alison had learned to detach from the malice of her egoic self. Then, she recalled her epic battle on the beach and her triumph over the neediness that once clawed at her soul. What had seemed like such a struggle was now only a dream. She sighed, *finally, I can relax and let go.*

Ian sat up, his eyes wide. "What's the point of all this violence and deception?"

Alison nodded. "I ask myself the same question." She pondered for a moment. "Why don't we explore our roots? After all, I remember Persephone saying, In ancient times, life was simple, and the blueprint, unmistakable."

Ian nodded. "Okay, I'm in."

They focused their thoughts on the origins of the story, and a swirling vortex pulled them into a stream flowing through time. They emerged into a cloudlike realm. Standing before them was a wooden doorway set within a massive stone wall.

"I wonder where we are," said Ian.

"There's only one way to find out," said Alison. She raised her hand and knocked firmly.

32

The Danaides

THE SOUND OF ALISON'S knocking reverberated through the air.

Instantly, a winged angel appeared.

She smiled. "Where are we?"

"You are standing at the gates of Heaven, where all the secrets of the human story are held."

"Oh," said Alison, her eyes wide. "Can we enter?"

He held up his sword. "Entry is forbidden." Then the angel paused and listened to his earphones. "Oh, I see," he said, lowering his sword. "Sorry about that. It appears the rules have changed. Higher powers are instructing me to let you in."

Alison and Ian exchanged glances.

"I have a question," said Alison. "Does everyone see the same thing?"

"It depends," replied the angel. "Each has their own unique perception and, therefore, what passes as truth for one may not be for another."

Alison's brow furrowed. "But I always thought there was only one reality?"

The angel gave a fleeting smile. "There is, but it manifests in countless forms. They say it is the boundless expression of a loving Creator."

Ian blinked. "So, why was the doorway closed in the first place?"

The angel's eyes flashed. "To prevent humans from entering the Garden of Eden."

"Of course." Ian's eyes narrowed. "But what was the *real* reason?"

The angel's eyes shone with an otherworldly light. "For those who desire a deeper understanding, you must climb the Sacred Mountain where all divisions created by the mind dissolve into One."

"Where is this mountain?" said Ian.

"You will see it as you pass through the gate."

Alison took a breath. "Is it dangerous?"

"The perils of the higher realms are not for everyone." With that, the angel flung open the gate, and a dazzling light blinded them. "Go forth into the sacred origins of your story."

They stepped through the doorway and found themselves under the iridescence of an opaline sky. In the distance rose a silvery temple, while the spectral glow of a lake shimmered in the foreground.

Alison looked around. "It's a wonderland!"

"Sure is," said Ian.

An ethereal energy swirled around them, and with a loud pop, Grace appeared.

"Hi, I didn't want to miss the fun." She looked around. "Wow, this place is surreal. Where are we?"

"We're in the realm of ancient secrets," Alison replied.

Grace's eyes widened. "Oh, you mean, like a storybook?"

Alison nodded, her gaze fixed on an ancient procession of women with jars on their heads. "Something like that."

"Strange," Ian said, as he watched the women disappear into a forest.

"Where are they going?" asked Grace.

"Let's find out," said Ian, striding out.

Grace frowned. "I'm not sure if I want to dig up the past."

"Come on," said Alison. "That's why we're here—to discover the secrets of the human story."

"Oh, okay," Grace sighed.

They walked through the forest and found themselves on the shores of a lake. There, a woman in sky-blue robes was scooping water into an earthenware jar.

Ian approached. "Ah, excuse me," he said.

Her eyes sprang open like a frightened doe. She dropped the jar onto the sand. The other women passed by as if in a trance.

Ian held up his hands. "Don't be afraid. I just want to know what's going on."

The woman's face paled. She backed away, then turned and ran into the trees.

Ian frowned. "I seem to have touched a nerve."

"How about I deal with this?" said Alison.

"Okay," Ian shrugged and walked away.

Alison looked down at the clay jar lying on its side. "Come on, Grace, let's find her."

"I don't think we should get involved," said Grace.

"Stay if you want, but it's our myth after all." Alison strode into the forest. She heard a rustle, and the woman peered out from behind a tree.

"Don't be afraid," said Alison. "We're not going to hurt you."

The woman stared for a moment, then stepped out. "We don't get many visitors here." Her hands tensed as if they longed to hold the jar. "I must get back."

They walked briskly to the beach. The woman bent down and gently righted the jar, then filled it with water and placed it on her head. Her face relaxed.

Alison smiled. "I'm Alison, and this is Grace."

"I'm Lydia, and these are my sisters." She waved at the ghostly forms walking past. "We are the Danaides." Lydia's expression turned solemn. "It is our destiny to carry these jars of water to the temple as punishment for our wickedness."

Alison blinked. "Sorry, what was that?"

"Well, it's like this. Long ago, I was one of the fifty daughters of King Danaus. We sisters were destined to marry our cousins, the fifty sons of King Aegyptus. Our father, Danaus, was a godly man who wanted to preserve our innocence, so he gave us daggers and ordered us to kill our husbands on our wedding night. One of the brothers, named Lynceus, was spared because he agreed to respect his wife, Hypermnestra's purity.

"They married, and it was not long after that he killed our father as revenge for the death of his brothers. Then, he and Hypermnestra started the dynasty of rulers in Argos. Meanwhile, my sisters and I found husbands, and we raised large families. However, after we died, we had to carry water to cleanse our sins," she sighed wistfully.

Alison nodded slowly. "Okay, but I notice you keep going back and forth to the lake. When do you actually bathe?"

Lydia shook her head. "That's the point. No matter how much water we carry, we can't seem to fill the tub."

"This is utterly pointless," whispered Grace.

"Oh, come on, Grace," said Alison. "I'd like to explore this further."

Grace sighed. "If you wish."

Alison turned to Lydia. "Would it be okay if we accompanied you?"

Lydia smiled. "Of course," she said, setting off with the jar on her head, her sky-blue robes swirling.

As Alison followed, it was as if she entered a trance-like state, one foot in front of the other. "I feel like I've been walking this path forever," she said.

"Me too," echoed Grace.

They entered the temple courtyard, where a group of sisters sat chatting in the sunshine.

Lydia led them up the temple steps. They entered the temple, its columns adorned with sacred symbols. Lydia placed the jar of water before the altar, bowing her head in silent prayer. Then she emptied the water into an azure-tiled bath and smiled sweetly. "We need more water," she said. Lifting the jar onto her head, she walked outside.

Alison looked around at the ancient columns. "Imagine how old this temple is."

"It's ancient, all right." Grace frowned. "Something about this place gives me the shivers."

Alison circled the bath and returned. "Perhaps that's because the bath is bottomless."

Grace's eyes widened. "What?" She walked to the edge and peered over. "Oh, my...," she gasped. "It's a giant hole."

"That's why it is an endless task," said Alison.

Grace shuddered. "Now I've seen everything."

A melody of voices drifted from the courtyard.

Alison stood and listened. "Can you hear their mournful song? A fruitless labouring to appease the emptiness within?"

"I can," said Grace. "Let's go."

They met Lydia on the temple steps.

Alison smiled. "Your myth may not offer you forgiveness, but I forgive you."

Lydia returned her smile, her eyes as clear as water. "Thank you."

Their song reached a crescendo. They cried out in unison before lifting the jars onto their heads.

Lydia watched her sisters walk single file through the temple gates, then she turned to Alison. "I must go."

The courtyard was silent. The air was warm, and birds twittered in the trees.

Grace sat heavily on the bench. "This story is no fun after all. It's confronting. It's—it's outside my comfort zone."

Alison sat beside her. "What did you expect, a garden of flowers and endless rainbows?" Her voice rang through the courtyard. "The human story arose out of emotional chaos, but it is through looking within and bringing the unknown to light that we encounter our truth."

"Well said!"

Alison looked up.

Ian stood in the gateway. "Is it safe to enter?"

"Yes, the women won't be back for a while."

"Why are they so scared?" asked Ian as he sat down.

"Perhaps they're fearful of the truth." Alison related the story of the Danaides sisters and the bathtub. She turned to him. "What do you make of it?"

Ian pondered for a moment. "I think it's a message about the human condition; the deeply buried feelings of guilt and shame."

"I agree," said Alison. "Not to mention the ongoing blame directed at women."

Grace closed her eyes. "I feel faint..."

"If only they could awaken from their dream," said Alison.

"I once read about *the observer effect*," said Ian. "Apparently, by observing something, you can change it. So maybe the fact that you've taken an interest in their plight will make a difference."

"I hope so," said Alison. Lulled by warm sunshine and the chirping of birds, she closed her eyes.

Suddenly, Grace sat up. "But why did they kill their husbands?"

Alison opened her eyes. "In those days, people spoke in symbols. And death... well, it represented some sort of change or ending."

"But it was outright murder!" Grace protested.

Alison nodded. "As long as we keep asking questions and following the bread-crumbs of answers, we will eventually uncover the truth of who we really are."

"Perhaps you'd like to hear what happened to me?" said Ian.

Alison nodded. "Oh, yes."

"I was walking along a path when a woman approached, so I ran into the woods to hide. Suddenly, I found myself trapped in the labyrinth of the Minotaur."

Grace's eyes widened. "Oh, dear. Did you see him?"

"No, but I heard his roar. My heart was racing and my knees shaking."

"Oh, Ian, how awful," said Alison. "How did you escape?"

"I ran blindly, but because I was in a maze, I kept taking wrong turns and ending up in dead ends. I was frantic, thinking I'd never escape, and then I realised this was showing me something about myself, so I sat down and focused on the One. It wasn't long before my mind settled, and I heard the words, 'The moment you latch onto anything as truth, no matter how credible it appears, you are lost.' That's when I released the fear and the universe appeared safe again. And so, I drifted back onto the path."

Alison smiled. "Wow, you're a hero!"

Ian brushed the hair from his eyes. "It was nothing."

Grace looked around at the high walls of the courtyard, her eyes pale. "This place is creeping me out. I just don't know, guys. I'm not sure if I'm up to being a hero."

Alison put her arm around her. "Oh, come on, Grace. Take your thoughts back to when you looked over the edge of the bath. Embrace the feeling of emptiness. It's only through bringing shadows into the light that we grow."

Grace sighed. "Oh, okay. I'll try." Her eyes clamped shut, and a wave of sorrow swept through her. All at once, a whirlpool of energy swirled, drawing her deeper and deeper into herself.

"Whoa!" she yelled. She threw up her arms, trying to hold on to something, anything, that would stop the sudden draft that took her higher and higher, her legs and arms thrashing helplessly in the tornado.

Alison jumped up. "What on earth is happening?"

"It's the Chaos," replied Ian.

"The what?" yelled Alison over the roar of the wind. "Get a grip, Grace!" she cried helplessly.

Grace spun endlessly through space. From within the swirling tempest, mythical creatures emerged, smirking and leering. She lurched from one image to the other.

"Come with me," called the Siren, tempting her with long, outstretched fingers.

"No, she's mine," bleated the goat-like creature with large horns.

"Over here," called a one-eyed monster. "I'll devour her."

"Ha! I've got her." A vulture grabbed her with its claws.

"Oh, no!" she screamed.

"You are unworthy. What about the children in your care? Do you feel guilty about not being able to protect them?"

"Yes, I do," Grace cried.

"Then you are doomed to suffer for eternity."

Grace struggled to free herself, but the vulture gripped her even more tightly until finally she passed out. The creature dropped her into the water with a splash, and she sank into the depths of the ocean. Weak with unspeakable guilt, she wished for the murky waters to obliterate her forever.

"Grace, where are you?" called Alison.

"I'm here... in the ocean of hopelessness," she murmured.

"No, you're not!" cried Alison. "You're a heroine! Don't allow those thoughts to separate you from your truth. Use your willpower to escape the drama in your mind."

Grace opened her eyes. Around her, weeds swayed. Water... so soothing. A school of fish darted through the rocks, chasing each other. The fish turned into children, who swam and tumbled around her.

"Forgive yourself," they said.

Grace's eyes flickered. "Am I dreaming?"

"It's not a dream, but your deepest self," replied a dolphin, nudging her from below. He pushed her upwards towards the light. Her face broke the surface, then a feeling of hopelessness came over her and she began to sink again.

A bearded, half-clad god emerged from the waves and swept Grace into his arms. He carried her swiftly through the waves to the headland, where he placed her on a rock. She gasped, water dripping. Shaking her hair, she saw a fishtail where her legs had been.

Staring up from the ocean, a half-submerged head, crowned with a mop of curly hair. The waves rolled over him, and he re-emerged.

"I am Poseidon!" His voice, like thunder.

Grace's heart beat in her chest.

Seeing her anguish, the great god's eyes softened. "Are you comfortable with your subconscious realm?" he asked.

Her breathing came in shallow gasps; her eyes unblinking. "No, I'm not," she replied.

"But why not? After all, you are part of the story of eternity."

"Then, why do I feel so separate?" she asked.

"Because you cut yourself off from your Source," he replied.

Grace stared at her fishtail, and a shiver ran down her spine.

"Can you not forgive yourself?" he asked.

She shook her head. "I can't," she whispered, tears brimming.

"Well then, we must put things right." Poseidon's hand plunged into the waves, and he took out a giant trident, its prongs luminous. "Awaken your third eye!" he roared as he thrust it toward her forehead. His voice carried over the sound of the waves as they crashed against the rocks.

"Trust the wisdom of the universe!" He cried as a bolt of energy pierced her mind.

Instinctively, her hands flew to her face, then suddenly, her mind calmed. Her skin felt cool from the sea spray. The air tasted fresh and salty. Dolphins leapt out of the water and landed with a silvery splash. Seeing them swim and dive, a sudden clarity flooded her—like the dolphins, she too was a part of this vast, living story.

"Are you ready to swim in the ocean of awareness?" challenged the god.

Grace nodded. "Yes, I am."

"Well, then my work is done."

Poseidon summoned his horse-drawn chariot. Taking the reins, he sped off through the waves.

Without hesitation, Grace dived into the ocean. She found herself immersed in a deep love that healed the pain and sorrow of many lifetimes. "This is wonderful!" Her laughter rang out. She propelled herself through the water as if she had done so all her life.

It was then that Grace's eyes flickered.

"Oh, thank goodness, you're back," said Alison. "Where were you?"

Grace rubbed her eyes. "Poseidon's watery depths." A smile spread across her face. "At last, I can see and feel again."

"That's amazing, Grace. Are you ready to continue?" asked Alison.

Grace turned to her with sadness in her eyes. "I'm sorry, Alison, but this path is not for me." She sighed. "But I'm not sure what else to do?"

Her thoughts reached an angel, who appeared before her. "Do not be distressed," he said with a voice serene. "You are free to choose again."

"Oh!" Grace exhaled. "I just want to find my tribe."

The angel answered, "Then it shall be."

In the distance, a group of people beckoned. Seeing them, Grace smiled. She turned to Alison and Ian. "Goodbye, dear friends, and thank you." And with that, Grace flew into her new life.

"I suppose we should go too," said Ian.

Alison nodded, and in an instant, she found herself on the sofa. She looked around, half-expecting to see Grace, but all that remained was a pile of cushions and a crumpled throw.

33

Aion

ALISON GAZED AT THE distant mountains. The air felt heavy with unspoken secrets. Suddenly, her eyes widened as a giant clock appeared in the sky. She gazed at the hands ticking slowly towards midnight.

"Hey Ian, what do you make of it?" she said.

Before he could answer, a deafening boom split the air. Another boom followed, and plumes of smoke billowed from the realms below.

The computer gave a beep. Ian looked down. Joel's face appeared. "Hi Ian."

"Hi, Joel, what happened?"

"A missile strike."

Ian frowned. "Are you okay?"

"Yes. But we're no longer safe, so friends and I are looking for somewhere else to stay."

"Good luck," said Ian.

"I'll talk to you soon," said Joel.

Ian closed the screen and then looked up at the clock. "Judging by the hands, I'd say *Chronos* is almost out of time."

Alison felt a shiver run down her spine.

Not long after, a flock of Observers circled overhead. On board sat the Professor, his cloak billowing. Flapping their wings, the birds landed; some smoothly, while others skidded and tumbled over each other.

The Professor strode towards them, and a ribbon of Observers waddling behind. He spread his arms: *"The sea roared, and the earth trembled as the gods clashed in battle. Their war cries echoed to the heavens, and their weapons struck with unrelenting fury."*

"Hello, Professor," said Alison. "You're in fine spirits today."

The Professor leaned on his staff. "One is always happy when events unfold precisely as they should."

Alison frowned. "But how can you say that when the clock has almost reached midnight?"

The Professor looked up. "So, it has." His eyebrows raised. "Once you understand the nature of eternal time, worry is merely optional." He smiled. "How are you settling in?"

"Quite well," she said. "We went back in time to the Danaides sisters."

"It was quite an experience," added Ian.

"So, you understand how this place works." The Professor smiled. "Fascinating, isn't it? Any thoughts about what you want to explore next?"

"Mm...," said Ian. "After experiencing the futility of striving to fill an empty bathtub, I'd like to find true fulfilment?"

"Oh, yes." The Professor nodded. "The ancients referred to this as *eudaimonia*. It is a state of complete and utter fulfilment. Naturally, you cannot find it in the world of form. It is only in here." He tapped his temple. He paused for a moment. "Perhaps you should climb the Sacred Mountain?"

"I'd like to," replied Ian.

"I'd like to climb the mountain, but I want to be prepared," said Alison, as she recalled the angel's message.

The Professor nodded. "It is wise to make preparations before breathing the rarefied air of *Aion*."

"Who is *Aion*?" asked Ian.

"The lord of unbounded time—and patron of this realm."

Ian frowned. "Why have I not heard of *Aion*?"

"Perhaps you are engrossed with the ticking clock of *Chronos*?" said the Professor. "*Aion's* time is vast and eternal. It is through the knowledge of the cycle that your awareness expands, and this broader perception of life would no doubt aid you in climbing the mountain."

"Can you tell us more?" asked Alison.

He nodded. "The cycle is the focus of my studies at the Library of Alexandria. If it is your wish, I can take you there."

"Yes, please." Ian and Alison replied in unison.

"Well then, let us turn our thoughts and go to the library."

The three stood silently, their minds attuned. A hush settled over them, then with a rush, a swirling vortex opened, drawing them into a fast-flowing stream. Suddenly, the motion ceased, and they found themselves on a lawn. In front stood a monumental building.

Alison gazed at the grand stairway and the symmetry of the columns on either side. "It's amazing."

The Professor's eyes glowed. "Indeed, my heart sings every time I enter its hallowed doors."

Ian gazed in awe at the wide entrance leading to the pool beyond. "I read that the library had burned down," he said.

"That is correct," said the Professor. "However, while the ravages of time and war laid waste to the earthly library, here it is preserved forever."

"When was it built?" asked Alison.

"The library was founded by the Ptolemaic kings of Egypt in the third century BC. They wanted to gather all the knowledge of the world in one place."

Ian's eyebrows raised. "How did they gather so much information? I mean, it wasn't like they could download it from the internet."

"Ian, really...," Alison chuckled.

The Professor smiled. "In those days, much of it came by sea. When ships entered the port of Alexandria, their manuscripts were taken to be copied by scribes. It was a trade of knowledge, a worldwide devotion to learning."

The Professor led them up the marble stairs. The scent of frankincense and myrrh greeted them as they entered the great doors. Shafts of light filtered through tall windows, and shelves stacked with ancient scrolls lined the walls. The libraries' silence was profound; the hush of learning.

Alison watched the scholars in linen robes move quietly among the shelves. She drew a sharp breath. "So many scrolls."

The Professor nodded. "Each is a vessel of wisdom." He led them through the library, pausing in front of a mosaic image, a winged man standing within a coiled serpent, its tail touching its mouth.

"Here we see a representation of *Aion*, the cyclical nature of time. It also served as a symbol of the city of Alexandria."

Alison grimaced. "Why a snake?"

"This is the Uroboros, one of the oldest symbols known to humankind. The Uroboros appeared in ancient Egypt, coiled around the sun god Ra as he sailed through the underworld. Later, it slithered into Greek philosophy."

"I heard that once a snake is injured, it bites its tail and dies," Ian said.

Alison frowned.

"Ian is right," said the Professor. "The great Ouroboros is a symbol of birth and death; creation and destruction. It is the symbol of an ever-turning cycle of time that repeatedly devours and renews itself again." He paused for a moment.

"If you look closely, you will see the four seasons. But these are not merely of the natural world. They represent the phases of the human story through a cycle of spring, summer, autumn and winter."

Ian nodded. "Interesting."

"Come," said the Professor. He showed Alison and Ian to a wooden table. Then, ascending a ladder, he returned with a handful of scrolls.

"These are the words of our ancestors, whose knowledge of the universe was vast. We begin with the Greek poet Hesiod, who lived around 700 BC. In his treatise, *Works and Days*, Hesiod spoke of four ages of humankind. He describes the height of civilisation as the Golden Age, symbolised by the softest and most radiant metal, gold. Then came the Silver Age, followed by Bronze and finally, the Iron Age, which is the hardest and darkest of all."

Ian and Alison sat, wide eyed as the Professor carefully unrolled a scroll. "Hesiod's account of the Golden Age," he said.

They lived like gods, without sorrow of heart.
Remote and free from toil and grief:
Miserable age rested not on them.
But with legs and arms never failing, they made merry
With feasting beyond the reach of all evils.
When they died,
it was as though they were overcome with sleep.
And they had all good things;
For the fruitful earth unforced bore them fruit
abundantly and without stint.
They dwelt in ease and peace upon their lands
With many good things,
Rich in flocks and loved by the blessed gods.

The Professor looked up. "It was a time of innocence, harmony and abundance." He then unfurled another parchment. "The Roman poet, Publius Ovidius Naso, born in 43 BC, tells a similar story of peace and harmony. This is from *Metamorphoses*."

Then it was an eternal spring;
And the gentle zephyrs, with their soothing breezes,
Cherished the flowers produced without sowing seed.

Soon too, the earth unploughed yielded crops of grain;
And the land, without being renewed,
whitened with the heavy ears of corn.
Then it was, rivers of milk and rivers of nectar flowed,
And the yellow honey came from the green holm oak.

Alison smiled. "The descriptions sound heavenly."

Ian nodded. "Vastly different from the world we know today."

"I agree," said the Professor. "The contrast between our conflict-ridden world and a world of peace and plenty is so great that most people can hardly imagine it."

Ian frowned. "Why did civilisation decline?"

"Good question." The Professor nodded. "The law of entropy states that systems move from order to disorder, from unity to scattered parts. In this way, history unfolded over eons, and all the while, the story adjusted to suit the people, the situation and the time."

"I see," said Ian. "It reminds me of a poem by *Lao Tse*."

"Let's hear it," said the Professor.

Ian took a breath.

The Tao gives birth to the One.
The One gives birth to the Two.
The Two give birth to the Three.
The Three give birth to the ten thousand things.
The ten thousand things
are bolstered by Yin and wield Yang.
Together, they harmonise as Breath.

"Perfect description." The Professor looked down at the scroll. "And now, to the Silver Age. Hesiod spoke of the second generation as less noble than the golden race. Innocence had waned, and humanity began to struggle. Life was shorter, harder, and they did not honour the gods."

The Professor moved to the other scroll. "Ovid describes it similarly."

Then fled eternal spring.
And the year was divided into seasons.
Men built shelters for themselves.

And tilled the reluctant soil.

"Sounds like the environment was quite different," said Ian.

"Yes," said the Professor. "Rivers altered their course, and the seasons came into being. For the first time, human beings faced challenges that forced them to adapt. Many were forced to move to more habitable places."

He looked down again. "And now for the Bronze Age. Hesiod called them a brazen race, sprung from the ash-trees; terrible and strong."

They loved the lamentable works of Ares
And deeds of violence...
Their armour was of bronze.
And their houses of bronze,
And of bronze were their implements;
There was no black iron.
These people were destroyed by their own hands
And passed to the dank house of chill Hades.

"This is the first we hear of Ares," said Alison.

"Indeed," said the Professor. "With the Bronze Age came the birth of the gods and goddesses. Ovid described these people as being inclined to arms, but not to impious crimes."

"So, they weren't all bad," said Alison.

"Oh, no," said the Professor. "Bronze Age people were, in the main, merchants, artisans and traders who worshipped the gods." He gazed into the distance and smiled. "They were also storytellers who appreciated the grandeur of the theatre of life. But as time went by, the population grew, and with it, the urge to conquer and expand their territories. And that's when the story took a turn. Until then, life on Earth was orderly and predictable. Now, it wasn't only nature causing problems, but also warring tribes."

"So, was this the beginning of the battle of good and evil?" said Ian.

"That is correct," replied the Professor. "Out of the conflict emerged another race. Hesiod refers to this as the Heroic Age—a return to nobility, when demigods fought at Thebes and Troy. Unlike the Bronze race, they were honoured. After death, they were granted a place in the Isles of the Blessed."

His tone grew grave as he looked down at the scroll. "And then came the Iron Age."

Ian shifted uneasily. "So, it just keeps getting worse."

"I'm afraid so," said the Professor. "Hesiod spoke of this age."

For now, truly, is a race of iron.
And men never rest from labour and sorrow by day,
And from perishing by night;
And the gods shall lay sore trouble upon them.

The Professor continued. "Ovid describes the Iron Age in terms of expansion and conquest."

The sailor now spread his sails to the winds
And with these as yet
He was but little acquainted;
And the trees, which had long stood on the lofty mountains,
Now, as ships bounded through the unknown waves.
The ground too, hitherto common
As the light of the sun and the breezes,
The cautious measurer marked out
With his lengthened boundary.

"Both Ovid and Hesiod refer to a sharp moral decline," said the Professor. "Ovid provides us with a vivid description."

The last age was of hard iron.
Immediately, every species of crime burst forth.
In this age of degenerated tendencies;
Modesty, truth, and honour took flight;
In their place succeeded fraud, deceit, treachery, violence,
And the cursed hankering for acquisition...
Men live by plunder; the guest is not safe from his host.
Nor the father-in-law from the son-in-law;
Good feeling, too, between brothers is a rarity...
Piety lies vanquished, and the virgin Astraea
is the last of the heavenly deities to abandon the Earth,
Now drenched in slaughter.

Ian exhaled. "Remarkable how they visualised the ages so accurately."

"Yes, their powers of visualisation were strong," said the Professor.

Alison tilted her head. "How about the goddess Astraea?"

"Interesting question," said the Professor. "According to Greek myth, Astraea accompanied humans during the Golden Age, when they were virtuous and no evil existed in the world. As time went on, humanity became increasingly violent and corrupt, and that's when she fled the Earth and became the constellation, Virgo."

"It seems to me humans lost touch with their very essence," said Alison.

"You are right," said the Professor. "As the Iron Age unfolded, human consciousness became increasingly entangled with matter and the physical form."

Ian frowned. "So, are we trapped in this Iron Age?"

"Not if we choose." The Professor's eyes glimmered as he drew out a smaller scroll. "Virgil was a Roman poet who lived in 70 BC. In his *Eclogue IV*, he wrote."

Now comes the last age of the Sibyl's song;
The great cycle of the ages begins anew.
A child is born who shall end the Iron race
And usher in a golden age once more.

"Just imagine... a peaceful world," Alison said with a sigh.

"So, the four ages aren't just warnings of ruin?" said Ian.

"No," said the Professor. "They hold the promise of return. The Golden Age arises again because *Aion's* time is not a straight road, but a wheel. After night comes the dawn; after winter, the spring. After all," he leaned closer, "if humanity can spiral down into sorrow, it can also ascend, like the Phoenix rising from the ashes."

Ian gave a smile. "It sounds like a game."

The Professor tilted his head. "Not a game in the sense of winning or losing. More like the universe breathing in and out; an endless dance of *Aion*."

"I have another question," said Ian. "I see how civilisation declined, but how does it reverse? I mean, how do we go from ten thousand things back to one?"

"Ah... but that's where you are mistaken." The Professor's eyes glimmered. "What you call *things* are not truly solid at all, but condensed energy—expressions of the consciousness that dreamed them."

Ian raised his eyebrows. "What, but how?"

"Think of the universe as energy. And energy can neither be created nor destroyed, only transformed. When chaotic energies come into contact with an unimaginably high energy field, the disordered consciousness unites. No longer separate currents, but one great ocean of divine love. That is why when our thoughts, words and actions align with the Source, we create a world of peace and harmony."

"Amazing." Ian exhaled. "All right, but what's the point of a peaceful world if we are only going to fall into chaos again?"

The Professor nodded. "A fair question. But you are viewing the world through *Chronos*, where time moves in short periods of harmony followed by war. Try zooming out. Imagine a place where peace and joy aren't rare visitors, but the air itself. That is *Aion*."

He leaned back, eyes distant. "From there, what looks like chaos to us might just be a ripple; a small wobble in a much greater rhythm. The soul's knowing. Not a moment of insight, but timeless awareness, where it feels like the ages pass like the blink of an eye."

"Oh," said Ian, drawing a slow breath. "I think I'm getting my head around it."

"Well, I'm struggling," said Alison. "It doesn't fit with anything I learned at school."

The Professor paused for a moment. "Well then, perhaps we should call upon a philosopher." He turned to Alison. "Do you recall Plotinus?"

"Yes." Alison nodded. "He studied in Alexandria, didn't he?"

"He did," the Professor nodded. "Plotinus was born in Egypt in 204 AD. He came to Alexandria and studied under Ammonius Saccas for ten years. Later, he joined a Roman campaign to the East, hoping to gain the knowledge of Indian sages, but fate turned him back. In the end, he settled in Rome, where he taught for the rest of his life." His eyes glimmered. "What do you think?"

Alison nodded eagerly.

"That would be great," said Ian.

"Then let us invoke his presence," said the Professor.

Silently, they focused their thoughts on the philosopher. The murmur of scholars dissolved, and they found themselves in a small courtyard within the ancient library.

34

Plotinus

HEARING THE SPLASH OF water and the hum of cicadas, Alison opened her eyes. The sun shone warmly. She blinked and looked around. A fountain murmured softly in the middle of the courtyard, while faded frescoes and oil lamps in niches adorned the walls.

The Professor led them to the shade of a spreading tree. Beneath its branches sat a solitary figure wearing a tunic and grey cloak. As they drew near, he looked up; his eyes, warm and welcoming, shone with a silence from beyond.

"Come in from the heat of the day," he said. "Shade is kind. It is the soul's memory of the calm light of God."

"Greetings, Plotinus," said the Professor. "I would like to introduce Alison and Ian. We have been discussing the cycle of *Aion,* and they have questions."

"Very good," Plotinus replied, settling onto the stone bench. "Let us contemplate life together, sharing ideas, but more importantly, the living experience of the soul." He gazed at Alison and Ian. "Where would you like to begin?"

Alison turned to the Professor. "Where to start?"

"What about your encounter with the Danaides sisters?" suggested the Professor.

"Oh, yes," she said, turning to Plotinus. "Ian and I enquired about the origin of the human story, and we were led to this ancient myth."

"Hmm, the Danaides," said Plotinus. He closed his eyes. All they heard was the whisper of the fountain. He opened his eyes once more. "What were your thoughts?"

"I understood the myth as symbolic of the emptiness of the human spirit," said Ian.

"Very good," said Plotinus with a nod. "You will make a philosopher." He paused. "This myth tells of the soul's fall into its lower form. When the soul forgets its source, it becomes an *eidōlon,* a mere likeness, pursuing the objects that delight the senses."

"You mean the soul no longer knows who it is?" said Ian.

"Exactly," said Plotinus. "It ceases to live from its own being. And so, try as it might, it cannot find lasting fulfilment."

Alison shook her head. "I felt so sad seeing the women working hard and achieving nothing." She paused. "And yet, perhaps it fulfilled a purpose—staying busy was a way to avoid the guilt they couldn't bring themselves to face."

Plotinus nodded slowly. "Another philosopher." He smiled.

"In the beginning, the soul was whole and complete, contained within the beauty and peace of God. It knew itself as spirit, distinct from the physical body. But then the soul decided to experience a world of opposites, and it fell into a material consciousness. The soul identified with the body was no longer itself, but someone who had forgotten itself and was living the life of another.

"The result of the fall was a feeling of shame, tiny at first, like a pea, but over time, it grew. To survive this inner ache, the soul silenced itself, forgetting its true nature and donning the mask of a human story. Yet, the shame lingered, giving rise to a restlessness like that of the Danaides, condemned to labour endlessly, pouring water into a bottomless bath. But their vessel never filled, and so their labour never ceased.

"The myth of the Danaides is the soul's journey of forgetting. And yet, the soul's true task is to awaken—to remember who it is. This is not the path of endless striving, but returning to what has always been. As Persephone rises, so the shadows dissolve in the presence of a greater light, allowing the true self to shine once again."

"I'm familiar with the story of Persephone," said Alison.

Plotinus nodded. "The story of Persephone represents the divided state of the human soul and the promise of our return journey and the eternal season of spring."

Alison frowned. "But the return journey isn't easy. We must face the inner critic who uses blame, judgement and criticism to keep us trapped in a false identity."

"That is a profound insight," said Plotinus. "The false self doesn't just wear a mask; it accuses and blames you for what you have become. It makes you believe you are not enough; it tells you if you were stronger, wiser, better, then others would love you. In this way, it tries to convince you that every failure is your fault. And so, the more you believe its words, the further you drift from your essence."

His gaze met Alison's. "It is the illusion of separation that you must overcome if you are to escape the prison of the mind."

Alison nodded. "So, I heard. But how do we break free?"

"Through remembrance." Plotinus sighed. "It is a wonder, isn't it? Even in this state of self-imposed exile, the soul carries a memory of the peace and harmony of the One. Many ask me who this One is, and I always reply, this is union, the soul becoming what it beholds. In that remembrance, the soul realises who it is—not a mask, but the eternal essence, a child of God."

"So, you mean, when people long for God, they are longing for what they are already part of?" said Alison.

"Exactly," replied Plotinus. "This world is but a reflection of what is real and eternal. You do not have to create something, but merely return to what you never truly lost—the realm of light where everything exists in its fullness."

"Who is God?" asked Alison.

Plotinus sat, his eyes serene. "It is natural for us to be drawn toward beauty. Anyone who has experienced it knows that God is beautiful and the very source of life, of mind, of being. Once you experience divine love, you can never compare the One with anything, nor can you ever admire or desire anything less. This is our deepest longing."

Ian frowned. "If the soul was so content when it was with the One, why did it ever leave?"

Plotinus took a breath. "You ask a deep question. Let us say that the soul does not leave out of force nor punishment. No, it descends freely, for it belongs to the nature of souls to take part in the drama of life. The soul delights in the play of images and in the spectacle of change. It wishes to weave its own tale, to be a spectator and actor all at once."

Ian nodded. "We always have free will."

Plotinus smiled. "You are right. We are never slaves. Even though sometimes it seems that way. Each soul has its own story of descent and return, a story written in the annals of time. Think of it as the call to leave and to return, to end in the One from which it all began."

Alison smiled, her eyes glistening. "You have a beautiful way of thinking about life."

"Most people don't stop to consider these things, but if they did, their hearts would overflow with happiness."

Alison felt the gift of his words and smiled.

Ian frowned. "You speak of the good, but what of evil and deception? These forces are rampant in our world."

"A worthy question, for evil and deception are things that few of us desire. But if the universe is to exist, all degrees of being must be present, from the highest to the lowest. Evil is the lowest rung in that order."

Ian frowned. "So, you're saying evil is not wrong?"

"Evil runs contrary to the goodness of the soul, so we must naturally resist it," said Plotinus. "But just think for a moment, if all were good, there would not be a universe at all, but only the Good itself. And so, understand that evil is not a principle in itself; rather, it is the absence of good, just as darkness is the absence of light and fear arises in the absence of love."

Ian nodded. "That way of thinking is natural."

"Exactly," said Plotinus.

"I am interested in hearing about love," said Alison.

"Oh, yes, love...," said Plotinus. He gazed at the clouds and sighed. "Often, I awaken to myself, as though freed from the body, and when I do, I sense a beauty most wondrous. Then, more than ever, I know I belong to a higher order and that true love is found there. This feeling of love is as natural as being in my home."

A stillness came over the courtyard, and the fountain's spray caught the sun in countless jewels. The moment expanded; the shimmer of water and the warmth of the air, woven into pure harmony.

Alison felt the softness in her heart. "So, union with God is not about escaping this world, but a homecoming?"

"Exactly." Plotinus smiled. "The soul does not ascend to something foreign but awakens to what it has always been." He paused, his eyes distant. "There exists not I, or you, only the overflowing fullness of love."

Ian nodded. "And so, you could say, the cycle of time is a return journey?"

"Indeed, when the soul has gone even to the furthest extremity, when it has poured itself out, then a weariness comes upon it. And from that weariness is born the desire to return."

Ian nodded. "It makes sense to me now."

"I understand too," said Alison. "But I still wonder about the role that the gods and goddesses play in the human story?"

"I too have long considered their role," said Plotinus. "It appears to me that the gods are not mere products of imagination, nor are they symbolic; they are real powers. Each god or goddess embodies a higher principle. Each is a facet of the divine dance between opposites of the divine masculine and feminine.

"Take Aphrodite, for example. She appears in two forms: the heavenly Aphrodite, the pure principle of love, and the Aphrodite born of desire. Similarly,

Athena represents the feminine intelligence, and yet she is the offspring of Zeus. And also, Persephone represents the soul seized by the mind, who takes her to the Underworld where she becomes entangled with matter."

"Interesting," said Alison. "But why was the goddess forgotten?"

"Oh, yes. I observed this myself—the goddess cast aside as humans attempted to master the lower realms. But, keep in mind that it may be the wish of the goddess, for she is a higher force, more comfortable not in the world of matter, but in the mysterious realms beyond. For the goddess descends, and ascends, she veils and reveals, she gives birth and then takes it away."

Alison's eyes widened. "I sense that the goddess and mystery go hand in hand."

"You could be right," replied Plotinus. "And the deepest mystery is that the goddess is not outside you. She is your breath, the energy of the soul. She is the rhythm of the universe, the tide that takes you away and draws you to your home."

"It seems to me," said Alison, "while God is beyond the story, it is through the goddess that we live and breathe?"

Plotinus smiled. "Fascinating, isn't it?"

Alison smiled and nodded. "Speaking of the goddess, we heard a prophecy that Metis would bear a child who would overthrow Zeus. And so, Zeus swallowed her."

Plotinus smiled. "The ancients used words wisely. Rather than speaking openly, they clothed such matters in stories and prophecies, so that only those with understanding might perceive their meaning."

"I see," Alison said.

"We also heard that Metis is free from Zeus' story," said Ian.

"Ahh…" Plotinus' eyes glimmered. "If that is so, then the veil of illusion will fall."

They sat quietly, listening to the sound of the water trickling over the fountain.

Plotinus turned to them and smiled. "Do you have any more questions?"

They shook their heads.

"Thank you. It has been illuminating," said Alison.

Ian nodded. "Very helpful."

"That is good. I have enjoyed our little talk immensely. No doubt we shall meet again," Plotinus said as he faded into the mists of time.

For a long moment, they sat in silence. At last, the Professor spoke. "Well then, it seems like you had a successful meeting."

"Oh, yes," said Alison. "Plotinus' view of life was fascinating. I got to see the world through ancient eyes. Not as something frightening, but full of beauty and love."

"His perception was cosmic," said Ian.

Their conversation was interrupted by the arrival of a server carrying a dish piled high with an array of delicacies. Another server arrived, bearing an ornate tea urn. They set the offerings on a table nearby, and the Professor invited them to partake.

Amidst the talk and laughter, they savoured the treats. Then, no sooner had they finished and said their goodbyes, Alison and Ian found themselves back on the sofa.

✳

Alison rested her head against the cushions. She closed her eyes, seeing the ages of Hesiod; gold, silver, copper and iron, each shimmering with its own light. She felt the pulse of time, holding her, guiding her and carrying her forward even when she could not see the path ahead.

She recalled the words of Ovid, filling her like an eternal spring, touching her with lightness, knowing that she was eternal—a soul having an earthly experience, always supported, always loved.

She recalled with hope Virgil's promise of renewal and a new age to come. Then, her thoughts turned to Plotinus and his call to beauty, goodness and the love of God.

Their voices spoke of a world half remembered, half dreamed: not merely fragments of a story, but a mirror of her soul. With each breath, she felt herself emerging from the shadows into a light she did not yet understand, but was ready, at last, to follow...

A beep interrupted her reverie. She heard Ian's fingers tapping on the keyboard.

"Hi Joel, are you okay?"

"Yes," said Joel. "We found a safe place to stay."

"That's good to hear. How are you holding up?"

"Better, actually. I'm finding my connection to God. There's this quiet strength that comes with it, like standing in the centre of a storm. Sometimes the darkness clouds my mind, and then suddenly it lifts, and I can see again."

"It's a spiritual war," said Ian.

Joel nodded. "Absolutely. It takes courage to stand apart from the noise; to question the story we've told and not let it define us. To remember who we are when everything around us tries to make us forget. It's like a battle for our souls."

"Yes," said Ian, softly. "It's the chaos that marks the end of an old era. And the beginning of something new."

"You're right," said Joel. "Out of the ashes, the Phoenix rises, but first comes the fire."

"The fire purifies," said Ian.

Joel smiled faintly. "Maybe that's what being a spiritual warrior means—walking through the flames without losing heart."

They said their goodbyes, and with a click, Ian closed the laptop.

"Life on Earth sure is tough," said Alison.

Ian nodded. "It sure is. The world needs warriors like Joel more than ever."

He stretched his arms. "So, are you ready to see the universe as *Aion* sees it?"

Alison gazed at the distant mountains rising like a purple wave against the horizon. "Yes," she breathed. "I'm ready."

"Then, let's go!"

The force of their combined thoughts surged, projecting them into an infinite expanse of space.

35

The Gorgon

ALISON AND IAN TUMBLED onto a hillock. Before them stretched a parkland bathed in golden sunlight, and through it meandered a river. The trees rose tall, and the air was alive with the melodies of birds and the gentle rustle of leaves.

Alison felt the soft grass beneath her feet. "We made it."

Ian smiled. "Almost," he said, gazing at the imposing mountain and the mist swirling around its peak.

They set off towards the river, Ian striding on ahead.

Alison strolled along the riverbank, where ewes with their playful lambs came to drink. Peacocks emerged from beneath a weeping willow. Males fanned their sapphire and emerald tails while females watched on with admiration.

As she walked, a burst of yellow caught her eye—daffodils shimmering in the sunlight. A pang of longing stirred in her heart.

"Oh, Persephone... I miss you." Her words drifted through the air.

A whisper came back on the breeze. *"I miss you too..."*

Before her, an ethereal figure formed—a goddess with long, dark hair.

Alison's breath caught. "Oh, Persephone... you're here."

'Only in thought,' the goddess replied, *'for my thrilling tale of abduction and return has reached its conclusion.'*

Alison shook her head slowly. "Does this mean I'll never see you again?"

'Once you shed your victim consciousness and embrace your true self, you have no need of my story.'

A soft breeze brushed Alison's cheek—a wave of love, so pure that it blurred the edges of her mind. It was a joy that she had not felt before.

Then, in the middle of her quiet bliss, she heard a breathless voice. "Did you see that?"

Alison opened her eyes. Ian stood in front of her, his face flushed. She took a sharp breath. "See what?"

He stared at her. "The star..."

"No, I didn't—is it, God?"

"I don't know, but it spoke to me."

"What did it say?"

"Hello."

Alison's eyes widened. "Nothing else?"

He shook his head. "No, just *hello*."

"Hello." She felt a tremor of mirth arising within. She grinned, attempting to hold back the floodgates, but then, overwhelmed by the sheer absurdity of it all, she let go, and a flood of hilarity burst forth in waves.

"Hello...!" She laughed until her jaws ached and tears rolled down her cheeks.

Ian went to speak again, but this only set off a fresh bout of hilarity. He shook his head and went back to the river.

"Are you God?" he asked, looking up at the star.

"Sorry to disappoint you. I'm a Daimone."

"A what?"

"A spirit of the Golden Age, guardians of human beings." The star twinkled. "We are intermediaries between gods and mortals. Our role was to report injustices to Zeus."

"But the name..." Ian frowned. "Daimone sounds like what we'd call a demon."

The star's light shimmered softly. "We are all spirits who inhabit the Earth sphere. But while there are limitless demons, there are only thirty thousand of us Daimones. Like the demons, we influence mortals, but while their role is to lead mortals into the abyss, we guide spirits to the light."

Alison joined him, breathless. "Did you sort it out?"

Ian nodded. "It's a Daimone, a spirit of the Golden Age."

"Oh, can it hear me?"

The star sparkled, sending rainbow shards of light into the air. "I can indeed. Let me introduce myself; I'm Prakash, your guide."

"A guide?" said Alison. "Perhaps you can tell us where we are."

The star blinked. "You are in a divine realm."

"But I don't see the gods and goddesses."

"They have the freedom to come here, but most choose to remain in the realms where their stories play out. As a soul, you have free will to experience whatever you choose." The star blinked. "Now, are you heading somewhere, or would you like to stay and enjoy the scenery?"

"We're here to climb the mountain," said Ian.

"Very good. In that case, you'll need my help," said the star.

Alison gazed at the mountain peak, hidden in the clouds. "Is it difficult?"

"It all depends. Many make it. Some do not."

"I plan on reaching the summit," said Ian.

"That's a great goal, but do you have the courage to face whatever obstacles come your way? The last seeker wanted to reach the summit, but he grew tired of the endless challenges and turned back."

"I'm not returning to my old story," Ian said with determination.

Alison looked up. "I want to explore the mystery of the goddess."

"Well, you have good intentions. Follow me," he said, gliding on ahead.

They trailed the star, their steps light.

They passed a herd of cows lying peacefully under the trees. A flock of brightly coloured parrots wheeled overhead, their cries bright against the sky.

"There are so many varieties of birds and animals here," said Alison.

The star blinked. "You are in a higher realm where the goddesses appear as symbols. Parrots are the transformational power of Persephone. The cows are goddess Hera's nurturing qualities, as are the myriads of stars that form the Milky Way. And the peacock's tail feathers are the symbols of her all-seeing eyes. The deer is the goddess Artemis."

"How lovely," said Alison, gazing at the deer on the river bank.

They came upon a pond, its surface shimmering in the sunlight. In the centre stood a large stone bowl with a sacred flame burning within.

"It must be Hestia," said Alison.

"Yes," blinked the star.

Alison gazed into the crystal-clear water, watching golden fish dart between the flowering lilies. Swans floated on top of the water like white sailboats.

"The goddess Aphrodite," the star offered. "The swan is her elegance, while the water is her boundless love."

Ian smiled. "Well, I think we're finally having our flowers and rainbow moment."

Alison laughed. "At long last."

Above them, the star blinked. "We must keep moving if you want to reach the foothills of the mountain by nightfall."

With a swish, Alison and Ian found themselves lifted into the sky, drifting as if on a ski lift above the fields. As the sun set, they landed in a clearing where a small temple stood half hidden among the trees. An owl hooted from a nearby branch.

Ian gazed at the temple. "Who is this dedicated to?"

"I guess it's Athena," said Alison.

The star blinked. "Affirmative."

Alison's eyelids grew heavy. She spied a mound of moss, and sinking into its softness, fell into a deep slumber.

Ian stared at the temple. He couldn't shake the feeling that there was something sinister lurking inside. He set aside his doubts and sat under a tree, resting his laptop against its gnarled tree roots. As he typed out a message to Joel, a movement caught his eye. He looked up to see a giant viper gliding down the temple steps. The creature's scales glistened in the moonlight as it slithered towards him.

His breath caught in his throat.

The serpent coiled, ready to strike, then its body contorted. Before him stood a winged creature, half woman, half nightmare, her wings like jagged knives. Deadly claws elongated her fingers, and writhing serpents hissed in her hair.

Ian froze, wide-eyed.

"What are you doing here?" She spat, her voice like a venomous whisper.

"I-I want to climb the mountain," he stammered.

"You are nothing but a frail human, a speck of dust!" Her eyes blazed. "I am the Gorgon, and I command you to return to the story of mortality where you belong."

Ian sat up straight and stared her in the eye. "I don't care what you say; I'm not going back. The story you speak of is based on lies."

"What? Who do you think you are?" The Gorgon lunged at him with blinding speed.

"Uh-oh," said Ian, springing to his feet. He fled into the forest, running faster than he ever had before. His lungs burned and his legs felt heavy, but he pushed upward into the mountain until, gasping for breath, he collapsed under a giant oak tree.

Just as he thought he was safe, the Gorgon appeared, her wings glistening in the moonlight.

"Think you can outrun your unresolved fears?" She said, the serpents swaying back and forth.

Ian felt his heart pounding. He spied a hollow in the tree trunk and crawled inside.

The Gorgon followed, staring him down.

Huddled in the corner, Ian's vision grew blurry, and the world seemed to shift. When his vision finally cleared, he found himself in an unfamiliar time and place. To his surprise, he wore a suit of armour. Then, he realised, he was no longer Ian, but Lord Stephen, a powerful knight! Every inch of him oozed strength, from his bulging muscles to his chiselled jawline. Beside him stood his mount, muscles rippling beneath its sleek grey coat.

Stephen stood proudly, for his reputation was unmatched. In past battles, he had proven his valour, growing rich in the spoils of war. With his warhorse at the ready, Stephen felt invincible, as if nothing could stand in his way. He mounted his steed, which promptly reared with high spirits while he sat calmly.

Then he saw her—a doe-eyed woman in a crimson gown, her hair tucked under a bonnet and her cheeks glistening with tears. She ran towards him with such longing in her eyes that it took his breath away.

"Stephen," she cried. "I await your return."

"Rest assured my dear, I will be victorious."

But fate had other plans. As Stephen lay dying on the blood-soaked battlefield, his final thoughts were of Lady Windermere. He desperately longed to see her again, but alas, fate did not allow it. His sorrow would forever remain etched in his memory—a tragic tale of love and loss.

Ian opened his eyes. His heart weighed heavily. Lost in a sea of grief and sorrow, a song echoed in his mind, taunting him with its truth.

Do you really want to hurt me?

The melody wrapped around him, whipping up emotions and memories he had long buried.

Do you really want to make me cry?
Do you really want to hurt me?

As the chorus rang out, the storm within him quietened, leaving him adrift.

The cackle of the Gorgon shattered his thoughts.

"You tricked me..." he said, tears of anguish rolling down his cheeks.

The Gorgon's eyes glowed menacingly. "No, you tricked yourself," she rasped. "There are more unfulfilled desires where that came from. What about your insatiable desire for wealth?"

Ian recalled his father, who had wanted him to be a real man. The weight of his father's expectations pressed down on him. He had become consumed by a relentless drive to achieve wealth and fame to earn his father's approval.

"Oh," Ian moaned. "I feel so hopeless..."

The Gorgon hissed. "That is because the ego can never be satisfied. Acknowledge whatever happened and release it, otherwise, I will turn you to stone."

"I'm trying..." Ian's head slumped forward.

The Gorgon's eyes turned from black to blood-red. "Well, try harder."

✳

A rush of energy flew by. Alison's eyes snapped open. "What was that?" she said.

Moonlight shone over the clearing, and she sensed an eerie stillness.

"Ian!" she called as she walked towards the tree. On the ground lay his computer. "Ian, are you there?"

Joel's voice replied. "Alison... is that you?"

She gazed down at the screen. "Oh, Joel!"

"Where's Ian?"

Alison shook her head. "I can't see him anywhere."

"What? But he just sent me a message."

She looked up. "Help, Prakash! Ian's missing."

The star expanded its light over the clearing. "You're right, he's gone. I have a riddle for you—what game involves ascending and descending?"

"What, a riddle?" Alison sighed. "Is it Snakes and Ladders?"

"Affirmative. In this game, humans wield immense power to alter their own fate, sometimes climbing to great heights but also succumbing to the weaknesses of their own minds... and the venomous whispers of the Gorgon."

"Hey, Alison," said Joel. "Wasn't the Gorgon the creature whose gaze turned people to stone?"

Alison gasped. She looked up. "Is that right?"

The star blinked. "The Gorgon on the shield of Athena frightened her foes."

"Athena... but why?" Alison looked down at the computer. "Hey, Joel, I have to find Ian before it's too late."

"Good luck," said Joel.

Alison slid the laptop into Ian's bag. Throwing it over her shoulder, she looked around. "Where to from here?"

The star blinked. "Thirty spokes on a cartwheel go towards the hub that is the centre."

"Oh," Alison sighed. "You mean all paths lead to the top of the mountain?"

"Affirmative."

Alison set off, her path lit by the light of the moon. It twisted and turned, leading her higher and higher. Her legs grew tired, and doubts crept into her mind. *I don't know if I can do this,* she thought as she gasped for breath.

The path grew steeper, and Alison stumbled over a loose rock. Struggling to get a foothold, she lost her balance and fell. Sprawled on the rocks, she let out a long sigh. *If only Ian was here... he would say that the way ahead is smooth, like water.*

Immediately, an enormous tiger padded alongside, his stripes illuminated in the moonlight. She looked up. Despite his size, she didn't feel any fear.

The tiger gazed at her through amber eyes. "What seems to be the matter?" he rumbled.

"I-I fell," said Alison.

"So, I see... a little balance issue, perhaps. Have you been drinking?"

Alison sighed, wishing she were anywhere but here. She rolled over and leaned on one elbow.

"Of course not," she said.

The tiger studied her for a moment.

"Bipeds are so unstable. We tigers don't have that problem." He ambled off into the darkness.

The star blinked above. "There you are. I wondered where you'd got to."

Alison sat up. "Oh, Prakash. I'm pleased to see you. Everything is falling apart," she moaned.

"Traipsing through a landscape filled with flowers and rainbows is not the same as reclaiming your power."

She sat up. "What do you mean?"

"The riddle lies within. You really want the ups. You want the good times—you don't like it when you fall. When you go down, you suffer. Think about it," said the star.

Alison thought for a moment and shook her head. "Give me a clue."

"You're hanging on images, attached to the kaleidoscope of changing scenes."

As Alison closed her eyes, she realised her knight in shining armour would not save her. Without a story to hold on to, she was completely alone. Her eyes sprang open. "In my panic, I fell into an old pattern of relying on others!"

The star blinked. "Very good. Now, ask yourself, who am I? What is real, what is true?"

Alison looked up at the exiled star, Astraea, in the constellation of Virgo. She sighed. "My true self feels so far away."

"What is the opposite of abandonment?" rebuked the star.

Alison drew a steady breath, and a flicker of understanding stirred. "Oh, of course... what was I thinking?" she whispered. "I've been abandoning myself to an old program."

Alison looked up once more. Above her, the Milky Way shimmered.

A star appeared with the pure radiance of Hestia, and she heard the whisper. *You were never apart.*

Above her, stars sparkled like diamonds—alive with the tender reunion of Persephone and Demeter, the steadfast flame of Athena, the boundless love of Aphrodite and the untamed spirit of Artemis.

Bathed in their light, Alison felt the goddess awaken within, a remembrance of her own strength, love and freedom, arising from her core. She smiled. "I'm not a victim, but a multidimensional being, strong, courageous and free."

The tiger appeared at her side. "Are you ready to move on?"

"Oh!" Alison looked up. Seeing his gentle eyes, she smiled. "Yes," she said as she struggled to her feet.

"Climb aboard," he said with a low rumble.

"What, ride the tiger?"

"Of course," he replied.

Alison clambered onto the tiger's back, burying her fingers in his fur. She hung on firmly. The tiger bounded over the jagged stones. Trees flashed by as the path wound its way upwards. Suddenly, the tiger swerved. Padding off the path, he made his way to a giant oak, cautiously sniffing the bark.

"We stop here," he growled.

"What?" said Alison as she slid down. The tiger climbed a nearby tree. He stretched out on a low-lying branch with eyes half-closed.

The star shone overhead. "Did you know that the oak tree is symbolic of Zeus?"

Alison shook her head. "No, I didn't." She ran her fingers over the bark, noticing its trunk split by lightning and hollowed out by the years. Peering into the hollow, she blinked. In the corner sat a figure hugging his knees.

"Oh!" she gasped. "It's Ian!" She bent her head and stepped inside, then froze. A pair of eyes gleamed from the shadows.

Alison stumbled back, then she turned and hurried out.

Once clear of the tree, she came face to face with the goddess Athena, robed in full battle dress.

"Do not be afraid," commanded the goddess. "Go back and face the Gorgon!"

Alison's eyes widened. "What did you say?"

"You want to rescue Ian, don't you?"

"Yes, but..."

"What happened to your courage?" Athena's eyes narrowed. "Remember who you are."

Alison took a deep breath. *I can't let this beat me.* She focused her thoughts on the light of God and stepped inside the hollow.

A pair of eyes glistened in the dark. "What are you doing here?"

"Rescuing Ian," Alison said firmly.

"No, you won't," the creature snarled. "Stay, and I'll turn you into stone."

Alison's gaze sharpened. "I refuse to give in to your little mind games."

She drew on the power of her connection with the One until the hollow glowed, faintly at first and then with a radiance that filled the space.

The light sent the nest of snakes on the Gorgon's head into a fury. They came to life, writhing and snapping. With an anguished shriek, the Gorgon flew from the hollow and fled into the night.

Alison followed, heart pounding.

The Gorgon landed on Athena's shield; its eyes fixed on her.

Alison stared in disbelief. "Athena? But... why?"

Athena gazed serenely. "Ian was weighed down with emotional baggage, so we merely helped him lose some weight." Then, spreading her wings, the goddess flew away.

Alison sighed. "Oh, dear."

The air was heavy with tension as she entered the hollow tree. "Ian, it's me, Alison," she said, resting her hand on his shoulder.

Gaining no response, she reached into the bag for the computer.

"How do you start this thing?" She said, randomly pressing buttons. She pressed the green button, and the screen lit up. "Good, now to get Joel on the line...."

Suddenly, Joel's face appeared.

Alison gasped. "I did it!"

"Hi Alison. Did you find him?"

"Yes," she said. "But he's not responding. Perhaps you could talk to him."

"Sure," said Joel. "Hi, buddy, it's me, Joel."

Ian's eyelids fluttered. Alison moved the screen closer and went outside; her eyes fixed on the hollow.

The tiger stretched, then manoeuvred himself into a more comfortable position.

Inside the tree, Ian trembled. "Joel, is that you?"

"Yes," said Joel. "How are you?"

"It's so dark. I don't feel a thing."

"I'm here for you," said Joel. "Picture a shining lotus flower. Just keep moving towards the light."

Ian's chest tightened, his mind a battlefield of painful memories. His breathing became shallow, and his body tensed. He imagined a lotus flower pulsing with golden light. Amidst his inner turmoil came a semblance of harmony.

"Keep going," said Joel, encouragingly.

Guided by the shimmering lotus and the steady presence of Joel, his inner turmoil subsided. Then, in a blinding flash, everything became clear. Ian realised that his constant pursuit of validation stemmed from a false belief; a sense of lack, that something was missing within.

Overwhelmed by the suddenness of it all, tears streamed down his face. He released all the pain and insecurities he had been holding onto for so long. A deep feeling of security washed over him, filling him with warmth. In that moment of clarity, he knew—nothing could ever change the simple truth that he was enough, just as he was.

Slowly, he opened his eyes. With faith, he affirmed, "I am who I am, a being of light!"

A smile spread across Joel's face. "That's it, Ian."

Outside, the wind gusted and branches swayed. Thunder rumbled, and lightning streaked across the sky.

Alison's heart pounded as she struggled to stay upright against the gusts. Hearing Ian's voice, she stepped towards the hollow.

Suddenly, the tiger dropped from the branch. Bounding towards her, he pushed her away as a bolt of lightning struck the oak with a deafening crack. In an instant, the tree burst into flames.

"Ian!" she cried, as the flames forced her back, leaping, twisting and casting a fiery glow. Tears flowed down her ash-covered cheeks.

Smoke and flame folded together, forming the outline of a bird, wings spread, tail streaming sparks. It rose above the burning oak, and then, with a rush of wind, the image dissolved into the night.

Alison stood, unsure if she had truly seen it or if her grief had conjured the vision.

Then, just as suddenly as it had started, the inferno calmed and, like a warrior emerging victorious from battle, Ian stepped out unscathed. His stance was steady, his eyes calm, and a quiet radiance shone from within.

In that moment, Alison sensed a deep knowing, as if something ancient and divine had awakened. "Oh, thank goodness you survived!"

Ian nodded. "Thanks to you and Joel." He gazed at her face, streaked with ash. "It was grand," Ian added softly.

Her brows lifted. "What do you mean? What happened?"

Ian's eyes grew distant, his voice low.

"There I was, stripped of everything; every illusion, every trace of ego. In that stillness, I met the Ouroboros, the spirit of the universe. I felt myself dissolve into it, as though I too were part of that eternal circle—no beginning and no end."

Above them, a puff of smoke shaped like a phoenix drifted across the morning sky.

36

Gaia

THE MOUNTAINSIDE RESONATED WITH birdsong, and sunlight streamed through the leaves. Alison stepped lightly, as though she had sprouted wings. Beside her, the tiger kept pace, while Ian, in a reflective mood, followed on behind.

A hush fell over the forest. The air seemed to hum with an ancient pulse.

Alison looked up at the star. "What secrets does this mountain hold?"

The star blinked. "The elements of water, earth, air, fire and ether weave the mysteries of Gaia's story."

Before the gods ruled the heavens,
Before kings claimed the land,
There was only Gaia, the primordial deity.

Unlike the gods, Gaia had no domain–
For she herself was the domain.

From the limitless expanse of Gaia came Ouranos,
the heavens and the stars.
Together, Gaia and Ouranos
created the mountains, the rivers, the forest, the wind
and the Great Sea.

But the world was empty
And so, they filled the land with life.

The story ended and they found themselves on a rocky outcrop where gnarled trees forced their way between the cracks.

"Looks like a perfect lookout," said Alison. "Let's stop and take in the view."

No sooner had she spoken than the tiger bounded onto the rocks.

Ian navigated the narrow path through boulders and overhanging branches. He paused, looking up at flickering eyes peeking through the foliage. "Who are they?" he asked.

The star glimmered. "Dryads or nature spirits. If you look carefully, you may spy the Oreads or mountain nymphs among the rocks."

Alison squinted into a rocky crevice. Shimmering eyes met hers. "I heard they are waiting for the Earth's renewal so they can roam freely once more."

"That is correct," replied the star.

They climbed higher until they found a place to view the pink and gold horizon. They saw a flotilla of lights rising gently from the world below.

"Why are so many souls leaving Earth?" Alison asked.

The star blinked. "Natural calamities, floods and fire."

"How sad. I hope Joel is safe," she murmured.

"So do I." Ian frowned. "I want to reach him, but I lost my computer in the fire."

Alison closed her eyes, sending the healing light of God to all who had suffered. And for a moment, she felt the universe breathe in unison with her. Then her thoughts turned to Joel. She opened her eyes. "Something tells me he's okay."

"I hope so," Ian replied.

A gentle breeze stirred the trees as an eagle circled high above. Alison felt weightless and free, unbounded by Earthly cares. As she gazed into the sky, she heard the element of air whisper, *'Slow down, let my presence remind you of the power of your thoughts and the joy of creation.'*

The whisper faded, leaving only the rustle of leaves.

The star signalled them to move on. The group descended the rocks and re-joined the path that wound its way through the trees.

Ian slowed. "I hear running water," he said.

The distant sound grew louder. Soon, they reached the banks of a fast-flowing river, its churning surface sparkling like diamonds. On the banks, ferns grew among the grey and white pebbles.

The tiger padded to the water's edge. Crouching down, he lapped.

Alison sat on a rock and trailed her fingers through the water. Bringing them to her lips, she tasted the freshness of mountain herbs. As she gazed at the flowing water, she heard a whisper. *'Slow down and let my presence remind you of the sacredness of your feelings and intuition.'*

The words rippled through her. *How long had she been rushing, trying to make sense of everything?* The water asked for nothing, only to be aware of the sacredness of her intuition and feelings.

The star glimmered above.

Ian looked up. "I think he wants us to cross."

"What?" Alison's eyes widened as she took in the current that threatened to sweep them away. Sensing her concern, the tiger's steady eyes met hers. Alison quickly climbed onto his back.

"Come on, Ian," she said, reaching out her hand.

Once onboard, the tiger stepped into the river, shaking his massive paw and sending droplets flying, before descending into the current. For a moment, the rushing waters swept them away, but the tiger quickly straightened, moving powerfully through the torrent, and then he bounded up the other side.

The tiger surged ahead, climbing higher and higher until he reached a grassy plateau. The fragrance of wildflowers and the chorus of birds filled the air. They passed groups of fairies gaily chatting as they weaved garlands of multicoloured flowers.

"Where are we?" asked Alison.

The star glimmered. "The Meadow of Harmony."

Near the pathway stood a temple, its columns weathered and covered in vines. Offerings of corn and wheat lay on the steps.

The tiger stopped, and Alison and Ian slid down.

The goddess Demeter emerged in a flowing green gown. Around her nymphs floated like satellites in the orbit of her love. In her presence, Alison and Ian felt their hearts expand.

She smiled. "I am delighted to see you again. Welcome to the temple of Gaia."

"We are honoured to meet the goddess of the harvest," said Alison.

"I no longer preside over the crops, but I sit in the temple and wait." Demeter's eyes looked downcast. "At this time, everything is topsy-turvy. Humans imagine they can control nature, while desecrating the very forces that sustain them."

Alison felt the air become heavy, as if Nature itself were mourning. She shook her head. "I don't understand."

Demeter sighed. "We are all part of Gaia's story. She gave us everything—the land, the rivers, the sky. She provided the perfect stage for the human story. Life flowed peacefully for millennia until the gods were reborn and the war for the cosmos began. That is when creation turned against her.

"Through it all, Gaia endured. She allowed the gods to build their castles upon her bountiful Earth, to carve their structures into her mountains, to fish her seas. She let them believe they had conquered her, for deep in her heart, Gaia knew no one could remain on the throne.

Demeter's eyes narrowed. "A time will come when Gaia will unleash her most formidable offspring—Typhon, father of all monsters, bringer of storms. A force of pure destruction, feared even by the gods."

Ian and Alison stood wide-eyed.

"What will happen?" Alison whispered.

Demeter's eyes gleamed. "The elements of air, earth, fire and water will rage and clash. Such is Typhon's might that even the ether will tremble."

A breeze blew through the temple, and for a moment, Time seemed to hold its breath.

Demeter's tone softened. "Do not let your heart grow heavy, for this is Nature's way of renewal."

"You mean the cycle of time will start again?" said Ian.

Demeter nodded. "That is so. Now, go forth on your journey with the blessings of the goddess." A gentle light shone in her eyes, and then she glided back into the temple.

As they descended the temple steps, Alison frowned. "I can't stop thinking about Typhon and the misery he will unleash on the world."

"It seems daunting," said Ian. "But think of it as birth pains. The new world will emerge as beautiful and pure as a newborn."

Alison exhaled. "You're right," she breathed. As she gazed across the grassy meadow, she heard the element of earth whisper. *'Slow down. Let my presence remind you of the strength that comes from being grounded in your truth.'*

The stillness of the land seemed to reach up through her feet, reminding her of the quiet power that endures beneath all change. For a moment she stood, belonging to the earth as much as it belonged to her.

Then, she and Ian climbed onto the tiger. His muscles coiled, and with a sudden burst, he leapt forward, bounding across the meadow. The wind blew through their hair. Ian threw his arms in the air in a moment of pure bliss, surrounded by the untamed spirit of nature.

The tiger slowed as it rejoined the narrow path that wound its way up the mountain. Above them, the sun shone brightly in a cloudless sky.

Feeling the warmth on her back, Alison heard the whisper of the element of fire. *'Slow down, be present. Let my glow remind you of the ever-turning cycle and the power of divine inspiration.'*

Its message burned gently through her, an ember of renewal, a call to live with purpose.

As they neared the mountain peak, the mist shimmered with a quiet radiance, and the sounds of nature fell silent.

Alison sensed the soundless element of the ether. In the stillness, she heard a whisper. *'Slow down. Be present to yourself as spirit. Let my essence remind you of what is light and pure.'*

She felt her thoughts dissolve into stillness, as though she were breathing light itself.

She turned to Ian. "I feel a lightness in the atmosphere."

"I feel it too," he said. "Reminds me of the words of the angel when he said it was a merging of everything into one."

High on the mountaintop, the tiger halted in its tracks.

Above, the star blinked through the mist. "Congratulations! You achieved your wish. You are at the gate of the Sacred Garden. May you find peace and happiness within."

"Thank you, Prakash!" they said in unison.

The star sparkled one last time and then vanished.

"I can't see a thing," said Ian as he slid down.

Alison landed on the ground and stretched out her hand. Her fingers touched the fur of the tiger, then her hand met Ian's. "There you are," she laughed.

Ian's fingers tightened around hers.

"Where's this gate?" she asked.

"I don't know," he replied. Then, he recalled the cryptic message in the star's last words: "Whatever you wish for, I guess?"

She laughed. "Mm... I wish for a golden gateway."

With that, the fog lifted, revealing a clear blue sky. A golden gateway stood before them, shining in the sunlight. The gates swung open, and fairies welcomed them with a shower of fragrant petals. Nature wrapped them in its warm embrace, guiding them deeper into the garden. Surrounded by trees and vibrant blooms, it felt like a symphony of colour and fragrance.

Alison stopped and stared in awe. A towering ridge of pink and white crystals caught the sunlight, casting prisms of glittering light over the trees. It took her breath away.

They reached a clearing. The tiger stretched out on the grass while Ian sat on a log, entranced by a family of wrens whose tiny wings fluttered as they took turns splashing in a pond.

Alison stopped to admire an orchid, its petals a brilliant shade of fuchsia. *How beautiful,* she thought, mesmerised by the intricate folds and patterns of the flower. Time seemed to stand still as her thoughts dissolved into the exquisiteness of a design that mirrored the vast pattern of the universe.

A low rumble broke her reverie. She turned to see the tiger approach with Ian close behind.

"There's a temple over there!" Ian pointed.

Alison followed them onto an arched bridge. Pausing at the top, she took in the manicured lawns and a fountain surrounded by ferns glistening from its watery spray. The sun's rays tinted the columns of the temple pink and gold.

They crossed through a rose garden, then kicked off their shoes and climbed the temple stairs.

The marble floor felt cool beneath Alison's feet. She looked around at the interior. It glowed softly in the lamplight, and the musical tones of a kithara floated through the air. The grandeur reminded her of an old movie set.

While Ian studied the miniature gold leaf paintings on the walls, Alison followed the tiger into the heart of the temple. There stood a statue of a goddess. The air felt charged with her energy, as if the very presence of the goddess infused it with her power, and her elegant form reflected in the crystal-clear waters of a pond.

Gazing at the goddess, Alison felt tranquillity wash over her. Then, hearing a chorus of joyful voices, she turned her head.

An ethereal woman approached, carrying a platter laden with fruit. Others followed, laughing and chatting among themselves.

"Welcome," said the woman as she carefully placed the fruit on the altar.

Alison felt a glimmer of recognition. *The Danaides...* she blinked. "Lydia, is that you?"

The woman smiled. "It is." She turned and gestured. "And here are my sisters."

Alison's mouth dropped open. She was about to speak when Ian's voice echoed. "Alison, where are you?"

At the sound of his voice, they startled.

Ian stood still. "Ahh," he said, backing away.

"No, stay," said Lydia, smiling shyly. "We sisters were under a spell that bound us to a futile task."

"You mean you're free?" said Alison.

Lydia smiled and nodded, her face reflecting the light from the pond. "It was thanks to you."

"But how did it happen?"

Lydia glanced at her sisters. "You dared to confront humanity's deep-rooted shame. At the same time that you broke free from your fears and insecurities, you freed us from our mindless servitude."

"That's incredible," said Alison, gazing at her with wonder.

Lydia met her gaze. "Once humans face their fears and embrace their true selves, divine light shines through and the old chains that once bound them to unconscious actions dissolve."

Ian came closer. "I had a feeling about this," he whispered.

Alison smiled. "You did."

The sisters bowed their heads in reverence. They left the offering for Alison and Ian to enjoy and drifted away.

"How lovely," said Alison, gazing at the plate of carefully sliced pieces of mango, apples and melons, dotted with plump, red grapes. In the centre sat an open pomegranate, its jewel-like seeds scattered over the offering. Alison placed a seed into her mouth. Remembering Persephone's story, she wondered. *Does this mean I'll return to the Underworld?*

The room faded as she sensed the hum of *Aum*. Then a voice whispered. *'There will come a time when you forget me and the home from which you came. But know that I will never forget you.'*

A hush lingered after the words. Then, gently, the temple breathed again.

Ian reached for a grape and popped it in his mouth. "Wow, this is delicious," he said, reaching for another.

The fruit pulsed with life. Bursts of flavour erupted in their mouths. They ate their fill and, feeling content and a little weary, made their way back to the entrance. They found the tiger stretched out on a rug. Ian nestled into his side and was soon asleep.

Alison sank into the soft rug, the warmth of the tiger's shoulder against her cheek. Sleep soon enveloped her, and the Oneiros led her into a garden of dreams. Moonlight shimmered through silver leaves, casting patterns upon the ground. Beneath an ancient oak stood Pandora, her hair woven with jewels. She regarded Alison's old clothes with a faint frown.

"Such attire does not befit you," she said, lifting her hands. In a burst of magic, a delicate silver circlet appeared on Alison's head. Around her wrist, there appeared a bracelet of memories, each charm a golden moment that had shaped her journey. Her old clothes shimmered and transformed into a silken gown. Last, Pandora pinned a dragonfly brooch to her chest, symbolising strength and resilience.

"That's better." Pandora smiled softly, then she melted back into the pantheon of stories.

Alison awakened, lingering in the remnants of her dream. She opened her eyes and saw Ian silhouetted against the soft light, dressed in a flowing white tunic and pants.

She blinked.

He met her gaze, eyes wide. "I met an angel in my dreams," he murmured.

"Clearly," she said, standing slowly. "You look... like a sage."

He smiled at the sight of her gown and the glittering jewels that caught the light.

"And you... look like the goddess that you are," he said softly.

The gentle breath of love that passed between them needed no words.

37

Metis

THE SILENCE OF THE temple deepened. The tiger turned his head. Outside, a soft radiance glowed. Suddenly, the light grew brighter, and a majestic goddess swept inside. "Welcome home, dear ones!" Her voice rang clear, like a temple bell.

Alison held her breath, and Ian's eyes widened.

The goddess approached, her cerise gown swirling. "I am the goddess Metis!"

Ian exhaled.

Alison smiled. "I've been longing to meet you."

The goddess drew them into her loving arms. "Did you enjoy my ever-changing garden?"

Alison smiled. "It's beautiful."

Metis's eyes sparkled. "The variety of flowers holds unique beauty, just like the infinite souls on this planet," she said wistfully. "If only human beings knew just how cherished they are."

Metis gestured towards the chairs. "It has been a long time; let us reminisce."

They settled onto the velvet cushions. The goddess extended her hand and stroked the tiger's head. "He never fails to bring them home."

Seeing the bond between them, Alison smiled. "Is he your companion?"

"Yes," Metis replied. "But I have others." She looked up. "*Leon!*" she called.

A lion roared in answer, then strolled majestically into the temple and sat by her side. More tigers wandered into the temple. They inspected the newcomers. Their curiosity satisfied, they stretched out on the rug.

Alison gazed at the goddess. "Mother Metis...," she began.

The goddess smiled. "What would you like to know?"

Alison took a deep breath. "I'm trying to recall if any of the Greek goddesses had lions and tigers."

"I doubt you would find any. The big cats are symbolic of my lineage, which traces back to the deities of ancient Bharat."

"Oh!" exclaimed Ian. "You mean India?"

"Not quite," Metis said. "You see, ancient Bharat stretched far beyond modern-day boundaries." She gazed longingly into the distance. "In those far-off days, there were no borders. Everything was in perfect harmony—the earth, the waters and the sky."

Ian's eyes widened in recognition. "Wait... the miniatures. Are you the goddess who rides the lion?"

Metis inclined her head. "Indeed, I am Shakti, the pulse of the warrior's strength, the fire that sustains the eternal battle of spirit." She raised her hands, and a luminous host of arms appeared, each one bearing a weapon formed from celestial light.

"The Trident holds the power of creation, sustenance, and destruction," she said. "The Discus turns the eternal wheel of time. The Sword of Wisdom severs illusion from truth. The Bow and Arrow sharpen focus and pierce the veil of the unseen. The Lotus radiates the purity of the spirit, and the Conch carries the eternal sound of Aum that echoes through the cosmos."

The goddess lowered her arms, and the weapons faded. "All are divine powers for destroying falsehood and restoring the original light of the soul." Her words faded, and the temple fell silent.

Ian sat, his eyes unblinking.

Alison felt the resonance of the goddess's words. "I don't understand," she said. "You say you're from Bharat, and yet you appear in a Greek myth?"

The goddess nodded, her gaze calm. "To understand means to step beyond the linear mind into the realm of paradox."

"Paradox?" Alison whispered, shaking her head. "It's just that I've spent so long with the Greek goddesses. I didn't expect... all this."

Metis smiled. "Reality rarely conforms to expectation. That's what makes it so fascinating."

Seeing the uncertainty in Alison's eyes, she rose from her chair. "Come," she said softly. "Let us sit outside under the stars. After all, *meta* means *beyond*."

The tigers circled the goddess. With a deep rumble, the lion shook his mane. They strolled through the temple with the lion leading the way.

"Do you know the significance of this temple?" Metis asked.

Alison gazed at the grand pillars and intricate carvings. "I imagine everything here is symbolic."

"Does it reflect the true self?" Ian offered.

Metis nodded. "You are both correct. This temple reflects the infinite light and beauty of the soul."

"I imagined nothing as lovely," said Alison as they walked down the stairs.

The scent of roses filled the night air. They sat beside the fountain; the moonlight reflected on their faces.

"Now, where were we?" said Metis. "Ah, yes—the paradox. How it is I have two forms and two separate myths?" Her voice softened. "Let's see if we can bring this story together as one. As I mentioned, in ancient times, Bharat's borders stretched far and wide. As the population grew, people migrated, each taking their own gods and goddesses. By the time the Greeks appeared, or Hellenes as they were known, the great kingdoms of the past had already faded, lost to the passage of time. And so, the mighty gods of old became known as the Titans—mysterious forces whose power and majesty had once brought harmony to the world."

"I take it that the Greeks created their own narrative," said Ian.

Metis nodded. "Isn't that what all conquerors do?" said Metis. "But fortunately, the ancient bards recorded the genealogy of the gods in story form."

"I'm getting the picture," said Alison. "You're saying that some gods and goddesses originated in Greece while others were adopted from previous ages?"

Metis nodded. "Correct."

"Excuse me, I have a question," said Ian. "If Metis means beyond, how was Zeus able to swallow you?"

"Oh, Ian...," whispered Alison. "That's a little insensitive."

"Sorry," said Ian. "I just want to hear her side of the story."

"Of course," Metis smiled. "Myths are metaphors that reflect the passage of the soul, which was originally pure and its powers, unlimited. However, once the ethereal soul entered a world bounded by the laws of a space-time matrix—it was as though it was swallowed up in the human story."

Ian nodded. "Oh, I see."

"I was once a Titan. We lived in a time when nature abounded with plenty and the earth was rich with gold and silver. Our king, known to the Greeks as Cronus, heard a prophecy that his kingdom would fall and, in an effort to hold back the march of time, he consumed his offspring: Hestia, Demeter, Hera, Poseidon and Hades."

Alison shuddered. "How dreadful."

"Cronus' wife, Rhea, thought so too. When she became pregnant again, she was determined to prevent her child from being swallowed and so, she handed her husband a stone wrapped in swaddling and sent baby Zeus to a remote island to be raised by nymphs. Zeus grew tall and strong under their watchful eye, and when he reached adulthood, he sought my knowledge of herbs to help him free his siblings.

"This golden-haired youth charmed me, so I agreed to make an emetic. In no time at all, Cronus had regurgitated his children. The Olympian gods and goddesses emerged fully formed and immediately planned the overthrow of their father. It wasn't long before conflict erupted as the Olympians clashed with the Titans. The Olympians won the war, and Zeus imprisoned the Titans in the pit of Tartarus with triple-thick primordial darkness. To ensure they couldn't escape, he arranged for the many-headed Hekatonkheires to stand guard at the entrance to the abyss.

"And that is how the Olympians gained control of the narrative and *Chronos*, the Father of Time, replaced Cronus."

Ian's brow furrowed. "That seems rather fantastical."

The goddess chuckled. "True or not, a story's success lies in its ability to endure the test of time."

Alison said, "But they didn't lock away all the Titans. What about Hecate and Epimetheus, for instance?"

Metis nodded. "You are right. Titans loyal to Zeus were absorbed into the Greek story; however, they lost their original powers."

"I see," said Alison.

"Once Zeus was proclaimed ruler of Earth and the heavens, he asked for my hand in marriage, but then came the twist. Zeus was delighted with the news that he was to be a father, but fear ate at his heart when he heard of my dream of a bright-eyed daughter followed by a son who would one day become the king of gods and men. And so, using his magical powers, he pursued me.

"Naturally, I resisted. At first, I changed into a hawk, then a fish and a serpent. Finally, Zeus tricked me into becoming a fly, and then he swallowed me whole."

Alison gasped. "A fly?"

Metis blinked. "It was not my finest moment."

"Did Zeus feel any remorse?"

"I can't say," said Metis. "However, not long after, he married Hera."

Alison frowned. "I heard it is not the happiest of marriages."

"I can attest to that." Metis smiled. "Their alliance is often strained—a cocktail of betrayal and jealousy."

Ian, who had been listening quietly, leaned forward. "I hope you don't mind my asking, but how did you survive?"

"Well, to be honest, I enjoyed Zeus' company. I found his boldness and ingenuity intriguing. Before I knew it, our thoughts had intertwined in a web of scenarios and campaigns." She smiled. "Zeus sought my wisdom, but equally, he ignored me."

"I see," said Ian. "And your daughter?"

"Athena was born from Zeus' head, clothed in my armour," said Metis. "She quickly became her father's daughter, forever weaving strategies to promote Zeus and defend his name."

"Athena is a force to be reckoned with," said Alison.

Metis' eyes sparkled. "Oh yes. Unlike Ares, who revels in strife and bloodshed, Athena is admired for her intellect and foresight. In ancient times, the goddess of war was able to defeat Ares, but then, the tables turned.

"The goddess, who was once in every corner of the ancient world, as creator, prophet and warrior, vanished; her voice buried beneath layers of silence. The wisdom once spoken in her name rewritten as sin. Over time, she was feared—and then forgotten."

Alison shook her head. "How did you make your escape?"

"Over time, I became jaded by a world obsessed with pleasure, comfort and entertainment. Humanity was driven by an endless quest for more. With that came wars—larger and uglier than before. Zeus detected my lack of interest. He offered incentives to stay, praising my wisdom and telling me he needed me and all that." Metis smiled. "I played along for a while until one day I asked myself; who am I? And the answer came: You are not a forgotten goddess, but a living force, unfolding through time and space. The Earth, the stars, the endless turning of creation—all are reflections of the vastness of your dreaming!

"My spirit stirred, urging me to act. As Zeus lay snoring, I slipped out of his mouth."

Alison smiled. "That's amazing."

"But that's not all," said Metis. "So it was, without the wisdom of the goddess, Zeus's façade soon crumbled—and that is how his kingdom fell into the hands of his son and rival, Ares."

"Oh... Ares," Alison grimaced. "We know him well."

Metis nodded. "Many loathe Ares, but equally, many bear allegiance to him. They gladly serve the god of war."

"But why?" asked Ian.

"Why indeed?" replied Metis. "As we know, Ares is neither majestic like Zeus, nor poetic and cultured like Apollo. He is not as clever as Hermes, nor as industrious as Hephaestus. He is neither a strategist like Athena, nor deep and meaningful like Hades, nor emotionally intelligent like Poseidon. Ares is a trickster. He is shrewd. He understands the human desire for power and uses it to his own advantage."

Ian frowned. "Why don't people see the deception?"

Metis gazed into his eyes. "Did you?"

Ian winced. "No, I have to admit I didn't."

Her eyes gleamed in the moonlight. "Clever, isn't it, the way humans are lulled into a false sense of security? They want all the good things, yet forget that every good casts its own shadow."

Her tone softened. "Still, there is wisdom in this. Everything has its purpose, even Ares. After all, it was the feeling of being trapped and jaded that stirred me from my slumber. No doubt under Ares' relentless command, many more will awaken from the dream."

Ian frowned. "But the question is, will humanity awaken in time, or will we continue to descend into the abyss?"

Alison gasped. "Don't prod the lion," she whispered.

Ian shook his head and shrugged.

The goddess turned to him, her eyes blazing. "After all you've achieved, you still have doubts?" She took a breath. "You underestimate the power of the human mind, or perhaps you've simply lost touch with reality. Either way, see for yourself..."

The goddess turned to the lion. "We're going down!"

38

The House of Ares

WITH A SWEEP OF her hand, the tigers gathered around, their amber eyes fixed on the goddess.

"Follow me," Metis said as she leapt onto the lion's back. With a bound, the lion soared into the sky.

Alison's heart raced as she scrambled onto the back of the nearest tiger. Another crouched for Ian. Once on board, the tigers leapt into the night sky. Alison and Ian clung tight, their hearts racing.

Flying swiftly, the tigers came alongside the lion.

"Where are we headed?" yelled Ian.

Metis turned to him, her hair flowing. "To the Thracian castle of Ares," she replied calmly.

Alison and Ian exchanged glances.

The big cats descended. Landing in the dim light of the courtyard, their paws kicked up a cloud of dust.

Across the yard stood sentries, their plumed helmets glinting in the lamplight. The dust cloud caught their attention, and they walked towards it.

Metis acted quickly, pulling Alison and Ian deeper into the shadows. Then, she pointed to the gate. At once, the lion and tigers bounded out of the courtyard and into the forest.

Startled, the guards came to a halt. "Did you see that?" one asked.

"Just some wild animals," another muttered. They walked away without a second glance.

"Whew, that was close," said Ian under his breath. He turned to Metis. "Won't they see us?"

"Not if you follow my instructions." Metis handed them each a cloak. "Hide your form with this is a cloak of invisibility. But you must also protect your mind by elevating your thoughts above the frequency of judgement or fear. Hold the image of a lotus in your mind: its roots growing deep in the mud while the flower opens to the light."

Metis pulled her cloak tightly around her and set off towards the entrance. Alison and Ian followed. They hurried up the stairs and along a dimly lit hall until they reached the door of the games room.

"I'll wait out here," said Metis.

Ian pushed open the door, and a wave of stale air wafted towards them, thick with cigarettes and beer. Chairs lay overturned, and glass crunched underfoot. Amid the chaos, music thudded like a defiant heartbeat.

Alison followed him inside. They stood near a cluster of toadlike creatures hunched over a computer screen, their eyes gleaming as they hunted for their next victim.

"I'm hungry for fear," croaked one.

"And terror," rasped another.

A bleakness rose in Alison's chest. She steadied herself with the image of the lotus, untouched by the mud. No judgement, her mind steady in the light.

The toads moved the marker over a house. Inside, a group was seated in the lounge room. The people appeared exhausted, as though they had walked a long way.

The toads croaked with anticipation.

"Let's make them doubt each other," said one.

"Yeah," said another. "Let's make them fight."

Their evil intentions sped through the air like flaming arrows, streaking toward the group. But these humans were no ordinary targets—they had mastered the *Deception Breaker*. The arrows struck the shields of light around their heads and ricocheted back, exploding through the computer screen in a blinding flash.

The toads shrieked in horror, covering their faces as the searing malice burned through their eyes.

Alison gave Ian a small nudge. He smiled and nodded slowly.

Suddenly, a caterpillar-like creature scurried past, its legs propelling it forward.

"Let me show you how it's done!" the creature squealed. It seized the mouse. "Groom them first," it said. "Distract them, offer them what they crave." It locked its thoughts onto a young woman. "Hey, beautiful," it purred. "You deserve more than this. I can give you everything you've ever wanted."

The woman's eyes blazed. "I will not be bought," she said. A powerful beam of light surged through the screen like lightning, knocking the creature to the floor. It lay on its back, its many legs twitching.

Ian grinned, then tilted his head to show that he had seen enough.

They slipped outside.

"All good?" asked Metis.

Ian smiled and nodded.

"They're holding a meeting," Metis whispered.

Metis navigated her way along the crowded corridor, followed by Alison and Ian. They glided into the hall, positioning themselves near the door.

The chairperson stood at the microphone. "Welcome to the plenary session of our Advanced Technology Conference. This is the final stage of our twelve-step program for world domination," she said. "Now, without further ado, allow me to introduce Bogaris, our conference leader."

The hall erupted in applause.

A godlike figure in a Roman toga stepped up to the lectern.

Alison's eyes widened. He appeared to have achieved his aim.

Bogaris gazed out across the sea of faces, and the room fell silent. "It is heart-warming to see so many familiar faces all gathered here tonight." He spoke at length about their achievements, praising their hard work. "All this could not have happened without the vision of our leader, Ares."

Suddenly, the doors flung open. "And now give a big welcome to his sons, Phobos and Deimos, who brought Ares' vision into the modern age!"

Faces turned as the gods strode through the door in matching business suits and ties. The gods raised their arms triumphantly above their heads. The audience stood up, clapping and cheering as they strode onto the stage.

Deimos stepped up to the lectern. "Thank you, thank you." His voice echoed loudly through the speakers.

The audience resumed their seats, hanging on every word.

"Fellow gods, colleagues and friends, we celebrate our victory over humanity. Through technology, we have reduced a once-proud species to pitiful slaves." Deimos scanned the audience. "They caress their beloved devices. Their new-found masters consume every aspect of their lives—sleeping, eating, walking, driving, all under the control of their technical overlords."

His voice rose to a fever pitch. "No longer are there any sovereign humans in this world. Only mindless drones enslaved by the gods of technology!"

The audience cheered.

Phobos took the microphone. "Our advanced use of technology is no more evident than with our advanced computer games. We have been able to pierce the veil of human consciousness in ways that mortals could never imagine. Through these games, we have extended our influence into every corner of the world."

Phobos flashed a grin. "It was a victory hard-won. Decades of planning, executed with ruthless precision. We gave them everything they desired—an ocean of comfort and entertainment. And now they're eating out of our hands. All this means we were successful!"

Phobos and Deimos turned to face the Ares' portrait.

Leaning into the microphone, Deimos' voice thundered. "Hail to Ares!"

"Ares! Ares!" echoed the audience.

"Victory is ours!" Phobos roared.

With this, the audience erupted into wild cheers, clapping and hollering as if they had been waiting for this moment their whole lives.

Phobos and Deimos took their seats.

The chairperson came to the microphone. Looking at the door, she smiled. "Now, I have great pleasure in welcoming Eris, the goddess of discord."

Eris sauntered through the hall in a tight black suit and dangerously high heels. The audience erupted in cheers and whistles as she ascended the stage stairs.

Ian's eyes widened.

The breath caught in Alison's throat as she recalled how they had fallen under her spell. Evoking the lotus, she reminded herself of the light.

Eris took the microphone. Despite her diminutive size, she exuded an overwhelming presence. Her voice rang out. "We are here to celebrate the victory of Ares, the rightful ruler of the air, land and sea."

She waved her hand. "And to each of you who has played a crucial role in his victory, I dedicate my latest song, *The Shadow's Triumph*."

The music sounded. Eris took a sharp breath before unleashing her words like a deadly spell.

Victory is ours.
We are free to rule the world.
Our dark forces have prevailed
And the light is no more.

We have crushed them
With our power and might,
Their armies have fallen
And their leader lies dead.

The streets are red with blood
And the air is thick with smoke;
Houses are burning
And families torn apart.

There is no mercy in our hearts
For those who dare to stand against us.
We are the rulers of this land
And all must bow before us.

No more will we hide in the shadows.
For now, we reign supreme.
Let all who oppose us tremble!
For they will never defeat us again.

Her performance ended with wild cheers, then Eris stepped down from the stage. As she left the hall, the audience chanted.

"Eris! Eris!"

Deimos and Phobos followed her out to the sound of cheers and clapping.

The chairperson stepped up to the microphone. "And now for the business at hand." One by one, speakers took the stage to voice their latest plans to further divide-and-conquer humanity.

As the speeches droned on, Ian grew restless. He turned towards the door.

Metis shook her head and whispered. "Let's just wait and see what else they have to say."

Ian took a deep breath, feeling the calmness of the lotus reaching to the light.

Finally, the chairperson introduced an expert on the human mind. Murmurs rippled through the hall as a man in a brown suit stepped up to the lectern. He scanned the audience with an unreadable expression, adjusted his glasses and glanced at his report. Then, speaking in measured words, he quoted the study funded by Phobos that confirmed the success of their technology in infiltrating the human mind. His study found that their computer games not only directed behaviour but also created unusually high levels of terror and dread. His voice droned on and on, quoting from the study.

When he finally finished, the chairperson opened the floor for questions.

A delegate stood up and mumbled into the microphone.

"I can't hear you," said the man in the brown suit. "Could you repeat your question?"

Someone flicked a switch, and the delegate's voice boomed through the speakers. "You say that the object of this game is to create fear. My question is, why are people no longer afraid?"

A sea of faces turned to the man who was so bold as to question the latest findings.

Another delegate stood up and took the microphone. "He's right. Humans are resisting!"

Murmurs spread quickly as tensions rose.

Another grabbed the microphone. "I've even seen them channelling the light!"

"Your report is corrupt!" yelled a delegate from the far side of the hall.

"There is no corruption," refuted the man in the brown suit, holding up the report as proof of his innocence.

The din in the hall rose with arguments back and forth. Some claimed the game was working, while others argued it had failed, calling out painful consequences.

Finally, Bogaris stepped up to the mike. "Please, let me explain!"

The expert quickly took his seat, and a hush fell over the hall.

Bogaris straightened his toga and looked out at the sea of wide-eyed delegates. "There may be a minor glitch in the program," he began, his voice smooth but taut. "I recall discussing this with Phobos after the launch. The problem occurred when we delegated the game to a human programmer for fine-tuning. Somewhere along the way, he must have tampered with the code, turning it from a one-way program into a competition of equal and opposing forces."

His eyes flickered. "By the time we realised this, the programmer had disappeared without a trace."

The tension in the hall was palpable. Suddenly, the noise level increased as everyone began talking at once.

Bogaris raised his hands, attempting to calm the delegates. When this didn't work, he leaned into the microphone. "What's the worry? Humans are weak and stupid. The fear of death works every time."

The delegates quietened. An official in the front row stood up, and someone handed him a mike. "Thank you for your explanation, Bogaris. I was at the launch and saw everything. The programmer's name was Ian. He and his female accomplice pulled off a daring escape."

The official threw the microphone down and, with a menacing glint in his eye, he pushed past people as he strode towards the stage. Mounting the stairs two at a time, he lunged at Bogaris, grabbing him by the collar.

"You were with that girl—the serving maid. You know more than you're letting on."

"How dare you?" muttered Bogaris, fury blazing across his face. He pushed the official, sending him sprawling across the stage.

The delegates leapt to their feet, shouting over one another. Within moments, the hall dissolved into disorder, fists flying as they revelled in the chaos.

Wild-eyed with fury, one voice rose above the rest, damning Ian's name for all eternity. The delegates cheered—at last, there was someone else to blame.

Ian's heartbeat quickened.

Metis caught his eye. "Congratulations, you created quite a stir," she whispered.

Ian took a deep breath and focused on the light.

The chairperson took the microphone, but the arguments started up again. Soon, they were shoving and trading blows.

Suddenly, guards in high-vis jackets burst through the door. Their boots thudded on the carpet as the team raced down the stairs. Moving swiftly through the brawling delegates, they quickly broke up the fights.

The chairperson called for order, and everyone returned to their seats, their once-confident demeanours somewhat dampened.

Alison whispered, "It appears victory is not guaranteed after all."

Ian smiled.

"Let's go," said Metis quietly.

They followed her down the hallway and into the courtyard, their faces glowing.

The lion, ever vigilant, sat waiting in the shadows.

Metis looked around. "Where are the tigers?"

The thud of boots grew louder on the drawbridge outside.

Alison held her breath.

The tigers emerged from the far side of the yard at the same time a group of soldiers marched through the gate. Seeing their black and gold stripes, the soldiers came to an abrupt halt.

A commander stepped forward, raising his hand. Slowly, he scanned. Pointing to the intruders, his voice rang out. "Take them—alive or dead!"

In a swift movement, Metis raised her hands. A radiant shimmer flared, and out of the air two swords appeared. "Use these to cut through the falsehood." She tossed the swords to Alison and Ian. "Remember who you are—immortal beings of light!"

They caught the glowing blades.

Metis leapt onto the back of the lion, and in an instant, she was gone.

The soldiers charged, their metal-plated boots clanging against the stone.

Ian swung his immortal blade with fearless precision, light bursting from each strike, but to his dismay, they rose again and fought on. "Nothing is real," he shouted.

Amid the skirmish, a tiger emerged from the shadows, his eyes fixed on Alison. She understood. Gripping her sword, she leapt onto his back, her eyes blazing with certainty. "I care not for the illusion of conflict created by the false self!" she cried. With one clean stroke, she sliced the air. The courtyard wavered—like a curtain torn from the scene from her story.

Ian's sword burned brightly. "I am not part of this cosmic struggle!" he cried, cutting through the last threads of illusion. He sprang onto a tiger's back, raising his sword high.

The courtyard fell silent. Then, with a rush of wind, the tigers bounded into the night sky—they were free!

39

Apokalupsis

ALISON GRIPPED THE FUR on the tiger's neck. Above her shone the stars. On and on they flew, as if passing through a canvas painted by the magic of the night. She melted into the deep resonance of Aum, where a higher power beckoned. *Come, child, to your home of light and be at peace once more.*

The tiger descended, landing softly on the grass. The temple stood before her, its columns glowing in the moonlight. Alison drifted up the stairs, aglow with the wonder of it all. Inside, she found Ian and Metis deep in conversation. The lion and tigers lay at their feet, their eyes half-closed, listening.

She heard Ian say, "Ares seems so sure he can control the world."

And Metis answered, "It's the ultimate misconception. No one can rule the world through physical power alone." A smile formed on her lips. "Legend had it that Ares became a fish."

Alison sat heavily. "A fish!?"

Metis smiled. "A prehistoric Lepidotus, to be precise."

"You can't be serious," said Alison.

"But I am," said Metis, with a twinkle in her eye. "No one, not even Ares himself, can outdo Gaia. As the legend goes, when she released the monster Typhon, Ares, along with the other gods, escaped to Egypt, and there he became a fish."

Alison laughed.

Ian sighed. "What with the chaos of Ares and the devastation of Typhon, what more do we need?"

The smile left Alison's face. "Ian's right. I don't want more strife. I just want to stay here for eternity," she said, gazing at the cool lines of the temple.

"I'm sorry, but apart from God, no one is free from playing a role in this drama," said Metis.

"Even Ares," said Ian.

"Even Ares," Metis nodded. "Despite his lies and dishonesty, he holds a special place in the story. You see, the god of war is central to the gods' agenda, which is to perpetuate the battle of good and evil so *they* prosper."

Ian's eyebrows raised. "We heard Hades speak of a war room."

Metis nodded. "Hades was referring to the council of the gods headed by Zeus. Ares was part of that council, but recently he broke away and formed his own assembly."

"What do these councils do?" Ian asked.

"They are the divine authorities who work behind the scenes, formulating rules and regulations on how the people should be governed, fed, taught, protected—or otherwise."

Ian's eyes widened. "Really?"

Metis nodded. "Under their guidance, civilisations rose to power and then fell." She paused. "The councils brought about many good things, like the flowering of art and literature and advancements in architecture and science." Her eyes narrowed. "However, I can tell you now, their attitude is not benevolent. To put it simply, the councils are not messengers of a loving God. They hide behind a smokescreen of selfless service, but in reality, they are working against each other to gain control of the planet's wealth and resources. That is why there has been so much conflict over the centuries."

Alison's eyes widened. "So, they actually need Ares?"

Metis nodded. "Ares' forces were maintained by the councils."

"You mention councils. Was there more than one?" said Ian.

"Oh, yes, the dynasty of councils has continued since ancient times. The Greeks knew them as the Dodekatheon; the Sumerians spoke of the Ukkin, the divine assembly; and the Babylonians knew it as the Puhru Ilani. The Egyptians revered the Ennead, and in ancient India, the gods gathered in the Sudharma Hall. Each was distinct, having its own gods of creation, order, and wisdom, yet all gave a place to gods of conflict and war."

"Whew," Ian exhaled.

Alison shook her head. "But why weren't we told?"

"Clever, isn't it?" Metis' eyes glimmered. "To hide behind a story that people were vulnerable and that their gods would take care of them? The fact was that because of their constant meddling in the story, humanity lost touch with their origins, their true essence and the power and potential within."

"So, you mean we've been manipulated?" asked Ian.

"Yes, and no. It's a collaboration, a two-way relationship. Humans always have the freedom to agree with or push back against their rules. The gods depend on humans for emotional energy and in return, humans depend on the gods for security, stability and guidance."

"So, it's an energy exchange?"

"Something like that," Metis said with a smile. Then she paused, eyes glowing. "Yet, as humanity increasingly attunes to a higher consciousness, the divine powers and virtues of the goddess will emerge once more and the world will be transformed."

"You mean the councils will be no more?" said Ian.

"That's right. There will be no need for advisors in the new world. It is only when consciousness falls that the councils come into force."

"Speaking of the new world reminds me of the prophecy of the child. Is it true?" asked Alison.

Metis smiled. "It is."

Alison's eyes sparkled. "That's quite a revelation."

Metis nodded. "At this time of the *Apokalupsis,* all is being revealed."

"Apocalypse?" said Alison, a shadow passing over her eyes.

"The ancient Greeks used the word *Apokalupsis* to mean revelation." She gave a knowing smile. "In this sense, the revelation of impermanence in the world. You get to see it for what it is—a grand story, a creation of the collective mind, the dream of separation—so that you might awaken to yourself and to God."

"Oh!" Alison's eyes widened. "You're different from the other goddesses. They never spoke of God."

"Ah, yes...," said Metis. "I carry the wisdom of the Greeks and the fire of the Titans, but beyond that, I hold the knowing of the soul's return to God."

"Can you tell us about God?" asked Alison, her voice almost a whisper.

Metis' eyes shone. "While in the world, I heard many versions. Some learned to love Him, and others learned to fear Him. Many would deny Him. But to truly know God, you must let go of everything you've been told."

As she spoke, a hush fell on the temple.

"God is not human," she breathed. "He is a living spirit, boundless and unchanging. You know Him not through the mind, but through the heart, and yet He does not demand worship. Like a loving father, He simply longs to share His wisdom, His power and His light."

Alison took a breath. "You speak of God as *He*?"

"Language cannot describe the paradox of the soul, as it expresses the energy of masculine and feminine. So, you can think of God as a Supreme Soul with the qualities of Mother and Father."

"You make it sound so easy; none of the worldly complications," said Alison.

Metis smiled. "It is when you realise that soul and God are woven from the same stardust."

Ian gazed at the goddess. "You've opened up in me a feeling of love, a sense that God is more than light. He feels *alive* with beauty and personality."

"Believe me, he has a charm. God embraces everyone with tenderness, and neither is He bound by time or space, so He responds instantly to your every question, your every thought or feeling." Metis gazed beyond the columns to where the pink haze of the morning light lit the sky. "And the sign of His love is His creation, a Golden Age of happiness and peace."

The air pulsed with a cosmic heartbeat, a feeling of ancient power.

Ian smiled. "Sounds like complete fulfilment. What do they call it—a state of *eudemonia*?"

"Yes," said Metis. "The new age arises out of the contentment of the soul, a world where there is no concept of life and death; no beginnings or endings. A thousand years with the awareness of being a spirit and yet living life on Earth."

Alison's eyes shone. "How beautiful," she breathed.

Ian frowned slightly. "But how did the world get to where we are now?"

Metis inclined her head. "The world as you know it is a simulation, a creation of the collective mind. Like any story, it unfolded one thought at a time." She nodded. "Think about it. Every thought, every emotion, generates energy that feeds a story. You keep it alive. That story spreads to others, and soon you have many minds dreaming the same dream."

Ian's eyes widened. "So, each of us contributes to this story?"

"Yes," said Metis, with a twinkle in her eyes. "The world is a mirror of the soul. In the beginning, when there were few humans on the planet, the story grew slowly. Now, with billions of minds, the story expands exponentially. Today, there is a war going on within every human mind. And so, the outer world reflects this inner conflict. But imagine a world where every soul is in the highest consciousness of peace. No division, no pain, no death. No beginnings or endings. Only a unified field of awareness, a flowing stream of living light."

Ian sighed. "What a dream..." Then a shadow passed over his eyes. "I just don't understand the point of a Golden Age if we're going to lose it all again?"

Metis gazed into his eyes. "Can you lose what you have not gained?" she said.

He tilted his head. "I hadn't thought of it like that."

"Of course not," said Metis. "Picture the ancient symbol of yin and yang."

"You mean the *Taijitu*?" said Ian.

She nodded. "Opposite forces create harmony and balance in the universe. Like the ocean, the universe is an ever-flowing tide from light to dark and dark to light, from self-awareness to forgetting and becoming self-aware again. It is a perfect balance, the eternal nature of things."

Ian was quiet for a moment. "I feel it," he said slowly, "it's like an inner knowing."

"Just as you know who you are," said Metis.

He gazed at the goddess. "But I feel weighed down, if you know what I mean. I don't feel like a soul having a human experience. I feel like a human trying to imagine myself as a soul."

"I also find it difficult," said Alison.

"I know you want it easy, but..." Metis leaned in. "Let me tell you a secret. Your higher self delights in this time of change and upheaval. Believe it or not, difficulties accelerate your growth far more than easy times. So, release any sense of guilt, doubt and fear and embrace these challenges as a stairway to the light."

The air stilled, and for a moment, it seemed Time itself was listening.

"You are givers and not takers," continued Metis. "Your light sustains the world. Know yourselves as sovereign beings and reclaim your power—not only from the goddess long forgotten but also from the gods you fear. Do not feed them your energy so that their story becomes your own."

Alison's eyes widened. "You mean Ares?"

Metis nodded. "Yes. Ares, the god of war; the warrior." She paused. "Embrace your inner Ares as the embodiment of courage." Her gaze deepened. "True courage does not march in the streets or demand the heads of others. True courage stands in calm confidence of knowing who you are. It is the strength to act from the loving remembrance of God."

"And what of Zeus?" asked Ian.

"Zeus, the king who sits upon the throne. And what is a king but one whose very thoughts, words and actions align with the divine will? The king moves a finger, and everyone obeys. Ask yourself: are you the ruler of your own reality, seated upon the throne of the self? Can you exercise your will with the confidence of one who knows who they are?"

Her voice softened. "This is the war for the self that lies beyond borders and boundaries, beyond race, religion, gender, colour and creed. It is about *you*, the soul, the spark of light who once parted from the Eternal One and entered the realm of myth, so that through the dream of separation, you may awaken to eternal life—and to God."

The air shimmered, and the tigers stirred, their eyes glinting in the morning sun.

Alison closed her eyes. A subtle energy flickered at the edge of her awareness. Threads of colour drifted around her: silver, sapphire, emerald... each shimmering with its own pulse, yet somehow incomplete. She felt these hues as stored emotions; fragments of her own energy scattered across many lifetimes.

She opened her eyes. "How do I heal and become whole?"

Metis nodded. "By looking inward and acknowledging the broken, shadowed, or unclear parts of yourself as colours born from the soul's light, interacting with the prism of life. Hold these colours in the pure white light of the Supreme Light. In that radiance, whatever was broken becomes whole again."

Alison felt her heart reach out to the light of God. One by one, she drew the many colours upward. Gradually, the hues dissolved, blending into a single radiance, clear, pure and still. Happiness filled her being as if it came from a deep well.

She opened her eyes and smiled. "It's like something inside me has been waiting to remember."

Metis returned her smile. "You see now, true power is not born of the world outside, but rises from the light of God within. The journey is both inward and upward—a homecoming of light unto itself."

A low hum of Aum rose, resonating within their hearts, a vibration that seemed to unite them. Metis extended her hand. A disc of light spun gently above her palm. "Take this gift of a discus and use it to end all illusions. Spin the cycle and know yourself as the powerful light that you are."

The spinning disk sent ripples of gold into the air.

Metis gazed into their eyes. "Be the messengers. Let your light guide others beyond the veil of appearances, toward understanding, toward themselves."

Her eyes shone with a love so pure that their hearts melted. "Remember," she whispered, "you are always and ever you..."

The scenery began to shimmer and blur until, with a sudden jolt, they tumbled onto the sofa.

"Oh!" exclaimed Alison.

Staring at them were the sapphire eyes of the Observers.

40

Typhon

ALISON RESTED HER HEAD against the cushions. She felt as if she were on a carousel spinning slowly through an endless space. In that moment, a veil lifted. She resonated with the stars—no longer separate but part of the cosmos. A soft hum stirred within.

Aum... Not heard but felt.

She saw every facet of her soul journey, an interplay of victory and defeat, light and dark—a never-ending dance of destiny. And in that moment, she knew in her heart, everything was perfect. Nothing needed to be changed. A stillness came over her, as though the world itself breathed through her. Symbols that once seemed distant—gods, stars, wings, light—were no longer outside her. A quiet remembering spoke to her in images, that the divine and the human were of the same breath.

The words of Hesiod echoed in her mind: *'We descended from the mighty gods, and to the gods, we will return.'* For a long moment she rested in that peaceful knowing.

A siren wail pierced the air, and her eyes sprang open.

The Observers hurried towards the cliff, but before they reached the edge, a powerful blast flung them backwards onto the rocks. Clouds of black smoke billowed from the earth below. Slowly, the smoke dispersed, and a skull with glowing red eyes hung in the sky.

"Leave this place at once or face your doom!" echoed a voice from within. And just as suddenly as it had appeared, the skull vanished.

Ian scanned the horizon. "The demons will stop at nothing."

The Observers emitted a series of high-pitched chirps before scattering for cover. Overhead, a warlike chariot thundered. It veered sharply before zooming into the distance.

Ian followed the chariot's path. "They know we're here."

"I didn't think they could reach us," said Alison.

His eyes narrowed. "Their technology has advanced. But then again, so has ours."

A formation of chariots streaked across the sky. Then, suddenly, one chariot broke away, its silver form gleaming.

"Here it comes," said Ian, his voice steady.

The wind caught Alison's hair. "We can't let them intimidate us," she said, holding up her hand. Swiftly, a spinning disc appeared. "We must release all thoughts fuelled by fear and remember who we are—beings of light!"

They elevated their vibrations, their silhouettes more akin to gods than mortal beings.

The chariot flew towards them, bullets ricocheting off the cliffs.

"AMPLIFY!" roared Ian.

The power of their consciousness ascended, transcending time and space and connecting with the supreme power of God. The air shimmered, revealing their form as powerful points of light.

The chariot circled and then zoomed toward them. It struck their energy field and veered off course, becoming a chaotic blur.

Just when they thought the attackers had left, another chariot appeared, hurtling toward them at deadly speed. They concentrated their energy again. Instantly, its detection system failed. Swerving wildly, the chariot careened off into the distance, leaving behind a sharp smell of burning metal.

Stillness spread through the air. The Observers emerged, spinning and twirling in delight. But their celebration was short-lived, as down below the drums of war pounded.

Alison and Ian joined the Observers, standing shoulder to shoulder at the cliff face.

The air trembled as the scene unfolded.

War clouds swirled, oceans churned with warships, and fighter planes zigzagged through the sky. It wasn't long before explosions rocked the earth and the roar of artillery filled the air. Grey smoke billowed, and the smell of fire carried on the wind.

The Observers sounded an alarm. Above them, the clouds split open and Ares, in his gleaming chariot, soared triumphantly across the sky. From his heavenly throne, he thundered, "The reign of Zeus is over. I am Ares, ruler of the world!"

In his moment of glory, the god of war revelled in his power and the rivers of blood that flowed at his command. The winds raged—a tempest of fury that carried his declaration to every corner of the globe. Some revered this awe-inspiring spectre while others shook their heads in disbelief.

Alison's eyes gleamed. "This tyranny must end once and for all."

"You're right," said Ian. "We need to activate the final stage of the *Deception Breaker*."

"What do you mean?" she asked.

"The *Deception Breaker* helped individuals to raise their vibration, but it didn't address the core issue of division. Through their narrative of fear, we see each other as enemies, and so they grow stronger while humanity grows weaker."

Alison nodded. "Of course, divide and conquer. But what can we do?"

Ian looked out at the stormy sky, his voice clear. "Metis spoke of the war within. The final stage isn't a weapon; it's love, pure and unlimited. We must unite our light with others and together we can dissolve the darkness in this world!" Ian shook his head. "But without my computer, I can't communicate with Joel."

The Observers gathered around, their voices rising and falling.

"Do you understand what they're saying?" asked Ian.

Alison leant in. "I hear the word angels... They're talking about being messengers, reminding us that our minds act as receivers and transmitters." She gazed at Ian, her eyes wide. "They're urging us to communicate through the power of the mind!"

"Telepathy?" Ian pondered for a moment, then he nodded. "Let's try."

Together, they concentrated on Joel.

Ian was the first to feel the connection, like two threads intertwining. Shortly after, Alison felt a fusion of divine love and harmony. It only took a second, and like a gentle whisper carried by the wind, Joel's voice broke through the stillness.

"Hey, guys," he said warmly.

Ian's eyes widened. "Hi, Joel. Our power of telepathy has returned!"

"Yes, it's amazing!" Joel replied.

"From here, we see that the forces of darkness have gained control," said Ian. "It's time to activate the final stage of the *Deception Breaker*."

"Okay, what's that?" Joel asked.

"To dissolve the darkness in the world, humanity must rise above their differences and unite as one," said Ian, with calm confidence.

"Sounds simple but difficult," said Joel.

Alison chimed in. "The main thing is not to have doubts, but to concentrate our efforts with complete faith."

"Sure," said Joel. "I'll send the message out."

The message of unity spread like ripples on a pond, both online and through the collective consciousness. People had grown weary of conflict and yearned for healing and peace. As hearts opened, the sense of separation dissolved. Those who once felt lost and alone now felt part of a worldwide family.

With the collective rise in consciousness, visions became commonplace—images of light, ancient goddesses, saints and prophets of old. Many glimpsed the vision of a father figure who belonged to all. They heard his gentle message: "Come, children, and be at peace once more."

They heard the chirrup of the Observers. Above them, the night sky had transformed into a theatre. Winged dragons—one fiery red, the other icy blue—circled each other, their scales glinting. Suddenly, they clashed and roared. With each swoop and dive, their wings unleashed gusts of wind that buffeted the earth below.

Ian smiled. "I saw these dragons in a video game."

Alison turned to him, her eyes large. "Oh! Who are they?"

"Celestial beings born from the elements. The red is passion and the blue is logic."

Alison followed the dance of two opposing forces, clashing in a vibrant dance against the backdrop of the night sky. She smiled. "Amazing how mythical creatures reflect the struggle of human emotions and desires."

Ian nodded. "The struggle ends when they realise opposites are just different sides of the same coin."

Then, as suddenly as it had begun, the game was over. The dragons hovered in midair, momentarily forgetting their original reason for fighting. With one last glance, they turned and vanished into the darkness.

Alison smiled. "Do you ever wonder how the demons are faring amid all this human indifference?"

"Most likely, they're hiding underground," he replied. "Without the battle of good and evil, they simply can't survive."

They glanced at each other and smiled. Neither spoke, but the energy between them spoke of their mistakes, forgiveness and a shared purpose. Together, they fell silent as they continued their vigil, spreading the radiance of God's light into the world.

✳

Time moved differently in the Realm of Possibilities. In *Chronos'* time, it may have been hours, days, or even weeks before the rush of wings and excited chirps rose to a deafening crescendo, urging them to the cliff face. Gazing over the edge, they witnessed an awe-inspiring sight. Below them, tiny lights twinkled like fireflies in the dark. From each soul, rays of light extended outward, like dendrites, joining with others to form a luminous web encircling the globe.

The goddess had awakened...

Alison and Ian beamed with joy. Their thoughts turned to Joel, and in an instant, they felt his presence. No longer were they mortals, but beings of light, united by a greater purpose.

It was not long before they felt the presence of other souls whose powers of telepathy had awakened. The love of the gathering was tangible; a sea of kindred spirits who recognised their cosmic origins. It emanated a radiance that pulsed with the living force of humanity—souls who had seen through the deception and were ready to reimagine a new reality and to be custodians of a new, beautiful world.

The gathering dispersed just as a chorus rang out—a spontaneous symphony of voices celebrating the One. The luminous web grew brighter as the collective joy of humanity increased. As more and more rejected the idea of fear and separation, the light expanded into a dazzling pyramid that reached towards the heavens. The Apex pierced the ancient veil that had long separated humanity from the heavenly realm. And with this, an immense flow of light poured onto the parched earth below.

Many felt the embrace of a great and pure love. For a moment, everything was weightless. Sorrow lifted. Pain vanished. The Earth breathed again.

From deep within came a single vibration... *Aum*... rolling through creation like a tide of remembrance. It moved through every heart, awakening the knowing that Heaven and Earth were one.

Then came the sound of countless wings, a shimmering chorus of angels. Light poured through the clouds, radiant and alive, as their message echoed throughout the world: "Prepare yourselves, dear ones, for all that is illusory will finish, and only that which is eternal will remain."

Some who saw them wept, while others stood in quiet wonder. Those whose connection with God was strong felt the joy of knowing that the angels above and the angels below were one.

Silence fell: deep, golden, endless. It was the silence after revelation, when even the wind was still.

Then the Observers hummed, soft at first, then they grew louder. Alison and Ian raised their eyes to behold a breathtaking sight—a goddess seated on a chariot pulled by white horses, flying gracefully across the sky.

The Observers hummed a story.

"What are they saying?" said Ian.

Alison leaned in. "It's Gaia surveying the Earth." Her eyes widened. "They say that thousands of years ago, the Olympians defeated her beloved Titans and locked them away in Tartarus. In her fury, Gaia vowed to release her most powerful child, the monster Typhon, to free the Titans from their prison." She listened again. "This monster will destroy the world of illusion, and the gates to Heaven will open."

Ian's eyes widened. "Really?"

Alison nodded, then she leaned in again. "They say, creation and destruction are not opposites but part of the same sacred flame."

"That reminds me, we must warn Joel!"

"Oh, yes," said Alison.

They focused their thoughts, and soon, they felt Joel's presence.

"The forces of nature are about to put right all that has gone wrong," said Ian. "In other words, Gaia is about to push the reset button. There will be chaos, but the goddess knows what she is doing. Continue to be a channel for God's light."

They felt a wave of love and appreciation as Joel's presence faded.

Gaia's chariot faded, and all was silent except for the distant sound of machine-gun fire. The air grew heavy. A clap of thunder sounded as if a fist had slammed against the sky.

As the echo faded, they realised this was no ordinary tempest—it was the monster Typhon. After centuries of imprisonment in the depths of Tartarus, the father of all monsters was ready to wreak havoc on the world.

Another clap of thunder echoed through the heavens, followed by Gaia's powerful command: "Cleanse and purify!"

Hearing these words, the Observers moved swiftly, settling themselves beside Alison and Ian.

Enfolded in their feathery cocoon, Alison drifted into the boundless expanse, where all that existed was the light and love of One.

Above, dark clouds gathered, blocking the moon and stars. Lightning flashed. The heavens opened, and rain pounded the earth. The wind howled so loudly that it drowned out all other sounds except for the screams of demons trying to escape their fate.

But this was only the beginning...

A low rumble sounded, barely perceptible at first, but growing in intensity. Suddenly, the earth split open, and with a deafening roar, the mighty Typhon emerged. Lightning flashed around him, revealing a hundred serpent heads, their hideous forms writhing and twisting.

The monster waved his arms, whipping up a windstorm that tore across the lands, lifting roofs, shattering windows and uprooting trees as if they were mere twigs. As the beast stormed across the continents, mountains trembled and buildings swayed. Wherever Typhon stepped, deep fissures burst through the Earth's crust. Rivers of lava consumed everything in their path.

The mighty armies of Ares fled in terror as Typhon rampaged through their ranks. In his rage, the monster tossed aside their battle tanks and planes like toys. Picking up giant boulders, he threw them at their warships. The rocks landed with thunderous splashes, sinking ships and creating towering tsunami that surged towards the shores, engulfing entire cities in their wake.

Meanwhile, the tremors set off warning signals, but it was too late. Somewhere in a war office, the plea for restraint had failed. In a blinding flash, a swarm of nuclear weapons was unleashed. One after the other, massive explosions shook the Earth, and once-bustling civilisations vaporised in an instant. Towers of smoke and molten dust billowed into the sky, concealing the sun and plunging the world into darkness.

With the power of the atomic forces spent, a hush fell over the world, broken only by the fading roar of Typhon as he melted into the night. But there was more to come—

A rumble sounded deep within the crust as magma surged like a molten sea. The poles moved and tectonic plates collided with unimaginable force, causing a massive wall of water to sweep across the continents.

Finally, the planet shuddered as it settled on its new axis.

For a moment, all was still—no wind, no sound. Only the soft exhale of a world reborn.

Once more, Gaia rode her horse-drawn chariot across the sky, surveying the Earth with satisfaction.

Alison opened her eyes. The clouds had cleared, and the moon glowed brightly. Stars glimmered in the sky. She blinked and then blinked again as she realised those were not stars but countless souls shimmering like pearls.

She watched in awe as the souls strung together, like strands of luminous pearls. Above, the brightest star shone like a beacon, drawing souls upward, to the place they had longed for—home.

Then, in the darkness, Alison heard the hum of voices and rustle of feathers as the Observers prepared to sing in the new creation.

In the beginning there was only Chaos,
a boundless, formless void.
From it emerged Gaia the Earth,
Tartarus the Deep,
and Eros, Love.

Gaia brought forth Uranus, the Starry Sky,
and together they birthed Aether's brightness
and the coming of Day.

Mountains rose; the sea stirred.
From the deep came the Titans,
Oceanus of the waters; Coeus and Crius, keepers of wisdom;
Hyperion of the sun; Iapetus the Bold; and their leader, Cronus.

With them came their sisters, radiant Thea, nurturing Rhea,
Themis of Justice, Mnemosyne of Memory, golden Phoebe of Light,
and gentle Tethys, mother of streams.

Exalted they rose, endowed with love and power—
children of the Creator.

The chorus faded. The world lay hushed in dawn's soft silence.

In the early morning light, Alison sensed the future like a fresh canvas waiting to be filled. She glimpsed herself as a vision of natural beauty watching with quiet joy her bright-eyed children walking among the gentle lions, lambs and peacocks. Beside her stood her husband, smiling as he watched their children at play. A family united in harmony and love.

But this was only the beginning. Time spread out before her in a heavenly vista—lifetime after lifetime of light-filled days filled with the idyllic awareness of being a soul having an Earthly experience. Whether in a male or female form, all the while, life flowed with grace and ease.

The Observers hummed softly.

Ian opened his eyes. His face radiated serenity and joy.

Seeing him, Alison smiled, and he returned it with the same gentle recognition.

A low hum grew. Above, the sky rippled with light as the planets aligned, suspended like lamps upon a cosmic stage.

The Observers sang their ancient names of the planets: *"Hermes, Aphrodite, Ares, Zeus, and Cronus."*

Their humming continued, ethereal voices rising and falling like waves upon the shore, carrying the memory of eons; of battles fought and peace restored, of humanity's long search for God and then the revelation that the divine had never been apart.

Alison felt the closeness of Ian beside her; witnesses to the unfolding of something greater.

They lifted their eyes to the heavens. From the radiant alignment, a goddess descended, draped in sunlight, the moon at her feet and a crown of stars circling her head. In her arms, she cradled a celestial child, glowing with light—a child destined to reign over a golden new world.

Ian's eyes shone with warmth, no longer questioning or striving, but fulfilled.

Alison smiled, grateful for the vision that promised lasting peace in the world. Even more, she was thankful for the peace that had settled in her heart. For in that stillness, she felt what souls had strived for since the beginning—the gentle presence of God.

Together, they watched the dawning of a new era. The age of the warlords had ended and the Golden Age had begun—

And in the stillness that followed,
a single note was heard through all things.
Aum... the sound of beginnings and endings,
echoing in the heart of the world,
joined in silence, older than time.

✳

Acknowledgements

My sincere thanks to spiritual teachers, friends and family for all their support and encouragement.

Thank you also to my editors and especially my friend, Robyn Stephenson, for her helpful critique and dedication to the story.

I am most thankful for the generous grant from the Creative Spirits Initiative, an arts fund administered by Brahma Kumaris Australia and established by Jaie Watts to foster spirituality through art.

And, to the Muses. May you ever inspire us.

Author

Johanne Shepherd was born in 1956 in Sydney and spent her early years in the coastal suburb of Avalon. After moving to Canberra, she completed her studies at the Australian National University and the University of Canberra.

In 1981, a course on Raja Yoga meditation sparked a deep interest in the spiritual path, leading her to travel through India and China to explore their ancient traditions. Her fascination with Greek mythology and archetypes arose years later, after reading *Goddesses in Everywoman,* by Jean Shinoda Bolen.

A lifelong writer, Johanne began formally studying the craft a decade ago, weaving together her interests in spirituality, mythology and storytelling. She lives in rural New South Wales, where she continues to write and reflect amidst the quiet rhythms of nature.

www.ingramcontent.com/pod-product-compliance
Lightning Source LLC
Chambersburg PA
CBHW031119210626
46816CB00016B/1723